SPECIAL MESSAGE TO READERS

THE ULVERSCROFT FOUNDATION
(registered UK charity number 264873)
was established in 1972 to provide funds for
research, diagnosis and treatment of eye diseases.
Examples of major projects funded by
the Ulverscroft Foundation are:-

- The Children's Eye Unit at Moorfields Eye Hospital, London
- The Ulverscroft Children's Eye Unit at Great Ormond Street Hospital for Sick Children
- Funding research into eye diseases and treatment at the Department of Ophthalmology, University of Leicester
- The Ulverscroft Vision Research Group, Institute of Child Health
- Twin operating theatres at the Western Ophthalmic Hospital, London
- The Chair of Ophthalmology at the Royal Australian College of Ophthalmologists

You can help further the work of the Foundation
by making a donation or leaving a legacy.
Every contribution is gratefully received. If you
would like to help support the Foundation or
require further information, please contact:

THE ULVERSCROFT FOUNDATION
The Green, Bradgate Road, Anstey
Leicester LE7 7FU, England
Tel: (0116) 236 4325

website: www.foundation.ulverscroft.com

As the fourth of six children, Debby Holt discovered at an early age the joys of losing herself in a brilliant book. After graduating from the University of Exeter with a history degree, she taught in a boys' comprehensive school, then gave up full-time teaching when her twin sons were born, and started writing when her fifth child began primary school. She has had over sixty-five short stories published at home and abroad, and has written seven novels in eleven years. She lives in Bath.

You can discover more about the author at www.debbyholt.co.uk

THE SOULMATE

Widower Henry Drummond is marking time, drifting towards retirement, until he accidentally saves a life — and realises his own is worth living. His daughter Maddie is at a wedding with the love of her life — but he is the groom and she is not the bride. Henry and Maddie realise they need to make some changes, preferably with a soulmate by their side. But as Henry's mother tells him, 'Love is a complicated business and it is not for the easily discouraged.' Strange encounters, humiliations and adventures ensue, but romance remains elusive. By the time family crises complicate things further, the quest has taken on a life of its own — with surprising consequences . . .

Books by Debby Holt
Published by Ulverscroft:

THE EX-WIFE'S SURVIVAL GUIDE
THE TROUBLE WITH MARRIAGE

DEBBY HOLT

THE SOULMATE

Complete and Unabridged

CHARNWOOD
Leicester

First published in Great Britain in 2016 by
Accent Press Ltd
London

First Charnwood Edition
published 2019
by arrangement with
Accent Press Ltd
London

A catalogue record for this book is available
from the British Library.

ISBN 978–1–4448–4054–4

Published by
F. A. Thorpe (Publishing)
Anstey, Leicestershire

Set by Words & Graphics Ltd.
Anstey, Leicestershire
Printed and bound in Great Britain by
T. J. International Ltd., Padstow, Cornwall

This book is printed on acid-free paper

1

Sixteen weeks after Maddie broke up with Freddy she received a jaunty 'Save This Date!' card in the post. A few months later, the wedding invitation arrived. Maddie could not imagine why she'd been sent it. Perhaps it was a challenge, she thought, in which case she was duty-bound to accept.

It was a costly decision. The wedding was held on the edge of a particularly charming Sussex village which boasted a variety of hotels, pubs and B&Bs, none of which were cheap. Then there was the new dress, and the new shoes that were currently crippling her feet as she ascended the hill along with other stragglers.

A voice called her name and she turned. Cassie Lucas was a former flatmate of Freddy; she had always regarded Maddie with an air of bewildered politeness, as if she couldn't quite work out why she was there. But now she seemed eager to catch up with her and quickened her pace. Maddie had to admire the way she negotiated the pot-holes in the lane, since it couldn't be easy. Cassie's heels were even higher than her own and she had to keep one hand on her head-gear — a tottering, pink crêpe flower confection — while her other kept tugging at the hem of her short silk dress.

'Hi . . . Maddie . . . ' The words emerged in little gasps as Cassie strove to catch her breath. 'I didn't expect to see you here today.' She put a supportive hand on Maddie's arm. 'It's very brave.'

Maddie resisted the impulse to shake off the hand. 'It's a wedding,' she said, 'not an assault course.'

'I know, but you and Freddy were together forever. Mind you, I know I'm too sensitive, everyone tells me that. But I couldn't watch any of my exes getting married. It would be like seeing my future with a big red line scrawled through it. I just couldn't do it. Do you know what I mean?'

Maddie did. It was painful to realise that Cassie was wiser than she was. She adopted a tone of brisk certainty. 'I'm very fond of Freddy. I wouldn't miss his big day.'

'That's so impressive,' Cassie sighed, 'but then so is Freddy. He always stays on good terms with his exes. I don't know how he does it. There are three others coming today.'

'You make us sound like a cult. Freddy's hardly Charles Manson.'

'You're seeing someone new?' Cassie's eyes shone with curiosity. 'Is he coming today?' And then as a voice called out, 'Hey, Babes, wait for me,' she smiled and said fondly, 'It's Jason.'

Jason was a tall, blond man with a strong jaw and perspiring forehead. He took possession of Cassie's right hand and exhaled loudly. 'I thought I'd never find a place. I've had to park on the bank.' He had the sort of voice that made every word he uttered sound extremely important.

2

'It must be a big wedding,' Cassie said. 'Jason, this is Maddie, she's one of Freddy's exes.'

'Hi, Maddie,' Jason said. 'Lovely dress.'

'It *is* nice,' Cassie said. 'It suits your height, Maddie. And the sash is very brave.'

By now they had reached the field and gave a collective gasp of stunned approval. A vast circus tent, royal blue with sunshine gold trimmings, gleamed in the bucolic landscape like a kingfisher in a cabbage patch. Behind it, a collection of vanilla-coloured canopies provided protection to the catering staff, while to the right, sundry knee-high hayricks were scattered around the grass.

Even while admiring the Big Top, the guests could not fail to notice the Sussex Downs making a stunning backdrop in all their late-summer glory: sloping hills criss-crossed with ancient trees and vast squares of varying colours — palest green, mustard-yellow, muted cream. A few puffy white clouds scudded across the sky, their transient shadows deepening the colours of the hills as they passed.

Maddie left Jason adjusting Cassie's head-gear, and walked on. Inside the Big Top, an excited mass of guests sat on chairs facing a platform adorned with two huge floral arrangements and a complex array of sound equipment. Maddie's eyes scanned the crowd and quickly found what they were looking for: a rudimentary bar at the back, manned by three attractive young men in white shirts and black waistcoats.

She was given a modest glass of white wine, which would have to do, and felt a spark of relief

3

as she spotted the bullet-shaped head of Gregory in the back row. He had saved a chair for her and was staring at his tablet, his dark brows knitted in concentration. She threaded her way between the rows, holding her glass high in the air, and took her seat, careful to adjust her brave sash as she did so.

'Gregory,' she said, 'thank you for being here today. I am *so* glad to see you.'

'Well . . . ' Gregory gave a slight awkward shrug — he never quite knew what to do with a compliment. 'I suppose I couldn't let you face this on your own.' He closed his tablet. 'You know Richard the Third?'

'Not personally.' Maddie was sometimes irritated by his habit of ruminating on random subjects but today she was happy to follow him down any conversational avenue, however abstruse.

Someone in a monk's habit sat a couple of rows in front of her. There were quite a few guests in interesting clothes. They would, Maddie knew, be friends of the groom. Her own outfit, a magenta pink dress with sky-blue sash and matching heels, defiantly designed to make an impression, was quite commonplace by comparison.

'Here comes Freddy,' Gregory said, 'in a *suit*.'

'He is the groom after all,' Maddie said, although she too was a little surprised that Freddy had bowed to convention. 'And, anyway,' she added, '*you're* wearing a suit.'

Gregory's suit looked as if it had been pulled from the back of an over-stuffed wardrobe which, knowing Gregory as she did, it almost certainly had been. And now, as she finally looked at Freddy, she could see that his was far more elegant: well-fitted, deep blue, with a red rose embroidered on the lapel of his jacket. His hair was quite long, which suited him, and he had grown a small beard, which did not. She'd heard he was rehearsing for a role in *Measure for Measure* at the Globe.

The last time she had seen him had been the evening she'd left him, ten months ago. Their final discussion had been stark and bitter and it felt odd to sit and watch him now, talking to people in the front row, his hands in his pockets and a broad grin revealing his teeth. Maddie recognised both the grin and the posture. The hands were hidden to conceal their inability to be still, and the grin was Freddy's default expression whenever he was nervous. There had been quite a few times when Maddie had spotted that grin across a crowded room; she would catch his eye and flash a matching grimace back at him. Usually, his features would relax into a genuine Freddy smile.

She was aware she had been expecting him to sense her presence and look across at her. She took a gulp of her wine. 'What *about* Richard the Third?'

'You must remember,' Gregory said. 'His bones were found under a Leicester car park back in February. Do you know how the scientists proved they were his?'

'I very much hope you'll tell me,' Maddie said.

'It was a match of mitochondrial DNA. That's

the genetic material passed down the mother's line. It's a perfect match between the skeleton and some Canadian called Michael Ibsen. The Canadian is directly descended from Richard's sister. Think about it. Ibsen's spit has provided the vital link across nearly six centuries.'

'Wow,' Maddie said. 'Imagine what happens when Ibsen goes to the dentist. Every time he washes his mouth out, he ejects a little piece of Richard the Third.'

'That's sort of true.' Gregory rubbed his chin with his hand. 'Isn't that extraordinary? I shall think about that next time I go to the dentist. I shall even *enjoy* going to the dentist.'

Maddie had known Gregory for fifteen years and been his business partner for two; she still wasn't always sure when he was serious. But all thoughts of Ibsen's history-laden spit vanished from her mind as Freddy's oldest brother stepped onto the stage, tapped his microphone and asked everyone to stand up for the bride.

Maddie craned her neck to catch a first glimpse along with everyone else. She had spent entire evenings staring at Facebook photos of Victoria but none of them did her justice. Victoria — at twenty-five, a long decade younger than Maddie — was the perfect bride, in a cream lace dress that looked like she'd been poured into it. There was no veil or headgear of any kind, just unadorned blonde hair falling down to her shoulders. She stepped up to the groom and Maddie watched Freddy's features relax into a genuine, rapturous smile.

The monk in front of Maddie stood up, made

his way to the stage and pushed back his cowl to reveal the face of Johnny Peters, an old actor friend of Freddy. Maddie had once spent a happy two hours arguing with him about *Othello* after seeing a production in which he and Freddy had small roles. She had been exercised by the fact that in the final scene, Othello had been far more upset by his fall from grace than he was by the fact that he'd murdered his innocent wife. Johnny insisted she had missed the point of the play but it still seemed to Maddie that Othello, like so many wife-murderers these days, felt it was quite forgivable to kill a woman if she made him unhappy.

Every groom, Maddie thought, should have friends in that profession. In his beautiful voice, Johnny read out one of Shakespeare's love sonnets and then summoned other speakers to the stage. There were pieces from *Jane Eyre*, *Pride and Prejudice*, *Captain Corelli's Mandolin* and *Dr Zhivago*, all of them thrillingly read and all suggesting that only love could make a person whole. Maddie began to feel as if she should walk around with a disabled sticker on her dress, emblazoned with the word SINGLE. She wondered if other unattached people in the audience felt the same. She glanced at Gregory, who was looking rather irritated. God knew what he was thinking but he certainly wasn't feeling bad about being single.

And now Johnny came to the microphone to announce that the bride and groom had written their vows and wished to declare them in front of their families and friends. Freddy and Victoria came to the front of the stage and turned to look at each other.

Freddy spoke first. His promises were touching, funny and sweet. 'I promise to try to be the man you deserve,' he said, 'and I want my last night alive to be with you.' He promised to love Victoria and cherish her and respect her always, and he promised to 'find some non-aggressive ways of discussing the cooking'.

Freddy had always found it impossible to be a bystander in the kitchen. Maddie remembered a time Laura and Ted were coming to supper while Laura was heftily pregnant with Billy. Maddie was making her favourite creation: flaked chicken in white sauce with carrots, green peppers and mushrooms. She had caught Freddy bearing down on the stove with curry powder and she said, 'If you even try to put that in my casserole, you're dead.'

'It's great,' Freddy had said, 'it's just a little bland.'

'I know it's bland. That's why I'm about to add a few drops of Tabasco to it.'

'Tabasco's good,' Freddy said, 'but curry powder is better.'

'Freddy,' Maddie said, 'this is my mother's classic recipe. I've been making it for years. You always think you can improve things and sometimes, you can't.'

Freddy had put an arm round her waist. 'I don't want to improve *us*,' he said. And then he'd kissed her and one thing had very nearly led to another, with Maddie only remembering just in time that her dinner was bubbling away like a demented dancer on acid.

When Ted and Laura left, Freddy had looked at Maddie and kissed her. Still kissing her, he'd walked her through to their bedroom. He'd pulled his jersey up over his head and she pulled her dress up over hers. She'd straggled, as she always did, to remove her bra, and with one quick movement, he'd released the hook.

'How do you *do* that?' she'd asked.

He'd laughed and pulled her to him. 'Just so you know,' he'd told her, 'I shall never, ever stop loving you.'

She blinked and found she'd missed every one of Victoria's vows. The woman on her right blew her nose very noisily and murmured, 'So beautiful . . . so very beautiful.'

Later, as they filed out of the Big Top, the woman blinked at Maddie. 'That has to be the most romantic ceremony ever! Didn't it make you want to howl?'

'It certainly did,' Maddie said.

★   ★   ★

Gregory had been refilling their glasses and as he came up and gave Maddie her wine, the woman stared up at him.

'Wasn't that lovely? Didn't you want to cry?'

Gregory responded with excessive force. 'No,' he said, 'I didn't,' and, as Maddie drew him away, he muttered, 'I never read *Jane Eyre* and I certainly shan't do so now. Mr Rochester calls out to Jane in the night and although she's miles and miles away she hears him speak and she tells

9

him she's coming and *he* hears *her* and,' Gregory shook his head violently. 'I mean, it's nonsense. You have to admit, it's nonsense.'

'It's *Jane Eyre*,' Maddie said. 'Thousands of readers have wept tears over that scene. Her soul went out to comfort *his* soul. They were soulmates. And don't roll your eyes at me — every dating site in the country is predicated on the belief that there's a soulmate out there for everyone, even for you, Gregory, though I can't imagine what she'd be like.'

'You see, even that's bollocks.'

'What? The idea that *you* have a soulmate? You might have a point.' She spotted her small godson charging out of the Big Top. A few moments later his father appeared. Ted wore a gold shirt and brown trousers and as he loped after his son, looked a little like an anxious giraffe.

'It's a construct that's riddled with flaws,' Gregory said. 'It's based on outdated biology and centuries-old mumbo-jumbo. A human being is a collection of molecules driven by genetic impulses. I refer you to Michael Ibsen's spit.' He loosened his tie. 'I blame Plato.'

'What does Plato have to do with it?'

'He believed that each one of us is part of a soul and the two halves are forever seeking each other out in order to form a whole. It's probably the single stupidest idea he ever had and it's responsible for all the romantic rubbish that people like you studied at university.'

'I had no idea you were such an expert on English Literature,' Maddie said, though actually, listening to Gregory ridicule *Jane Eyre* was

10

like watching a rare, delicate flower wilting under a spotlight. She supposed it *was* a ridiculous story and was rather pleased that Gregory had drawn its weaknesses to her attention.

★ ★ ★

The afternoon continued to unroll with impressively organized ease. Guests were encouraged to sit around the hayricks while caterers delivered picnic bags containing baguettes, tomatoes, cheese and fruit. Maddie sat with Laura and Ted and little Billy.

Maddie had met Laura on their first day at university and had been impressed by her passionate views on the planet. Within a few weeks of their arrival, Laura had set up a society called 'Population Overload', which aimed to promote the idea that having more than one child in such overcrowded times was a crime against humanity. She had produced a flyer with the title *Bugger Breeding*, a slogan almost perversely designed to confuse. And now here she was, almost seven months pregnant with her second child, a twenty-first-century criminal who showed not a sliver of remorse.

Gregory had promised to join them all for lunch but had been diverted. They could see him sitting with a group of very young women, listening intently to a beautiful girl with long red hair and a diaphanous green dress.

'How does he do it?' Laura asked. 'They must be Victoria's friends. They look like they've hardly left school.'

'You've known Gregory too long,' Maddie said. 'He's actually very attractive. When I was a student, I was quite smitten by him.'

'Were you?' Ted reached for a strawberry. 'I never knew that.'

'It was in our first year,' Maddie said. 'I liked *him* and he liked *me* and we kept waiting for the other to say something. And then other people came along and the moment passed. Which is just as well since we were far too young and we'd never have stayed together. We wouldn't be friends now and we certainly wouldn't be running a business together.'

Ted put an arm round Laura. 'We stayed together.'

'I know,' Maddie said, 'but you two are freaks.' They *were* extraordinary. They'd got together in their final year at university. They'd toiled away throughout their twenties, Ted in I.T. and Laura in fashion journalism. And now here they were in their mid-thirties, working together in Laura's ethical fashion business, bringing up one child and expecting another. They were definitely freaks.

'Gregory would look great,' Laura said, 'if only he dressed better. And he shouldn't cut his own hair. I'm always telling him to go to a proper hairdresser.' The sun was at its brightest now and she put a hand over her eyes. 'He does have a nice smile. He's smiling a lot at the moment. I've never seen him smile so much.'

'He didn't want to come, you know. I virtually had to force him to accept his invitation.' Maddie glanced down at her godson. 'Are you

12

going to eat your tomatoes? I'll have them if you like.'

Billy scooped them up and emptied them onto Maddie's lap before running over to the Big Top. Maddie watched him jumping back and forth across the guy ropes. 'That Big Top is amazing. I wonder where they found it.'

'I thought you'd remember,' Ted said. 'That last time we had supper with you and Freddy, I mentioned my little brother's latest exploit . . . '

'Oh God, I do! He and his friends take these things round the country, hiring them out and putting them up. So this is Joe's tent?'

'Freddy rang us about it a couple of months ago. It's all worked out rather well. We've rented a small cottage in the high street for a few days. Joe is going to babysit for us tonight. In return he can stay with us in comfort instead of sleeping in his big smelly lorry.'

'I remember meeting Joe at your wedding,' Maddie said. 'He was rather sweet and very confident.'

Ted grunted. 'Well, now he's just confident.'

Maddie stood up. 'I suppose I ought to circulate. I might go via the drinks tent.' It had been clever of Freddy to remember that conversation. It upset her that he had filed it away for future use.

★ ★ ★

She wandered round the field, greeting Freddy's old friends and having almost identical conversations with each of them: 'It's so good to see you

13

again . . . How are you? . . . We mustn't lose touch just because . . . ' The voices were laced with well-meaning, but not entirely convincing, resolution. It was a chastening thought that she and Freddy had shared their lives for two full years and yet only three of her friends had been invited to his wedding: Gregory, Laura and Ted. Four, if one counted Billy. Maddie didn't blame Freddy for this. She had made precious little effort to see *his* friends in the last ten months and was now reduced to mouthing social niceties at most of them. She suspected Laura and Ted had only been invited because of the tent.

She would have liked to talk to Freddy's sister, Georgia, but whenever she saw her she was surrounded by friends and family and children. Georgia lived in Clapham with her husband and three sons and had regularly invited Maddie and Freddy to Sunday lunch. A sad by-product of the split with Freddy was losing touch with his parents and many siblings. They had always embraced her as one of their own and she'd been grateful for it. Given the permanent, gaping wound within her own family, she found the careless, easy closeness they had for each other particularly warming.

She saw Freddy's parents talking to a man in a black-and-white striped suit and waved. Freddy's mother, Kate, waved back and murmured to her husband. As they walked towards her it was obvious that they were apprehensive. The conversation that followed showed that neither of them quite knew how to talk to her. In fact, Kate's tactful attempts to steer a path through the minefield were more difficult to cope with than her husband's unerring ability to detonate every mine in sight.

'Maddie,' Kate said, 'how lovely to see you. I had no idea you'd be here. You look gorgeous in that dress! Matthew, doesn't Maddie look gorgeous in that dress?'

'Maddie never fails to looks gorgeous,' Matthew said. 'I've always maintained that every one of my sons has excellent taste in women. I have four quite stunning daughters-in-law and . . . ' A sudden, panic-stricken expression crossed his face, 'though of course you're *not* a daughter-in-law, Maddie, but you *might* have been and I suppose what I'm trying to say . . . '

'Maddie knows very well what you're trying to say.' Kate's complexion had gone very pink. 'So there's no need to say it. Now tell us, Maddie dear, how is your business going?'

Maddie made her excuses as soon as she could — it was obvious that Kate found the meeting excruciating — and, walking with great purpose to nowhere in particular, found herself face to face with the bride and groom. She had known this would happen sooner or later but it didn't stop her brain sending busy messages to every fibre in her body: don't blush, stare them in the eye with easy confidence, keep your shoulders back and your chin up, don't laugh for no reason, smile for long enough to be friendly but not for so long that you look like you're mad.

Freddy, like his mother, professed to be delighted to see her. One might have thought he had spent the last hour combing the field for her.

But then, Freddy *was* an actor.

'It's so nice to meet you at last,' Victoria said. 'Freddy's told me so much about you.'

Victoria was genuinely friendly. It was clear that she had an open, kind-hearted nature. She also had unblemished skin, slight arching eyebrows and a figure as slender as a silver birch. In comparison, Maddie felt like a gnarled old apple tree. 'I can see you make him very happy,' she responded. 'You both look very, very happy!' She sounded like a stuck record.

'We'd better get on,' Freddy said. 'It's back to the tent for the speeches, I'm afraid.' He gave her a brief smile but it was clear his mind was already on the next stage of the proceedings.

She had, she saw now, made a huge miscalculation arising from a misplaced sense of her own importance. Freddy hadn't sent her an invitation as a challenge. Why should he? He had no residual feelings for her; he was besotted by Victoria. He had invited Maddie to his wedding because he was a nice man who bore no grudges.

So now it was back to the tent, and Maddie listened as Victoria's father talked about his daughter's unerring ability to win the hearts of all who met her. Freddy's oldest brother told funny stories about Freddy and finally Freddy himself stood up. He was visibly more relaxed than he had been during the ceremony.

Like the good actor he was, he understood the importance of timing. He moved to the front of the stage and glanced amiably round his audience until there was an expectant hush. 'At the beginning of this year,' he said, 'I was sitting

16

in a reception area, feeling pretty low.'

Maddie stiffened. *Was he going to mention her?* 'A few weeks earlier I'd been promised a fantastic part in a new American TV series; it was a role that was guaranteed to make my fortune. Then my agent rang to say my part had been written out and instead he sent me to audition for a non-speaking role in a chocolate bar advert.' *He wasn't going to mention her. Of course, he wasn't.* 'Anyway, I sat in my chair, musing on the fickleness of fate and TV executives and suddenly this amazing woman flies through the door and alights on the chair next to mine and tells me, very apologetically, that she's afraid she and I are going to have to kiss each other.'

Everyone laughed. Maddie, following suit, heard her own laugh sound like a hyena being strangled.

'I told her quite sincerely I didn't mind at all and a few minutes later we were both ushered through and I did indeed have to kiss her.' Freddy paused and gave a shrug. 'I know. It's a tough life being an actor but someone has to do it. Our auditions were successful. The advert will be on your TV screen any day now. I, for one, will be eternally indebted to Crispy Crackle Chocolate Bars.' He stopped to clear his throat. 'Within the week, I knew I wanted to many Victoria. It took a little longer to persuade *her* to marry *me*. I firmly believe that there is one person for everyone and I know that I am Victoria's and she is mine. She is loyal, supportive, kind and true. She has taught me what love really means and I want to spend the rest of our lives proving that I'm worthy of her.'

The applause was tumultuous. If Gregory were next to her, he would probably whisper some critical remark about sentimental rubbish but Gregory was now sitting with the red-haired girl and Maddie was surrounded by people cheering Freddy and shouting, 'Bravo!'

In the evening, there were hot dogs and pizzas, and a band — friends of Victoria or Freddy or both — provided the music. Maddie talked to Johnny Peters' girlfriend who was pregnant — quite a few women here seemed to be pregnant — and she danced with Freddy's father and Gregory and Ted. She went out of the tent to get some fresh night air. Groups of people stood around a bonfire and candle torches were dotted around the field. The sky was dark now, an inky panorama patterned with dusky blue streamers.

★   ★   ★

She caught sight of Freddy's sister leaving the drinks tent with her hands cradled round a plastic cup. Maddie took a deep breath and walked across to her. 'Georgia, I've been trying to say hello to you all day.'

'Hello, Maddie.' Georgia enunciated the words slowly. 'I'm a little drunk. It's a good wedding, isn't it? It's nice to see you.' She frowned. 'Actually, it's quite strange to see you. Why are you here?'

Maddie had been asking herself the same

question. It was obvious that as far as Freddy's family was concerned, she was about as popular as Banquo's ghost. 'I was sent an invitation,' she said. 'It seemed churlish to turn it down.'

'I see.' Georgia nodded gravely and took a sip of her wine. 'It's funny how things turn out. I always thought you and Freddy were made for each other.' She glanced across to the Big Top and waved at someone. 'I'd better go. I've promised my husband a dance and no-one else will dance with him. He has very heavy feet.' She patted Maddie's arm with her free hand. 'Have a nice life, Maddie. I always liked you. Goodbye.'

It was then that Maddie decided to leave the party. She walked carefully down the bumpy lane, cursing herself for not bringing a torch. The entire occasion had been unremittingly grim. In her mind a host of newly minted images were already hardening into intractable memories.

Her mother used to say that one should never indulge in self-pity more than once a week. Maddie agreed with the maxim. She had thrown herself into her work throughout the last seven days and had resolutely refused to think about what might have been. Now she felt entitled to wallow. Freddy's family had firmly relegated her to The Past; Freddy had barely noticed her, his attention totally given over to a vacuous twenty-five-year-old who, worse still, probably wasn't vacuous at all since everyone loved her so much. Gregory, her very best friend who had only agreed to come today in order to support her, had hardly spoken to her since the picnic lunch. When she left she had spotted him dancing enthusiastically with Victoria's red-haired friend. And all *she* had to show for the day was an overdrawn credit card.

She emerged onto the road and began to walk up the main street of the village, grateful for the light provided by houses on either side.

She heard someone calling, 'Maddie? Maddie Drummond?' and turned. A young man with unruly black curls stood smoking in the front garden of a neat little cottage on the other side of the road.

She crossed the street and stopped outside his gate. 'It's the tent man! Hello, Joe. How clever of you to recognise me.'

'I could never forget you, Maddie.' He threw away his cigarette. 'You've left early. The night's still young.'

'It's been a long day and I'm ready for bed.'

Joe walked down towards her. 'Fancy a nightcap? I've some wine in the fridge.'

'It's tempting,' Maddie said, 'but I've drunk too much already. What I need is water. I'll see you, Joe. I loved your Big Top.'

As she walked on up the street she heard him call, 'I can give you water!' and smiled. It was ridiculous how a flattering comment and a blatant proposition — even if it came from Ted's cocky little brother — could uplift the spirits.

She let herself into her lodgings and walked up the stairs to her room. She felt, quite suddenly, overcome by exhaustion. She was sure she would fall asleep as soon as her head hit the pillow.

Two hours later she was still awake, Georgia's words reverberating round her mind with ever-increasing intensity: *I always thought you and Freddy were made for each other.* So did I, Maddie thought, so do I.

The wedding had proved to be a wake, an overdue burial of all her fantasies of a future with Freddy. She had, after all, been right to come today. She had seen at first-hand that she'd comprehensively and finally lost the love of her life. She had needed to understand this. All she had to do now was to work out where she went from here.

2

It had often occurred to Henry that small decisions could have vast unforeseen consequences. Certainly, if he hadn't fancied an omelette for supper that evening, life for many people would have been substantially altered.

There were no shops in Higgleigh that sold free-range eggs after six; so, at the end of his working day — in fact, his working week, although after four months Henry still felt surprised by this each and every Thursday afternoon — he decided to visit the mini-supermarket round the corner from his office in Colchester.

On the way back to the car park, Henry stood by the road, waiting for the lights to change. Behind him, a former office building was being converted into flats. A radio blared out music while men worked on the scaffolding. A group of teenage girls stood laughing on the other side of the road, flicking back their hair, their white shirts only a little shorter than their black school skirts. Their confidence was plain to see and Henry felt a momentary gratitude that he was no longer a boy. He noticed Jeremy's secretary, Audrey Pennington, standing a few feet away from him. He'd have said hello but she was engrossed in her mobile. Henry wondered if he was the only adult in England who had never ever been engrossed by a mobile.

The next few seconds passed in a ghastly slow-motion sequence. The men at the top of the scaffolding shouted a warning and Henry looked up as a large iron bar headed straight for Audrey's head. With a speed and agility that, later, Henry thought was little short of miraculous, he lunged forward to grab her by the waist and brought her crashing down on top of him. Someone, possibly Audrey, screamed and for a few moments the two of them lay in a sideways embrace like a spooning couple in bed. Henry's free-range eggs exploded across the road and the iron bar plunged like a thunderbolt onto the pavement, cracking the hard stone beneath it.

Henry was tall but also very thin. Audrey, while shorter, was considerably more substantial and his muscles creaked in protest. After onlookers helped them to their feet and workmen made shaken and breathless apologies, it was Audrey who helped Henry across the road to the car park. 'Are you all right?' she kept asking, 'are you sure you're all right?'

When they arrived at his car, Henry forgot about his own aches and pains because Audrey murmured, 'I think I might be . . . ', sank against the car and was caught by Henry once again.

Audrey lived in Wivenhoe, a small Essex town a few miles to the south-east of Colchester. Henry insisted on driving her home and assured her it was almost on his way, although in fact Henry's house in Higgleigh, Suffolk, was a good fifteen miles in the opposite direction. As they made their way through the rush-hour traffic, Henry kept glancing across at his passenger and was relieved to see the colour coming back to her face.

'It was the shock,' she said. 'I keep seeing that bar . . . If you'd not been so quick . . . ' She put her hand to her throat. 'You saved my life, Henry.'

'I wouldn't say that,' Henry murmured. He was terrified she might start to cry. 'I saw you staring at your mobile,' he said. 'I remember feeling very impressed. The firm gave me a smartphone last year and I still can't make head nor tail of it. The buttons are too small for my fingers and it only rings once so I hardly ever hear it and when I do, I have no idea how to answer it.'

'My husband's the same.' Audrey's voice was firmer now. She craned her head forward. 'This traffic is terrible. It's not usually like this. Something must have happened.'

They had left Colchester now and still the cars were only inching along. 'I was looking at a text from my younger daughter,' she said. 'Alice met her boyfriend when she worked in Pakistan and now he's come to join her here, In order to stay he has to take a test. He's had to buy this big book about England and has to learn every bit of it. You wouldn't believe what he has to know. My daughter sends me these questions he has to answer and I don't know any of them and . . . Good heavens!'

The mystery of the traffic jam had been solved. Sprawled across the road was a beaten-up car with words emblazoned in red along its side: *We Teach You to Drive Safely!*

Just in front of it, a van lay drunkenly concertinaed on the bank. A lone policeman waved Henry past.

Henry took the right turn towards Wivenhoe. 'They say things happen in threes,' he murmured.

'I've always thought,' Audrey said, 'that you'd have to be very brave to be a driving instructor.' They both fell silent and Audrey only stirred to give him directions to her home.

He stopped at the end of a row of semi-detached houses, each with white-fronted garages and neatly tarmacked driveways. Audrey's garage door was open and she murmured that Michael was probably stuck in the traffic. Insisting that Henry stop for a cup of tea, she put him in her front room and retired to the kitchen, returning a few minutes later with a tray on which sat a floral teapot, matching crockery and a plate of shortbread biscuits.

She seemed fully recovered now. Noting Henry's interest in a framed photo on the mantelpiece, she set down the tray and said, 'That's Alice on the left. Hannah's getting married next April. I need to lose two stone for the wedding. I've joined Weight Watchers.'

'I don't think you need to do that,' Henry said. She was a little plump but not unpleasantly so.

'That's very kind of you . . . '

'Not at all. I was saying what I thought.'

Audrey passed Henry his tea. 'Hannah's fiancé is very nice. He's called Edmund. His mother . . . ' She sighed. 'His mother is very slim.'

'I see,' Henry said, accepting a shortbread biscuit.

'His parents have offered to hold the reception at their house in Berkshire which is very generous but . . . '

There was the sound of a key in the lock and Audrey immediately stood up. 'We're in here, Michael!' she called.

A bald-headed man came in. He had big, black-framed glasses like the ones Henry wore. Audrey went straight across to him. 'Oh Michael, this man saved my life!' she said, and burst into tears.

★ ★ ★

By the time Henry left, the roads were much easier. Even the A12 was relatively empty. In the pale evening light, the Suffolk countryside seemed particularly lovely; the copper beech trees were at their best at this time of year and the banks along the Higgleigh road were full of wild flowers. A tribe of wild geese formed a perfect V against the soft pinkish sky. He thought how odd it was that a few hours ago he had only known Audrey as Jeremy's secretary, a woman who always smiled at him when he said hello to her. Now he knew that she had a nice husband called Michael, a daughter called Alice with a boyfriend from Pakistan and another daughter called Hannah whose future mother-in-law would possibly be a problem.

Back at home, he eased himself out of the car and reached for the keys to his house. 'You're a hero,' Audrey's husband had said and, remembering, Henry straightened his shoulders as he walked through the green gate and up his garden path.

When Henry and Marianne married, they lived in London before moving to Colchester. The first time he'd taken her to Higgleigh to meet his parents, she'd enthused about the town with its timber-framed buildings and wide high street. On Maddie's seventh birthday, his mother had sent them the particulars of a modestly priced house in Belton Street and had written on a torn-out piece of paper: 'What do you think?'

Marianne fell in love with the place as soon as she saw it. 'I always wanted a dolls' house when I was little,' she said, 'and here it is!'

It *did* look like a dolls' house. Dating back to 1790, it stood in the middle of a walled garden: red-brick walls, tiled roof, tall sash windows almost hidden by the wisteria covering the front of the house. A detailed examination explained the low asking price. It needed everything doing to it: a new heating system, re-wiring, proper insulation, damp proofing, repairing and re-stringing the sash windows. The list was endless, Henry said, and the garden was a wilderness.

The house had been used to billet sick soldiers in the Second World War and an internal wall had been knocked down to make way for all the patients. Its latest owner, crippled by illness for several years, had used the huge room as a bedsit. His daughter had finally persuaded him to move into a home and was anxious to sell the place quickly.

'But Marianne,' Henry said, 'it would take years to get this right.'

'We *have* years,' she'd said. 'This room will make the perfect family kitchen. And imagine getting out of the car on Belton Street and walking through the door into our own private world. It will be heaven!'

It *had* taken a long time, although Henry had underestimated Marianne's tirelessness. Four years after her death, the house remained a testament to her enthusiasm and energy and love.

As Henry entered the hall, his mother's French bulldog shuffled and snuffled across the flagstones towards him. Ivan had gleaming black fur with a jagged white dash along his back. He possessed small, squat legs, erect little ears, huge bulging eyes and a head that was far too big for his body. His face looked like it had been bashed inwards by a giant fist. When he was excited, as he was now, it sounded like a golf ball was stuck in his throat. In all the excitement of the near-accident Henry had forgotten that he was looking after him and he bent down to stroke his fur. 'Hello, Ivan,' he said, 'you poor old boy, you must be starving. Did you think I'd left you forever?'

As soon as he'd given Ivan his supper, Henry made straight for the drinks cupboard, taking out the bottle of whisky and carrying it to the table. 'You should have seen him,' Audrey had told her husband, 'he didn't flinch; he just leapt forward like an acrobat. He saved me. Everyone said he saved me.' Henry smiled. He'd thought he was long past saving anyone and not even his mother would call him an acrobat.

It was while he poured his whisky that he noticed the three eggs sitting in their basket on the dresser. His first thought was that he would be able to have an omelette after all. His second was more sombre. If it hadn't been for his appalling memory he would have driven straight home and Audrey's skull would have been crushed by the iron bar. He sipped his whisky and winced as a shaft of pain raced through his lower back. He would have a bath tonight.

He made his omelette and read the paper while he ate it. After he had cleared up the kitchen, he thought he might watch a little television and went through to the sitting room, closely followed by Ivan. He wondered what Audrey and Michael were doing. He felt restless and, as he walked towards the television, was relieved to be interrupted by the ringing of the telephone.

It was Nina. 'Hi, Dad,' she said. 'We'll be a little late for lunch on Sunday, I'm afraid. Expect us about half one. Robbie has a load of paperwork to do this weekend.'

'He works too hard,' Henry said.

'Tell me about it. That's what happens when you start a new business. There are always things to do.'

Nina should know. When people asked Henry what she did, he told them she was an *organiser*. Nina, like her mother, had always been good at organising. As a teenager, her boyfriends invariably played in bands and Nina had proved adept at finding them engagements or 'gigs', as she called them. From there, she had gone on to organise parties and celebrations and sometimes even weddings. She booked bands and caterers, she found the venue, she even designed the invitations. Once Megan was born, she embraced full-time motherhood with equal enthusiasm. These days she helped at Chloe's playgroup, she was on the parent-teacher committee at Megan's school and she ran her household with huge efficiency. She was a very impressive young woman and Henry looked forward to impressing *her*.

'I saved someone's life today,' he said, with what he hoped was an air of unstudied nonchalance.

'Did you? I wish someone would save mine. What happened?'

Henry told her about the eggs and the iron bar and Audrey fainting by his car. And he could tell by all her questions that he *had* impressed her.

'Dad, that's amazing,' she said at last. 'Well done!'

'Thank you,' Henry said, and then as an afterthought, 'Why does *your* life need saving?'

'Oh, I'm just a little down at the moment. Now that Robbie's parents have moved away, life is so much more difficult to sort out . . . '

'They've moved away?' Henry said.

'We threw a leaving party for them six months ago. You came to it. You only stayed for about five seconds but you did come to it.'

'Of course I did.' Henry remembered it now: there had been a strong smell of beer and the place had been crammed with people who talked too loudly. He said, 'They moved to Devon. I can't recall why.'

'They retired there to be near to Robbie's sister, which is great for her but a disaster for me. They were always looking after the children, and now Robbie's started his business we need every penny and I can't afford to pay babysitters. Sadie's having a birthday supper next week and I can't go because Robbie will be in London. It's just a pity, that's all.'

It had never occurred to Henry that Nina might get tired or dispirited. Tonight, she did sound dispirited. He said slowly, 'I could look after the girls for you.'

A stunned silence greeted this offer before Nina said, 'But Dad, that's not what you do.'

'I know,' Henry said, 'but perhaps I should.'

'The girls would be asleep,' Nina said uncertainly. 'You wouldn't have to do anything. Dad, it would be great! I'd so love a night out!'

'Well,' Henry said, 'a night out you shall have!'

After he rang off, he returned to the kitchen to make a cup of tea. He should have remembered about Robbie's parents and should have offered to help before now. He'd never been very adept with small children. Marianne had been capable enough for both of them. His guilt threatened to puncture his mood and he decided to ring his older daughter to tell her about his adventure.

'I wish I'd been there,' Maddie said. 'I can't imagine you leaping forward and saving a woman from certain death.'

Now Henry came to think about it, he

couldn't imagine it either. 'Audrey Pennington definitely said I leapt,' he said.

'Well,' Maddie said, 'you are an undisputed hero. Where do you go from here?'

Henry knew he was not always very good at understanding his daughters. He and Marianne used to ring Maddie at university and Henry would chat to her first and think she was fine and then Marianne would talk and start asking questions and it would turn out that Maddie's heart had been broken or her latest essay had been trashed by her tutor. Tonight, however, Henry was aware that the accident had sharpened his senses and he could tell that his daughter's voice was a little flatter than usual. 'How are you?' he asked. 'Is everything all right?'

'I'm fine.' There was a pause. 'I went to Freddy's wedding on Saturday.'

'Did you? That was very . . . very . . . '

'Very *what*?'

'Well, it was very . . . ' If Marianne were here, she would roll her eyes and grab the phone from him, 'very . . . *nice* of you to go. Did you like the bride?'

'She was lovely. I'm sure she and Freddy are made for each other.'

'I'm glad,' Henry said. 'I always liked Freddy.'

'I know you did. Dad, I'd love to chat but I have some calls to make. I'll speak to you soon, all right?'

Henry put the phone down and felt another sharp twinge in his back. He would go and have that bath. He took Ivan out into the garden and waited. As usual, Ivan looked, as if he had no idea what he was doing there. 'Come on, Ivan,' Henry said. Ivan made his way to the flowerbed with a distinct lack of enthusiasm. He stretched his back legs behind him, lowered his behind and proceeded to relieve himself while staring at Henry with mournful eyes. Henry shivered and he and Ivan made their way back to the warmth of the kitchen. Henry said good night, switched out the lights and made his way slowly up the stairs.

He ran his bath and climbed very gingerly into it. Every bone in his body seemed to ache but he didn't mind. He regarded his bruises as battle scars. Four years ago he had assumed that the rest of his life would be a mere postscript to everything that had gone before, that he would slowly slip into retirement and old age. But now — 'You saved my life' Audrey Pennington had said, and *he had*.

'Where do you go from here?' Maddie had asked. The question was both unnerving and a little exciting. He was sixty-two and he had thought he was old. But he wasn't. He had saved a life today. He had been like an acrobat.

Everything was different.

3

When Maddie decided to leave Freddy, the first person she rang was her aunt. Colette said — as Maddie had known she would — 'You can stay with me for as long as you like. It will be lovely to have your company.'

Maddie sometimes wondered how often Colette recalled that wildly over-optimistic assertion. There were the evenings when Maddie wept with lavish incontinence on Colette's sofa and there were weekends when she would leap from her laptop, demanding that her aunt see the latest perfect flat she could rent in some exciting part of London. On those days she would assure Colette it was exhilarating to be single again, free to settle where she wanted and see whomever she wished.

She started seeing a man she met through work: he was forty-nine and divorced. He was wealthy, attentive, kind and a little too needy. After two months he asked her to marry him. He offered her love, security and a nice house in Dulwich. She was shocked by the fact that she nearly accepted his proposal. For the time being, she decided, it was safer to be single.

Meanwhile, Colette had been doing research of her own. It might be sensible, she suggested, for Maddie to live near her place of work. Maddie knew she was right. Encouraged by Gregory's example, she had been on the verge of

34

planting her first foot on the property ladder a few years ago. But then she had met Freddy and property ladders had seemed pedestrian. And when she and Gregory set up their company they could only afford to pay themselves modest salaries.

The sad truth was that it was difficult to be a free spirit without sufficient financial resources. Reluctantly, she gave up all thoughts of Vauxhall or Clapham or Camberwell or Brixton and settled for Crystal Palace, a sprawl of a town that owed both its name and its fame to a building that had burnt down over half a century ago.

The flat Colette had found was in an old house that must once have been lovely. The big hall with the sweeping staircase was all that remained of its former glory — the dark green stair carpet was frayed and stained and the wallpaper was thin and grey with age.

By contrast, the flat on the first floor was light and bland, with wood-effect flooring, chalky white walls and sundry Ikea units. It stood politely waiting for someone to give it a personality. Once Maddie brought in her pictures and books, her lamps and her rags, she was sure she could oblige. Best of all, it was only a few minutes' walk from Gregory's place.

Gregory's road, unlike Maddie's, was wholly residential, lined on either side with purpose-built houses, each comprising a trio of flats. Gregory had one on the lower ground floor, and its large sitting-room doubled as their office. After Maddie moved, she suggested to him that they start their working day earlier to ensure a calmer system. Gregory agreed with the principle but found putting it into practice difficult since he had an innate dislike of early mornings. They reached a compromise. On Mondays and Fridays, they would start at eight thirty and on other days they would begin half an hour later. Since then there had been quite a few Mondays when he was washed, dressed and ready for work.

Today, she let herself in, walked through the narrow corridor into the sitting room and found Gregory in front of his computer, dressed in his pyjama bottoms and one of his ugliest sweatshirts. She peered over his shoulder at the screen. 'Gregory,' she said, 'what *is* this?'

'It's a 'Life in the UK' test,' he said, without looking up. 'If you come to this country and want to stay, you have to take it. It's unbelievable. There are questions a six-year-old could answer, like *The Prime Minister is a very important man in the country: True or False?*, and then,' he paused to scroll down the list, 'you suddenly get these questions about Wales: *What percentage of the population lives in Wales: 5%, 6%, 7%, 11%?* And look at this: *How many members does the National Assembly for Wales have: 50, 60, 70, 80?*' He glanced up at Maddie. 'Do you know the answer to either of those?'

'Of course I don't but . . . '

'Hang on, let me give you two more then I'll stop. *What are the two characteristics of civil servants: friendliness and efficiency/long holidays and quick service/political neutrality and*

36

professionalism/political correctness and slow but careful service?'

'I'm not sure. It can't be friendliness and efficiency. My Uncle Edward was a Permanent Secretary and I can't imagine him being friendly to anyone.'

'Well, there you go. And finally: *Many people remark on the great variety in the British land-scape: True or False?* Has anyone ever said to you, 'It's a funny thing about the British land-scape, you know, it has such a great variety'?'

'To be fair,' Maddie said, 'it *is* pretty varied. Suffolk's very flat and Dorset has hills . . . '

'Most countries have varied landscapes. Israel's the size of Wales and it has deserts and mountains and the Dead Sea.'

Maddie took off her jacket. 'Can we get to work now?'

'This *is* about work. You know Amira?'

'I should do. I was the one who interviewed her.'

'She wants to be an English citizen. She's had to buy a colossal book and she's supposed to memorize it all so she can answer these questions. I said I'd help her.'

This was why Gregory exasperated and impressed Maddie in equal measures. She had known when he'd first suggested joining forces that he'd be a difficult colleague. Erratic in temperament, he could spend a day complaining of headaches or heartburn and then the next morning she'd wake up to find he'd texted her a dozen great ideas during the night. His view of time-keeping was abysmal — he'd missed more trains in one year than most people did in a lifetime. Quick to take offence and impatient of sloppy thinking, he was also capable of unexpected kindness. Maddie had known that Amira was struggling with her homework but it hadn't occurred to her to offer to help. On the other hand, she thought, there was a time and a place for everything.

Her eyes swept over the sundry motivational directions stuck on the wall round his computer, stopping at the highest one. 'Look,' she said, 'I refer you to your friend Lord Chesterfield: 'One yawns, one procrastinates, one can do it when one will, and therefore one seldom does it at all.' I'll make us some coffee. I bet you haven't even showered yet.'

'Actually,' Gregory said with dignity, 'I have. But I *will* go and shave.'

Gregory's small galley kitchen was in its usual state of disarray. When they had first agreed to base their office here, Maddie had told him sternly that housework was not part of her job description. As a matter of principle she continued to resist an instinctive impulse to clear the sink, but it wasn't easy. She had to remind herself that one of the tenets of their mission statement was developing a sense of respect and equality between the sexes.

She and Gregory had set up Plug Clubs two years ago, armed with their savings and a hefty grant from a courageous bank manager who had somehow been persuaded by their pitch. They had eight after-school clubs now, dotted around South London. The idea was simple: school premises were hired along with retired teachers and university students who provided basic courses in drama, music, sport, philosophy and debating. Sandwiches and cakes were provided by teams of home-based cooks. The clubs were not cheap but, as Maddie said, they were less expensive than nannies, and special rates were offered to those with low incomes.

The first year had been manic and there were still days when they worked late into the evening. Crises were normal. Only last week Gregory had to take a Philosophy group in Forest Hill. He'd been very smug the next day, telling Maddie that the children had loved his graphic recreation of Socrates' suicide. With any luck, today would be uneventful. Maddie hoped so; she'd agreed to meet Amy in town at seven and she had no wish to keep her waiting. Amy was a stickler for punctuality.

Gregory came into the sitting room, newly shaved and now dressed in a tee shirt and tracksuit bottoms. Maddie poured his coffee and sipped her own. 'Did you have a good weekend?' she asked. 'Did you get to see that girl you met at Freddy's wedding? What was her name? Araminta?'

'Actually,' Gregory said, 'she prefers to be called Minty.'

'I'm not surprised.'

'And while it would be nice to chat about her . . . ' Gregory paused to take a sip of his coffee, 'I'm afraid it would be a clear case of procrastination. I think it's time we got down to work, don't you?'

Maddie had met Amy years ago when she'd
started her worst-ever job as a lowly marketing
assistant with a TV production company. She
and Amy suffered equally from the volcanic
rages of Monsieur DuPlessis, their managing
director. His default method of management was
to lose his temper. His face, a tomato sizzling in
oil, would twist with derision and his Gallic
consonants would spit across the room like
venomous arrows. He expected his employees to
work themselves senseless despite the fact that
he left the office after lunch every Friday in
order to catch the shuttle back to Paris to spend
the weekend with his wife and son. No one was
surprised when Madame DuPlessis left her
husband — the only mystery being why she had
ever married him — but within a few months, his
rages had moved from tyrannical to almost
certifiable. The company was heading for the
rocks and Maddie and Amy were two of the first
rats to leave the sinking ship.

Amy found a job with a charity and Maddie
re-trained as a teacher. In the next few years they
continued to see each other regularly. Amy
would moan about immature boyfriends and
Maddie would rant about her disastrous career
choice. And then Amy met John and meetings
became rather more sporadic. Maddie thought
John was kind and polite and deadly dull. Last
year she and Freddy met up with them in
Hampstead. They had gone to the theatre and
had a meal together afterwards. It had not been a

success. Freddy had loved the play and John had hated it but was too polite to say so. Maddie and Amy were both nervous, sensing almost at once that their partners had nothing in common.

A week earlier, Maddie had a call from Amy, suggesting they meet for a meal. 'I've broken up with John,' she said. 'I could really do with some brilliant Maddie-style advice.'

The restaurant served good pizzas and moderately-priced wines. It also had the charisma of a doctor's waiting room, with black and orange walls, thin black plastic tables and chairs and lighting that was a little too bright. Maddie arrived first and ordered a bottle for the two of them, an act designed to stifle the guilt she felt: she had turned down two invitations to supper from Amy in the last ten months and was only here now because John wasn't.

The waitress, a girl with pencilled eyebrows, an overactive ponytail and sprayed-on enthusiasm, had just opened the bottle when Amy arrived. Grief suited her. She had a new haircut, she'd lost weight and wore a black dress that Maddie instantly coveted. 'Amy,' she said, 'you look fantastic!'

Amy sat down and patted her hair. 'You don't think it's too short?'

'Absolutely not, and I love the fringe.'

'It hides the worry lines.' Amy scanned the menu. 'Let's order, shall we?'

She had always liked her food and Maddie was relieved to see that she chose a pizza rather than some rabbit-food salad. Having called and despatched the waitress, Amy put her hands on her lap and asked, 'How's work? Is Gregory driving you mad?'

Maddie responded with a few funny stories, all received with a polite, if perfunctory, display of amusement. It was obvious that Amy was in no mood for small talk, which suited Maddie since she was curious to know how a couple who talked about pension plans could decide to split up. She put a hand on Amy's arm and said, 'Tell me about John.'

Amy's body seemed to sag. 'It's a long story,' she said.

'I like long stories.'

Amy smiled. 'It *is* nice to see you.'

'It's nice to see *you*.' Unencumbered by lovers, it was easy to remember why they used to be close. Amy gave a little sigh as if exhaling what little energy she possessed. 'It started back in June. John had these tummy pains. They got worse and worse. He had all sorts of tests and was admitted to hospital. The doctors thought it might be his kidneys and then they thought it was something else. He nearly ended up with a colostomy bag. Luckily a bright young junior doctor discovered his appendix had been ruptured. A part of it had fallen into his pelvis which stopped his gut working. It was rather gruesome, really.'

'It sounds terrifying. Poor John.'

'I suppose.' Amy took a sip of her wine. 'His mother came up to see him. We spent a lot of time together and while he was in the operating theatre I told her we'd been trying for a baby.'

'Oh my God,' Maddie said, 'I had no idea.'

'John didn't want anyone to know. He said it would jinx things. We'd been trying for fourteen months. Can you imagine what that's like? Every four weeks you find out you're not going to have a child and it gets so you can't walk past a baby shop without crying . . . Anyway. I told his mother and she looked at me as if I was mad and said, 'But, Amy, surely you knew John can't have children?''

'Oh, Amy, you poor thing . . .' Maddie had no idea what to say. There was a time when she and Amy had told each other everything and it wasn't Amy's fault that they had drifted apart. There had been regular invitations to supper, chatty messages via Facebook, a bouquet of flowers when she moved to Crystal Palace. Come to think of it, there'd been a distinct absence of chatty messages in the last few months. *I should have known something was wrong,* Maddie thought. *I should have got in touch.*

'Hi, ladies!' The waitress was back, a plate balanced on either palm. 'Who wanted the pepperoni?'

Maddie raised a hand and nodded her thanks as the pizza was put in front of her. The waitress served Amy and smiled at them both. 'Enjoy!' she said.

Amy waited until they were on their own again and leant forward. 'Don't you hate being called 'Ladies'?' she hissed. 'It makes me feel like we're old-age pensioners.'

'We probably are as far as she's concerned,' Maddie said. 'So what happened next? What did you do?'

'I went home, packed my bags and took a taxi to my mother's house in Richmond. We drove each other mad for a few weeks and then I found a flat of my own.'

'Yes, but . . . Surely you talked to John about it?'

'I visited him in hospital. He confessed that he hadn't dared tell me. He thought I'd leave him if I knew the truth. It took quite a while to explain that I was only leaving him now because he *didn't* tell me. Think about it. Every month he'd watch me fall apart and never said a word.' Amy bit her lower lip and blinked twice.

'If it's any consolation,' Maddie said, 'I never thought he was right for you. If you want to know the truth, I found him pretty boring.'

Her remark, crass though it was, had the desired effect. Amy no longer looked like she was going to cry. 'If you want to know the truth,' she said, 'I never liked Freddy either.' And now she smiled, a proper Amy smile. 'I wish you could see your face.'

'I'm just surprised,' Maddie said. 'Why didn't you like him?'

'Do you remember how dull that play in Hampstead was? At supper afterwards, he went on and on about it, what an amazing piece of theatre it was, how brave the director was. What is brave about directing a really dull play that no one but the actors can understand? And why do actors always think their profession is so much more important than anyone else's?'

'I don't know,' Maddie murmured. She was stunned by Amy's judgement. No one could ever accuse Freddy of being boring. Except Amy, apparently.

'You might be right about John,' Amy conceded. 'It doesn't matter now. I spent three fertile years with him. I'm thirty-six and on the dust heap.'

'Listen,' Maddie said. 'You are younger than Jennifer Aniston, Sandra Bullock and Meryl Streep and they're all still gorgeous. You'll meet someone else.'

'I'm *thirty-six*. How many attractive men of my age do you know who aren't married or gay or just a little weird?'

'Well . . . ' Maddie began and then stopped. She'd been about to mention Gregory but Amy would simply think that proved her point; she had never understood Gregory.

'You and I,' Amy said, 'are competing with girls in their twenties who have no need for fringes because their foreheads are unlined. We are pariahs.'

'Amy, that is *so* ridiculous,' Maddie said. 'This is the twenty-first-century. You've been reading too much Jane Austen. You've had a big shock and you're not thinking straight . . . '

Amy shook her head. 'Do you know what men see when they look at us?'

Amy's Cassandra-like gloom was becoming oppressive. 'They see two fascinating, attractive, worldly wise women.' Maddie glanced around the room for support. A middle-aged man sat chatting too brightly to a sullen teenage girl who was almost certainly his daughter. Four young men at the table next to them were trying to catch the attention of three young women at the table near the door. A couple talked earnestly in a corner. No one was looking at Maddie or Amy.

'Men see the clock on our shoulders,' Amy went on. 'They know we want babies and they run a mile.'

'They don't know anything of the sort. I mean, it's probably not a good idea to meet a new man and ask him straightaway if he's able to impregnate you . . . '

'I'm serious, Maddie, I want a baby. Don't you?'

'I don't want one *yet*. And there's no immediate urgency anyway. I know hordes of women who've had babies after forty.'

'Do you?' Amy demanded. 'Do you really?'

'Yes. Yes, I do.'

Amy lowered her voice. 'I've been looking on the internet,' she said.

Oh God, Maddie thought, and reached for the wine.

'Did you know,' Amy whispered, 'that you can buy sperm online?'

'No,' said Maddie, 'I didn't.' It was going to be a long evening.

★   ★   ★

The idea that any woman would choose to be a single parent seemed to Maddie to border on insanity. Her birthday present to Nina this year had been a promise to babysit her nieces for twenty-four hours. The day had dragged by in a miasma of food-crusted bibs, foul-smelling

46

nappies, repeated readings of the same boring story about a child falling off her swing and elaborate constructions of Duplo buildings, which Chloe would knock down while Megan burst into tears. Maddie had stumbled into bed at ten and been woken by Chloe two hours later. She would never forget the giddy joy she had felt the next morning when she'd welcomed back Robbie and Nina and waved goodbye to her charges.

She could understand Amy's urge to be a mother — there had been moments in the last five years when she'd envied Nina — but it seemed reckless beyond belief not to exhaust every chance to share the burden. Over coffee, Maddie made one last attempt to save Amy from herself. 'Can I make a suggestion? Wait six months. Sign up with at least three dating sites and look for a mate. My sister's best friend did that last year and now she's in love with a very cool photographer. If, at the end of six months, you've met no one who takes your fancy, feel free to have as many babies as you like. But in the meantime — look online. It's fun and it's safe. You meet contenders in a public place and leave when you like. Everyone does it.'

'Do *you* do it?' Amy asked.

'Well, not as yet,' Maddie admitted. 'I've been too busy building up the business but . . .'

'If *you* do it,' Amy said, 'I'll do it. I can't do it on my own. I need support.'

There was no point in explaining that their circumstances were entirely different. Amy had a mulish look on her face that Maddie knew only too well. If she didn't agree, Amy would go home and start injecting herself with all sorts of dubious bodily fluids.

'All right,' Maddie said. 'You're on.'

In fact, Amy's dilemma had helped resolve her own. It was possible that Amy's desperate desire to produce a baby arose partly from a wish to punish John but, even if it was a straightforward physical yearning, a six-month delay could hardly dent her chances very much.

Maddie refused to be rattled by Amy's dark warnings. She felt no primeval urge to breed and had no interest in finding a future husband, let alone a future father of her children. Ever since Freddy's wedding ceremony, she had been increasingly annoyed by its prevailing message that one could only be fulfilled as part of a couple. What she wanted, she saw now, was to prove it was possible to create a rich and balanced life without ever putting on a wedding dress. What she wanted, in fact, was not a new man but a steady procession of men. With any luck, online dating would provide them.

4

The drive to Ipswich took only twenty minutes and Henry arrived at Nina's small terraced cottage promptly at seven thirty. He eased his long legs out of the car, pushed back his hair, adjusted his glasses and composed his features. His face displayed, he hoped, a generous degree of calm enthusiasm for the task ahead. He was about to look after his sleeping grandchildren. How difficult could it be?

Nina must have been looking out for him from the sitting room. The front door was flung open immediately and she gave him a radiant smile. She was dressed in knee-length red boots, a short pink dress and the black tailored jacket he and Marianne had given her on what turned out to be Marianne's last Christmas.

'Nina,' Henry said with feeling, 'you look stunning.'

'I feel I haven't dressed up in years! If Chloe wakes up — though she won't — you can give her some water and put her back to bed. Her green cup is on the table. The girls are both asleep. The nappy bag is by the television but you won't need it. Robbie has promised me he'll be back by nine. Help yourself to coffee or tea. If anything goes wrong, ring me. And thank you!'

There was a quick hug and then she left, her scent lingering in the air. Henry sat down on the sofa and opened his book. He was touched by

Nina's gratitude and felt ashamed that he'd never offered to babysit before. He must do better in future.

Half an hour later, there was a loud rap on the door. Henry froze, terrified the noise might wake his charges. Then he got up and opened the door.

The man in front of him was dressed in jeans, a grey shirt and a heavy ribbed jersey. He wore no mac or coat despite the unsettled weather. He looked like he might once have been a rock star — a moody, introverted rock star rather than a glittery, excitable one. He had black hair and one of those thin, barely-there beards that seemed to be fashionable, though they made no sense to Henry. He presumed it must take a great deal of time to keep them so extensively pruned.

'Is Nina around?' the man asked.

'I'm afraid not,' Henry said. 'I'm the babysitter. Can I help?'

The man glanced up at the charcoal-coloured sky as if seeking inspiration. 'Nina's helping me plan my wife's birthday party. I wanted to sort out a few details with her. But she's not here.'

There seemed no sensible response to this and, since Henry had no wish to remain standing at the door for longer than necessary, he didn't attempt one.

'Has she gone somewhere nice?' the man asked.

'She's out with her girlfriends.' Henry cleared his throat. 'Can I take a message?'

'No. No, I'll give her a call later this week. I'm sorry to bother you.' The man smiled at Henry as if he'd just that moment remembered his manners.

'That's all right. Goodbye now.' Henry closed the door and a few moments later walked over to the window. His visitor still stood outside, as if rooted to the path. Only when he caught sight of Henry peering out at him, did he give his stiff smile again before walking down the road.

Henry sat down on the sofa. He felt a little disturbed by the strange man. He hoped he wasn't a potential burglar but of course that was silly since he obviously knew Nina. He took his phone from his jacket pocket and put it on the small table next to the standard lamp. There was nothing remotely smart about this mobile, thank God. It was twelve years old and enabled Henry to make calls and receive them and that was quite enough.

Nina and Robbie had moved to this house seven years ago. Nina had painted the whole place in mint green and pink, bedecking the walls with pictures and photos displayed in old frames she'd picked up in junk shops. She disliked overhead lighting and the sitting room was served by two standard lamps that provided a comfortable but effective glow. Henry picked up his paperback and sat back against the cushions.

He had barely read a page when a sound from upstairs made him sit up. Henry leant forward, desperately hoping the sound would subside. It didn't. In fact, it increased in volume. At first it was a little like a faulty machine gun but, as Henry raced upstairs, it developed into a volcanic eruption.

51

Pausing only to glance at the miraculously sleeping Megan on the top bunk, Henry whipped Chloe from under her duvet and carried her down the stairs and into the sitting room. 'Hello there, Chloe!' he said, jogging her up and down in a cheerful manner that didn't fool Chloe for a moment. Her face was red with rage.

'Mummy!' she yelled, twisting her body and flailing her arms. 'I want Mummy!'

So do I, Henry thought, as his nose was assailed by a hideous smell which was possibly the reason for Chloe's distress. He reached for the nappy bag, found what he assumed to be the changing mat and wasted precious Chloe-soothing moments trying to work out how to use it. Having discovered that it unfolded into a T-shape, Henry now had to place Chloe on it; a very difficult task given that she showed no signs of wanting to do anything other than yell for her mother. It was only when Henry had the ingenious idea of offering her his car keys that she agreed to lie down for him.

* * *

Henry doubted that the keys would keep her happy for long. Reaching for the wet wipes, he tried frantically to mop up the brown excrement with one hand while taking out a new nappy with the other. He was not fast enough for Chloe, who dropped the keys and directed her right foot at Henry's face, just missing an eye. Henry, stunned by the blow to his cheekbone was too late to prevent the left foot pressing down onto the soiled nappy and then directing it against his shirt.

Henry wasn't sure how he did it but he finally fastened her clean nappy and then her pyjama bottoms. Chloe began crying for her mother again. Henry, desperately searching the room for inspiration, remembered that Chloe loved listening to people on the phone. 'Shall we call Aunty Maddie?' he asked, putting her down on the sofa.

Chloe's face, beetroot-red with swimming eyes, nodded.

Henry put the phone between him and Chloe and rang Maddie's number, only to hear her infuriatingly bright voice tell him that she wasn't there right now but ... If Henry was disappointed by this, Chloe was incandescent, trying to grab the phone and calling for her aunt. 'I tell you what, Chloe,' Henry said in desperation, 'shall we call your Great-aunt Colette? Shall we call Coltie? Won't that be fun?'

There followed an unseemly battle to be the first to say hello. Fortunately, Colette was not deterred by the heavy breathing that was Chloe's default method of talking on the phone. Henry broke in to say, 'Colette? Can you help me? I'm babysitting and Chloe's woken up and wants her mother and I don't want to ring Nina but ... '

'Put the phone to her ear,' Colette said. 'I'll try the troll song. You never know.'

Henry had no idea what she was talking about but he did as she said and, a moment later, he and Chloe could hear Colette's thin, tuneless voice warbling, 'I'm a troll, fol-de-rol, I'm a troll, fol-de-rol and I'm going to eat you for supper!'

Chloe was transfixed. She allowed Henry to sit her on his lap and the beginnings of a smile appeared on her face, disappearing as soon as Colette stopped for a moment. Henry said urgently, 'Carry on! She loves it!'

Poor Colette must have sung for at least ten minutes before — joy of joys — Chloe's small body had fallen back against Henry's arm.

'Colette,' Henry whispered. 'I think she's asleep. I'll try to put her down. I'll ring you back.'

He put the phone down and carried Chloe upstairs, holding his breath as he bent down to put her back in her bed. She stayed asleep. She *stayed asleep*. Henry felt like cheering.

He tiptoed back downstairs and rang his saviour. 'Colette, you're a genius,' he said. 'You did it! How did you know what to do?'

'It was probably luck.' Colette sounded pleased with herself, which was quite fair. 'I know Chloe loves the troll song so I thought it was worth a try.'

'Well, I'm in your debt. I was getting desperate. Thank you. I'd better go and clear up all the nappy stuff now but I am most grateful.'

'I'm glad I could help. Good luck for the rest of the evening.'

Henry turned his attention to the mess on the floor. He scooped up the dirty nappy, folding it into a tight ball. He took it through to the kitchen and dropped it into a plastic supermarket bag before taking that into the yard and dropping it into the dustbin. It was raining slightly now but Henry stood for a few moments, enjoying the fresh air.

Back in the sitting room he dealt with the sea of nappy wipes on the carpet. He had never changed a nappy before. He couldn't believe that one small child could produce so much poo, some of which was now on his shirt. He dealt with that last of all, removing the stain with a combination of water and kitchen paper. By the time he'd finished, there was a big, wet, uncomfortable patch on the front of his shirt. In addition, Chloe's right foot had proved to be far more powerful than might be expected of a two-year-old child; his cheekbone throbbed.

Henry returned to the sitting room and sank onto the sofa. His initial elation at getting Chloe to sleep had evaporated. He felt tired, battered and bruised. Nina's sitting room was cold. He went through to the kitchen and spent a fruitless twenty minutes looking for coffee. The only tea bags he could find were ones made of nettles or blackberries or anything at all other than genuine tea. What he really wanted was a glass of whisky. He took a glass of water back to the sitting room and noticed with horror a suspicious brown stain on Nina's pale green carpet.

Fortunately, once he found a floor cloth, he was able to eradicate the offending mark and he had no sooner picked up his book again than he heard the key in the lock. 'Hiya, Henry,' Robbie said. 'How's it been tonight? Have the girls been all right?'

Physiognomy could be deeply misleading. Marianne's mother had been a great beauty with

55

wide expressive eyes, yet she had the soul of a harpy. Robbie looked like a thug and was one of the kindest men Henry knew. He was almost as tall as Henry but much broader, with tattooed, muscular arms and a broken nose. He shaved what little hair he still possessed and looked more than ever like one of those celluloid action-men, ready to kill at the slightest provocation.

Robbie's father had left home when he was fourteen and Robbie, according to his mother, had stepped up to the line, taking on a paper round and doing all the household repairs. He left school at sixteen and trained as a plumber. By the time he was twenty-two he was able to pay for his sister's wedding. ('He didn't have to,' his mother had told Henry. 'I'd married Gary by then and he's a generous man but Robbie said it wasn't fair.') At the age of twenty-six he bought the house in Ipswich and now he had started his own heating business. His idea, he told Henry, was to make enough money to retire in ten years. In the meantime, he was working all hours and tonight he looked even more exhausted than Henry felt.

Henry said, 'The girls have been fine. How are you? I hope you don't get home this late every night.'

Robbie managed a weary smile. 'I try not to,' he said. 'I keep telling Nina, a few years of hard graft and then we'll move somewhere nice, sip cocktails on the lawn, have holidays in Thailand . . . In the meantime, I need a beer. Do you want to join me?'

Henry was pretty sure that all Robbie wanted to do was crash out in front of the television. 'I think I'll get home,' he said. 'Tell Nina that a man called about a birthday party for his wife. I suppose I should have taken his name.'

Robbie took off his jacket. 'I wouldn't worry. Thanks for coming here tonight. It meant a lot to Nina. We're both grateful. You're a very good grandfather!'

Henry was almost out of the house and he knew he had to say something, because the truth was that he wasn't a good grandfather and he knew he should do better. 'I was very pleased I could help. Tell Nina I'm happy to babysit any time she wants.'

Robbie laughed. 'Henry, that's a very dangerous offer to make. Are you sure you know what you're saying?'

'Yes,' Henry said. 'Yes, I do.'

★ ★ ★

The next day, Henry drove up to Southwold to take Ivan back to his mother. Many years before, his brother Edward had tried to get his son to call his grandmother 'Grandmother Teresa'. The best the eighteen-month-old Roland could manage was Granty. The soubriquet had soon been adopted by everyone, much to Granty's relief. She had always loathed her first name, with its sanctimonious associations.

She had returned a few days ago from her annual holiday in Devon. This consisted of a week in Totnes with her oldest son and his wife, followed by a restorative fortnight with her best friend, Elizabeth, in Exeter.

Granty and Elizabeth had known each other since their schooldays. Granty married early, had three sons in quick succession and embraced her role as the wife of a prominent businessman. She accompanied Henry's father on his frequent trips abroad, gave useful dinner parties and ensured his home life in Higgleigh was comfortable. Meanwhile, Elizabeth trained as a doctor and moved to Exeter, where she married a dentist and had two sons while enjoying a busy career as a GP.

Despite their divergent paths, their friendship had never wavered. Henry's childhood had been punctuated by bank-holiday visits from Elizabeth and her family. Henry's father and Elizabeth's husband would scoop the children up and take them off on expeditions to Flatford or Mersea, waving goodbye to Granty and Elizabeth as they cooked together in the kitchen, talking non-stop. The party would return in the afternoon for a delicious tea of scones and cake to find the two women still in the kitchen, still talking non-stop.

When Elizabeth's husband died, Granty went straight down to Devon and remained there for six weeks. When Granty's husband died, Elizabeth invited her to come and live with her in Exeter. Granty told Henry that she refused the invitation because she wanted to remain in Higgleigh near him and his family. Henry had cause to doubt this explanation since only six months later, Granty decamped to Southwold. He suspected that the real reason she shunned

Exeter was that Granty had no wish to live near Elizabeth's serious son and saintly daughter-in-law a mere ten minutes away.

It was obvious, too, why Granty had chosen to move to Southwold. Every time he visited, Henry felt a rush of nostalgia. A succession of scenes flooded his mind: the careful precision with which his two older brothers built their sandcastles, and the huge responsibility he had felt in being charged with the collection of water for their castle moats; his father rhapsodizing about the joys of egg sandwiches as they ate their picnics on the beach; the games of Monopoly in the evening and the long and heated discussions that accompanied them. Henry was sure that there must have been downsides to their annual summer holidays there — his brothers often cited the draughtiness of their rented house — but he couldn't remember any.

Southwold was a pretty good place in which to grow old. It was flat, it had decent pubs and tea-rooms, nice shops, sedate residents and a splendid seafront. Henry's mother lived in a small pink cottage with white railings and a grey door. It had a compact kitchen and garden, two low-ceilinged bedrooms, a bathroom and a wide sitting room with an enormous red-brick fireplace and walls studded with ancient beams.

The house was bright and clean thanks to the administrations of Violet Wesley, who had long since achieved god-like status in the eyes of Granty's children. Violet's grandfather had arrived from Jamaica in 1956 and ended up in Lowestoft. According to Violet he had developed a reputation as the hardest working decorator in the neighbourhood and had clearly passed on his work ethic to his granddaughter. Originally hired to clean the house two mornings a week, Violet now worked there four mornings and did everything from making beds to shopping, cooking, gardening and reminding Granty of family birthdays.

Consequently, Granty's sons could relax in the knowledge that their mother was well cared for. She certainly looked far younger than her eighty-seven years. Today she wore trainers with green corduroy trousers and a ribbed, primrose-coloured jersey. Her short grey hair, brushed back from her forehead, revealed a face with black eyes whose sparkle defied the patchwork of lines around them. She knelt down to embrace Ivan, who produced ecstatic little noises like water escaping down a plug hole. Standing, she gave her son an extravagant hug. 'Henry,' she said, 'my hero! I'm so proud of you!'

Henry felt a little embarrassed by his earlier eagerness to parade his life-saving achievement to his mother and his daughters. 'Really,' he murmured, 'it was nothing very much, after all. I was in the right place at the right time.'

'You saved a life, Henry. What can be greater than that? Come and have a sherry.'

Violet had lit a fire in readiness for Henry's visit and he and his mother settled with their drinks on the sofa. Granty's cat, Lupin, lay on the floor in front of them, purring softly. Ivan padded through behind Henry and lay down by Granty's feet. The sunlight from the window played on the cut-glass vase on top of the bookcase. It would all be very peaceful, Henry thought, if it weren't for the fact that Granty was fizzing like a glass of newly opened tonic water.

'Before we talk about *you*,' she told Henry, 'I want to talk about Daniel.'

'Who's Daniel?' Henry asked. He had a familiar sense of foreboding. It was Granty's practice to walk Ivan along the seafront, and she often struck up conversations with other dog-walkers, all of whom, it seemed to Henry, had complicated legal problems which Granty was confident Henry would solve.

'He's Violet's brother, Henry, I've told you about him before. He's a care assistant in Great Yarmouth and he has a sweet dog called Grover who barks quite a lot when Daniel's at work and Daniel's neighbour has threatened to throw poison over the fence if Grover doesn't calm down. Henry, what should Daniel do? Should he alert the police? The man sounds like a psychopath.'

'Well,' Henry said. 'If Daniel's neighbour *did* throw poison over the fence, he could call the police and . . . '

'And poor Grover would be dead!'

'There is one solution,' Henry said. 'Daniel could give Grover away to someone who isn't at work all day.'

'There speaks a man who's never owned a dog. I'll tell you something, Henry. If it wasn't the dog it would be something else. The man's obviously a bully and when a bully tastes victory, he wants another bite. Look at Hitler! I'll tell you

61

what I will do, I shall write to my M.P..'

'That's a good idea,' Henry said. He felt very sorry for Granty's M.P.. She wrote to him at least once a month. 'Tell me about your holiday,' he said. 'How were James and Lorna?'

Granty took a sip of her sherry. 'They get odder all the time. It must be Lorna's influence. James was such a sweet little boy. At mealtimes we sit round the table and they take it in turns to make random statements. Lorna will say, 'If only we could ban ready-cooked meals, obesity would cease to be a problem.' And James will nod and remain silent and then thirty seconds later, he'll say, 'I think the church organist is tone deaf,' and so it goes on. If I try to respond they look at me in wonder, so instead I make my own little statements. I made up one about the need to cull poodles and even that didn't get a reaction. *And* their house was freezing. I was very glad to get away to see Elizabeth.'

'You always *are* glad to get away and see Elizabeth.'

'I know but I always forget.'

'How *is* Elizabeth?'

'Oh, she's fine. Elizabeth is always fine. That's what's so marvellous about her.'

It was only now that Henry noticed there was something forced about his mother's habitual energetic cheerfulness. He said, 'But . . . ?'

Granty sat for a full few seconds saying nothing at all, an act that was sufficiently extraordinary for Henry to be seriously worried.

'Do you remember Elizabeth's brother, Peter?' she asked.

'Uncle Peter and Auntie Sarah? Of course I do.' How funny, Henry thought, that even now, old as he was, he still referred to them as Uncle and Auntie even though they weren't actually relations at all. Uncle Peter and Auntie Sarah had lived in a big house in Wiltshire. They used to go and stay with them en route to Elizabeth's house in Devon. Henry and his brothers adored the house because it had two staircases at either end and they'd spend hours racing up and down them. Uncle Peter was a huge, affable man who liked building bonfires, while Auntie Sarah was a tiny, bird-like woman who made the best chocolate cake in the world.

'They moved to Exmouth ten years ago to be near their daughter, Migs.'

'I remember her too. She always wanted to join in our games.'

'She and her husband have a very upmarket guest house. Anyway, Elizabeth and I visited Peter and Sarah and . . . It was sad, Henry, it was very sad. A year ago, Peter was told he had motor-neurone disease and now everything — everything except his brain — is shutting down. The day we visited, he'd received a neck brace in the post and he was wearing it and they were both so pleased . . . He can hardly move, his voice is slurred, he has trouble with breathing . . . He's like a great felled oak tree, Henry, and he and Sarah are so brave and upbeat and determined to make the most of every day together . . . ' She took out a tissue and blew her nose. 'I can't talk about it now . . . Tell me your news. How are the children?'

Henry cleared his throat. 'Nina's fine. I looked after the girls the other night. Maddie went to Freddy's wedding a couple of weeks ago, which I thought was rather odd.'

'What did she say? Did she find it difficult?'

'I didn't like to ask. She said Freddy and his bride were made for each other.'

'Oh dear. Poor Maddie. I wish we could find someone new for her. And what about you? How are *you*?'

'I'm very well.' Henry took off his glasses and began to clean them with his sleeve. 'In fact,' he began, 'I have something momentous to tell you.'

Granty put her sherry glass down on the coffee table. 'Do you, Henry? Tell me at once!'

★　★　★

As Henry drove back to Higgleigh with his homework on the passenger seat, he knew he had only himself to blame. He felt rather like Dorothy must have felt when she'd been picked up by the typhoon — or was it a tornado? — in *The Wizard of Oz*. He had wanted to distract Granty — he could never bear to see her unhappy — and he had succeeded.

He had said, 'I want to find a wife, Granty,' and it was only when he said it that he knew it was true. The idea that an eighty-seven-year-old resident of Southwold would be able to give him tips on the contemporary dating scene was even more preposterous than his mother's suggestion that he should try to make a point of flirting with a different woman every day. Henry should have

64

known better. He had long since learnt that the enthusiasm and energy with which Granty invariably approached a new project rarely produced the results she anticipated.

He remembered a particularly hideous visit from his mother-in-law twenty years ago. Anouk was French and had returned to Paris after the death of her second husband. She used to descend on them every year for three weeks in September and this visit had been particularly unbearable. She took it upon herself to correct her granddaughters' deportment, their manners, their intellectual and sartorial sloppiness and finally their lamentable inability to converse in what Anouk insisted was their mother tongue despite the fact that their mother was half-English and had been born and bred in England. Anouk also felt it necessary to remind Marianne of the boyfriend she had given up in her teens, a god-like paragon who had gone on to become an obscenely wealthy banker. When she wasn't belittling Henry's bourgeois credentials as a provincial solicitor, she reminded Marianne constantly, shooting knowing glances in Henry's direction, that she had never regretted leaving Marianne's father for Marianne's now deceased stepfather. This was all the more galling since Henry knew that this stepfather had been a wholly unpleasant influence on the lives of Marianne and her sister. Henry could not understand why Marianne, so fearless in her dealings with the rest of the world, could be so cowed in the presence of her mother. The only time she showed any anger was when Anouk

65

made disparaging remarks about Colette.

One evening, Henry, needing to release his impotent fury, had called in on his parents after work. The following evening, Granty came round with a speech that was clearly carefully planned. Much later she confessed that she'd prepared it along the lines of Harold Macmillan's 'Wind of Change' speech to the South African Parliament. She began by embracing Anouk as a fellow grandmother and mother-in-law. They both shared a difficult task, she said, their status in the family required huge levels of tact and toleration and kindness since their supreme role was to support and encourage harmony in the home of their children. She suggested that any attempts to alienate Marianne from her husband would be entirely counter-productive and concluded by saying that, 'It's obvious to me that you are far too intelligent to attempt any such action.'

When she'd finished, Anouk exploded in a furious denunciation of Henry and Granty and the appalling petit-bourgeois family in which Marianne was trapped. Fortunately, the tirade was in French, so Granty remained blissfully ignorant of the insults raining down on her. When Anouk was finally silent, Granty embraced her once more and said she must get home to cook some lamb chops for supper. The next morning, Anouk decided to cut short her visit and left. So, perhaps, Henry thought, turning into the long drive that led up to his house, his mother's intervention had been a good one after all.

At home he sat down with a cup of tea and inspected her list.

1: Contact your old friends and let them know you are available for dinner invitations.

Henry thought of all the dinner invitations he had turned down in the four years since Marianne's death. His friends had long since given up trying to lure him from his home. Henry didn't blame them. Short of issuing a public proclamation that he was now available, he didn't see what he could do.

2: Join local societies and classes — Aerobics? Painting? Tapestry? French or Spanish?

This, Henry thought, was not a bad idea. Presumably, one didn't have to engage in polite conversation since one would be listening to the teacher, and if one *did* have to talk, the subject matter need only be about the aerobics or the painting or the tapestry. He wasn't enthused by any of the suggested classes but it must be possible to find an interest that was, well, interesting. Marianne's death had acted like a blowtorch on his life, scorching all earlier hobbies and passions in the face of the terrible, irrevocable absence of Marianne. He liked cooking and he had once thought he might like to paint. He would go to the library and see what was available. He put a tick in the margin.

3: Join a dating agency and be prepared to have an open mind.

The first time Henry saw Marianne was on a February morning in 1971. Henry was sitting with two friends in the student union coffee bar. His friends were having an argument about a girl they both liked and since they had been having the same argument for at least a week, Henry was not paying much attention. His eyes slid across to the queue by the canteen and he saw a girl talking with great animation to a boy with Clark Kent glasses. The girl had an enormous shoulder bag and at one point she shoved it back across her shoulder and then apologised profusely to the unfortunate person whose arm had been hit by it.

What was extraordinary was not the girl — she was certainly attractive but her frayed jeans and over-sized jersey indicated a complete lack of interest in personal appearance — but Henry's reaction. 'That's the sort of girl I'd like to marry,' he thought.

All these years later, he still couldn't understand what it was about Marianne that had provoked that feeling. She was clearly vivacious, but Henry knew other girls who were vivacious. She was neither particularly slender nor tall, qualities that had always been essential as far as Henry was concerned. He could remember that he had no wish to leap up and go after her. But the thought had remained with him: that's the sort of girl I'd like to many.

Weeks later, he'd spotted her again. She was talking to a friend of his in the university bar. He could still remember the excitement he'd felt as he introduced himself. But that was then and this was now.

He stared again at his mother's list. Being prepared to have an open mind meant approaching women for whom one felt no excitement or anticipation or attraction. In such clinical circumstances, how *did* one converse with strange women? Henry had no idea.

4: Ask your daughters for advice. Nina and Maddie will know far more than we do about flirting and first dates.

There was so much wrong with this suggestion that Henry could barely bring himself to re-read it.

5: Go to art galleries. I have read two novels recently in which the hero met the love of his life at an art gallery.

Henry pictured himself standing in an art gallery for hours on end, scrutinizing the visitors and then being asked to leave by suspicious attendants. He and Marianne had once gone to the opening of an exhibition in London; a schoolfriend of Marianne had three paintings on display there and had taken Marianne off as soon as they arrived. A rather striking woman in a red hat had approached him and asked his opinion of a very odd painting that looked as if it had been daubed with dog poo. Henry had said a little cautiously that it seemed to be quite *dark*. She told him she'd produced it three months ago on the day she discovered her younger sister was having an affair with her husband. She had been very keen to regale Henry with all the details and had become so animated that she had spilt her red wine down Henry's shirt. He had not been to an art gallery since.

6: Consult Colette. She's been married twice and has an encyclopaedic knowledge of romantic films.

Henry had never understood how someone like Colette could have had two husbands. He couldn't imagine Colette encouraging the advances of anyone. It had taken her years to relax in his company and he was her brother-in-law. But then nor could he imagine her having the confidence to create and develop a successful business of her own, which only went to show that he didn't know her as well as he thought he did. Even so, he thought, he would have to be truly desperate to ask Colette for advice in finding a mate.

7: *Buy a dog. Women always like men with dogs.*

Henry knew this was true. Everyone liked people with dogs. In the last few years, Henry had looked after his mother's dog every time she went away and Ivan's gargoyle-like appearance always attracted admirers. On the other hand, Ivan's charisma was not so evident at home. He always defecated just outside the back door, he would fart every time he settled on Henry's lap and he could bark for hours at the birds who'd taken up home in Henry's trees.

8: *Contact Louise!*

The last time Henry had seen Louise was at least forty years ago. He could still remember the acute misery he'd felt as he stood on the station platform and waved goodbye to her. Only his mother could imagine it would be a good idea to contact her now.

9: *Get advice from William. Give him a ring.*

And now at last, Henry's mother hit gold. Henry's friend, William — a telegenic academic, writer of sundry articles and essays on the differences between the sexes, subject of innumerable adoring interviews by female journalists, and a man who continued to attract quite effortlessly any woman who aroused his interest — William would know what to do.

5

In the six months Maddie had lived in Crystal Palace, she had failed to catch even a glimpse of Mrs Pritchett, the lady who lived in the downstairs flat. Now she never would. When she came downstairs late on Saturday morning, two men were delivering a bookcase into the flat and a male voice called out, 'That goes in the bedroom. Put it in the bedroom.'

For a moment, Maddie thought of introducing herself, but they were obviously busy and she didn't want to be late to meet Colette. As she stepped out of the front door she noticed that Mrs Pritchett's name by the doorbell had already been replaced. She wondered if Guy Neale would be as unobtrusive as his predecessor.

She was looking forward to her lunch with Colette. Her meeting with Amy had depressed her and, in every way but one, her aunt was an excellent role model for her life as a contented single woman. At fifty-eight, Colette was well dressed and attractive, if a little too thin, with a pageboy hairstyle that suited her short nose and clear blue eyes. She had a thriving business, running basic literacy courses for the many under-educated employees in sundry offices and companies throughout the country. She'd been married twice and, although she never talked about her marital experiences, Maddie had vague recollections of her second husband, a big, gentle man who, according to her possibly faulty memory, had spent many hours helping her and Nina to dress their dolls in sickly confections of pink organza and satin.

Granty had been responsible for the dolls and the dresses. She had always delighted in giving her granddaughters presents designed to enrage their mother. On Maddie's eighth birthday, Granty had given her a framed poster of Disney's Snow White with the slogan, 'Some Day my Prince Will Come', spread across it. Maddie's mother shuddered every time she saw it.

Colette had done well. Twenty years ago she had bought a two-bedroom house in Blackheath which was worth a small fortune now. In the two months Maddie had lived there, she had grown rather fond of the vast heath spreading out from the elegant nineteenth-century church at its centre. Blackheath had a fabulous farmers' market every Sunday that sold artisan bread, luscious cheeses and organic meat. It boasted a variety of places where one could order great coffee and, best of all, it had an excellent secondhand bookshop. But today, as Maddie left the station to walk through the village, stopping to buy wine for her aunt, she knew Crystal Palace suited her better. There were rather too many well-heeled young families here with beautifully dressed children and designer buggies. She wondered if Colette ever minded being childless. She had always been an affectionate aunt and was now an equally interested

73

great-aunt, but she also loved her career. It wasn't a bad sort of life, Maddie thought; she'd be all right with a life like that.

Colette was on the phone when she opened the door to Maddie. 'Seriously, Granty, don't waste your time watching that one . . . A good rom-com needs a hero who's handsome *and* vulnerable. Jude Law couldn't look vulnerable to save his life . . . I have to go now . . . Your granddaughter's arrived. Do you want a word with her?'

Maddie stepped into the hall and exchanged the bottle for the handset.

★ ★ ★

'Darling Maddie!' Granty always felt it necessary to speak very loudly on the phone. 'Why are you visiting Colette when you never visit *me*?'

'It takes half an hour to get here and at least half a day to get to you. When I get a car . . . '

'You've been saying that for years. By the time you do buy one, I'll be dead and then what will you do?'

'I'll sit by your grave and cry, 'Why, oh why, didn't I listen to Granty?''

'Very funny, darling. Well, I'll see you at Christmas, I suppose. Be sure to give me a ring soon and we'll have a proper chat.'

'Will do.' Maddie walked through to the kitchen and found Colette opening the wine. She kissed her aunt and put the phone back on its stand. 'Granty sounds very jolly.'

'She's always jolly,' Colette said, scrutinizing

74

her recipe book through her glasses, 'and right now, she's very excited about your father.'

'He's not still going on about his heroic act in Colchester, is he?'

'It was a wonderful thing to do.' Colette raised her head and lowered her glasses. 'I think it's been very good for Henry. It's given him confidence. Did you hear he babysat for the girls on Thursday? Do pour us some wine. I'm not at all sure this lunch is going to be any good.'

Colette always said that. She was a competent cook rather than a natural one. Cooking had been a hugely important part of Maddie's parents' lives together and Maddie had inherited their pleasure in creating meals out of odd ingredients that happened to be around. For Colette, preparing a meal was fraught with anxiety and she could only relax once it was on the table. Today, she had made an onion tart and as she slid it into the oven, Maddie said, 'It looks great to me. Can I do anything to help?'

'I've made the salad. We can relax till the tart's ready. So tell me your news: what have you been doing?'

People had always remarked on the physical difference between Maddie and Nina but they had more similarities than their mother and their aunt. Marianne had had thick, untidy blonde hair, talked a great deal and loved gardening, cooking and entertaining. Colette's brown hair was always neat, she had never had, or wished to have, a proper garden and, in the company of people she didn't know, spoke only sparingly. Her default position at Marianne's parties had been to station herself by the door and gradually ease herself out into the hall and upstairs to the TV room with her nieces. What she did share with Marianne — apart from a difficult childhood — was the same delighted laugh and a talent for listening.

So now as Maddie described the latest problem at work — a team leader in Bromley who was great with the children but increasingly critical of Maddie and Gregory — Colette gave no instant opinion but simply asked the odd question, leading Maddie to reach her own conclusion, which was that Heather would have to go.

And then the timer went and for a few moments Colette was all panic and worry as she took out the tart and expressed doubts about her pastry. Finally, they sat down and of course the tart was fine and the two women had another glass of wine to celebrate. Maddie told Colette about Freddy's wedding, including the literary cocktail of readings about love.

'I remember going to a wedding years ago,' Colette said. 'A friend of mine was marrying a Shakespearean scholar and he made a long and very touching speech, peppered with quotes from *Romeo and Juliet*, *Anthony and Cleopatra* and the letters of Abelard and Heloise. And even then I thought, that's all very well but those three couples ended up enduring violent deaths, castration and separation. Five years later, my friend fell from the balcony of a holiday apartment.'

Maddie blinked. Colette had always been

reticent about her life but whenever she did mention some personal experience it invariably seemed to be a little odd. 'What do you mean? Do you think her husband pushed her?'

'I'm not sure. I think he might have done. I often think that of all the emotions, romantic love is the least reliable.' She glanced at Maddie's empty plate. 'Would you like some more tart or some fruit?'

'I couldn't manage anything else. That was . . . '

The phone went and Colette picked it up, listened for a few moments and put the receiver down against her shoulder. 'Maddie, upstairs in my room there's a jersey I don't like. Why don't you go and try it on?'

Maddie pushed back her chair. As she walked up the stairs she heard Colette's voice, strained and stiff. 'So how did you find my number? I'm sorry?'

On Colette's bed was a long jersey in Maddie's size — twelve — rather than Colette's ten. A further indication of Colette's deviousness was that the jersey was crimson: a colour that Maddie liked and Colette did not. Colette enjoyed buying clothes for her nieces but was embarrassed by gratitude. She habitually pre-tended her purchases were cast-offs, though when she once offered Maddie a very short and clingy canary-coloured dress her ruse broke the bounds of credibility.

Maddie tried on the jersey and liked it too much to take it off. She gave a quick glance round the room and remembered that she never felt comfortable in there. The glossy photos on the walls unnerved her, reminding her that many people, especially her aunt, had secrets that could never be explained or understood.

She stopped halfway down the stairs. Colette sounded angry now, and upset. 'You can't expect me to come . . . I won't do it . . . I don't care . . . Please don't call me again, I'm going to go now.'

Maddie took a deep breath and charged down the stairs. 'Colette,' she cried, 'this is lovely! I don't believe for a moment you bought it for yourself and you must stop doing this but I *do* love it.'

Colette's eyes were suspiciously liquid but she clapped her hands together and said, 'It's perfect for you, I knew it would be!'

Maddie spent the next forty minutes chatting about films and books and dating sites and was rewarded with a few genuine laughs. There was no question of asking about the phone call. Colette had never been one to share her problems. It was clear that she'd been badly shaken and Maddie left sooner than intended. She wished she'd had the courage to ask about the phone call; she felt she'd let down the aunt who'd listened so patiently to her many self-indulgent tirades about Freddy. It was at times like these — self-critical times — that she most missed her mother.

★   ★   ★

The removal van had gone when she got home. On impulse she knocked on the door of Mrs

Pritchett's flat and a voice called out, 'I'm coming! Don't go away!' A few moments later, a man stood looking down at her: tall, slim, well-dressed, bright-eyed, with short, dark hair. He was a definite improvement on the absent Mrs Pritchett.

'I'm sure you're busy,' Maddie said. 'I won't keep you. I live upstairs and thought I should say hello. I never actually met your predecessor, which makes me feel rather guilty. I'm Maddie.' She extended her hand which was taken in a quick, strong grip.

'It's good to be interrupted. I was putting up pictures. Come and see my new home.' He stepped to the side of the door and welcomed her in with an exaggerated flourish. 'What do you think?'

Maddie had always imagined Mrs Pritchett as a sad old recluse surrounded by significant mementoes, so she was surprised to find that Mrs Pritchett's hall, sitting room and kitchen was large and open-plan with fashionable sludge-green walls and genuine wood flooring as opposed to Maddie's cheap laminate.

'This is really nice,' Maddie said. 'Did you meet Mrs Pritchett?'

'No. She travels abroad a lot. Apparently she moved here to be close to her mother. When her mother died, she decided to sell up and move to New York.'

'Well, I love her flat. I love *your* flat, I should say.'

'I can't offer you tea or coffee but I have wine in the fridge. Will you join me for a glass? I could

79

do with a break from the pictures.'

'If it were me,' Maddie said, glancing at the packing cases strewn around the floor, 'I'd leave the pictures till last.'

Guy walked over to the gleaming black retro fridge — this was the sort of place that aroused serious consumer envy. 'The point is,' he said, 'once I've put my pictures up, I'll know where to put everything else. The pictures come first.' He gave a glass of wine to her and smiled. 'Cheers! It's very nice to meet you.'

She raised her glass, her attention caught by two pictures on the wall. The first resembled a mess of green ink dropped on white blotting paper, a piece of art on which Maddie felt entirely unable to comment on. The second was a poster for a film called *A Place in the Sun*, the names of the stars emblazoned in white against a fiery red background and the faces of Liz Taylor and Montgomery Clift close together, her perfect eyes gazing wistfully upwards and his staring moodily down. 'They're so beautiful,' Maddie murmured, 'They're *both* so beautiful. They even have the same eyes.'

'She was nineteen when the film came out,' Guy said. 'Did you ever see it?'

'No. Was it good?'

'You'd probably think it hopelessly dated but it's one of those stories where everyone has Big Responses to every situation and *very* big emotions, so there's a huge amount of emoting and passion and heartbreak and tragedy. There's one scene where the two stars are dancing together and the camera is all over those two

80

amazing profiles. He tells her he loves her, she tells him she loves him, and then she murmurs 'Tell Mama', and then, 'Tell Mama'. And in those two words you have everything that made her so wonderful. I first saw that film on television on a damp Sunday afternoon. I was thirteen and she was my first big crush.' He took a gulp of his wine. 'Molly Ringwald was my second.'

'*Pretty in Pink*,' Maddie said, 'is my all-time favourite film. Blane was my ideal boyfriend.'

'Blane was your ideal boyfriend? Blane was a vacuous pretty boy who never said a word.'

'Yes, but when you're a teenager you think boys who say nothing must be really deep and interesting.'

'That's interesting,' Guy said. 'That explains why I was so spectacularly unsuccessful with girls throughout my teens. I tried too hard and I never stopped talking.'

Maddie laughed. 'I should let you get on. I only came in to say hello.'

'I'm glad you did.' He picked up the bottle. 'Do you want one more for the road?'

'I shouldn't,' Maddie said, and held out her glass.

6

Henry had high hopes for his consultation with William. Marianne had always maintained that William could only cope with romanticized versions of women rather than the real thing and it was true that he had his limitations. Henry could remember her throwing her hands in the air: 'Why do you think he loves the Pre-Raphaelites?' But this didn't detract from the fact that William was second to none in his ability to attract those women he wished to attract. Had William possessed a Richard Burton voice or superstar looks, this might not have been as impressive as it undoubtedly was.

William came from Birmingham, a region not noted for its seductive accent. He was of average height with rust-coloured curls and a nose that was too big for his face. He wore suits that never seemed to fit him and bit his nails when thinking, a habit that the youthful Henry had been warned by his mother was singularly repellent to the opposite sex. And yet William's women were invariably sylph-like sirens who adored him. If anyone could tell Henry how to appeal to the opposite sex, it was William.

William was based in London but, ten years ago, encouraged by visits to Henry and Marianne, had bought what he called his country retreat in nearby Dedham, a pretty little village a few miles from Higgleigh. The Grade Two-listed thatched cottage was tiny but perfect for William's needs. It had no spare room, thus making it impossible for his sister to visit; it had a combined kitchen and sitting room, ideal for a man who spent as much time cooking as he did; it had a small enclosed garden that required little work; there was a narrow study just wide enough to house his father's imposing Victorian desk; there was a big bathroom and an equally spacious bedroom with strawberry walls, exposed ceiling timbers and a deep coffee-coloured carpet. It was, in short, an ideal house for a man with sybaritic tastes and no personal ties.

Initially, Henry and Marianne had hoped they'd see more of William as a result of his purchase. Unfortunately for them, it coincided with his increasing popularity as a literary pundit on television and radio. When he did get away, he was usually accompanied by his woman of the moment and, while he was tremendous company on his own, he was very boring when he wasn't.

This evening, he was on his own. He had come down for ten days, he told Henry, to kick-start his latest book, a study of his favourite diarists through the ages. 'I've been re-reading Pepys,' he said, ushering Henry into the kitchen. 'He's just as good as I remember him. He had kidney problems, bladder problems, pains in his eyes, appalling allergies and agonizing ulcers and yet he still found time to reorganize the navy, converse with the best scientists of his day, enter Parliament, have countless sexual encounters and produce the most extraordinary diary in history. I tell you something, Henry, everyone should read him. You'd soon stop complaining about your health if you read Samuel.'

'When have I ever complained about my health?'

'I seem to remember you went on in interminable detail about your stiffening joints last time I saw you.'

Henry settled onto William's comfortable two-seater sofa. An old friendship, he reflected, was like a marriage: one understood the patterns of the conversations. William's idle comment about Pepys had not been idle at all. It had opened the door, preceding with the customary insult to Henry to the topic that was currently preoccupying William.

'I am supremely unconcerned about my stiffening joints,' Henry said. He accepted a large glass of wine from his friend and asked the question he knew was expected of him. 'How about you?'

William gave an unconvincing shrug and began mashing peppercorns with his pestle and mortar. There was an enticing smell of garlic wafting towards Henry from the oven, and on William's shiny black work surface stood a plate on which sat two big, brown and meaty steaks. Henry always ate well with William. He drank well too and was always careful on these occasions to book a taxi.

'The thing about modern medicine,' William said at last, his face a little flushed after his exertions with the peppercorns, 'is that the cure is almost as bad as the symptoms. No one ever tells you about the side effects. I have problems with my cholesterol so I'm given statins and suddenly, hey presto, I have aches in all sorts of places I didn't even know about and, worse still . . . Are you using statins, Henry?'

Henry had been watching William paint the steaks with oil. He presumed he would then dip them in the mashed peppercorns. He shook his head. 'No, I'm not.'

'You should talk to your doctor. Mine is convinced that every man over sixty should take them. But the ones I'm on now have begun to . . . To be honest, Henry, I think they affect my libido. So now I have to buy these hideously expensive pills and every time I plan to have sex I have to cut one of them up a couple of hours beforehand. The other night, Lydia came over and we had a row and she stormed out and all I could think was that I'd wasted one of those bloody little pills. I suppose it's not something you have to worry about.'

'No,' Henry said. 'I suppose it isn't.'

'Well, you're very lucky.'

Only William, Henry thought, could make a comment like that. He asked, 'What was the argument about?'

'It was all very silly. Lydia is thinking of leaving her husband. It's crazy. They're very good friends and he's always been happy to let me see her. I would never have got involved if I thought he minded. You know what I'm like. I don't mess around with married women.'

Henry was sure he could remember at least two previous women friends of William who'd been married at the time but he said nothing.

William was quite capable of sitting down and giving him a long, laborious and probably incomprehensible explanation of why the previous women — like Lydia — were special cases. William was a past master at justifying dubious actions and Henry was hungry. He said, 'You've been seeing Lydia for two years now. That's a long time for you. I'd have thought you'd be pleased if she was suddenly free.'

'I'm simply thinking of Lydia. She and her husband have been together a very long time. They have family. They share a big house. They're always entertaining their children and grandchildren.'

'And if Lydia moved in with you, you'd be able to enjoy the many visits of her children and grandchildren. I see your problem.'

'That's remarkably cynical, Henry. I repeat: I'm thinking of Lydia.'

Henry said hopefully, 'Do you have something cooking in the oven?'

'Garlic tart,' William said. 'I hope you like goat's cheese.'

'I love it,' Henry said.

The garlic tart proved to be excellent, as were the steaks. Once he had food in his stomach, Henry was more than happy to listen to William describe the dying embers of his affair with Lydia. It was apparent that she had committed the cardinal error of believing William's earlier protestations of love. To be fair, William had almost certainly believed them as well.

'The trouble with you,' Henry said, accepting another glass of William's excellent Rioja, 'is that you actually like spending a lot of time on your own. I'm afraid I'm not very good at that.'

William leant forward and briefly squeezed Henry's hand. 'I'll tell you something, Henry. I thought you'd fall apart after Marianne died. You've been very strong. Marianne would be proud of you.'

Henry shuffled in his seat. He was never very good at accepting compliments, especially when they weren't warranted. 'You have a new picture,' he said, 'where the noticeboard used to be.'

'Ah,' William smiled. 'It's only a print but I found a good frame for it. I went to the Pre-Raphaelite exhibition back in January. I won't even ask if you saw it. You're such a philistine.'

Henry could imagine Marianne rolling her eyes at him. He lowered his glasses gazed across at the picture. 'She's a beautiful woman,' he said. 'Who is she?'

'Funnily enough, she's called Mariana. Millais was inspired by Tennyson's poem . . . ' William cleared his throat. '*She only said, 'My life is dreary/He cometh not, she said;/She said, 'I am aweary, aweary,/I would that I were dead.'*'

'She sounds very sorry for herself.'

'She has every right to be. Look how lovely she is — the curve of her figure, the grace of her hand. You see the autumn leaves on the carpet? That shows the passing of time. She's locked in a loveless marriage and is wasting her life, waiting for the lover who does not come.'

'More fool her,' Henry said, 'she ought to get out more.'

William grinned. 'The trouble with you, Henry, is that you have no soul.'

'Though actually,' Henry said, taking off his glasses and speaking with careful deliberation, 'I have been thinking about autumn leaves lately.'

'They're a bugger, aren't they? I've only been away a week and there was a mountain of them outside the front door when I got here on Thursday. I suppose it's all the bad weather we've been having.'

'I'm speaking metaphorically,' Henry said. 'I'm getting on, I'm getting old.' He put his hands on the table. 'I want your advice,' he said. 'I want to get married again.'

William's face registered a variety of emotions: shock, embarrassment, possibly even disapproval. He said, 'Have you met someone? Has something happened?'

'I'm lonely,' Henry said. 'I haven't met anyone but I'd like to. The trouble is, I have no idea how to go about it and even if I saw a woman I'd like to get to know, how would I approach her?' He leant forward. 'When you see a woman you like, what do you do? How do you catch her interest? What do you *do*?'

William had begun to bite his nails, a sure sign that his faculties were engaged. Now he took his fingers from his mouth and sat back in his chair, his arms folded round his waist. 'I suppose,' he said slowly, 'that if I see a woman I really like, I try to catch her eye and then — if that's successful — I smile at her in a special sort of way.'

'How is it special?' Henry asked. He felt he should be taking notes.

'I maintain eye contact and I don't blink,' William told him. 'It's a serious smile.'

'I see. And when you smile, what happens?'

'Well . . . usually . . . she smiles back and then I'll go and say something.'

'What do you say? What can you say?'

'It's easy by then. I tend to apologize for staring; I confess that I felt I had met her before, which is actually true because I only approach a woman with whom I feel I have a definite connection . . .'

'Isn't that simply a dressed-up term to mean that you fancy someone?'

'You are such a cynic, Henry. How did Marianne put up with you?'

'I don't know.' It was easy to tease William for trying to elevate a simple, basic impulse; it was easy but, just possibly, it was unfair, since Henry couldn't help feeling William had made a valid point. The first time Henry saw Marianne, he had a strong if irrational instinct that he would always be comfortable with her. And he'd been right. 'So I've stared at my woman. I've smiled. I've approached her and explained I thought I knew her. Now what do I do?'

'It's easy,' William said. 'You just . . .'

'You have to understand,' Henry said, 'the last time I chatted up a woman was over forty years ago. I don't remember much about it, which is probably just as well.'

William opened his mouth and shut it again. He went over to the wine rack below the picture of Mariana and took out a bottle of red wine. 'I think we need another drink,' he said.

★ ★ ★

It was William's fault. If Henry hadn't received his masterclass the night before, it would never have happened. Unfortunately, the very next day, Henry was in the library changing his books when he saw her.

She was tall and slim with a pink and grey jersey; her long legs were encased in lemon-coloured jeans. She had a narrow, elegant face with short, blonde hair swept back from her face, exposing a high, flawless forehead. She looked radiant and fresh, Henry thought, and more to the point, she reminded him so much of Louise that for a moment he wondered if it *might* actually be her.

Even as he stared at her, he knew it was impossible. The focus of his teenage dreams would be the same age as him and there was no way this woman was over sixty. Also, her eyebrows were arched whereas Louise's had slanted upwards, as if poised in a state of permanent interrogation.

Aware of his scrutiny, the woman looked across at him and that was when Henry did what William had advised: he did the smile. It was, he realized almost immediately, a terrible mistake. He suspected his smile had somehow emerged as a grimace. She responded with a small startled frown, followed by a polite but bewildered lifting of her mouth. And then, pausing only to take a leaflet from the desk, she made a hasty and determined retreat to the door marked Exit.

It was mortifying and humiliating. Even in the midst of his self-laceration, he somehow had the presence of mind to take one of the leaflets before he left. When he emerged onto the street, he was relieved to see she had disappeared.

7

The last week had been a bad one for Maddie. Having agreed with Gregory that it was time to confront the Bromley team leader over her continuous complaints about their programme, Gregory acted with characteristic decisiveness. Early on the Monday evening the two of them drove to Bromley in Gregory's Fiat Uno and rehearsed what they were going to say.

It was as unpleasant as they'd feared. Maddie began mildly enough, voicing their disappointment over Heather's negative attitude. Heather went straight on to the offensive, reminding her employers of her twenty-two years of experience at the cutting-edge of education, dismissing their own far more modest qualifications and accusing them of only being interested in monetary gain. When Gregory pointed out that he'd earned far more money as a business consultant, she inferred that he must have his own reasons for working with children. At that point, Maddie lost her temper and ten minutes later, Heather walked out and said she would not be coming back.

Gregory volunteered to take her place at the Bromley club until they found a replacement. This made sense since he had his car and was far more patient with the children than Maddie was. On the other hand it meant that Maddie was now responsible for researching venues for the proposed new club in Peckham. And both of them were shaken by the venom Heather had displayed. It was always depressing to be actively disliked by someone and it was doubly hard to be disliked by an employee. There was no consolation in realizing that she was a particularly unpleasant person since it only proved they'd been wrong to take her on in the first place.

On Wednesday evening, Maddie returned from a trudge around five uninspiring locations to find a long email from Amy describing a drink she had had with an online possibility. 'He said,' Amy wrote, 'I looked older than my photo. He talked for an hour and a half about his unfaithful ex-wife and offered to have no-strings sex with me. I thought you said this would be *fun*. And by the way, aren't you supposed to be doing this too?'

Spurred by her conscience, Maddie spent a dispiriting hour after supper looking at the details of possibly desirable males. She discovered that they all had a sense of humour, many of them were fun-loving, some looked for 'like-minded free spirits', and at least three liked 'swimming in the sea in January'.

On Friday there was only the weekend in Higgleigh to look forward to. Her lack of enthusiasm made her feel guilty. Her father always did his best. He'd collect her from the station at Manningtree and ask about her work. Once home, he would open a bottle of wine and they'd chat about family matters while he prepared the meal. Over supper, she'd produce a rainbow-coloured version of her social life and later they'd watch a little television. Finally she'd go up to bed and feel awful because the truth was that within half an hour of being at home she couldn't wait to leave.

Once upon a time, Maddie would have gone home confident in the knowledge that when she unburdened herself of all her professional and personal disasters, her mother, with one knowing comment, could transform her mistakes into amusing and unimportant anecdotes. Marianne had always been the star of the show, while her father had been the supporting act. Maddie accepted that life was different now. It was only when she went home and felt the sadness seeping through the house that she felt her own loss so acutely she could hardly bear it.

When she arrived at the station, she could see her father leaning against his car and she called out to him. He closed his book, gave a broad smile and strode towards her. He looked the same — tall, thin, hair a little messy and in need of a good cut, glasses halfway down his nose. But there was something different about him. For a start he didn't ask the usual polite questions.

'I'm reading a book,' he said as he turned on the ignition. 'William lent it to me. It's a biography of Samuel Pepys and it's riveting. I've just read this description of an operation he was given to remove a stone in his kidneys. The doctors trussed him up like a chicken and then — remember there were no anaesthetics in those days — they drove an instrument through his penis to position the stone, made an insertion

94

between his scrotum and his anus and got the stone out with pincers. Can you imagine anything more terrifying? I'll tell you something, it makes a man grateful to be living in the twenty-first-century . . . '

He continued to entertain her with stories of Samuel Pepys for the rest of the journey. They were all very interesting, if delivered in a manically enthusiastic manner. Once home, he put her case at the bottom of the stairs and said, 'Come into the kitchen and we'll have a drink before supper. I've prepared everything so we can sit down and relax . . . and just talk about things.'

Maddie had rarely seen him so un-relaxed. She hung her coat on the stand and followed him through to the kitchen. There was a colander of washed spinach leaves on the draining board. The fresh scent of mint emanated from a saucepan simmering on the stove. Two glasses and a bottle opener were ready and waiting on the table, along with cutlery and a couple of red paper napkins. It looked rather festive.

Maddie had always loved this room. It was hard to imagine that it had housed gallant wounded soldiers seventy odd years ago. At its far end there was a wood-burning stove, a two-seater sofa and a small table and chairs. Tonight, for the first time in ages, the stove was lit and was giving out a warm, comforting glow, reminding Maddie of when the kitchen had been the living, breathing heart of the family home.

Once Henry had poured the wine, he stood for

a moment and then reached into the pockets of his jacket. He had given up smoking years ago but still reached into his pockets when nervous. He made for a chair opposite Maddie, sat down, raised his glass and said, 'Well then!' with an enthusiasm that was as urgent as it was uncomfortable.

She watched her father fold his arms and then unfold them. 'Dad,' she said, 'is there something you want to tell me?'

'I think so,' he said. He cleared his throat. 'I'm not sure. The thing is . . . I have been thinking I'd like to get married again.'

Various possibilities had been chasing through Maddie's mind: illness, retirement — he'd already gone down to four days a week — plans to move, plans to travel. But this pronouncement was so extraordinary that she could think of nothing to say.

'You're horrified,' he said. 'You're appalled. I can see you're appalled. You're probably right.'

'No, no. I'm just surprised, that's all. Who is she?' She saw him look at her blankly. 'I mean, who are you going to marry?'

'Oh,' Henry smiled. 'I have no idea. I only decided a few weeks ago. Do you think it's ridiculous?'

She thought it was unbelievable. 'Of course it's not. It's unexpected, that's all.'

'I wanted you girls to know. I meant to tell Nina but I lost my nerve. I've told your grandmother.'

'Has something happened? Have you been thinking about this for a long time?'

96

'Oh no.' Henry shook his head. 'It was saving Audrey Pennington. Ever since your mother died, I felt I was marking time, until . . . Well, I was marking time. And now, now I think perhaps I shouldn't be.' He stood up abruptly. 'That's all I had to tell you, really. I probably won't do anything but I thought you'd like to know. Anyway, I'd better see to the vegetables.'

Maddie couldn't recall a time when her father had spoken so freely about his feelings. He reminded her of a shy tortoise pushing its head out from under its shell. She might be stunned by what he had to say but she felt gratified and touched by his wish to confide in her. Now she could see he was regretting his frankness, so said with deliberate carelessness, 'I've been thinking about things like that recently. It's quite a coincidence really.'

Her admission had the desired effect. He turned and smiled. 'Have you? How very interesting. That's quite extraordinary.'

'Freddy's wedding set me thinking and then I met up with an old friend who's left her partner and I told her she should join a few dating sites. She said she would if I did. You should do that, Dad. Everyone does it.'

'Perhaps your generation does but I'm not sure about mine. Besides, I'm beginning to think . . . ' He stirred the spinach in the wok and added seasoning. 'Granty's made a list of suggestions. Do you want to see it?'

'I would *love* to see it.'

Henry strode across to one of the drawers in the dresser. He pulled out a plastic orange folder

97

and extracted a sheet of paper covered by Granty's familiar looping scrawl. He handed it across to Maddie. 'I'm not sure of some of them,' he said, 'To be honest, at the moment I'm not sure of any of them.'

Maddie studied the first item on Granty's list. '"Contact your old friends and let them know you are available for dinner invitations.' Well, that's sensible. They must know loads of widows and divorcees.'

'The trouble is,' Henry said, 'after Marianne died, I received all sorts of invitations and turned them down. I can't just ring up and say, 'Hey, I want to know you again.''

'Dad,' Maddie said, 'if you're serious about this, you have to have courage. Everyone likes to be useful. You call your friends and you say you miss them. Tell them you're lonely. You can't afford to stand on your dignity. They'll want to help you. People do.'

'I know. You're probably right.' Henry didn't sound convinced.

'"Join local societies and classes — Aerobics, painting, tapestry, French or Spanish."' She had a fleeting image of her father's long limbs flailing helplessly in a sea of women in leotards. 'It's not a bad idea,' she said. 'But make sure you join something that *interests* you. I mean, I can't see you enjoying tapestry.'

'No,' Henry said. 'I wouldn't enjoy tapestry.' He took a casserole dish from the oven and set it on the stove. 'And then she suggests a dating agency and I have to tell you that the thought of sitting in some restaurant waiting for a stranger to come over and take a look at me, knowing that I'm taking a look at *her* . . . No, it's too horrible. I couldn't do it. And *then* she goes on about flirting and first dates . . . It's all hopeless.'

Her father was looking unhappier by the minute. Certainly, Maddie couldn't imagine him engaging a stranger in polite conversation, much less batting delicate compliments across the table. Granty's other suggestions — stalking women in art galleries, seeking advice from Colette and buying a dog — were equally fanciful. She watched her father serving out the meal and returned to the list. 'Who's Louise?'

'I had a crush on her all through my teens. Her parents lived next door to mine. She's Granty's goddaughter. She lives in Inverness. Her husband died two years ago and Granty is convinced we'd be perfect for each other.'

'What do *you* think?'

'I haven't seen Louise in a very long time and I don't want to go to Inverness, much less live there.'

'Fair enough. 'Get advice from William . . . '?'

'I've done that,' Henry said, 'and it was a total disaster. He told me to smile at a woman I liked and I did that and . . . '

'What? What woman? What are you talking about?'

'I saw a woman in the library. She looked very . . . nice. I smiled at her, well, I tried to smile, in the way William had told me to: staring at her and not blinking and then smiling seriously — very difficult — and . . . It was awful, Maddie, she looked at me as if I were mad.' He shook his head as if trying to dislodge the memory from his head. 'The whole thing's hopeless, I see that now. Let's have supper. Tell me about *your* life. That's far more interesting.'

'No, it isn't. My life is spectacularly boring at the moment. And I think you should start getting out and looking for a partner but I'm not sure this list will help you. You can't take advice from people like Uncle William because they're totally different from you. You need to take it one step at a time and try different things at your own pace and in your own time . . . ' She saw him shake his head and said quickly, 'I have an idea. You want to find a mate. So do I. Let's start a campaign. We can report back to each other. Let's make a rule that we *have* to do something every week to . . . further our chances. We can pool resources, trade experiences. It's much easier to attempt something like this if we support each other.'

He put his hands in his pockets and stared down at his shoes and then very slowly, raised his head. 'Maddie,' he said, 'I'll do it! You will help me and I will help you. Thank you. It will be an adventure. The only thing is . . . What happens now?

⋆   ⋆   ⋆

Maddie was under no illusions as to the immensity of the task she had set herself. In order to propel her father back into the land of the living she would have to provide him with weekly bulletins — true and unvarnished — of her own attempts to find a partner.

On the train back home she sat staring out at the increasingly urban landscape, pondering her dilemma. What she had to do, she supposed, was to regard this unwanted homework as a hobby, a light-hearted social diversion. Love was out of the question but sexual adventures were not. From now on she would try much harder to seek out companions. Any humiliations, misunderstandings and tedious dates would simply be collateral damage. She would be fulfilling her promise to her father *and* to Amy.

When she got back home she found an envelope had been pushed under her door. It contained an invitation from Guy to his housewarming party the following Friday. She was relieved. She would go to the party; she would chat someone up; and she would duly report back. She might even chat Guy up. In fact, she would definitely chat Guy up. Week One's bulletin would be taken care of. Hopefully within the year, Amy would find a new man and her father would have recovered old friendships and built new ones. At which point she would be able to dismiss forever all those men with a great sense of humour who were waiting to swim with her in January.

8

Henry had put the library flyer on his noticeboard and through the following week he was constantly aware of its presence: both a mocking reminder of his inappropriate behaviour in the library and a challenging invitation to rectify his mistake.

The flyer advertised a forthcoming talk about Queen Victoria and her children. A local historian called Beryl Antrobus had written a book on the subject and the talk would apparently be controversial and stimulating.

WAS QUEEN VICTORIA AN APPALLING PARENT? IF SO, WHY? BERYL IS CONFIDENT HER TALK WILL PROVOKE A LIVELY DISCUSSION ON WHAT MAKES A GOOD PARENT. 'IF YOU DOUBT YOUR PARENTING SKILLS,' BERYL SAYS, 'COME TO MY TALK. I PROMISE YOU'LL FEEL BETTER AFTERWARDS!'

Henry thought he would very much like to go to Beryl's talk. He had huge doubts about his parenting skills. Marianne had always had enough for both of them and he knew that, since her death, he had been sadly wanting as a father.

If he did go, he would be terrified that the beautiful lady might be there. On the other hand, if she *wasn't* there, he would be bitterly disappointed. The fact was that he *had* to go. He had precious little to report back to Maddie so far. His only achievement since their meal had been to cut out an item in the local paper about Pilates classes. Maddie had said — a little unfairly, he thought — that it only counted if he actually *went* to the class.

So now — even though every fibre of his being baulked at the idea — he was on his way to Higgleigh Town Hall on a cold October evening. The advertisement had suggested comfortable clothes, so he was decked out in the old drawstring trousers he used for decorating and a faded blue polo shirt. Even if there were a dozen gorgeous unattached women at the Pilates class, he couldn't believe that any of them would find a man in paint-spattered drawstring trousers remotely attractive.

As he walked up the steps to the hall, he could hear a buzz of conversation behind the doors. He almost turned back, and was only stopped by the memory of his mother's latest exhortation. 'Searching for love is a complicated business,' she'd said. 'And it's not for the easily discouraged.'

How right she was, thought Henry, how right she was. As he went through the doors, he felt like a boy starting at a new school. There were about fifteen people in the room and they all seemed to know each other. Only two of them were men. Henry was pleased to see that they were as badly dressed as he was. One of them was overweight with a red face and even redder ears, and the other wore a T-shirt that said, 'Keep Calm and Do Some Exercise'. A group of four athletic-looking young women laughed together in one corner while the T-shirt man chatted to a group of older ladies in another. The rest of the class stood on their mats, stamping their feet like portly race horses waiting for the starting gun.

Henry hovered by the door, still tempted to retreat. He was forced to move forward by a friendly wave from a pretty young lady with a tablet and a notepad. She couldn't be more than twenty-five and was dressed in purple lycra which on anyone else would be quite unpleasant.

'I'm Daisy,' she said. 'We haven't seen you here before, have we? Did you read about us in the paper?'

Henry nodded. 'I thought I'd . . . I've never done anything like this before . . . I thought I'd see how I got on . . . It's probably way beyond my . . . '

'You'll be fine,' Daisy promised. 'As this is your first time, it's only five pounds.'

She looked at him expectantly and Henry took out his wallet and gave her the money. She rewarded him with a smile and a blue-rolled mat.

'Just do what you can,' she said, 'and be sure to follow my instructions. You'll get better every lesson. Trust me, I know what I'm talking about.'

Henry was sure that she did. Daisy was a glowing testimonial to the positive effects of Pilates.

'You're here to enjoy yourself,' she told him. 'And you're here to become flexible. You'll be amazed at what you can do. Enjoy!' She gave him another ravishing smile and suggested he might like to go and stand next to Geoffrey.

Henry followed her gaze. Geoffrey turned out to be the overweight man who was currently doing a few ostentatious press-ups. Henry decided he didn't like Geoffrey.

'Right,' Daisy started up the music on her tablet and clapped her hands together. 'Let's get going, shall we?'

Neither Henry's body nor Henry's mind were equipped for organized exercise. Henry felt — and knew he looked — like an arthritic scarecrow. When Daisy told the class to curl their pelvises, Henry's brain directed the message to his spine; when Daisy wanted a single leg stretch, Henry's other leg insisted on joining in. When Daisy said in a happy voice, 'Now touch your toes,' Henry lost the will to live and his hand barely managed to reach his knees. When Daisy asked everyone to 'roll up off the floor', Henry knew he was in trouble. Every time he tried to roll up off the floor, he collapsed back onto it and when, at last, he made a final furious effort, he felt a sharp pain in his lower back and, with an agonized grunt, fell back onto the mat like a sack of potatoes dropped from a great height.

What followed were the most embarrassing moments of his life. The white-haired woman to his left who must have been at least seventy and had done all the exercises with apparent ease, got to her feet and asked, 'Are you all right, dear?'

Daisy came over at once. 'Oh, Henry,' she said, 'didn't you hear me? I *told* you and Geoffrey not to do this one. It's not suitable for beginners.'

Geoffrey, who did press-ups, was a *beginner*?

105

Geoffrey looked down at Henry with a sorrowful expression. 'She did say that,' he said. 'I thought you were being a little over-ambitious.'

Henry meekly allowed himself to be raised from the floor by the surprisingly strong arms of Daisy. He apologized profusely to everyone for interrupting the class and murmured that he was absolutely fine but that perhaps — just this once — he would opt out of the rest of the lesson.

He limped home slowly. Every time he tried to quicken his pace, he received another flash of pain in his lower back. He had never been any good at physical exercise. He should have remembered that at school he had been the last one to be chosen by team captains every single time. At home, he shuffled up the stairs, ran himself a hot bath and took fifteen minutes to take off his clothes and lever himself into the water.

'You'll find it easier next time,' Daisy had assured him. 'Trust me!'

But Henry no longer trusted Daisy and he knew that, if he lived to be a hundred, he would never ever attend another Pilates class. The honour would be Geoffrey's alone.

★　★　★

Henry was still walking with care when he went to the Queen Victoria talk three nights later. The library was one large room, divided into sections by grey metal bookshelves on castors. For the talk, they had been wheeled back towards the windows in order to accommodate four rows of blue plastic chairs, most of which were already taken. Either Beryl's flyer had been a success or there were plenty of Queen Victoria fans in Higgleigh.

Henry glanced around for a place to sit and stiffened. The beautiful lady was sitting in the third row. There was a space next to her which she might have reserved for a friend or husband. Even if she hadn't, she might, with justification, suspect Henry of stalking her if he tried to sit there.

His indecision was ended by a voice calling, 'Henry! Over here!' and, with mingled relief and disappointment, he made his way to a familiar face in the second row.

Tessa Goodbody was an old friend. Years ago, she and Marianne had been in Samaritans together. Henry had always liked her husband, Frank, who had as little interest in talking about his job as Henry did about his own. The Goodbodys had been one of the many couples who had invited Henry to supper after Marianne's death. A year ago, Frank had died after a brief illness. Henry had written a note of condolence to Tessa and had received a heartfelt response by return of post. He had done nothing more, assuming a little too readily that she, like him, would wish to retreat from the world.

He sat down beside her and said, 'Tessa, how are you?'

She raised her hand in an indecisive gesture. 'Oh, you know . . . ' and Henry nodded, because he did. 'I went to see a medium last month,' she

107

said, and then catching Henry's horrified glance, added quickly, 'She was performing at a theatre in Colchester. The place was packed. I just thought . . . well, I don't know what I thought. At one point she asked, 'Does anyone here know a Malcolm?' And you'd think that among all those people, someone would, but it was a minute or so before a woman stood up and said that her husband's middle name was Malcolm. And then the medium came out with all sorts of amazing stuff about him. But afterwards I thought, why would the woman's husband choose to offer his *middle* name? And then I remembered that Frank always loathed psychics and would be hardly queue up in heaven to speak to one. So I won't be going again.'

'Very wise,' Henry said. He remembered both Goodbodys had been churchgoers. He himself had gone through a phase the previous year of trying to believe in eternal life but it hadn't worked. He found the idea of immortality ridiculous and even if there were a serene and peaceful heaven, he couldn't imagine Marianne enjoying herself there.

The room fell silent as Wendy Miller, Higgleigh's sole librarian, walked in, escorting a confident-looking woman with a smooth helmet of blonde hair and very shiny lips.

'You are in for a treat tonight,' Wendy assured her audience, 'Our guest is a formidable authority on the subject of Queen Victoria and has some quite shocking things to tell us about the way she treated her children. Please give a big hand to Beryl Antrobus!'

The audience duly obliged. Henry wished he had the courage to see if the chair next to his lady had been taken. Stop it, he told himself, concentrate on Queen Victoria.

Concentrating proved to be surprisingly easy. Beryl Antrobus was a good speaker with a fascinating story to tell. She said that Queen Victoria was a monster. She had nine children and was horrid to all of them. She hated being pregnant and resented the fact that her condition interfered with her sex life. Her oldest daughter, Vicky, was married off to a Prussian prince and despatched to Germany at the age of seventeen. For the rest of her life, increasingly lonely and isolated, Vicky received hundreds of letters from her mother packed with unsolicited advice and severe reprimands. The Queen despised her oldest son and did her best to keep her other children under her strict control. Her youngest son, Leopold, suffered from ill health which she used as an excuse to keep him at home throughout his childhood.

Tormented by the bullying tutors his mother chose for him, he was desperate to escape, but his mother refused to let him go to school. According to Beryl, the Queen believed that the sole purpose of her children was to support their mother.

Henry leant forward, his hands gripped together, and at the end of the talk he clapped louder than anyone. Wendy stepped forward again. 'I'm afraid we have no time for questions but Beryl will be signing her books if you wish to purchase them. And may I remind you that in

109

two weeks' we are lucky to be hosting a stimulating talk on bee-keeping by local expert Fred Martin.'

Henry turned to Tessa. 'That was good, wasn't it?'

Tessa nodded. 'It was fascinating! The more one hears about our royal family, the worse it appears to be.'

'I agree,' Henry said. A fleeting glance revealed that his lady was buying a copy of Beryl's book and engaging the author in animated conversation. If Henry had brought his wallet with him, he would have felt strongly tempted to do the same.

'It's very good to see you, Henry,' Tessa said. 'You became such a hermit after Marianne died.'

'I know.' Henry hesitated. 'I intend to get out a lot more. That's why I came tonight.'

'I'm glad to hear it. I wonder if . . . No, it's a stupid idea. I'm sure you're far too busy.'

'Tell me,' Henry said.

'I wondered if you'd like to join our book group. I'm afraid we have no men at the moment but we'd welcome any who wished to attend. We meet every month at The Frog and Whistle if you're interested.'

Henry's back gave a twinge. A book group full of women seemed far more enticing than Pilates with Geoffrey.

'I'd love to come,' he said. 'When's the next meeting?'

'We had the last one a few days ago, which means that you have a month in which to read *Middlemarch*.' Tessa stood up and glanced across towards Beryl Antrobus. 'I'll ring you with the date and time. I'm going to join the queue. What about you?'

The queue was very long. His lady was still at the front, still talking to the author. There was no way Henry could even imagine approaching her. 'I think I'll get along home,' he said. 'It's been very nice to see you.'

He struggled to his feet and walked out of the library. The sky was almost dark now. It had been raining and the road glistened. Across the road, smokers from the pub stood on the pavement, inhaling furiously, discussing the football. An elderly couple emerged from the Chinese restaurant. As they walked past Henry, the man said, 'Good evening, Mr Drummond,' and Henry said, 'Hello there!' recognising him too late as a client probably five years younger than himself. Henry supposed that anyone looking at *him* would think he was elderly. That was a disturbing thought.

He heard footsteps behind him and he looked back to see who it was. His heart did a little flip and he gave a cautious nod as he slowed to let her approach.

She seemed to have forgotten the smile incident. She said, 'Did you enjoy the talk?'

'I found it fascinating. I had no idea Queen Victoria was quite so unpleasant.'

'I thought it was very one-sided. I told Beryl Antrobus so. I mean, think about it: what did she tell us? The queen loved sex and hated pregnancy. Amazing! She missed her husband and found it difficult bringing up her children on

111

her own. Wow! There were times when she found her offspring irritating and she wasn't afraid to tell them so. Extraordinary! If all that makes her a bad mother, then so are we all.'

'My wife loved being pregnant,' Henry said.

'Well, she was lucky. I was sick every morning, had constant indigestion and got leg cramps in bed. For the last two months I could hardly move. And don't even get me started on childbirth.'

'I wouldn't dream of it,' Henry assured her.

'The first time took forever,' the lady said. 'I thought he'd never come out. He was over nine pounds.'

'Oh dear.' Henry couldn't imagine how such a slim lady could produce a nine-pound baby. 'I'm sure you found him beautiful once he was born. I'm sure you didn't think he was . . . What did Victoria call one of her babies? A 'very nasty object'.'

'Actually, Adam was spectacularly ugly at first, which is funny, because he grew up to be spectacularly good-looking. I do concede that I never found him nasty.'

Henry laughed. 'I'm glad to hear it.' He realized with regret that he was near his street and that he had to say goodbye. 'I live in Belton Street,' he said. 'It's been a pleasure to talk to you.' He extended a hand. 'My name's Henry by the way.'

She put her hand briefly in his. 'And I'm Ellen. Thank you for letting me sound off at you.'

As he crossed the road he resisted the

temptation to look back at her, and walked on down Belton Street. Presumably she regarded his earlier *faux pas* as an aberration. He felt enormously grateful to be given a second chance. She was really quite lovely, and both articulate and interesting. Perhaps the talk *had* been one-sided. He wasn't wholly convinced by her defence of Victoria but at least he no longer regarded the monarch as a monster. More importantly, Ellen, he felt, now saw that *he* wasn't a monster. She wouldn't have told him her name if that had been the case. Henry walked back home with as much of a spring in his step as was possible given his back trouble.

Cleaning his teeth that night, Henry's mind swung between plans to read *Middlemarch*, thoughts about Ellen and reflections on Queen Victoria and her nine unfortunate children. It was only when he awoke the next morning that he realized that for the first time since Marianne's death, he had gone to bed without thinking of her.

9

Guy's party proved to be an entertaining if chastening experience. Maddie arrived late, having had to make a long-planned visit to a school in Streatham. Guy's door was open and before going in she stood for a moment and surveyed the scene inside. At the far end of the room a big man dressed entirely in black stood eating his way through a large plate of cocktail sausages. There was a very attractive couple near the blotting-paper picture. The woman had black hair and a pale, luminescent complexion, and was pregnant and wearing a tight red dress; the man had strikingly blond hair and dark eyebrows. They were talking to two elderly people who looked like they'd stepped from the pages of a nursery-rhyme book. The woman wore a belted floral dress and flat shoes. Her hair was tied back in an old-fashioned bun and she had rosy cheeks, twinkling eyes and a sturdy figure. Her partner was tall and thin and dressed in a wrinkled grey suit with a check shirt and a tweed tie.

On the other side of the room, a group of people listened to a man with extravagant eyebrows, while a large woman with a husky laugh was clearly enjoying talking to Guy. He had the knack, Maddie thought, of making anyone he talked to feel special. It was a great gift.

And now he saw her and came over to her. 'Maddie,' he said, 'I was beginning to worry about you . . . ' The pregnant woman had come over to join them and Guy took her hand. 'Maddie, this is Jess, my business partner. I told you we represent artists, didn't I? She is the calmest, most unflappable woman I know and I'm very, very lucky. Jess, this is Maddie, who lives upstairs and is going to be a very good friend. I'll go and get you a drink, Maddie . . . '

Maddie smiled at Jess. 'He's a very charming man,' she said.

'Oh yes. He likes to be liked of course . . . God, that sounds bitchy, doesn't it? I suppose I'm a little jealous of him, if you want to know the truth. Plus, my back is aching. I find pregnancy is a brilliant excuse for all sorts of bad behaviour. Leo can't wait for it to end. I could talk to you forever about my problems with wind.'

In fact, unlike some of Maddie's pregnant friends who assumed she was desperate to know about cramps and sickness and over-sensitive nipples, Jess was refreshingly uninterested in talking about her condition and instead gave Maddie a potted history of other guests in the room. 'You see Bill over there? He describes himself as a behavioural artist. He sets up situations — in his last one, he had a couple arguing in Paddington Station and he filmed the reactions they aroused — and over there is Martha, who does amazing things with mannequins. Guy and I spend our days trying to find sponsors for these people . . . '

115

And now Guy was back with a glass of wine for Maddie and a request for Jess. 'Can you talk to Bill?' he asked. 'He's eaten all the sausages and now he's started on the sandwiches ... Maddie, my parents want to meet you. Come and say hello.'

It seemed odd that the nursery-rhyme couple could produce such an elegant, confident son. They seemed bemused both by his flat and his friends and latched on to Maddie with evident relief, sensing that she too was an alien here. The other reason for their interest was soon apparent. Having ascertained that she was single, they were anxious to tell her that Guy would make a perfect husband and a brilliant father. Eventually Jess's partner, Leo, came over to join them — Maddie suspected he'd been sent by Guy to rescue her — and told her that someone called Garth was dying to meet her.

Garth turned out to be the man with the big eyebrows who did a very good job of concealing his desperate desire to be introduced. Once she realised he was a man who preferred to pontificate rather than engage, she found it quite pleasant to hear his views. He had interesting ideas on education and was convinced that politicians should listen more and talk less.

When Guy's parents left, the room relaxed. Voices were louder, laughter less restrained, discussions more heated. Maddie, finishing the smoked salmon sandwiches with Jess, nodded towards Guy's framed film poster and asked, 'Have *you* seen that film?'

'You can't be a good friend of Guy's and *not*

see it. I can tell you all you need to know about both the film stars in it. Did you know they were very close friends? Montgomery Clift was gay but he never loved anyone like he did Liz Taylor. Six years after that film was made he had a terrible car accident after leaving her house. His face was smashed up and he lost some teeth. He'd have died if it hadn't been for her. He was choking on his broken teeth when she found him and she pulled them from his mouth. After that, he got addicted to prescription drugs and alcohol and he died of a heart attack a few years later.'

'That's so sad.' Maddie glanced through the doorway into Guy's bedroom and froze. Guy was kissing Leo. She blinked and instinctively turned to her companion, who regarded her with sympathetic amusement and said, 'It *is* confusing, isn't it?'

★ ★ ★

'So it turns out,' Maddie said, over lunch with Gregory the next day, 'that Leo and Jess had been in a relationship for three years before he realised he was gay. But she wanted a baby and so did he, so now she's pregnant, they're still sort of living together and he's fallen in love with Guy, who is happy to be an honorary uncle because it turns out he'd like a child too . . . '

'It all sounds very sensible,' Gregory said. He picked up her carton of pasta salad. 'Do you want any more of this?'

'No, you finish it.' Maddie watched him heap

117

the rest of the salad onto his plate. She could never understand how he remained so thin when he ate so much. 'I must say I feel very silly. I thought he liked *me*.'

'I'm sure he does. You should be flattered. He's not trying to get you into bed so there's no ulterior motive. He is simply attracted to your compelling personality.'

'I think it's more to do with the fact that he has extremely good manners and . . . Gregory, are you listening to me?'

'I was thinking,' he said. 'It might be rather nice to be a father.'

'I've never heard you say that before. Things must be going well with the dainty Minty.'

'A very unpleasant note creeps into your voice whenever you mention Minty. She can't help having a funny name.'

'I don't mind her name. I just find it difficult to watch my best friend copy my ex-boyfriend. It must be the season for child brides.'

'Minty isn't a bride and she's not a child. She's actually a very intelligent woman.'

'And I'm very happy for you.' She caught Gregory's eye. 'Really, I am. I'm sorry. I know I'm being a cow. I'm in a bad mood, that's all.'

'To be honest,' Gregory said, 'even if Guy *had* been after you, I'm not sure it's wise to have an affair with your next-door neighbour.'

'It's not just that. When I left the party last night I had two messages waiting for me and I could have done without both of them. Amy remembered that I have a birthday quite soon and is paying for us to go on a speed-dating evening. And if that wasn't bad enough, I've had my first invitation from a dating-site man. He wants to meet for a drink next week.'

'You never know,' Gregory said, 'he might turn out to be the man of your dreams.'

Maddie directed a sour look at him. 'He doesn't exist,' she said.

★   ★   ★

Nathan had said he was abnormally tall and would be wearing a sickly green shirt. Maddie told him she'd be sure to wear her mustard-coloured dress. He had obviously been eyeing the door; as soon as she entered the place he stood up and waved. He *was* tall — not exactly a giant but taller than her father who was six feet four.

'Hello,' he said. 'You noticed the sickly shirt?'

She smiled. 'It's a very nice shirt. You observed my mustard-coloured dress.'

'It's a lovely dress. Let me buy you a drink.'

He looked like a grown-up Just William. He had curly brown hair, small dark eyes and a dented nose that suggested a certain amount of schoolboy battering. He wore a good suit, although its elegance was rather spoilt by the fact that his brown tie was at half-mast.

'I'll get it,' she said. 'I hope I haven't kept you waiting too long.'

'It's not your fault. I'm always ultra-punctual when I'm nervous.'

She liked that he admitted his nerves. She ordered a spritzer and saw him checking his phone but noticed with approval that he switched it off when she joined him again. She set her glass on the table, took off her jacket and sat down opposite him. 'I've never done this before,' she said. 'So I have no idea of the etiquette. Do we fire questions at each other or what?'

'I don't know,' he said. 'I *have* done this before without great results so it's the blind leading the blind, I'm afraid. We could start with questions.' He swung his long legs to the side of the table. 'Are you a London girl born and bred?'

'I was brought up in Suffolk,' Maddie said, 'but I've been here for years.'

'I have an aunt who lives in Lavenham. I like Lavenham but I don't like my aunt so I very rarely go there.'

'Why don't you like her?'

Nathan frowned and rubbed his chin. 'She's one of those people who make a point of speaking their minds. In practice, she thinks this gives her licence to be as rude as she can be about the many character flaws of her nephews and nieces. Do your parents still live in Suffolk?'

'My father does.' She took a sip of her drink. 'My mother died four years ago.'

'I'm sorry. How did she die?' He hit his forehead with his hand. 'That was a singularly crass question. You don't have to answer it.'

A man in a navy blue suit and a bright red shirt sat alone at the next table. Maddie wondered if he too was anticipating a conversation with a stranger. She stared levelly at Nathan. 'She was sitting in her car. She'd just been to the dentist. A woman drove straight into her. Apparently she'd been distracted by her children in the back.'

'That's terrible.'

'Yes, it was. What about *your* parents? Are they still alive and well?'

'They're alive. My father lives in the south of France with his second wife and my mother nurses her bitterness in Hertfordshire with daily doses of gin.' He caught her eye. 'I'm sorry, this is all very grim, isn't it? I'm beginning to see why I'm not very good at this sort of thing.'

She laughed. 'I think you're doing very well,' she said. 'Tell me more about yourself. Do you have any brothers or sisters?'

'My brother,' Nathan said, 'is married to Cressida.' He relayed this information in the manner of a fishmonger throwing down a piece of plaice on his cutting board.

'What's wrong with her?' Maddie asked.

'Oh God!' He pushed his hands through his hair. 'What can I say? Cressida is brilliant at spending money, or rather she's brilliant at spending my brother's money. She gave up her career to look after her children, which was very noble of her since she had a fascinating job as an estate agent in Knightsbridge. They have a nanny, a gardener and a cleaner and my brother worries about her over-tiring herself. She suffers from a multitude of ailments with endlessly shifting symptoms. I see them as often as I see my aunt which is not very often because, it might surprise you to hear, Cressida doesn't like me very much. I don't visit my father either. Would

121

you like to hear about my father?'

By the time he'd finished describing his quite stunningly dysfunctional family, Maddie had finished her drink. He offered to buy her another. 'You can stay a little longer can't you?' he asked. 'Won't you have one for the road?'

She'd forgotten she'd warned him she could only stay for a brief drink. 'I'd love a white wine,' she said, 'just a small one.' She noticed that the man in the red shirt had been joined by a female companion. It was with a slight feeling of smugness that she saw that they were struggling to find things to talk about.

★　★　★

Really, they had nothing in common. Nathan had been to public school; he worked in the City; he liked to ski in Switzerland and scuba dive in Mallorca. His favourite film was *Saw* and his favourite author was Andy McNab. But he did make her laugh. Reluctantly, she turned down his offer of a third drink and said she must go. They swapped telephone numbers and he apologized for talking too much. On the way back home she kept remembering things he'd said and found herself smiling like an idiot.

At home, she ate a pizza and watched a serial about a psychopath terrorizing a housewife. He'd terrorized her the week before in her remote weekend cottage and now she'd happily gone back there to be terrorized again. The plot was ridiculous but Maddie enjoyed it.

She awoke the next morning with the happy

realization that she hadn't once thought of Freddy the day before. Over breakfast, she switched on her phone and discovered she had a message from Nathan.

She sat staring blankly at the image that came up on her screen. Nathan had taken a photo of his penis, poised and ready for action. She put her phone down and wondered what he expected her to make of it. She could think of no conceivable reason why he would do this. Perhaps he'd been abused as a child, or watched too much porn, or was simply unhinged. He had seemed so nice and he looked like Just William.

She felt such a fraud. She had told herself she'd embarked on the dating campaign to help her friend and support her father. But, first with Guy and then with Nathan, there had been that seductive little wriggle of hope leading her to believe that she might, just might, get lucky and find a man with whom she could live and love. She was such a fool.

She picked up the phone and sent him back a message: *I'm on Cressida's side.*

10

Two weeks previously, one of Henry's old colleagues, Brian Haddon, a nice man who'd only retired six months before, had complained of a headache. Three days later, he had died. His death shook everyone at the office. People walked through their lives as if they had all the time in the world but, just occasionally, something would happen to reveal that each of them was accompanied by a tall, dark companion whose scythe was waiting to strike at random, on a whim.

Henry didn't want to die on his own and he was increasingly sure he didn't want to live on his own either. What had begun as an amorphous feeling of restless energy had crystallized into a concrete determination to find a permanent partner. Maddie's involvement had made a crucial difference. Her support and readiness to pursue a similar goal had legitimized his plans. The very fact that he had to report back to her every week kept him focussed on the task ahead. Admittedly his achievements so far had been pretty modest. Meanwhile Maddie had made new friends at her neighbour's party and had joined a dating agency. Better still, she had even had a date as a result and although it hadn't led anywhere, she had not been put off trying again. Henry still wasn't sure about dating agencies for himself and he certainly had no time to join one at the moment. It was taking a great deal of time to read *Middlemarch*. It was a very long book.

At home that evening there were two messages on the answerphone. The first was from his sister-in-law. 'Henry? It's Colette. I'm very happy to offer my services if you want them and if you don't I'm sure you'll be fine but if you *do*, don't hesitate to ring and I'll speak to you soon . . . '

Henry had no idea what Colette was talking about. He wondered if she'd finally lost her marbles. The horrible thought occurred to him that his mother had co-opted her as an adviser on his romantic aspirations, a possibility that was as embarrassing as it was unwanted. He wasn't sure whether to ring her or pretend he'd never heard the message.

The second was from Nina. 'Dad, I want to ask a big favour. Robbie's away on the second weekend in November, which is a pity because Maddie's invited me to London for her birthday celebrations and I'd really love to go. Could you have the girls for twenty-four hours? I've talked to Colette and she says she's happy to come up and help if you want. They'll be quite easy and I'd be so grateful. Ring me!'

The first time Henry had babysat his grandchildren, Chloe had defecated for England. The second time, last Thursday, Megan had been unable to sleep and he'd had to read endless stories about a very boring child who liked to explore other planets. Nina had returned to find her father and daughter both unconscious on the sofa.

Colette wasn't going mad; she was offering him a life-line.

★ ★ ★

The Frog and Whistle was Henry's sort of pub: fairly large, unpretentious, with a broad clientele. It was a place where one could find old-age pensioners playing backgammon at one table and a group of excitable young adults at another. Thanks to the smoking ban, the young adults spent most of their time on the pavement. In fact, Henry enjoyed their sporadic high spirits, while glad to be reminded that he no longer needed to be so relentlessly sociable.

He arrived late for the book group, owing to a call from Maddie who wanted to make sure he was happy for Nina to come to London for her birthday. 'You would say if it was too much for you? You don't have to do it . . . '

He'd assured her that he was very much looking forward to having the girls to stay and, besides, Colette would be helping him so it would be a piece of cake. 'I'd better go,' he'd added carelessly, 'I have a book group to go to.'

He had high hopes for the evening. He had finished *Middlemarch* the night before, racing through the final chapters in order to find out if Will and Dorothea would get together in the end. He was eager to share his thoughts. At the pub, he bought a beer and hurried through to the room at the back.

Two small tables had been put together and seven women sat round them, chatting amicably while sipping their drinks. Henry caught Tessa's eye at once and she cried out, 'Henry, you've come!' as if she hadn't rung last night to confirm that he would. Henry was warmed by her welcome. It was difficult not to feel a little intimidated by the all-female group.

Tessa was not the only familiar face. He recognised two of the others. Andrea and Jill had daughters who'd been in Maddie's class at school. The other four were called Becky, Christine, Flicky and Helen — though Henry had no idea which name belonged to which woman. They seemed happy to include him. Henry said he was very pleased to be there and that he'd *loved* reading *Middlemarch*. 'It's a very big novel,' he said, 'and I did get confused by the large cast of characters but I never found it boring.'

'That's good to hear,' Andrea said, without noticeable enthusiasm. 'But what we do in these evenings is to let the member who chose the book give her assessment first. There will be plenty of time for you to tell us what you think, never fear!'

'Of course.' Henry nodded, 'that sounds very sensible.' He remembered now that at parents' evenings, Andrea used to enrage Marianne by asking the English teacher a long series of earnest questions, ensuring that by the time he and Marianne reached the front of the queue, there was only time for a quick, 'Everything all right?' which, luckily, it invariably was.

'Right.' Andrea put her hands together. 'Would you like to kick off with your thoughts, Becky?'

127

The woman who was Becky cleared her throat. She was quite young — in her early forties, Henry reckoned. She wore a pale yellow dress and a pink cardigan and her light brown hair was tied back in a neat plait. Henry could imagine her in her kitchen, singing while she made the family supper.

'First of all,' she said, 'I feel I should apologise for making everyone read such a huge novel. The thing is, I always wanted to read it but I knew I'd never feel I could spare the time without the book group keeping me focussed.'

There was a ripple of agreement round the table, concluded by a 'Too right!' from Jill. Jill's daughter had been a friend of Maddie in the sixth form. Henry wondered if they were still in touch.

'But I'm so glad I *did* choose it,' Becky continued, 'because it's the most glorious love story! I fell hopelessly in love with Will Ladislaw. He's not shackled to any particular class, he's not interested in worldly possessions, he's artistic, he likes children, he's a good friend to old little Miss Noble and he's completely true to Dorothea. I did find her a little less easy to love. She was so very noble and so very good. But I did come to care about her and when, near the end, she cries, 'Oh I did love him!' my heart broke for her.'

'Excuse me, Becky, can I say something?' A woman with short hair and long earrings put her hand up.

'Of course, Christine, go ahead.'

'Am I the only one who finds Dorothea a pain

in the neck? Am I the only one to think that she is priggish, insufferable and, most of all, stupid? It's clear as day that anyone who marries Mr Casaubon is asking to be bored out of existence.'

Christine's questions both finished on a tone of upward inflection. Henry had been tempted to respond to them with a 'No, you are not!' but he suspected they were rhetorical and Christine did not look like a woman who would welcome unsolicited interruption. He couldn't imagine Christine singing while she made the supper. Come to that, he couldn't imagine her doing anything so humdrum as cooking.

'But that's why George Eliot's so clever,' Becky said. 'I know that everyone else can see how tedious Mr Casaubon is. And of course Dorothea is hopelessly blinkered by her desire to do good. And yet, by the end of the book, we love her and we want her to be . . . '

'I didn't,' Christine said. 'I thought her sister was far more interesting.'

Tessa spoke for the first time. 'Even if you can't like her,' she said, 'you have to agree that the love story between her and Will is just lovely. I'm with Becky. I cried!'

Henry had been wishing to speak for some time and since both Christine and Tessa had interrupted, he couldn't think Andrea would mind if he did so too. 'The thing is,' he said, 'I don't think *Middlemarch* is primarily a love story. I think it's a book about bad marriages and why people make them. Dorothea marries Casaubon because she thinks he's a wise, noble man who can teach her about life. Dr Lydgate is as idealistic as Dorothea but he's attracted to Rosamond's beautiful face and he *assumes* she's sweet and tender when he sees her crying.'

Becky had leant forward and was studying Henry with rapt attention and Tessa murmured, 'Very true.' Encouraged, Henry cleared his throat and carried on.

'In fact, of course, she is a shallow, mercenary egotist without an ounce of self-doubt in her soul who slowly destroys her husband. I have to say I think Rosamond is one of the most terrifying characters ever written. Can you imagine what it must be like to be married to someone with whom you have nothing in common? It must be so lonely. It must make you question everything about yourself.'

It was a long time since Henry had spoken at such length and with such energy about anything. But then, it was a long time since he had been in a situation where his opinions were received with such flattering attention. Later, he decided that the attention had gone to his head. His enthusiasm was only checked by a sudden, rasping sound as a chair was pushed roughly backwards. Becky stood up and murmured, 'I'm sorry . . . I'm sorry . . . I have to go.' Her companions watched as she fled from the room, through the main area of the pub and out onto the street.

Henry was aware, as the faces of the remaining women turned towards him that he was somehow to blame. He said, 'I'm so sorry. I didn't mean to . . .'

'It wasn't your fault.' Tessa's quick response

was kind if not convincing. 'You were saying what you thought. You couldn't know that ... It's just a little unfortunate, that's all.'

The woman with earrings looked severely at Henry. 'Becky's been having a few problems. Your comments on bad marriages were a little close to home.'

Henry was appalled. 'I'm so sorry. I had no idea.'

'Of course you didn't. Why should you?' Tessa was being very kind. 'You mustn't blame yourself. And I thought what you said was most interesting.'

'If a little simplistic,' the woman on his right said. '*Middlemarch* is a vast, panoramic novel that's concerned with the position of women, social history, the decline of religion and the elevation of work as a possible alternative.'

A slightly stunned silence followed this assessment and Henry felt that he wasn't the only one who had failed to notice all or indeed any of these elements.

The woman with earrings leant towards Henry. 'Flicky is a retired English Literature professor. She's always able to tell us what a book is really about.'

She gave him an understanding smile and Henry smiled back. He remembered her name was Christine. He thought, not for the first time, that it was far too easy to make a sweeping judgment about a person. It was now quite easy to imagine Christine singing in the kitchen. Presumably, poor Becky didn't sing at all.

11

There was something wrong with Nina. For a start, her determination to come down for Maddie's birthday was odd. She had never shown much interest in celebrating it in the past.

'It's a lovely idea,' Maddie told her, 'but Amy's paid for me to go on a speed-dating evening with her . . .'

'I'd love to do that,' Nina said. 'Give me the details and I'll get myself a ticket.'

'You can't do that. You already have a perfectly decent partner. It's greedy to want more than one. And besides, I have no idea how much it costs.'

'I can afford it. I sold Chloe's camping cot and a whole lot of baby equipment to a friend's sister last week. I've never gone speed-dating. Robbie won't mind. He knows you'll look after me.'

'Even Robbie won't agree to stay at home with the girls so you can look for men!'

He won't have to. He's got a stag weekend in the Lake District. I'll ask Dad to have the girls for twenty-four hours. He does babysit now, you know.'

'Sitting on a sofa for a couple of hours is very different from looking after them for a weekend. He'd be terrified.'

'I'll ask Colette to go up and help him. She'll be happy to help out. Oh, Maddie, do let me come. I need to get away. Please.'

'If you can fix it, yes of course. Are you all right, Nina? There's nothing wrong, is there?'

★ ★ ★

'I'd like a break, that's all. Robbie's so often away now and the girls are pretty full-on. I'm thirty-three and I feel like I'm fifty. Do you know what I mean?'

Maddie did, although she wasn't sure Amy would. To have her own family was Amy's Holy Grail. She might find it difficult to appreciate Nina's weariness with her own domestic idyll.

★ ★ ★

When Nina arrived late on Saturday afternoon there was something slightly manic about her, like someone finally allowed out of school. 'Oh Maddie, I love your flat! It's so clean and tidy and bright! It's so *civilized*.' She threw herself onto the sofa. 'I could sit here all night, you know,' and promptly stood up to go to the window. 'And you have a church opposite you! I forgot you had a church!'

'It's a pretty ugly one,' Maddie said. Nina's admiration of her domestic environment was beginning to grate. Nina lived in a pretty Victorian terrace in a quiet lane in Ipswich. There was no comparison with Maddie's utilitarian flat in a crumbling house in an undistinguished road in an even more undistinguished part of south London.

Now Nina was on the move again, kneeling

133

down to open the rucksack she had left in the corridor. 'I've bought you a birthday cake. I made it this morning.' She handed over a Tupperware box to Maddie and took an envelope from the pocket of her parka. 'There's a candle and candle holder in there. One must do these things properly.'

Nina was a superb cook. She was relaxed now, enjoying her second cup of tea, pleased with the success of her cake. Maddie, too, felt soothed and calmed. There was no need to worry about Nina. She was a woman who could produce a superb coffee and walnut sponge, decorate her house and organize her family. Like everyone else, she needed to get off the treadmill occasionally.

After tea, Nina delved into her rucksack again and gave Maddie her birthday present: a photo of Maddie with her nieces, inside one of Nina's vintage frames.

'I have to say,' Maddie said, 'this is the best birthday present I've received.'

'Be honest. It's the only one you've had.'

'Not true. I had an umbrella from Gregory because I keep taking his. I got a scarf from Colette, a book from Granty and . . . '

'A cheque from Dad. And tonight you get to go speed-dating. Lucky Maddie!'

★ ★ ★

On their way downstairs, they met Guy on his way up. Maddie made brief introductions and Guy said he was delighted to meet Maddie's

134

sister and did they know that they had exactly the same manner of talking?

'Jess asked me to ask if you're busy next Saturday,' he told Maddie. 'It's her birthday. Leo's making a special meal.'

'I'm pretty sure I'm free. I'd love to see Jess again.'

'Good, we can go together. Have a good evening.'

Nina said nothing till they hit the pavement and then put her arm through her sister's. 'Now *he* is lovely and he's your next-door neighbour! Why bother with speed-dating?'

'One, he has a very nice boyfriend and two, speed-dating was not *my* idea.'

'If you go with the wrong attitude,' Nina said piously, 'you will have a bad time. You have to be positive. And remember that your friend has spent good money on your behalf, and so have I. My ticket cost an arm and a leg.'

'I didn't ask either of you to spend any money at all.'

'That's not the point. Accept our generosity with grace and optimism. This evening could change your life.'

'It might change *your* life and then what would you do?'

Nina bent down to scoop up an empty cigarette packet. 'I'd be rather pleased,' she said.

★ ★ ★

The organisers had gone to some trouble to provide the right atmosphere. Muted lighting

135

helped disguise the fact that the Caesar Bar was as huge as a railway concourse. The small interview tables had a tea light on each of them, which was nice, although the plastic number cards were a sobering indicator of the point of the evening.

The air was thick with nervous excitement and studied confidence: the bar was doing great business. Amy, Maddie and Nina stood in a huddle, drinking the house punch, a lurid orange confection that tasted like cough medicine. Amy had been unnerved by Nina's presence at first, but Maddie felt she was proving to be a Godsend. It was impossible to be nervous while she kept up whispered and scurrilous descriptions of every man who walked in. By the time the MC stepped forward, dressed in a blue suit, grey shirt and a fixed smile, Maddie was even ready to enjoy herself.

First name labels, he said, should be collected from the table by the doors, along with individual scorecards. The ladies would sit at the numbered tables while the men would rotate. Every four minutes, the bell would ring, signifying that it was time to move on. This, Maddie thought, was matchmaking for the Ritalin generation. Heaven forbid that one should have time to attempt a serious conversation.

'Feel free to stay behind afterwards,' the maestro said. 'Remember that everyone here tonight is between the ages of thirty and forty-two, so already you have something in common!'

'That's a good opening gambit,' Nina murmured. ''Hey, what do *you* find it's like to be between the ages of thirty and forty-two?''

And now here was Maddie, seated at Table Seven, smiling a little too hard as a man called Francis approached. He had to be at least forty-two. His shoulder-length hair tied back in a ponytail suggested he was a fully paid-up member of the Peter Pan brigade. She found him irritating immediately, which was fine. She could feel her combative instincts simmering hopefully.

He took out a notebook and checked a page, before sitting back in his chair, legs apart, one hand on his knee. 'So . . . ' he squinted at the label on her dress, 'Maddie, are you looking for love or just a good time?'

'Well, Francis,' Maddie said, in the happy knowledge that all her prejudices had been confirmed, 'I suppose most of us are looking for love at one time or another. What are *you* looking for?'

Francis gave an eloquent shrug. 'I want to find a soulmate. I won't settle for less. The woman I love will like picnics in the park and cycling in the rain; she'll wake up on a Saturday and say, 'Let's find a train and go to Brighton!' She'll be crazy and fun and she'll live for the moment.'

The man was a walking date-agency advert. 'Why is it fun to cycle in the rain?' Maddie asked. 'And do you *know* how much it costs to catch a train without booking in advance? I'll tell you something, Francis, spontaneity is a very expensive luxury.' She was enjoying herself now. She had imagined stilted attempts at flirtation but this was fun: setting out to annoy someone who deserved everything she could throw at him. She leant forward. 'Do you see what I mean? If you follow the spontaneous path, you won't bother with pensions or insurance or birth control and at some stage you'll be old and poor with too many children and not enough money and constant health issues because of all those ill-advised cycle rides.'

'Well,' Francis gave a mirthless laugh, 'my parents would love you.' Francis didn't. Francis loathed her. He was already checking out the other tables. 'That's why speed-dating works, don't you think? In other circumstances it could have taken an entire evening to see we're not compatible. I'm afraid I'm a spontaneous man at heart.'

Maddie was pretty sure that, whatever the circumstances, she would know in twenty seconds that Francis wasn't her soulmate. She couldn't help thinking that a man who brought ready-made questions to the table was not a man who embraced spontaneity. It was probably just as well that the bell rang before she could point this out to him. Francis leapt from his seat without bothering to say goodbye.

The next one wore a brown jacket, white shirt, V-neck jersey and navy trousers. He had an egg-shaped head, big ears and a nice, if nervous, smile. Unlike Francis, he had the good manners not to cast his eyes at neighbouring ladies.

Maddie cast a quick glance at his name tag. 'Hi, Warren! Do you live round here?'

'No,' Warren said. 'I live in Coulsdon in Surrey

but I should tell you that it has very good train connections to Charing Cross.'

'Well,' Maddie said, 'that's good to know.'

'I should also say right away that I'm thirty-nine and looking for a serious relationship. I have a steady job, I bought a house two years ago, I keep myself fit, I can cook, I'd like to have children . . . Do you have questions you'd like to ask me?'

'I'm not sure.' Maddie, daunted by his list of attributes, couldn't think of anything.

'Let me show you something.' Warren took out of his briefcase a small leather photo album. 'When I bought my house, everything needed doing to it. I like a challenge.' He opened the album. 'That's the kitchen. Notice all the storage space and the twin Belfast sinks. I found them at a reclamation site.'

'Well,' Maddie said, 'I do like Belfast sinks.'

'And look at the sitting room. I made the units myself. Can you see the small cubby-hole, purpose built for the remote controls? People always seem to lose remote controls.'

'I suppose they do.'

'This is the bathroom. You'll notice there isn't a bath. Showers are far more cost-effective and they're better for the environment, of course. This is the sitting room from a different angle. You can see how light it is . . . '

The bell went while Warren was showing her his second spare room.

The next one, Colin, had his questions written in a notebook, like Francis. He was in his mid-thirties, Maddie thought, with the sort of face that would have looked enchanting when he was a baby.

'So,' he said with slow deliberation, 'if you were a colour, what would you be?'

Maddie hated questions like this. 'I'm not sure. Perhaps I'll go for grey. What about you?'

'Yellow, definitely yellow. Yellow and grey go well together.'

'Do they?'

'I think so. Now, how would your best friend describe you?'

'Oh, I don't know. Grumpy and bad-tempered, I expect.' Maddie's friend, Carla, at school, had loved quizzes with questions like these. They had once spent an entire lunch hour answering a *Cosmo* questionnaire designed to reveal whether they were optimists or pessimists. 'How would *your* best friend describe you?'

'To be honest,' Colin said, 'he'd probably tell you I'm way too serious. He's a spur of the moment sort of man. My last girlfriend left me because she said I was too predictable and reliable. Women don't like that, do they?'

'I'm not sure,' Maddie said. 'I was just telling someone that I disapprove of spur-of-the-moment people. In romantic comedies, the heroines are always women who collide into men on their bicycles or spill wine by mistake or jump into a pool with their clothes on and . . . Can you honestly tell me you'd like someone who messed up your bike or your shirt or spent the best part of an evening with clothes that dripped water on you? Isn't it better to be organised and reliable? I like reliable people.'

140

'We can be a little dull,' the man said, 'but thank you. I shall remember what you said. Do you have any questions you wish to ask me?'

Maddie supposed she should have brought some beforehand, like Francis. She felt sorry for Colin. His last girlfriend sounded horrible but it would hardly be tactful to ask about her. Two tables away, Warren was showing Amy photos of his house while at Table Two, Francis was talking with great animation to Nina. Maddie leant forward and said earnestly, 'Tell me, Colin, would you call yourself an optimist or a pessimist?'

★　★　★

The second part of the evening was far more entertaining, possibly due to the two glasses of cough mixture Maddie drank in the interval. Not surprisingly, none of the seven new contenders proved to be impressive but she did at least tick the last one as a Friend. Michael was a short man with thick glasses and mole-like features. When Maddie asked him about his hobbies, he told her that he loved German expressionist films of the 1920s, adding with a small smile that, 'This might explain why I don't have much success with women.'

★　★　★

Jess's birthday celebration the following Saturday was a far quieter affair than Maddie's but no less entertaining. Jess lived in a small, conventional semi-detached house in Sydenham with a neat front garden and a small lawn. Inside was different. The rooms were painted in warm, earthy colours and the walls were host to original art works. Most extraordinary was the furniture, hand-painted and decorated with quotations, symbols and flowers.

Anyone looking through the window would see two couples enjoying a splendid meal together. Guy and Leo teased Jess about her current love of spinach and marmite. Maddie described each and every conversation she had had at the Caesar Bar the previous week; and the four of them had a good debate about the best way to bring up a girl in a society plagued by online bullying and general sexism. Leo favoured strictly limited access to modern technology while Guy went for feminist indoctrination. Jess suggested that Maddie and Gregory establish karate classes for girls at their after-school clubs. And all the time, Maddie marvelled at the calm affection Jess displayed towards her former lover and her best friend.

Now the two men were in the kitchen, washing up and making coffee. Jess smiled across at Maddie and said, 'I suppose it is rather odd, isn't it?'

'You make it work though. I think you're amazing.'

'What's the alternative? Lose my two best friends and the business Guy and I have spent years building up? I'm going to have a baby. She'll have a great father in Leo and a good godfather in Guy. I think I'm pretty lucky. All right, it's not exactly normal but . . .

'Well,' Maddie said, 'who's to say what's normal these days? My father's best friend has been married twice and has an American son he's not seen in decades. I mean, so long as you're happy . . . '

'I know,' Jess nodded. 'I'm lucky. Most of the time, I do feel I'm lucky. I thought I'd missed the boat and here I am, forty-one today and a baby due in January . . . '

'You're forty-one?' Maddie cried. 'Guy didn't tell me you were forty-one. How old is Leo?'

'He's three months older than me.'

Maddie sat back in her chair. 'You look amazing,' she said. 'You both look amazing. Your child has got incredible genes. She'll probably end up advertising moisturizing cream and giving you free samples for the rest of your life. What more could you want?'

'Not a lot,' Jess agreed, 'just so long as she's a karate queen too.'

★ ★ ★

On Sunday morning, Maddie had two phone calls. The first was from Nina, who told her with great triumph that she'd been asked out by Francis and two other men whose faces Maddie had already forgotten. The second was from Amy, who was meeting Warren for lunch the following Saturday. 'It's funny,' she added as a *non-sequitur*, 'I've always had a thing about Belfast sinks.'

143

12

As Henry said to Colette, some valuable lessons had been learnt, not least of which was to remind Nina to bring Chloe's buggy in future. He should have realised that the walk to the playground was far too long for Chloe's small legs.

'I don't know about that,' Colette said. 'I do know I should have stayed away from the merry-go-round.'

That *had* been unfortunate. Henry was pushing Chloe on the swing when Megan wanted to go on the merry-go-round. Colette had whirled her around a few times and then Megan wanted to push Colette. Megan had enjoyed this activity a little too much and Henry, glancing across at them, noticed just in time, that Colette's body had sagged alarmingly and that her face, when briefly visible, had gone a very nasty shade of green. He rushed across to halt the proceedings and she had staggered over to a bench where she had stayed for at least ten minutes.

In fact, that whole outing had been problematic. They had bought ice-creams for the children on the way home and Chloe had no sooner finished it than she was sick. Colette supposed it was the effect of the swing and later, Chloe had happily eaten all her tea including Greek yogurt and banana. It was a great pity that she soon threw that up and even more of a pity for Colette since the vomit fell all over her voluminous brown jumper. That the jumper had shrunk in the dryer was a blessing in disguise, Henry said, since it fitted her far better than it had done before.

It had been an exhausting twenty-four hours but at least the girls had been returned to their mother in relative good health and good humour. Colette had been terrific, and surprisingly good company; the best part of the weekend had been the Saturday night long after the girls were in bed and supper had been cleared away. Henry and Colette retired to the sitting room to finish off the wine and Henry put a fresh log on the fire.

'This is nice,' Colette said. 'I adore my little house but there is nothing like a log fire to make one feel totally relaxed. The wine helps, of course.'

'You deserve it,' Henry said. 'I'd never have got through today without you.'

'I don't think that's true for a moment but it's kind of you to say so.' She put her glass down on the tea chest. 'I want to hear about your project. Granty's told me all about it. She's convinced you'll be married again in no time.'

'Ah,' Henry said. He might have known Granty would tell Colette. He took a sip of his wine and realised that he didn't mind. 'To be honest, I'm not very good at it. I think I'm trying too hard. It was always so easy with Marianne and, of course, I was much younger then. It doesn't help that I rattle around on my own here and *ponder*. I do a lot of pondering.' He raised a hand and let it drop. 'I'm sorry. I'm aware I sound pathetic. You've been on your own for far longer than I have and you seem to manage perfectly.'

'Well,' said Colette, 'it's different for me. I have Hugh.'

Hugh? Henry paused. It was so pleasant to sit here in front of the fire with the children asleep and the wine in his hand and now . . . there was Hugh. Perhaps this was the time to say something, to bring it out into the open but . . . He couldn't do it. He could almost hear Marianne hissing in his ear. Henry's silence didn't seem to bother Colette, who was gazing rather dreamily at the fire. Marianne had mentioned more than once that her sister only mentioned Hugh when she was really at ease. 'And so,' Marianne would say, 'we have no right to intrude.'

'The thing is,' Colette said, 'both my marriages were spectacularly unsuccessful. You're different. You're good at marriage, which has been very lucky for me. Thanks to you and Marianne, I have Granty, I have my nieces and now I have Chloe and Megan, too. That's enough. But you're different. You should be a husband again and I know you will be. You just need to get out there.'

'I'm going to London next Friday,' Henry said.

'Are you going on a date?'

'No, nothing like that. An old friend of Marianne lives in Devon with her husband. She comes up to London every year to do her Christmas shopping. This is the third year running she's suggested we have lunch together. I felt I couldn't say no.' Henry shifted in his seat and paused again. 'I thought I'd visit an art gallery in the morning.'

'Henry,' Colette said, 'you're blushing.'

'I'm sure I'm not.' Henry smoothed the crease in his trousers. 'The thing is, I'm supposed to report back to Maddie every week and it's extraordinarily difficult to think of things to tell her. So I thought I'd go to an art gallery and see if . . . '

'I think that's an excellent idea,' Colette said. 'My friend Marilyn met her second husband at the Tate. They got talking at a Francis Bacon exhibition.'

'Did they? That is very interesting. Are they happy?'

'I think so. I'm not sure he likes Marilyn's dog very much. To be fair, neither do I. He has acute halitosis and there's something wrong with his salivary glands which means he slobbers over everyone.'

'How very unpleasant. I'm not sure I could live with a slobbery dog. I suppose if one liked someone enough . . . ' He picked up his glass. 'I thought I'd go to the National Gallery. I'm meeting June in Leicester Square.'

'I'm sure you'll have a very interesting day. You must be sure to let me know if anything happens. I have a good feeling about it.'

★　★　★

147

Colette's feeling proved a poor guide. Henry wandered around a couple of rooms in the National Gallery, all full of over-excited school-children and camera-toting tourists. He went through to a third, attracted by a huge portrait of Charles the First on his horse. It was funny, he thought, how of all the various monarchs only five had faces that were instantly familiar: Henry VIII, Elizabeth I, Queen Victoria, Charles I and Charles II. This Charles had a sad, effeminate appearance with his long hair and thin, pointed beard. He didn't look very comfortable on his horse; it seemed far too big for him.

Someone else had joined him. A quick sideways glance indicated that she was female and attractive. Should he casually turn and voice his thoughts about the portrait? His heart beat a little faster and then, just as he was about to speak, a masculine voice said, 'He looks lost on that horse, don't you think? Of course, he was only five foot four.'

The speaker stood on the other side of the woman, his hands in the pockets of his jeans, his eyes fixed on the painting. Henry knew — he just knew — that the comment was directed at the woman.

'Really?' said the woman. 'But his son was Charles II and he was very tall. I wonder where he got his height from.'

'His grandmother, Mary, Queen of Scots, was almost six feet and in those days,' the man gave a smile that seemed to Henry to ooze smugness, 'that was tall!'

Perhaps the woman liked smug men. 'That's

so interesting,' she said. 'Are you a historian?'

'I'm a psychiatrist,' the man said, 'but I do love history.'

Very clever, Henry thought bitterly. Just throw in the 'I'm a psychiatrist' and watch her melt. Henry wouldn't be surprised if he *wasn't* a psychiatrist. He was probably a sad person who haunted galleries looking for attractive woman. He could see now that the two of them were quite a bit younger than he was. He left the couple — he already thought of them as a couple — and made his way to the gift shop. He bought a tea towel for Colette just to prove he'd been there, a scarf for his mother, some soft toys for his granddaughters and a very classy diary for Maddie with a Pre-Raphaelite cover that reminded him of William.

The fact that he had done the bulk of his Christmas shopping in thirty minutes restored his spirits and he walked briskly to the restaurant June had chosen, a large, busy place that was a pretty good imitation of a French brasserie, with lots of mirrors and plants, attractive young waiters and long tables with uncomfortable-looking benches. When Henry gave June's name he was relieved to be shown to one of the few secluded tables with high-backed settles. He asked for water and ordered a bottle of Sauvignon. June, he remembered, was very fond of dry white wine.

He had just approved its taste — feeling, as he always did in these circumstances, rather a fraud — when June arrived, looking just as he remembered her; hair short and brunette,

149

darting green eyes and a crimson and very mobile mouth. 'Oh Henry, you've got us wine already, how terribly efficient. I can't believe this is happening at last. It's so good to see you. You haven't changed at all!'

'Neither have you,' Henry said, rising from his seat and helping her with her coat. June did look good. She wore a black-and-white dress with pearls round her neck. Henry was glad he'd decided to wear a suit.

'It took a lot of courage to ask you here,' June said, sitting down and reaching for the wine before Henry could offer it to her. 'You've turned me down so often. I was beginning to think you'd crossed me off your list.'

'I'm sorry,' Henry said. 'I became rather a hermit after Marianne died. I neglected all my friends and probably my family as well. It was very self-indulgent behaviour, I'm afraid.'

'I'd probably be the same in your shoes.' June took a sip of her wine. 'Oh, that's good! I don't blame you at all. I can't imagine life without Ludo. But it's *lovely* to see you. Do you remember that camping holiday in France? We always knew when you and Marianne made love because your girls would wander into our tent and tell us you'd sent them over so you could do 'some thinking together'. Such a lame excuse, Henry!'

He chuckled. 'I'd forgotten that!'

'And then one afternoon you walked into *our* tent while Ludo and I were having a good time and you didn't seem to wonder why we didn't come out. You just kept reading us some article

150

on La Rochelle and it was only after we managed to grunt some comment from behind our curtain that you walked out and left us in peace. Happy days!'

'Maddie had a huge crush on your Matthew that holiday, and Sally and Nina were inseparable. How is Sally now? I haven't seen her since her wedding. Marianne kept going on about her husband's beauty.'

'Oh God, Henry, they divorced in the spring. I shall tell you *all*! Let's order first. I want three courses, I warn you, I shan't eat this evening and Ludo told me the meal's on him. He sends his love, by the way. Oh Henry, isn't this fun?'

It *was*. Henry heard about Sally's ex-husband, who'd apparently developed an addiction to gambling. He talked about Maddie and Nina, and June reminded him that they'd always hoped Matthew and Maddie would end up together and she wished they had because, 'Matthew's wife is humourless. I try to be a good mother-in-law but it's not easy. She has this habit of criticizing Matthew in a jokey sort of way that is actually as fun as a cobra about to spring. I have to be careful: I loathed my own mother-in-law. Marianne was very lucky with *your* mother.'

'They had their differences,' Henry said. 'Granty was always very naughty about Marianne's feminist views.'

'I remember our history lessons at school. Mr Edkins would make some patronizing statement about the Suffragettes and Marianne's hand would shoot up at once and she'd ask him if he

151

thought they'd been wrong to campaign for the vote; he would take off his glasses and say, 'You make me so tired, Marianne.' She picked up the empty bottle. 'Shall we have another glass each? It's nearly Christmas, after all!'

It was pleasant to sit and talk about Marianne. Henry had discovered in the last few years that most people disliked talking about his wife. It was almost as if she'd done something shameful by failing to stay alive. Even Nina and Maddie rarely talked about their mother. Perhaps it was his fault; perhaps they thought it would upset him. June showed no such reticence. 'I do miss her,' she confessed. 'She could be such fun and yet so ferocious! We were doing homework together once and her stepfather came in. He hardly noticed Marianne but he chatted away to me and after he left us, she gripped my arm and told me I was never to smile at him again. I made some silly comment about his beautiful eyes and she nearly leapt on me. That's when she told me about Colette.'

Henry put down his glass. 'What about Colette?'

'I'm sure you know. He tried to assault her or something — Marianne wouldn't go into detail. I don't know what she did about it but I understood then why he was so odd with her. He was scared of her. I can just imagine Marianne in full flight! She must have told you.'

'No,' Henry said, 'no, she didn't.'

'Well, it's a long time ago but I remember the past as if it were yesterday. Ludo says I have a memory like an elephant.'

152

'How *is* Ludo?' Henry asked.

'He's fine but the last few years have been testing for us. He's lost his sex drive, Henry, which is a pity because I haven't.'

'Oh dear,' Henry said, and then again, 'oh dear.'

'It's all right. We've reached an understanding. He knows I love him and I know he loves me and that's what matters. Now tell me, what are your plans for the rest of the afternoon?'

'Well,' Henry said, relieved at the change of subject. 'I thought I might go and find a present for Nina. She likes jewellery so . . . '

'Stop right there. I bought a necklace for Sally this morning but now I have my doubts. My hotel is only round the corner. If you like the necklace you can buy it off me. What do you say?'

★ ★ ★

On the journey home, Henry reflected that at some level he had known that the invitation was more than it seemed. They had gone to her hotel, she had locked the door and kissed him. 'You know I've always fancied you,' she said and she kissed him again and this time he put his arms round her. It had been surprisingly, deliciously easy. Afterwards, they lay side by side and June talked about Ludo.

'He's such a dear,' she said. 'He wants me to be happy. There's a man I see in Dawlish now and again. Poor Ludo can't do it anymore. He tried for a while but his heart wasn't in it and we both agreed it was better to adapt to the situation. What I'm saying, Henry, is that you don't need to feel guilty.'

In fact, Henry thought, staring out through the train window at the vague dark shapes of houses and trees, he felt guilty about *not* feeling guilty. To hold a woman close again, to feel her breasts and her thighs, all of it, everything, had been sublime. The entire afternoon had been marvellous.

There had been just one moment, one shadow. June had assumed — why should she not? — that Marianne had told him the true nature of her stepfather. It hurt that Marianne hadn't told him. Perhaps she felt it wasn't her secret to reveal. Henry thought of Colette sitting bravely on the merry-go-round while her face got greener and greener. He remembered the first time he met her, so shy she could hardly speak to him. Even then, the older sister had been protective of the younger. He was glad that their stepfather was dead. As a rule, Henry didn't believe in violence, but in this case he would have been prepared to make an exception.

13

Laura and Ted had bought their house in Walthamstow five years before and every time Maddie visited them she wished they hadn't. First, their three-bedroom, brick-fronted Victorian terrace had already trebled in value and was a constant reminder that they — like Gregory — had shown great foresight in buying a property before house prices soared to levels Maddie couldn't hope to afford.

Secondly, in order to get to Walthamstow, she had to make a long, laborious journey on a cold November evening via train *and* tube. Tonight, Maddie was making the long trek northwards due to a three-line whip from Laura. 'Once the baby arrives, we'll be too tired for anything. You *have* to come over.'

Gregory had been invited too but had a long-standing engagement. Four times a year he and three friends met for a games marathon. His friends were, respectively, a deputy headteacher, an IT consultant and a barrister. Their collective idea of heaven was to spend an entire weekend moving small plastic figures around a hand-painted battlefield made of papier mâché. Maddie had never met a woman who liked such things.

When she rang the bell, Laura opened the door and, sucking in her breath, put a hand to the small of her back.

'Laura?' Maddie put out an arm. 'Are you all right? You're not about to have the baby, are you? I warn you, my midwifery skills are non-existent. I also have a tendency to panic.'

'I've had these for weeks now,' Laura said. 'I had the same thing with Billy.'

'I've bought him a present,' Maddie said. 'You must give it to him after the baby's born.'

'I'd have kept him up for you,' Laura said, 'if you'd got here earlier.'

'For your information, it's taken me an hour and a half to get here. Not that I'm complaining.'

'Excuses, excuses,' Laura said. 'Come on through. We have Joe with us tonight. He's been erecting a pagoda in Epping Forest for some trade fair tomorrow. He's upstairs in the shower which means we have at least an hour on our own.'

There was, not surprisingly, a note of tension in Laura's voice and as she put a hand to her back once more, Maddie hoped she was right about the pains. In the kitchen, Ted was stirring something on the stove and stopped to give Maddie a hug. 'I seem to remember you agreed at Freddy's wedding to come up here more often,' he said. 'Almost three months later . . . '

'Don't you start,' Maddie said. Their kitchen reminded her of Nina's house. It wasn't just the high chair or the box of toys; there were finger paintings on the walls and pots of crayons and playdough on the shelves. Children, Maddie thought, created so much *stuff*.

She accepted a glass of wine from Ted and, as Laura eased herself onto a chair, intercepted a look between them. 'You two,' she said, 'is everything all right?'

Laura said carefully, 'Everything is fine but there's something we have to tell you and I can't relax until we do. Of course, you might already know.' She took a deep breath. 'Two months ago, Freddy and Victoria moved up here. They only live five minutes away.'

She stared expectantly at Maddie and Maddie, frowning, stared back at her.

'Is that *it*? I thought you were going to tell me something important. I'm honestly not bothered. It's not my business who your neighbours are. Why would I mind? Do you see them often?'

'We've seen quite a lot of Victoria,' Laura said. 'I mean, she's virtually our next-door neighbour. Freddy's on a regional tour of some Pinter play. That's partly why they're here. You see, Victoria's sister, Eve, lives on our road. You'd love her, Maddie. She's great fun and her youngest is the same age as Billy.'

'That's nice,' Maddie said.

'Yes.' Laura wrapped her hands round her glass of water. 'Victoria's parents own a flat here. They bought it when Eve started having babies. Anyway, when they realized Freddy would be away so much they suggested he and Victoria might like to live in it for a while.'

'That's nice for Freddy.'

'It's nice for both of them. Victoria's on her own so much and now she's near to her sister, and her parents come up for odd weekends. Victoria's been doing quite a bit of babysitting for us, actually. Billy loves her.'

157

'That's great,' Maddie said. She caught Laura's eye. 'I wish you'd stop looking at me like I'm about to have hysterics. Seriously, it's fine. You don't need to sound so defensive. I never expected you to break off relations with Freddy just because I did. That would be petty and bitter and I'm not like that. Or at least,' she corrected herself, 'I try not to be.'

'I know that. It's just that we didn't want you to think . . . We wanted you to know that our first loyalty will always be to you, that's all. There's something else. Do you remember that zombie-serial job Freddy nearly took in the States?'

'How could I forget?'

'Well, he's flying out there in a few weeks for exploratory talks, whatever that means. Apparently, the writers are toying with the idea of introducing the character he was originally going to play. If they *do*, he and Victoria could be living in the States next year.'

Both Ted and Laura stared at her, waiting for her to look hurt or pleased or something. Maddie hated the fact that she was conscious of having to appear disinterested and calm. The fact that Joe chose that moment to appear made her almost limp with gratitude.

'Maddie!' he said, 'Magnificent Maddie! You brighten up this drab and dreary kitchen!'

'Oh God.' Ted shook his head. 'I can smell the aftershave from here. I'm sorry, Maddie. He invited himself. There was nothing we could do.'

Maddie was glad he was here. She wouldn't have minded so much about her friends' cosy

158

new friendship with her ex-boyfriend's wife if it wasn't so obvious that they thought she *would* mind. It was a relief to sit quietly while Joe chatted on about pagodas and guy ropes and the possible purchase of the world's biggest yurt.

Halfway through the meal, Laura grimaced again and this time she didn't dismiss the pain. She stood up and pressed both her hands on the table. 'I think,' she gasped, 'this time it's different.'

Everything happened rather quickly after that. Laura went upstairs and Joe called a taxi while Ted and Maddie worked out a plan. Since Joe had to leave for Epping first thing in the morning, Maddie would stay with Billy until either Ted or his mother arrived to relieve her. When the taxi arrived, Laura came downstairs, clutching her stomach and trying to talk about nappies and Weetabix.

'Laura,' Maddie said, 'I've looked after my nieces. I'll find everything. Don't worry. Go!'

She and Joe watched in silence as Ted helped her to the waiting car. Maddie sighed with relief as the door closed. 'I hope they get there in time.'

'She'll be fine,' Joe said. 'I'd better ring Mum.'

He was on the phone for a long time, which was good for Maddie. While she washed up the dinner she could at last process the news of Freddy. It was extraordinary to think that the America job had come back to haunt her.

Only a year ago he had burst into their tiny flat with a bottle of champagne and demanded that she kiss him. Living with an actor was all ups and downs: the joy of a success that invariably led to heady plans for a glittering future; the down of a rejection that brought soul-searching and gloom along with clouds of financial insecurity. 'I didn't tell you about the audition,' Freddy said as he poured the champagne. 'To be honest, I never thought I had a chance. This is big, Maddie. This is *really* big.'

He'd got a part, he told her, in a brand new TV series in America. He talked about big names, big production values, big money and then he said, 'We'd move to California in January. Can you imagine? It'll be a whole new life.'

'But Freddy,' Maddie said, 'I can't leave England. What about Gregory? What about my business?'

Those two questions led to their first and last serious quarrel. She couldn't understand that it hadn't even occurred to him that her career mattered to her. He couldn't believe that she wouldn't want to join him in his dazzling new adventure. He dismissed her suggestion of a transatlantic relationship and she brushed aside his picture of her settling down to a possible new existence as an all-American mom. So the row continued and both of them said things they would later regret. At one point, Freddy stormed out, saying he'd stay the night with Andy, which might have been all right if Andy hadn't shared a flat with Esther who'd been trying to get into Freddy's trousers for years. Esther, being Esther, felt it incumbent on her to ring Maddie the next morning to let her know she'd finally succeeded.

So she left him. It took her a few weeks to decide she'd made a mistake and, by the time she'd heard of the premature demise of the American job, it was too late. Freddy had met Victoria.

Maddie finished the washing up and noticed the unopened bottle of red wine she'd brought. Ted had been about to open it when Laura had stood up with a face as white as chalk. It dawned on Maddie that she had to stop thinking about what might have been. There was something very wrong with a woman who obsessed about a long-defunct relationship minutes after one of her oldest friends had staggered off to hospital to give birth.

Joe came back to the kitchen. 'You wouldn't believe my mum,' he said. 'She wanted to drive up right away. I talked her out of that but she's leaving first thing in the morning.'

'That's fine,' Maddie said. She picked up the bottle opener. 'I think this calls for a drink, don't you?'

She wasn't sure exactly when she decided she'd go to bed with Joe. It might have been when he confessed he'd always fancied her, or perhaps it was when he told a story about his schooldays that made her laugh. At any rate, she didn't regret her decision. Sex with Joe was the equivalent of a fantastic, endorphin-raising workout. When eventually she fell back against the pillows, she went to sleep at once.

In the morning he kissed her when he left and she rolled over and went straight back to sleep. When she heard Billy crying it took a few moments to work out where she was. She jumped from the bed and raced through to his room. He stood in his cot, his face red and puckered with tears.

'Billy!' she cried. 'It's Maddie! Here I am!'

He raised his arms and when she lifted him out he flung them round her neck. Poor little Billy, she thought, he had no idea what was about to hit him. Her parents had enjoyed recounting the various methods she'd employed as a toddler to try to kill her new baby sister. Maddie was convinced that most of the stories were apocryphal but even so, she and Billy would soon both be paid-up members of the First Child Club.

Ted rang at nine, exhausted but happy. 'Viva was born at five,' he said. 'Mum's on her way to you. She'll be with you quite soon. If you hang on till midday, we'll be coming home with her.'

'I love the name,' Maddie said. 'Is Laura well enough to come home? Shouldn't she stay in hospital for a while?'

'The doctors say it's all right and she's fretting about Billy. Hospitals don't hang about these days. Is Billy all right? Has he had any breakfast? Is he upset we're not there?'

Billy was sitting on the floor, doing his best to dismantle a Duplo house that had taken Maddie at least ten minutes to assemble. He saw her looking at him and called out imperiously, 'Mad-die!'

Maddie smiled across at him. 'Did you hear that? I hate to tell you but he's not remotely bothered by your absence. He ate two Weetabix, a boiled egg and three soldiers. Get back to Laura and we'll see you both later.' She put down the phone, her brain adjusting to the fact that Ted's mother would soon be here. 'Billy,' she said, 'we have a lot of tidying up to do!'

Ted's mother arrived an hour and a half later and Maddie was abruptly jettisoned by Billy in favour of his granny. Maddie made a quiche and salad for the family's lunch and then — realizing that Granny would be sleeping in the spare room — raced upstairs to strip the bed and put on clean sheets. Fleetingly, she thought of Granny's younger son gripping her buttocks a few hours earlier. She was in the cellar starting up the washing machine when she heard the commotion of the baby's arrival upstairs.

Later she would recall the precise moment that Freddy ceased to matter to her. She had finally been given the chance to hold the baby. Viva stared up into Maddie's eyes, her bow-shaped mouth slightly open as if she wanted to speak, her tiny fingers curling round Maddie's thumb. Maddie looked at her, and smiled, and fell in love.

14

Henry had not been looking forward to the December meeting of the Higgleigh Book Group. Partly because Andrea had selected *Eat, Pray, Love* as her choice of the month. Henry had quite enjoyed the eating section but the rest of it had sent him — literally — to sleep. He had decided after last month's debacle to keep his opinions to himself and, since it was difficult to talk constructively about a book he had been unable to finish, this was probably just as well.

The main reason for his apprehension was Becky. He was worried she wouldn't be there because her absence would be *his* fault and he was worried she *would* be there because he'd have to say sorry.

He was walking along the pavement trying to construct a tactful apology when a voice said, 'Henry? It *is* Henry, isn't it? I always get names wrong! We met at the Queen Victoria talk.'

How could she imagine he wouldn't remember her? Tonight, Ellen was decked out in a warm coat, big earrings and heels. She was meeting someone, he thought, and felt a twinge of jealousy. He smiled, although after his last disastrous attempt in that area he was careful to make it a moderate sort of smile. 'Ellen,' he said, 'how nice to see you.'

'You must go to the library as soon as you can,' she said. 'Our historical expert is on the move. She's doing a talk in Dedham next month. It's on Prince Albert this time and she's produced another classic flyer. The library has got loads of them. We should go, don't you think?'

He was thrilled by that 'we'. 'We should,' he agreed.

'Hang on.' Ellen produced a card from her bag. 'There. You can get me by phone or by email. I'm happy to drive us there.' She glanced at her watch. 'I'd better go. See you soon!'

Henry dared not look after her. He walked on and, once he was out of range, stopped under a street light to peruse her card. 'ELLEN ANDERSON: curtains, upholstery, cushions.' On the bottom left-hand side were her contact details. Ellen Anderson was a lovely name: soft, almost lyrical. 'We should go, don't you think?' She had said it so easily. There'd been no need for her to suggest it; she must want his company. It was most likely that this was all she wanted but even so, it was a start. Ellen — Ellen Anderson — had stopped him in the street to ask him out. That was something. That really was something.

He walked on, crossed the road and went into the pub. At the bar, Becky was asking for a lime and soda. Henry cleared his throat and said to the barman. 'I'll pay for that. And I'll have . . . a gin and tonic please.' As Becky tried to protest, he quickly said, 'It's the least I can do. I felt terrible last month, blundering in with my silly comments . . . '

'You didn't. You mustn't think that. You said

165

nothing wrong, it was me. I just . . . And you really don't need to buy me a drink . . . '

'Please,' Henry said. 'It will make me feel better.'

'Well, in that case . . . ' she said, and laughed.

Despite her reassuring comments, Henry still felt it better to keep quiet this month. He did try to follow Andrea's impassioned espousal of her book choice but his mind kept buzzing between Ellen's invitation and Becky's genuine laugh. Neither he nor Becky had touched on the cause of her distress but he felt there was a glimmer of understanding between them and just possibly the beginning of a friendship.

Christine's voice cut through his thoughts. 'I'm sorry, Andrea,' she said, 'but I thought it was a load of sentimental rubbish.'

The clever professor lady — he couldn't remember her name — gave a magisterial nod. 'I'm afraid,' she said, 'I agree.'

Andrea turned to Henry. 'You've been very quiet,' she said. 'What do *you* think?'

'I think,' Henry said cautiously, 'I always slept well after reading a chapter or two.'

★ ★ ★

The meeting ended a little early that night. Andrea said she was tired. She also said — possibly as a reward for his tactful response — that Henry could select January's book. 'Is there anything you'd like to recommend for us?' she asked him.

It came to Henry, like a bolt from the blue,

that there was. '*One Hundred Years of Solitude*,' he said and felt himself exhaling as he did so.

That night, he went round to his wife's side of the bed and looked down at her bedside table. He had long since cleared everything else that had belonged to Marianne. The last morning of her life he had brought her a cup of tea and found her sitting up in bed, glasses on, book in hand. 'Henry,' she said, 'this is absolutely brilliant. It's about generations of family who are all so *unhappy*!'

He'd put the cup and saucer down by her bed and said, 'It sounds like a pretty miserable book to me.'

'But it isn't,' she'd persisted. 'It's extraordinary. It makes me . . . glad to be ordinary! I feel so lucky!'

He'd grunted some reply about being late for work and the horrible client he had to see, and as he'd gone down the stairs, she'd called out to him, 'I love you, Henry!'

And that was it. Those were the last words she said to him. He'd clattered downstairs, his head full of land-registry forms and difficult clients and for the rest of his life he'd regret that he hadn't called after her, 'I love you too.'

That night, when he'd finally gone to bed, he'd seen the book and felt such hatred for it that he'd wanted to pick it up and hurl it into the bin. It had made her feel lucky and a few hours later some stupid woman had driven into her stationary car and killed her. He had stared down at the book but he couldn't even touch it.

Now, four years later, her book still sat where

167

she'd left it. He took a deep breath and put out his hand. He picked the book up and felt almost breathless. Where the book had been was a pale rectangular shape. 'Henry,' he said aloud, 'you need to dust this room more often.'

He climbed into bed and put on his glasses. Then he opened Marianne's book, settled back against his pillows and began to read it.

★ ★ ★

In the good old pre-austerity years, Henry's firm used to hold its Christmas party in a country hotel, bringing the employees there by coach and treating them to a festive supper and open bar. These days it was held upstairs in the reception room of a Colchester pub. The lavish dinner had been replaced with plates of smoked salmon sandwiches but at least the bar was still free.

Henry was one of the few people who chose to drive rather than rely on taxis or public transport. This meant that every year he had the dubious privilege of watching those about him become increasingly unguarded and loquacious. He would usually wait till the dancing started before slipping away, grateful that he had another three hundred and sixty-five days before the next time.

Tonight he was rather enjoying himself. That morning he had received a Christmas card from June and Ludo. Beneath their signatures, June had scrawled a hasty message: 'Hello, Tiger! I might need to come to London in February!!' Henry's confidence had fizzed like bathcubes in hot water and hours later, continued to do so. This evening, he found it quite easy to chat to people he would normally take care to avoid and they, in turn, seemed quite happy to talk to him. Redmund Cockings, dynamic forty-one-year-old head of litigation kept his mobile in his pocket throughout their conversation and, even better, refrained from asking Henry about his retirement plans. Josie Miller, widely assumed to be having an affair with their CEO, told Henry he had a definite sparkle in his eyes.

'That's because I'm talking to you,' Henry said, hoping he'd remember to report this outrageous piece of flattery to Granty.

'Henry,' Josie murmured, 'you're a very naughty boy. I want a dance later.'

'I'll keep you to that,' Henry said. He caught the eye of Audrey Pennington across the room and went to say hello. Ever since the incident with the iron bar, she had made a point of chatting to him at work, asking about his daughters and telling him about her own.

'I have some news,' she said. 'Hannah's fiancé has had an argument with his mother.'

'I'm sorry to hear that,' Henry said.

'Yes, I know, it's very regrettable *but* . . . ' Audrey's eyes shone, 'as a result, he and Hannah have now decided they want to get married at St Mary's Church in Wivenhoe, which is lovely for Michael and me. It's our own church and we have a host of friends who'll do the flowers. They're having the reception at a pub in Alresford. Michael goes there every Friday so you can imagine how he feels!'

'That's wonderful,' Henry said. 'I know you weren't too happy about the wedding taking place in Berkshire.'

'It was a little disappointing,' Audrey conceded. 'There's something else I want to tell you. Hannah is very keen for you to come to the wedding. Of course you won't know anyone but you're welcome to bring one of your lady friends and you would be an honoured guest.'

Henry was touched and gratified that Audrey presumed he had an army of lady friends. 'I'd be delighted to come,' he said.

'I shall be sure to tell Hannah. She's so busy at the moment. I can't wait for Christmas. Alice and her boyfriend are coming; Hannah's arriving on Christmas Eve. She and Alice are so funny; we're not allowed to get rid of any of the old decorations and most of them are falling apart!' She smiled up at Henry. 'We'll be toasting *you* this year, you know.'

It was very pleasant to be regarded as a saviour. Henry continued to chat to Audrey until he was summoned to the dance floor by Josie. He found himself clapping away at 'Hi Ho Silver Lining', swinging his elbows around to 'Satisfaction', and dancing an uncomfortable waltz with Josie, who told him he was a natural, a comment that would have surprised Marianne; this was something else he would have to report to his mother.

He woke up the next morning with the distinct impression that there was something important to think about. It was not Josie's compliments — neither of which, seemed worth reporting to

170

anyone — and it was certainly not Don Bardgett's recipe for Christmas punch, which sounded both lethal and disgusting. He frowned, recalling the various conversations he'd had the night before. And then he remembered. It was Audrey. She'd been chatting about her children and the importance of the Christmas decorations. That was it.

For the last few Christmases, Henry had bought one of those artificial trees made from sparkly silver tinsel. Apart from displaying his Christmas cards, this was his sole attempt at decorating the house. Each year he was aware of the three big boxes in the attic and each year he felt unable to get them out.

Marianne had adored Christmas. She liked big trees with weeping pine needles that would only stand upright after hours of careful adjustment. That first terrible Christmas after her death, he had set up his new scratchy little silver tree in the sitting room and no one, not Colette nor his daughters nor even his mother, had made any comment about it.

This morning, after breakfast, he went up to the attic and switched on the light. He went across to the boxes and stared down at them just as he had gazed down at Marianne's paperback a fortnight ago. He opened the first box. In here were all the homemade ornaments: cut-out Christmas trees and cotton wool Santas brought back by the girls at the end of their school term; cinnamon sticks and dried orange pieces, all of which had long lost their scent, lovingly preserved in layers of tissue paper. There were

171

cardboard stars with lashings of golden glitter — Nina had always gone overboard where glitter was concerned — plaster of Paris angels and a knitted Father Christmas made by Maddie for some domestic-science competition. All this treasure, Henry thought, sitting here patiently in the dark.

★　★　★

Every Christmas Eve, he collected his mother from Southwold and every year he wondered at the amount of luggage she needed. This time there were two suitcases, five large carrier bags and a dog basket. Henry checked Ivan was settled in the back, said, 'All right then?' and turned on the ignition.

'I wonder if I should bring a blanket for Ivan?' Granty said. 'Your house is colder than mine.'

'I've put the heating up,' Henry said. 'We've already gone back twice to get his dog biscuits and his extension lead and *that* was quite unnecessary. I've a spare dog lead at home.'

'You don't have an *extension* lead. Ivan is a free spirit. He doesn't like to be restricted when he goes for walks.'

'I can't think why,' Henry said, easing out onto the road. 'He only goes at a snail's pace anyway, and he stops every five seconds so he can smell all the dog turds.'

'Don't listen to him, Ivan.' Granty beamed at her son. 'So is everything organised? When are the others coming?'

'Nina, Robbie and the children will be here

172

tomorrow in time for lunch. Maddie's driving up with Colette this evening. I'm going to make a chicken pie for supper. You and Ivan can keep warm in front of the fire.'

'I'm very happy to help with the cooking. I still have a few presents to wrap. Colette's only arrived yesterday though I ordered it weeks ago.'

'What have you bought her?'

'A box set of Doris Day films. Last time she came to stay, she took me to the cinema to see *Les Misérables* which was extremely long and very depressing. I thought it was time to show her what a real musical is like.'

'I wouldn't have given her Doris Day. If you wanted quality, you could have bought her *West Side Story*, or *Cabaret* or *All That Jazz*. I love *All That Jazz*.'

'Honestly, Henry, you're as bad as Colette. Why do you want to watch a musical about people dying or being horrible to each other? There's quite enough of that in real life. I don't want to come out of a cinema humming songs about dying.'

'Well,' Henry said, 'perhaps you're right.'

Granty took off her gloves and bent down to put them in her bag. She straightened her back and stared out of the window and then sighed. 'Elizabeth's brother died three weeks ago.'

'I'm sorry.' Henry reached for her hand and briefly squeezed it. 'You should have told me. I'd have taken you down to the funeral.'

'I couldn't go. It's taken me ages to shake off that flu. To be honest, I'm quite relieved I couldn't. I've never been very good at funerals. I wrote to Sarah. She sent me a very sweet letter back. She's a remarkable woman.'

They drove on for a while in silence and then as Henry joined the A12, he said, '*Singing in the Rain* — that's a great musical.'

'It *is*, Henry. And what about *Guys and Dolls*? Marlon Brando couldn't sing but he looked so beautiful it didn't matter.'

'I'd say the same about Grace Kelly in *High Society*.'

'I'm not sure she *did* sing in that film, I think she just wafted about. Now, Julie Andrews really *could* sing. How could I forget *The Sound of Music*?'

'I'd rather watch Grace Kelly waft about than listen to Julie Andrews sing about edelweiss.'

'I always thought,' Granty said, 'that Louise looked a little like Grace Kelly.'

Henry nodded. 'She did. That's probably why I liked her.'

'I heard from her last week.'

Henry turned to look at her. He noticed that she didn't return his gaze. 'Did you?' he asked warily.

'Yes. I'd written in my Christmas card that I'd love to see her again. I said that you and I were thinking of going to visit Edinburgh in the spring.'

'Granty! That's a lie!'

'It isn't. I *am* thinking of it and I'm far too old to go to a strange city on my own. I had a very enthusiastic letter back. She looks after her grandchild during school time — her daughter teaches, you know — but she could come down in the half-term, that's . . . ' Granty took out her pocket diary. 'That would be February the seventeenth to the twenty-first.'

'You've already put it in your diary! Was I ever going to be told about this?'

'I'm telling you now. You'll love it. We'll both love it.'

'You'd hate Edinburgh in February. It'll be freezing.'

'Nonsense. I have my lovely thick coat.'

'I haven't seen Louise since I was twenty . . . '

'Exactly. You have unfinished business.'

'No, I do not. I tried to ask her out when I was seventeen and that didn't work and I tried again when she was twenty and she wasn't interested. Do you really think that forty-two years later, she'll look into my eyes and say, 'You're the one,'? She was always very bright. She'll know what you're trying to do. It will be excruciating.'

Only if you let it be. She's my goddaughter and I haven't seen her in years. You're doing a favour to your frail old mother . . . '

'There is nothing even slightly frail about you,' Henry said, 'so don't give me that. How do you know I haven't arranged to go on an exotic holiday next February?'

'Have you?' Granty asked.

'No,' said Henry, 'but I'm seriously beginning to think about it.'

★ ★ ★

Henry had sat Granty down with a glass of sherry in front of the fire when the doorbell rang.

175

He went through to the hall and opened the door wide. 'Welcome!' he said. 'Happy Christmas!'

Maddie's head was swathed in a thick scarf. 'Colette's car is freezing,' she told him. 'Something's gone wrong with her heating.'

'Come on into the sitting room,' Henry said. 'You can thaw out in front of the fire. We'll take your cases up later.'

Maddie and Colette followed him in and Maddie gave an audible gasp. A large pine Christmas tree, its tip scraping the ceiling, stood twinkling in the corner of the room, bedecked extravagantly with most of Marianne's collection. More Christmas lights were threaded a little drunkenly round the cards on the mantelpiece. Sprigs of holly sprung from the pictures on the wall and tiny wooden angels hung from the chandelier. Henry looked anxiously at his daughter. 'What do you think?' he asked. 'Is it too much? I never had much to do with this side of . . . '

'Daddy,' Maddie cried, throwing her arms round him, 'it's beautiful!'

'Henry,' Colette said, 'it's magnificent!'

'That's what I told him,' Granty said, rising from her chair. 'It's been a very long winter but Henry's brought Christmas back to us at last!'

15

Maddie had never enjoyed introspection; in her experience it invariably inflated straightforward, simple decisions into complex and nebulous choices swayed by suspect impulses. In the last few months, Joe had spent four nights with her. On the fourth night he had asked her casually what her plans for New Year were. She was spending it with friends, she said, what was *he* doing?

'I'm not sure,' he shrugged. 'I was hoping I might spend it with you.'

'Yeah, right!' she'd laughed. But she was worried. Joe, the perfect partner for occasional sex, showed worrying signs of not understanding the nature of their arrangement. She began to wonder if she'd been right to sleep with him, and then she began to wonder exactly *why* she'd slept with him. Lust was the obvious answer. Had she also been affected by the conversation with Ted and Laura about their increasing closeness with Freddy and his wife? Had she, in some oblique and pointless way, wanted to prove that she didn't care at all about Laura's praise for Victoria and Victoria's amazing family by sleeping with Ted's younger brother? This is what happened with introspection, it produced preposterous and unpleasant conclusions that were never quite preposterous enough.

Meanwhile, she was trying to come to terms

with the amazing discovery that she was broody. At least, she was able to keep the unfamiliar urge under control. She hadn't yet reached the point — unlike Amy, it seemed — where she'd accept any man who could promise a nice sink. She certainly wasn't ready — as Jess appeared to be — to accept a sexless private life with a part-time, platonic partner.

But it *was* depressing. Her current plan to find the father of her yet-to-be-conceived child was proving as unsuccessful as her plan to enjoy guilt-free, occasional sex. In the last fortnight she had met three men for drinks. The first had checked his mobile repeatedly during her attempts at scintillating conversation. The second had blown his nose very loudly every few minutes. (Note to self, she had thought: never go on a first date while in the grip of a bad cold.) The third had gone on interminably about some engineering project with which he was closely involved.

The good news was that none of them had sent her photos of their penises. The bad news was that all of them had been extremely dull. To be fair, they had probably thought the same about her. It was not easy to be interesting on demand.

So it was a relief to come home and a total delight to find the Christmas decorations back in action. It was some time since Christmas Eve had been such fun. Granty, in particular, was on fine form, contributing to the family obsession with *Doctor Who* in her own inimitable way. 'I wouldn't say no to the present doctor,' she said.

'He might want to go back in time to my past youthful glory of course but then again he might — being so much older than me — like to spend a jolly evening with an octogenarian.'

'I'm not sure,' Colette said, 'that the doctor is terribly interested in sexual shenanigans.'

'That's a relief,' Granty said. 'I was thinking we might have a few games of Scrabble together. Incidentally, Henry, there's a Scrabble Club in Southwold now. You should start one up in Higgleigh: there's a legion of single women in the Southwold one.'

'That's why Henry doesn't need to worry,' Colette said. 'At our age, there are far more single women around than single men. Henry just needs to make it known that he's available.'

'You might be right,' Granty said. 'I remember when Elizabeth's cousin got divorced. He was a far less attractive prospect than Henry. He couldn't cook, he'd lost his hair and he made a whistling sound every time he talked — I think he had something wrong with his teeth. But Elizabeth gave a dinner party for him and he liked one of the guests and they married five months later.'

Henry frowned. 'Didn't he keel over with a massive heart attack six months after his wedding?'

'He did,' Granty conceded. 'But at least his final months were happy. Mind you, Elizabeth did wonder about his heart attack. His wife had already been widowed twice before. I must ask Elizabeth if she ever married again.'

'Well, don't ask on my behalf,' Henry said. 'I'd

179

rather not get involved with a woman who's had three husbands die in her care.'

'I'm sorry to hear that, Henry,' Granty said. 'If you're going to find a wife, it's important to keep an open mind.'

★　★　★

Nina, Robbie and the children arrived at eleven the next morning. The girls, dressed for some reason in their Halloween outfits, sped round the house like fireworks, barely able to comprehend their good fortune in having Granty, Coltie, Maddie *and* Granda all together at once. Megan explained to each in turn that she'd been a fairy in the school Christmas show and had thus been able to reprise her Halloween costume, a long-sleeved pink T-shirt and matching tights, a silver tutu and plastic wings. While Megan performed pirouettes round the kitchen, Chloe, possibly the most un-frightening witch ever, roared at anyone who talked to her, her bright eyes showing through the green tresses of her wig.

Maddie could see that her father was finding it difficult to prepare the Christmas lunch with all the commotion. She suggested a trip to the playground might be in order, an idea immediately endorsed by Nina and Robbie. Colette and Granty volunteered to assist the cook and waved the walkers off with more than a hint of relief. The rest of the party donned coats and scarves and took Ivan, who had to be pulled from the house by means of his extra-long extension lead.

There were few people out on the street which Maddie thought was just as well since Megan raced along the pavement on her scooter at a breakneck pace.

'I can hardly bear to watch her,' Maddie said. 'God help any pedestrians in her path.'

'She has it down to a fine art,' Nina said. 'See?'

Sure enough, Megan came to an abrupt stop as a couple walked towards her. She stepped off her scooter, waited till they passed and then went on her way again. Maddie wondered if she could ever be as relaxed with children as Robbie and Nina. There was Robbie, walking along with Chloe on his shoulders, her face almost obscured by her green wig and her arms jiggling around in the air, while Nina walked beside him, unconcerned by the diminishing figure of her older daughter in the distance.

Maddie had her work cut out in looking after Ivan. His extension lead seemed to have a life of its own, extending to its full length at the most inopportune moments.

The couple had reached them now and were clearly amused by Chloe's appearance. The man — seriously attractive — wore jeans, a dark jacket and a tartan scarf, his companion a red coat and black woolly hat. Ivan, despite Maddie's best efforts, jumped up at the man, making weird grunty sounds of welcome.

'I'm sorry,' Maddie told him. 'This lead is hopeless.'

'He's lovely.' The man bent down to stroke

181

Ivan's ears. 'What's he called?'

'Ivan,' Maddie said, 'as in Ivan the Terrible.'

He laughed. 'It's very nice to meet you, Ivan!' As he and his companion went on their way, Maddie couldn't resist turning round. The man had turned too and for a moment their eyes met. 'Merry Christmas!' he called back to her.

'He was nice,' Maddie said. 'I love men with strong chins.'

'He liked *you*.' Nina sounded rather put out.

'I liked *him*. Pity about the woman. She was much younger than him too. That's what happens now. Men who should be with mature and fascinating women like me choose to be with callow young things in their early twenties. I can't understand it.'

'You two are amazing,' Robbie said. 'How can you tell how old the woman is when half her face was covered with that hat? And how can you tell the man liked Maddie just because he stroked Ivan?'

'He was stroking Ivan but he was smiling at *me*,' Maddie said.

'The only reason he did that' Nina said, 'was because I have MUMMY written in invisible ink all over me.'

'Rubbish,' Robbie said, 'you look lovely.' He paused and then added hastily, 'You *both* look lovely.'

'I would just like to point out that *I*'ve had no time to put on make-up,' Nina said, 'and I'm wearing a very dull anorak and I have a rucksack on my back. Maddie's wearing a super-cool leather jacket and she has her face on.' She

182

glanced up at her younger daughter. 'Who am I, Chloe?'

'Mummy!' Chloe crowed, 'Funny Mummy!'

'There you go,' Nina said. 'Funny Mummy will probably be on my gravestone.'

They had caught up with Megan now, who was waiting impatiently to be allowed to cross over to the playground. Once there, Robbie made straight for the climbing frame. Megan abandoned the scooter, Chloe gave Nina her wig and both of them hurried off after their father.

'He's so good with the girls,' Maddie said. 'You're very lucky.'

'He's feeling guilty.' Nina stuffed the wig in the rucksack and joined her sister on the bench. 'He's hardly seen them lately. I've told him if he carries on working so hard, I'll up sticks and go off into the sunset with Francis.'

'Who's Francis?'

'You must remember Francis. He's my number one speed-dating conquest. He's asked me out three times since then.'

'Have you not told him you're a happily unmarried mother of two?'

'Certainly not. It's far too much fun getting his emails.'

'I almost feel sorry for him. Do you remember the man with the photos of his house? He and Amy are seeing each other now.'

'They're not! *Why?*'

'Amy wants babies.' Maddie watched Robbie help Chloe crawl along the horizontal bars of the climbing frame. 'So do I.'

Nina squeezed her sister's hand. 'Clive's

looking forward to seeing you tonight.'

'Is he? That's exciting.' Maddie had forgotten about the evening gathering of their old teenage friends. Crystal and Martin, childhood sweethearts, now married with two children, had bought their first house last year and celebrated with a party on Christmas Day. It had been such a success that they'd decided to throw one again. Last time, Maddie, fresh from her break-up with Freddy, had spent most of the evening with Faye and Bella, who were both newly separated from their husbands. The three of them had had a great time, competing with horror stories of their ex-partners. Maddie had had an appalling hangover the next day.

'Actually,' Nina said, 'Clive might be a little too fond of his beer but he's all right and I'm not saying that just because he's Robbie's best friend. He wants children too, you know. He's great with Megan and Chloe. And he does adore you.'

Maddie removed her hand from Nina's clasp. 'I know why you're doing this. You're just jealous because that man fancied *me*. It's very infantile behaviour.'

'I know,' Nina said. 'I *love* being infantile.'

★   ★   ★

The present-opening session was unusually protracted. Last Christmas it had been a far more sedate affair without Robbie, Nina and the children, who had spent the day with his family. Today, all the adults admired the playdough set

184

for Megan, the musical teddy for Chloe and all the other wondrous gifts pulled from Nina's copious carrier bags. Once the children, sated at last, sat quietly playing with Megan's set of *Little Mermaid* figures, the grown-ups could attend to their own parcels. Even then, there were distractions.

Robbie's present to Nina was a bright pink duffel coat, bought on the advice of her sister. The coat elicited a cry of joy from Nina, who insisted on doing a catwalk over the wrapping paper. A few minutes later, Robbie took another present from the bag. Small and thin, it was wrapped in green paper with Nina's name written on it in pen.

'It was put through the letterbox last night,' Robbie said. 'I put it in the bag with the other things and forgot all about it.'

'Oh really?' Nina smiled and took the present. She unwrapped the paper and took out a dark blue box from which she extracted a string of pearls. 'Robbie,' she said, 'it's beautiful. You shouldn't have . . . '

'I didn't,' Robbie said. 'There must be a note with it.'

Nina smoothed out the wrapping paper. 'There isn't.'

'Let me have a look at that,' Granty said. 'If there's one thing I know about, it's jewellery.'

'This morning,' Henry told her, 'you said if there was one thing you knew about, it was roast potatoes.'

Granty held the pearls up to her eyes. 'These are real,' she said. 'They're lovely, Nina.

185

Someone's been extremely generous.'

Nina gave a shrug. It was a rather elegant shrug but it was an uncharacteristic gesture. 'I expect they're from a client.' She sounded bored. 'People are always giving me things.'

'He must be a very rich client,' Granty said. 'I tell you something. They'd go beautifully with a wedding dress.'

'That must be a record,' Henry said. 'Robbie and Nina have been here for at least six hours without you mentioning the W word once.'

'I only do it,' Granty said, 'because I'm so fond of Robbie. I'd like him to be my legitimate grandson-in-law. You know that, don't you, Robbie?'

'I do and I'm very touched but . . . '

'He doesn't believe in marriage,' Nina said, 'and neither do I.'

'I don't know what's wrong with you and Maddie,' Granty grumbled. 'I loved being married. It's a very sound institution.'

'I believe in marriage,' Maddie said, 'I just have to find a bridegroom.'

Nina smiled sweetly at her. 'Clive believes in marriage,' she said.

★   ★   ★

Crystal and Martin lived on the new estate in Higgleigh. Their kitchen had shiny blue units and surfaces and a shiny blue fridge. The garden was small but the connecting roads on the estate were safe and perfect for two young boys with state-of-the-art bicycles. In fact, the boys

186

— Maddie was shocked to discover — had now become gangly teenagers and tonight were handing round canapes.

'They're a credit to you,' Maddie told Crystal, 'They are so polite.'

'I'm glad you think so,' Crystal said. 'We don't see any of that usually.'

'If I had children,' Maddie said, aware she was using this wistful preface far too often at the moment, 'I'd far rather they were polite to others than to me.'

'Why can't they be both? They only agreed to help tonight if we let their friends stay over . . . Hi, Bella! Hi, Pete!'

Bella, closely followed by the husband she'd described last Christmas as the lowest of the low, air-kissed her hostess. Pete, carrying a box of beers, said, 'Watcha, Crystal. Hi, Mads, where shall I put these?'

Crystal led Pete away towards the trestle table in the TV room, barking instructions at her sons as she did so.

Maddie turned her attentions to Bella. 'Nina told me,' she said, 'that you two were back together.'

Bella gave a sheepish smile. 'I held out for a while but Pete's mum suggested counselling and . . . Well, there are worse things than infidelity, I suppose. The alternative wasn't that great. Who'd want to be single at thirty-five?' She caught Maddie's eye and grinned. 'Oh God, I'm sorry!'

'That's quite all right,' Maddie said. 'I'm thirty-six now.'

187

'It's different for you,' Bella said. 'I have a three-year-old who missed his dad and . . . '

Crystal's son, Ace, appeared with a glass for Bella and a half-full bottle of white wine. 'Here you are, ladies,' he said, filling Bella's glass and re-filling Maddie's.

Faye appeared with another empty glass, which Ace filled with a smile. As he went on his way, the three women stared after him and Faye spoke for them all, 'He is so charming!'

'Last year,' Maddie said, 'we three promised to be sisters in singlehood. Tell me the worst, Faye. Are you back with Luke?'

Faye wasn't. She was now with Craig who had split up with Marnie who was now with Luke. There were advantages to remaining in the town in which one had grown up. Lovers could be recycled. As if to confirm this depressing observation, Clive now appeared and gave Maddie an enthusiastic hug. 'Maddie!' he exclaimed, 'when are you returning to Higgleigh?'

Faye and Bella gave Maddie a knowing smile and melted away, obviously assuming it was only a matter of time before their friend understood that she and Clive were meant to be together.

'So tell me, Mads,' he said. 'Do you have any one special at the moment?'

'I'm working on it,' Maddie said. 'How about you?'

Unfortunately, Clive assumed she really wanted to know and he was anxious to let her know that the two of them were free to be together.

'It's not very practical,' Maddie said. 'My job's in London.'

'You could commute. And when we have children . . . '

'We're going to have children? How many are we having?'

'Three would be great. But I'd manage with two . . . '

'That's considerate of you.'

'I'd like a boy though,' Clive said. 'I could take him to the footie with me.'

'You could take a *daughter* to the footie.'

'I could,' Clive agreed. 'We could all go together.'

Maddie laughed. She wished she *was* attracted to Clive. He was kind and funny and he'd make a great father. Come to think of it, he too had a Belfast sink in the house he'd bought two years ago. She moved on to greet another old schoolfriend who was holding a baby, miraculously sleeping amidst all the noise. Everyone here had babies or toddlers or children or teenagers. Most of the conversations ended up being about breastfeeding or potty-training or schools. Maddie lost count of the number of times she offered congratulations on advanced reading skills or precocious comments or first steps or a super-human ability to defecate in a potty rather than on the floor. And meanwhile, no one seemed interested in her career or possible achievements. 'I hired a car and drove round Madrid this summer on my own,' she told Faye, the one person who did seem interested. But as soon as the words were uttered, she could tell that Faye thought it was an admission

189

requiring pity rather than admiration.

At least in London, Maddie felt relatively normal. Here in Higgleigh, she was a rare, exotic fish, or rather a pathetic little pilchard left behind while her friends frolicked in the sea with their young. She was beginning to feel sorry for herself. It was probably time, she thought, to go easy on the alcohol.

Later, she wished she'd paid attention to her inner voice of caution. At some point she went upstairs to the bathroom and met her sister coming out. 'Nina,' she said, 'I'm glad I've got you on your own . . . '

'If you want my advice,' Nina said, clutching her glass in one hand and Maddie's arm in the other, 'you and Clive are made for each other. You're perfect. He's perfect. We're all family and friends and . . . '

'I'll think about it,' Maddie said. 'But Nina, just tell me . . . about this afternoon. Who gave you that necklace?'

Nina unhooked her hand and her eyes slid away downstairs towards the party. 'I told you . . . It was probably some client.'

'We both know that's not true. I watched you when Granty went off on her when-are-you-getting-married thing. You looked so relieved we'd stopped talking about the necklace. Are you seeing someone?'

Nina drained the rest of her wine. 'Look,' she said, 'it's under control and it's none of your business, but if you must know . . . ' She made a cutting movement with her hand, 'it's under control.'

'For God's sake,' Maddie hissed. 'Robbie's a star. You have to be mad. You'll lose him if you carry on like this, you'll lose him and you'll always regret it.'

Nina's eyes came back to focus on Maddie. 'Do you really think,' she asked softly, 'that you're in any position to tell me how to keep a guy?'

It was a rotten thing to throw at her. 'Just so you know,' Maddie said, 'at this precise moment, I don't like you very much. I don't like you at all.'

This wasn't the worst moment of the evening. That came later when a rather tipsy Clive tried to kiss her and she pushed him away. She knew immediately that she'd overreacted — perhaps it was the wine or perhaps it was the fact that she'd spent too much time pretending to admire all the many talents of her friends' brilliant children. Whatever the reason, she didn't mean to snarl, 'I don't want to kiss you, Clive. You're fat and you're dull and I've never ever fancied you.'

Clive didn't say a word. He just looked at her with wounded eyes and turned on his heel. A group of their friends stared at her and Pete said, 'I've got to tell you,' he said, 'Clive's a great bloke and you are one cruel bitch.'

16

Reading Marianne's book had not been easy. Henry had wanted to like it for her sake, and while he could appreciate her enthusiasm he couldn't understand it. There was all the magic for a start. What was one supposed to make of the beautiful young girl who floated up and away into the sky? And then there were the people who died and kept popping up again. None of it made any sense and all the characters had similar names so it was impossible to work out who was doing what to whom, especially when the *what* involved incest or murder or both.

Often, after a trip to the cinema with his wife, Henry would complain that one of the characters had behaved in a way that made no sense at all and Marianne would say, 'You always have to be so *sensible*, Henry. You just have to accept that sometimes, the rest of us do things that aren't sensible.' As far as *One Hundred Years of Solitude* was concerned, there was no sense anywhere. And even if he accepted all the magic and the dead people, it was difficult to like a story in which every single person had an unhappy ending.

When Henry finished it, he was hit by a black cloud of depression. Since Marianne's death, the book had acquired an almost totemic status for him and now he had read it and he hadn't liked it. He felt he had let Marianne down. Worse, he felt she had let *him* down. When Tessa rang in early January to remind him of the next meeting, he was half-inclined to make an excuse. He wasn't sure he wanted to talk about his book, he said, he didn't think he had anything interesting to say about it.

'I always think that,' Tessa said cheerfully. 'If it's any consolation, Frank used to say that people who found themselves interesting were always the biggest bores! Just tell us if you liked it.'

So Henry went and told the group he hadn't liked it at all. 'It's probably my fault,' he said. 'My wife loved it. But I found it difficult to follow and the ending was so sad . . . ' He really couldn't go on. He looked around for help and Tessa came to his aid.

'I found it quite absorbing,' she said. 'It was like reading *The Arabian Nights* and the characters were very interesting. My heart went out to poor Amaranta . . . '

'Poor Amaranta!' Andrea stared at Tessa in horror. 'She was a bitter and twisted woman who drove the man who loved her to suicide, *and* she went on to do disgusting things to her nephew!'

'That's true,' Tessa said, 'but she was such a sad woman. I suppose she was frightened of men and didn't understand . . . '

'Well, I'm sorry,' Andrea said. 'That's like forgiving Hitler because he was an unsuccessful artist or condoning Napoleon because he was so short. It doesn't matter *why* people do things, it's what they do that counts. My sister-in-law is rude to my children every time she sees them. I might know that it's because her own offspring are fat and ugly but it doesn't stop me blaming her for being unpleasant.'

'Well,' Tessa said, 'I can see that must be difficult but perhaps if you tried to talk to her . . . '

'I do! I have! You wouldn't believe the number of diets I've sent her over the years and . . . '

'I think,' the professor said, 'we are getting away from the book. I am glad you suggested it, Henry. It's a long time since I'd read it and I enjoyed it all over again. I'm not a great fan of magical realism but this is an outstanding example of it and I see now that it's rather prescient. We know far more these days about the importance of genes in our make-up and yet here was Marquez telling us nearly fifty years ago that families continue to make the same mistakes again and again. I don't think the final ending *was* sad. You do at last get a genuine love affair in the family.'

'But the baby is born with a pig's tail,' Henry exclaimed. 'And they all die!'

'Yes, but they had to die,' the professor said calmly. 'Everyone had to die. The village had become as corrupt as the family. I think it was a very satisfactory ending.'

As always when the professor spoke, there was a brief, respectful silence. And then Becky said, 'I suppose it depends what you mean by satisfactory.' She smiled and caught Henry's eye and for a moment again he could imagine her singing in her kitchen as she made the supper.

194

★ ★ ★

Afterwards, Henry walked back along the high street with Becky and she asked him, a little tentatively, about Marianne. He had no idea why he found it so easy to talk about his wife to a young woman he hardly knew. Perhaps it was because it was dark or because of her earlier conspiratorial smile. But he told her about that last morning and his hope that somehow the novel would make sense of everything that had happened.

'In fact,' he said, 'it does nothing of the sort. She was reading a book she loved. Now I've read it and I didn't like it. It's been rather an anti-climax.'

'I don't agree,' Becky said. 'If all this makes you sad, it's only because you disagree with her and you can't talk to her about it. At least you cared about her opinion. That proves to me that you had a good marriage. Think of all the couples who live together and never talk at all. There is nothing lonelier than being in an unhappy marriage.' She stopped and wrapped her scarf tightly round her neck. 'This is where I turn off. It's been very nice to have your company . . . '

'I wouldn't dream of letting you walk home alone,' Henry said. 'I'll see you to your door.'

'Really, there's no need. Higgleigh is hardly a hotbed of vice and depravity.'

'The walk will do me good. And I've been talking far too much about myself. You can tell me about your children while we walk.'

195

And so Becky told him about fourteen-year-old Ned who wanted to be a scientist and sixteen-year-old Toby who'd started seeing a girl who came round all the time and never raised her eyes from her phone. 'Toby and I used to be so close,' Becky sighed, 'and now he has eyes only for her and she never speaks! What does he see in her?'

Henry told her about Nina, who had gone out of her way to have unsuitable relationships throughout her teens and had ended up with the nicest man in the world, and Becky laughed and said that was very reassuring.

A car drew up beside them, with a squeal of brakes. Becky murmured, 'It's my husband,' as the driver leant across and opened the passenger door.

Becky's voice was quite different now: clipped, tense and hard. 'Hello, Alex,' she said. 'Henry was walking me home.'

'Good evening,' Henry said, lowering his head to smile at a man with shaggy dark hair and fierce eyebrows.

The man looked at his wife. 'Are you getting in?' he demanded

Becky climbed into the car and shut the door. She unwound her window, glanced up at Henry with an apologetic smile and then turned to her husband. 'Henry has joined the book group,' she told him.

The man stared at Henry. 'I didn't know it had started taking old-age pensioners,' he said. And then he drove away.

The outrageous rudeness of the man almost

winded Henry. For a few moments he stood frozen looking after the car. Then, slowly, he turned away. What was it Andrea had said earlier this evening? *It doesn't matter why people do things, it's what they do that counts.* There may have been a multitude of reasons for Becky's husband's behaviour but the effect of it was to make Henry feel that in walking Becky home, he'd laid himself open to ridicule. As far as her husband was concerned, he was an old man who'd sought out the company of an attractive woman young enough to be his daughter. And actually, Becky hadn't wanted him to walk her home. Now he came to think about it, the entire book group was probably humouring him. He wouldn't be surprised if all the pub regulars were laughing at him as he sat there surrounded by women. Shame coursed through his veins. He wouldn't go back next month. He didn't want to read the book for February anyway; it was some self-help book about learning to understand oneself and one's place in the world. Henry might not understand too much about his place in the world but right now he was pretty sure that it didn't reside anywhere near the Higgleigh Book Group.

★ ★ ★

At least there was the trip with Ellen to look forward to. Henry had picked up the latest flyer at the library. It bore a remarkable resemblance to the earlier one:

WAS QUEEN VICTORIA AN IMPOSSIBLE

WIFE? DID SHE DEMAND TOO MUCH OF ALBERT, DAY *AND* NIGHT? BERYL IS CONFIDENT HER TALK WILL PROVOKE A LIVELY DEBATE ON WHAT CONSTITUTES A GOOD MARRIAGE! 'IF YOU HAVE ANY DOUBT ABOUT YOUR OWN MARRIAGE,' BERYL SAYS, 'COME TO MY TALK. I PROMISE YOU WILL FEEL BETTER AFTERWARDS!'

Henry prepared carefully for the evening. He wore his best casual trousers, his black jacket, a check shirt and his charcoal-coloured jersey. After eating a light supper, he brushed and flossed his teeth and applied a few drops of the cologne Maddie had given him for Christmas.

Ellen had told him her house was the strawberry-coloured cottage opposite the antique shop. At seven o'clock he knocked on her door, feeling ridiculously excited, and smiled when she appeared. 'I have to tell you,' he said, 'that my daughter, Maddie, has always loved this house.'

'My son Adam does too,' Ellen said. 'It must be the thatched roof. Adam says it's like the witch's house in *Hansel and Gretel*.'

Her car was a lilac, soft-top Volkswagen. When he climbed in beside her, he noticed with pleasure that she too was wearing scent — an enchanting lemony one.

'I shouldn't be coming out tonight,' she told him. 'Adam and my granddaughter are coming tomorrow and I haven't even made the beds yet.'

'You look far too young to be a grandmother,' Henry said. Her short blonde hair gave her a boyish air and her loop earrings added a feminine touch to her grey trouser suit.

'I don't know about that,' she said. 'Izzy is off to university in the autumn.'

Henry studied her in amazement. 'I don't believe it,' he said.

'Oh Henry, I do like you,' she laughed. 'I had Adam at seventeen and *he* was a father at twenty-two. I couldn't believe it when he told me but, as he reminded me at the time, I was in no position to criticize. At least he got married, which is more than I did.'

'That must have been difficult. How did he cope? How did *you* cope?'

'When I had Adam, my mother was amazing. I wish I could say I was as good as she was when Izzy was born but I worked full-time and had a daughter just starting secondary school so it was difficult to be of much help. Adam's wife decided to give up her studies and she never let Adam forget her great sacrifice. She's one of those women who are never to blame for anything. It was Adam's fault she got pregnant, it was Adam's fault she decided to leave university and it was Adam's fault that she missed her carefree social life. Meanwhile, he was expected to do everything once he got home. Luckily she fell in love with someone else after five years and left him, for which I give daily thanks.'

'Did he marry again?'

'You must be joking. She put him off that for life. I despair of him sometimes. He adores Izzy but he's never wanted more children and Izzy is lovely. Fortunately she takes after her father rather than her mother. As you can see, I'm not entirely objective when it comes to my family.'

199

'And you have a daughter. Was that another teenage pregnancy?'

'Oh no, I was thirty by then. Her father and I lasted almost two years before he buggered off.' She glanced at Henry and laughed. 'We're all hopeless at choosing partners. We go for bad people, I'm afraid. Hannah spent most of her teens with a boy who introduced her to drugs, sex and extremely second-rate rock and roll. And now she's just left a hideous man who tried to micro-manage her life. I don't know why we can't do relationships. It must be the genes.'

'How very interesting,' Henry murmured. 'It's *One Hundred Years of Solitude* all over again.'

'I love that book. Why are we like that book?'

'Oh, you know,' Henry said vaguely, 'repeating the same mistakes . . . '

'How funny. I always thought it was about South America. Do you remember that terrible scene where three-thousand people were massacred?'

Henry gave an indistinct grunt because he was ashamed to realize he'd already forgotten it. But he could listen to Ellen talking about the brutalizing nature of war all night. Her voice could make even the most depressing subject sound enthralling.

When they arrived at the village hall, the room was fairly full although most of the front row was empty. Henry, following Ellen, noticed with dismay that she had made for the centre seats in the front. The light of battle was in her eyes as she whispered, 'This will be fun!'

There was a hush as a middle-aged lady in an

over-tight green dress walked towards the trestle table on the platform, followed by the redoubtable Beryl Antrobus and her male companion who noticed Henry and grinned.

'Do you know him?' Ellen asked.

'He's an old friend,' Henry murmured. 'He has a house here.' He wondered if William had ditched his married friend for the author.

The woman in the tight dress cleared her throat and spoke in a voice of barely suppressed excitement. 'Good evening, everyone. It's wonderful to see so many people here tonight, particularly since we have not one but two celebrities for you! Those of you who live in Dedham will know that we are lucky enough to count William Carter as a resident here, so I don't need to tell you that he is a brilliant academic and an ever-popular TV star. William is a friend of Beryl and so I have asked him to introduce her.' She turned to the ever-popular TV star and threw out her arms as if wanting to embrace him. 'Over to you, William!'

★ ★ ★

William stood up and pushed a hand through his curls. He wore his old brown tweed suit and a dull green shirt. He waited for the applause to die down and looked around at the audience. 'Beryl and I are old friends,' he said. 'She is a consummate expert on the life and times of Queen Victoria and her ability to understand the connections between past and present is second to none. I have often heard her speak and I can

201

assure you, you won't be disappointed. So without further ado I will step aside and let her weave her very particular magic.'

As William sat down he smiled — not at Henry this time, but at Ellen. He didn't just smile. He did *the* smile. Henry stared indignantly at him and then glanced at Ellen.

Ellen was smiling back at William.

Henry hardly heard Beryl's talk. He was aware of various phrases — *a voracious sexual appetite* and *an over-controlling nature* were two of them — but all the time he was conscious of Ellen sitting beside him, her scent wafting around him, her eyes fixed unwaveringly on William.

When questions were invited at the end, Ellen raised her hand straight away. Henry thought he saw a wariness on the face of the author.

'I wanted to ask Beryl,' Ellen said, 'if she doesn't think it's a little unfair to go on about Victoria's excessive love of sex? Surely Albert was quite happy to oblige his wife? Many people would think he was a very lucky man.'

There was no denying William's interest. When Ellen spoke he leant forward intently and when she finished he nodded approvingly at her. Henry couldn't bear to watch. Afterwards, William came straight over to them. In other circumstances, Henry would have enjoyed watching a master craftsman at work. In a matter of moments, William had found out her name; a few minutes later he received her card and, before he reluctantly returned to his dear friend Beryl, he had arranged to ring Ellen about some curtains he needed for his bedroom.

What made it worse was that William knew that Henry knew that he had never before expressed any interest in putting up any curtains in any of the rooms of his house, least of all his bedroom.

17

When Maddie returned from her less than joyful New Year's Eve celebration, she found a note under the door from Guy: 'Baby Phoenix safely arrived!' Was Phoenix a boy or a girl? Jess had always assumed the baby was a girl. Maddie made a mental note to buy a card for the happy family, though she couldn't face seeing them just yet. She wanted to wait until her black mood had passed.

There had been many times over the years when Maddie had felt she'd outgrown Higgleigh. Now that Higgleigh had outgrown *her*, she felt like a boat that had lost its mooring. More than once she had picked up her phone in order to apologize to Clive but each time she decided it would only make things worse. In time she hoped he'd understand her cruel outburst had been fuelled by drink. Which it had been, give or take a few dollops of general jealousy, bitterness and self-loathing.

At least she didn't feel guilty about Nina. Every day Nina failed to ring proved that she was as stubborn as ever. If Nina wanted to mess up her life, Maddie thought, she was free to do so. Meanwhile, the framed photo of her two little nieces was a daily reminder that at some point she would need to contact them. But not now, not while she felt so low.

Joe came round for supper and told her he'd

missed her, which was nice. He'd had a great New Year's Eve at home in Hampshire with his old schoolmates. They'd ended up playing forfeits and Joe had had to eat a raw chilli. 'What about you?' Joe asked. 'Did you have a good time?'

'I didn't eat any chillies,' Maddie said, 'but otherwise it was fine.'

This was a lie. New Year's Eve had been appalling. After the Higgleigh horrors, Maddie had looked forward to a laid-back break in the country. Sinead and Paul were old university friends who lived in a small village in Somerset. Four years ago, pre-children, they had hosted a brilliant end-of-year party. Maddie and her then boyfriend, Laura and Ted, plus Gregory, and Luke, a lanky mathematician who had shared a house with Maddie in their final year, had all gone along. This time, Laura and Ted were busy with Billy and little Viva, Gregory was partying with Minty and so it was just Maddie and Luke.

As soon as Maddie arrived it was obvious something was wrong. Paul was relentlessly cheerful, Luke was gloom personified and Sinead was upstairs putting the children to bed. She had bought a chicken for supper and had left her husband to deal with it. This in itself was ominous since everyone knew Paul could barely boil an egg. Paul gazed hopefully at Maddie and asked her if he should throw it in the oven. Maddie took charge; she told Paul to peel potatoes and suggested Luke might like to open one of the bottles they'd bought.

Two drinks later, Paul revealed that his parents

had been to stay for Christmas, and the children — like all children, Paul was quick to say — had been a little over-excited by the festivities. His mother had pointed out that her own children had never been any trouble, possibly because she'd elected to be a full-time mother. Sinead had said jokingly — and if ever there was a loaded adverb, Maddie thought, it was that one — that she seemed to recall Paul telling her about the occasion he and his brother had opened everybody's presents before their parents had woken up. From there, the argument had escalated to the point where Sinead had told his mother that her full-time mothering had produced a son who had no idea how to cook or clean or do anything of any use in the house at all. Christmas, Paul said, had been like a battlefield in which he was left to fend for himself in no-man's land.

When Sinead came down she barely greeted her guests, but noted that Paul — surprise, surprise, — was sitting down with a drink while poor Maddie was doing all the cooking and, by the way, would it be too much to ask him to go upstairs and read a bedtime story to his older daughter who had been waiting for him for at least forty minutes?

So then Paul disappeared and Sinead gave her own account of a Christmas in which her husband had failed to support her in the face of a full-on attack from her mother-in-law. Finally she said, with a laugh that was brittle enough to slice an ice cube, 'Enough about our woes!' and made the mistake of asking Luke how he was.

Luke, who'd been washing the spinach throughout Sinead's diatribe, revealed that his girlfriend had chosen to terminate their relationship on Christmas Eve for reasons that made no sense to him at all. He was so upset by this injustice that he had to stop washing the spinach, which was probably just as well since he had directed microscopic attention to each and every leaf he'd looked at.

A few minutes after midnight, Paul was asleep on the sofa, Sinead was weeping and Luke, who had put on the television to check the time for the countdown, was convinced that the fact that they'd missed it was a sign that the new year would be a bad one for all of them. Maddie was inclined to agree with him.

Remembering this now, Maddie said it had been nice to see old friends. 'I must say,' she conceded, 'it was better last time around when Laura and Ted were there. Did you see them at Christmas? How's the baby?'

'Beautiful,' Joe said. 'Sleeps like a baby, if you know what I mean.' He opened the wine he'd bought and poured a generous amount into their glasses. 'I told Ted about us.'

Maddie had been about to put the macaroni cheese she had made into the oven, but now she slammed it down onto the stove. 'I wish you hadn't. Why did you do that? There isn't an 'us' to tell!'

'Am I missing something?' Joe asked. 'I thought we'd been spending quite a bit of time together lately.'

'I've cooked a few meals and we've had sex a

few times. That doesn't constitute a relationship.' She took a gulp of Joe's wine. It was rough. Joe's wine was always rough.

'I'm sorry to be obtuse,' he said, 'but could you tell me what *does* constitute a relationship?'

Maddie pushed past him to get to the fridge. 'I'm simply trying to say . . . Oh, it doesn't matter. Do you want salad or green peas with the macaroni?'

'Either. Both. I don't care. I wish you'd answer my question. What am I doing here? Is it just sex you want? Is that all?'

Maddie pulled the lettuce from the fridge and closed the door. 'Be honest, Joe. If I'd told you that first night at Laura's that I wanted a serious relationship, you'd have run a mile.'

'I might have done then but it's completely different now.'

'You do see that it's only because I've made it quite clear that I don't want anything serious that you now decide that you do? Listen.' She paused, conscious that she needed to choose her words with care. 'I like spending time with you. I like having sex with you. If you met someone tomorrow I'd say goodbye with no hard feelings. That's a pretty good deal, don't you think?'

She smiled up at him and he waited for at least three seconds before sweeping her into his arms. One of the great delights of Joe was the ease with which she could arouse him. For a thirty-six-year-old woman who had already discovered that anti-wrinkle creams don't work, it was a welcome morale boost.

★ ★ ★

The next evening, she had a date. She had never felt less like being scintillating but at least this man sounded promising. His photo on the website showed an aquiline nose, red hair swept back from his face and pale blue eyes that stared straight at the camera. Walter was an accountant who liked theatre, cinema and historical biographies. There were two firm marks in his favour: he apologized for his career choice and he did *not* say he had a sense of humour. There was one further good sign: he'd suggested a wine bar which did excellent nibbles, which indicated that he, like Maddie, had no wish to chew his way through a meal with a stranger who might prove to be a disappointment.

As usual, she was late and recognised him at once. He wore a smart grey suit and she imagined that his red hair was longer than that of most accountants. She was impressed by the fact that he'd already taken possession of a bottle, two glasses, a bowl of hummus and two mugs full of crispy chips.

'Good evening,' he said, rising from his chair and extending his hand. 'Let me say right away that if you don't like the Chardonnay or the chips and the hummus, feel free to go and order what you want. I've come straight from work and I'm starving.'

'So am I,' she said. 'I'm sorry I'm late but I live in Crystal Palace and it's quite a trek . . . '

'If you will live out in the sticks . . . '

'Actually,' Maddie said stiffly, 'Crystal Palace

209

is a pretty interesting place.' Her affection for the town had crept up on her in the last few months and it surprised her to discover how proprietorial she felt towards it.

'I was joking,' he said. 'I'm sure it's lovely. I can see you've marked me down as a superior bastard . . . '

'*You* must think I'm completely humourless. I'm sorry.' Maddie gave an awkward shrug. 'It's been a long day.'

'Let's start again,' he said. 'Can I pour you some wine?'

'Please.' She glanced around the bar. She liked it. It was busy, humming with different conversations. Nearby, a group of Italians were having a spirited discussion involving huge gesticulations. At the bar, a trio of young men were trying to impress two extremely pretty girls who sat in confident silence, aware they needed do nothing but radiate loveliness. Maddie began to relax. Judging by the tricky introductions, this date wouldn't last long and in the meantime she intended to enjoy the wine and the chips.

She picked up her glass and had a sip. The wine was good, cold and very dry. She said, 'This is the first time I've been out with an accountant.'

'I can see from your tone,' Walter said sadly, 'that it will very likely be your last. I never intended to be an accountant. I wanted to be a rock star and when that seemed unlikely, I thought I'd become a glamorous entrepreneur — another Richard Branson, only more success-ful.'

'What went wrong?'

'I don't know. My father craftily suggested I got a serious qualification first and then I was offered a job with a nice salary and suddenly, hey presto, I end up being a snooty London-bastard accountant.'

Maddie smiled. 'I don't think you're a snooty London-bastard accountant.'

He beamed at her. 'That's a relief. What did *you* want to grow up to be?'

Maddie sat back and unbuttoned her jacket. 'I intended to be a pioneering headmistress. Instead, after university, I went into marketing and when that went belly-up, I retrained as a History teacher and discovered there was nothing more terrifying than entering a classroom full of thirty-four teenagers bursting with hormones. I continued to be terrified on a daily basis.'

'I had a friend who was a teacher. He had a breakdown and fled to South America. He's probably a drug baron now. Have you stuck it out?'

'I nearly did. I stopped being terrified, but to be a good teacher you need shed-loads of patience and I never had that. Eventually, I was rescued by my friend Gregory, who suggested we go into business together. So we did and I've never regretted it.'

'What sort of business is it?'

'We run after-school clubs. It's very hard work and often quite scary but at least it's never boring.'

'It can't leave much time for a social life. Is

211

that why you're reduced to having tricky conversations with boring accountants?'

'I don't think you're boring,' she said, 'and I could ask you the same question.'

The sides of his mouth twitched. 'But I asked you first.'

She helped herself to a chip. 'I suppose it's the usual thing. I've wasted too much time on the wrong men and messed up relationships with the right ones.'

'But the wrong ones are so much fun,' he said. 'It's funny how things work out. In your twenties you have all the time in the world and before you know it you're approaching forty and planning your pension.'

'I thought you *were* forty.'

'Thank you for reminding me.'

'It's a pleasure.' She hesitated. 'It's quite rare for a man to be single at forty.'

He stared at her and then smiled and shook his head.

'What is it?' she asked. 'Did I say something wrong? It was just an observation.'

'Did you know that you have a very expressive face? Let me reassure you. I am not an overgrown adolescent or a man with weird psycho-sexual issues. Cross my heart and hope to die.'

'I didn't think that you were . . . '

'You are such a bad liar. For most of my thirties I was in a serious relationship. It didn't work out which is why I'm here tonight enduring the third degree . . . '

'Listen,' Maddie said, 'I'm not trying to offend

212

you. I was just making conversation.'

'I find your conversation very unsettling. It's probably because I like you. That doesn't happen very often. It makes me defensive.'

'You don't have to be.' She looked directly at him. 'I like you too.'

'Thank you.' He reached for the bottle and re-filled their glasses. 'Do you have any more uncomfortable questions for me?'

'None at all. I think we should try to talk about something safe and uncontentious. Let's talk about films. What is your favourite film at the moment?'

So they talked about films and TV. Walter confessed he was disappointed by the second *Homeland* series and Maddie said she'd loved it. Again and again, she felt his eyes on her face.

When they finished the bottle, he asked if she'd like another and she shook her head. 'Any more and I'll get the wrong train home.'

'You needn't get a train,' he said. 'My flat's only twenty minutes away.'

She smiled. 'It's tempting. It's also premature.'

'Why? It's why we're here, after all.'

He'd taken her hand. She said, 'Is it just sex you want? Is that all?'

'Isn't that enough?'

It came to her that she'd echoed word for word Joe's questions to her. It made her uncomfortable. She removed her hand from his. 'I'm afraid,' she said, 'it isn't.' She picked up her bag and stood up. 'I must go. It's been a lovely evening and I've enjoyed meeting you. Goodbye, Walter.'

It was raining outside. Maddie pulled up the collar of her jacket and walked briskly towards the station.

'Well, Maddie Drummond,' she told herself, 'you so deserved that.'

★ ★ ★

Three evenings later, she was walking up the stairs towards her flat, with the music of Paolo Conte coming from Guy's as an accompaniment. Her phone buzzed and she pulled it out. The message read, 'Rebuff fully justified. Can we start again please?'

Maddie smiled and put her phone back in her bag. She continued up the stairs and then paused and went back down to Guy's flat.

He looked surprised to see her. 'Hello, stranger,' he said. 'What can I do for you?'

'I was thinking,' she said. 'When am I going to see baby Phoenix?'

18

Henry knew that William would ring him sooner or later and he wanted to be ready for it. There was no point in giving vent to the furious bile clogging his arteries. He could imagine William calling Ellen: 'I've just had a rather disturbing call from my old mate, Henry. He says the two of you are in a relationship and so of course I must step back . . . ' No, Henry decided, the only way to cope with William's predatory intentions was with guile and subtlety. He'd never shown much aptitude for either of these but there was always a first time.

For a start, he could mention Ellen's children and refer to the many problems they had. He would not be lying, after all. Hadn't Ellen told him that they both suffered from unsuccessful love lives? He could simply refrain from telling William that they were in fact adults who no longer lived at home. He could advise William to steer clear of a fragile woman whose heart had been frequently broken. Again, this was true. Hadn't she told William she always fell for bad men? Which explained, he thought gloomily, why she'd been attracted to William.

It was difficult not to be disheartened. The shaming meeting with Becky's husband and the cataclysmic encounter between William and Ellen underlined the fact that Henry's search for a partner was still deeply unsuccessful. It was difficult to give Maddie even slightly positive reports. At least she *had* things to report. She had a date this very week. Perhaps he should join a dating agency too. He would ask June on Thursday what she thought about that.

June was the one bright spot on the horizon. It was a pity he felt unable to tell Maddie about her. She was meeting a girlfriend for lunch on Thursday and had booked the same room as last time. She'd suggested a small Italian restaurant for dinner and Henry was already counting the hours.

★ ★ ★

He sat in the quiet carriage on the way to London with a biography of Sir Laurence Olivier given to him by Colette at Christmas. 'He married his third wife at fifty-three,' she'd told him, 'when he wasn't much younger than you.' Henry was enjoying the book, although it did seem to him that a man with the looks and fame of Sir Laurence would find it much easier than Henry to persuade attractive women to many him at any age.

His concentration was broken by an annoying sequence of staccato sounds and realized with horror they emanated from the pocket of his jacket. Too late, he remembered Robbie had changed his ringtone after he'd complained about the ineffectiveness of his old one. The lady opposite him, a terrifying woman with glasses attached to a red string round her neck, stared at

216

him furiously. He pulled out his mobile and saw William's name. It was typical of William to ring at the most awkward time possible.

'William,' he hissed, 'I'm on the train. I'm in the quiet carriage.'

William's voice sounded unconcerned. 'Get out of it then,' he said. 'I need to talk to you.'

'Hang on a moment,' Henry said.

The woman with the glasses spoke. 'This is the *quiet carriage.*'

'I know that,' Henry said, 'which is why I'm trying to get out.' His overnight bag was by his feet and he wondered if he should take it with him but decided that any possible thief would take one look at the woman and go on his way. He apologized to the man on his right who stopped reading his paper and sighed over-dramatically as he let Henry out.

Muttering under his breath, Henry made his way through to the gap between the carriages. There were three young men already there, drinking beer and laughing immoderately at nothing very much.

Henry found a place by the door and said tetchily, 'William, I can't talk for long, it's very uncomfortable here and . . . '

'Never mind that,' William said. 'I want to thank you for introducing me to Ellen.'

'As far as I remember,' Henry said, 'I did nothing of the sort. You barged in and introduced yourself.'

'She's making me some beautiful curtains,' William said.

'I thought you didn't like curtains.'

'It depends who's making them. I'm completely smitten, you know, and she's amazingly perceptive. She's invited me to supper this evening.'

'Has she?' Henry felt a shaft of jealousy. He had an image of Ellen opening the door of her strawberry-coloured cottage and beckoning William in from the pavement. 'How do you know she's perceptive?'

'We talked about her children,' — damn, thought Henry — 'and I told her about my own disastrous love life . . . '

'It hasn't been disastrous; it's been spectacularly successful!'

'She thinks we're two of a kind. She reckons we are drawn to people we know will abandon us.'

'William,' Henry cried, raising his voice above those of the beer drinkers, 'it's not that way at all. You're the most prolific abandoner I know.' He sidestepped a stream of beer cascading from the upturned can of one of the young men. 'I can't speak now. I can hardly hear you.'

'What are you doing on the train anyhow?'

'I have an exciting assignation.'

'Good old Henry. That'll be the day. I must try and get you together with Charity. She's single too . . . '

Henry switched off the phone. He remembered Charity. She and William had been an item for over a year. She had once caused Marianne to choke on her Brussels sprouts after describing William as the most honest man she knew.

Henry was going straight to the restaurant to save time. June disliked eating late. 'It's my only concession to age,' she'd told Henry. 'I can't cope with bed on a full stomach these days.'

June was ferociously well-organized. She'd emailed the menu to him the day before, so that she could make their order if he was held up. In fact, he was only a few minutes late but she'd already instructed the waiters and there was wine on the table.

'Dear Henry,' she said, pouring him a glass. 'Do you remember the last time we met?'

'It's engraved on my memory,' he told her.

'I was so nervous. I had determined to seduce you and I plied us both with wine. And this time, I can just relax and enjoy your company and know that . . . ' She stopped to give him a sideways look. 'Are you all right for tonight? Do you still want me?'

She had quite a carrying voice and he was glad she'd chosen a place with discreet nooks and crannies. He leant forward and murmured that he very definitely did.

Over dinner he told June about William and Ellen and was greatly cheered by the fact that she had failed to watch even one of William's many appearances on television.

'I think it sounds quite promising,' she said. 'All you have to do is to wait for William to leave her. Then you can step in and be the rock on whose shoulder she can weep copious tears before falling into bed with you.'

'I can't see that happening,' Henry said.

'You underestimate yourself,' June told him. 'You always did. How's Maddie's love life going?'

'She had a date this week. She hasn't rung so I presume it wasn't fantastic. She's such a lovely girl, what's wrong with all these men?'

'The trouble with that generation is that they know too much. When I was a girl, we fell in love and married, we had children straight away and learnt to adapt. The young today expect too much. They have a good time, they meet someone to love, have a few arguments and walk out of the door. And then in their thirties they decide they want a family and suddenly they come up against a big brick wall with the word COMPROMISE emblazoned across it. And of course they have no experience of it. I tell you something, Henry. I wouldn't be young again now.'

'Neither would I,' Henry said, 'as long as I have friends like you to talk to.'

'I hope I can offer more than talk.' June finished the last of her lemon tart. 'Would you like some coffee or . . . ?'

Henry raised a hand for the waiter and pulled out his wallet.

It was while they were putting on their coats that Henry spotted Colette in one of the booths. He took June over and said, 'Isn't this extraordinary?'

Colette raised startled eyes to his face. 'Henry!'

'You remember Marianne's friend, June?'

Henry said, beaming at his sister-in-law.

'Of course I do!' Colette's smile seemed to be a little stiff. 'How are you, June?'

June laughed. 'It's been a very long time!' She glanced expectantly at Colette's companion.

Colette noted June's interest. 'This is my friend, Roberta,' she said.

'Hello there.' Roberta's voice was low and husky. She was a big, broad-shouldered woman with enormous auburn hair and very long eyelashes. She had a disconcerting stare — possibly, Henry realized, because it was directed straight at *him*.

'I'd love to talk,' June said, 'but I must get back to my hotel. It's been lovely to see you, Colette.'

It seemed terrible to leave so abruptly. On the other hand, conversation was certainly proving difficult. Henry said, 'I'm enjoying the book on Olivier, Colette. It's very good.'

She smiled faintly. 'Thank you.'

Out on the pavement, Henry relaxed. 'What a very odd woman! Did you see that hair?'

'It was a wig,' June said, 'and that was no woman. She was a transvestite.'

'A transvestite! What do you mean?'

'Transvestites are men who like to dress up as women.'

'I know that but . . . What is Colette doing with a transvestite?'

'Perhaps she likes transvestites. I seem to remember she was always rather timid with boys.'

'She's had two husbands,' Henry protested.

221

'And then of course there's Hugh . . . ' He was thinking aloud, almost unaware of June. He was shocked. He had never seen such an incongruous sight. The contrast between small, slight Colette and that big, hulking woman who apparently wasn't a woman was bizarre, not to say unnatural. It made him feel quite uncomfortable. How had Colette met such a person? He felt June pull his arm.

'Henry,' she said. 'Tell me about Hugh.'

He shouldn't have mentioned him. As they crossed the road, he said earnestly, 'If I tell you, you must promise to tell no one.' He shook his head. 'It doesn't matter. It's not important.'

'Now you *have* to tell me. And who would I tell? Come on, Henry, who is Hugh?'

Henry sighed. 'Have you heard of Hugh Grant?'

'Have I . . . ? Are we talking about the drop-dead, most gorgeous actor on earth Hugh Grant? Henry, Henry, talk to me! Is Colette having an affair with *Hugh Grant?*'

'Yes. No. I mean, not exactly. She's never actually met him but . . . It started long ago.'

'What did? You're not making any sense.'

'She used to drop him into the conversation and at first we'd just sort of smile, you know? And she didn't do it very often but when she came to stay we'd hear her talking to him in her room and it got to the point where it was difficult to say anything. I mean, Marianne went to stay with her and saw all the photos in her room and tried to . . . but she decided he made her happy and so . . . ' He was aware of June

222

staring at him and raised a helpless hand. 'I just went along with Marianne. I don't know much about imaginary lovers, to be perfectly honest. What I don't understand is — not that I understand any of it but still — why is she there with that . . . that person?'

'Did you see they were holding hands before we joined them?'

'No,' Henry said. 'I'm rather glad I missed that.'

'Well,' June said, 'whatever makes you happy . . .'

'She didn't look very happy.'

'She wasn't happy to see *us*. She couldn't wait to see the back of us. That's why I thought we should make a speedy exit. I think we interrupted a delightful tête-à-tête and I suspect she was profoundly embarrassed that we saw her with 'Roberta'.'

'Is Colette a *lesbian*?'

'If she is,' June said, 'she's a very complicated one.'

'Oh dear,' Henry said again. 'What on earth do I say next time I see her?'

'You just proceed as normal. Don't look so worried, Henry. Life's full of surprises.' She squeezed his hand. 'I'm rather hoping you'll give me a few surprises in a moment.'

⋆ ⋆ ⋆

The next morning on the train, Henry made sure his phone was switched off. He took his seat by the window and pulled out Laurence Olivier.

He should be feeling happy. He had enjoyed an extremely active night with June, with the promise of more delights to come in a month or two. But he was worried about Colette. She had always been kind to him. In that first black month after Marianne's death, she had driven up with a hamper of food and it must have been difficult chatting to a man who could barely string two words together. It upset him to think she might be worried by his reaction to the company she kept. He wished he could reassure her that he quite understood, even though he didn't. Worse still, he felt ashamed of telling June about Hugh. He picked up his book and tried to concentrate but it was impossible. He had let Colette down. Marianne would have been furious with him and she would have been right to be.

19

'Do you like the name?' Jess asked. 'Mum hates it.'

'I adore it. Just assure me he's not a symbol of new life rising from the ashes of your misery.'

'I hadn't thought of that. I must try it on my grandmother. She's convinced he's called Felix. I've told her at least six times. 'Grandma,' I tell her, 'it's Phoenix, not Felix.' Do you want to take him?'

Maddie held him in the crook of her arm. The fingers on his left hand played an invisible piano in the air while he stared up at her with the calm, unblinking gaze of one alien to another. 'He looks like Leo,' she said.

'Don't tell Mum,' Jess said. 'She hasn't quite grasped the concept of co-parenting. She's been here for a week now — she's leaving tomorrow — and every day she asks, 'Will Leo be staying here tonight?' and shakes her head when I say he won't.'

'Guy says he's over the moon. Leo's phone has nothing but baby pictures.'

'I know. We're both appalling. We've become our own worst nightmares.'

'I'd be the same if I had a baby like this. He's so small but he feels sturdy and safe. He's really beautiful, Jess.'

'I know.' Jess gave a beatific smile. 'He's all I ever wanted.'

A few days later, Maddie was on an exploratory trip to Shoreditch to look at a couple of possible school venues. She and Gregory had argued long and hard about expanding their empire. Gregory was all set to zoom off to Birmingham and Manchester and they had finally reached a compromise. They'd open four more clubs across the capital first and see what happened. She and Gregory spent a great deal of time briefing the schools in question and had already begun going through the credentials of possible instructors.

Maddie had had high expectations that day, confident that she'd done her homework. In her experience, headteachers were happy to rent out their buildings, particularly since the children would be employed in mind-expanding occupations. But the first headteacher had found fault with every one of the activities on Maddie's programme. Finally, Maddie asked with carefully restrained exasperation why he'd agreed to meet her if he disagreed with the syllabus.

'I didn't read it,' he said. 'You sent it by email. I don't have time to go over every email.'

The second school had been equally time-wasting. The head was charming and took copious notes of everything Maddie told her. Then, she'd smiled sweetly and said it all sounded fascinating but that her daughter was in the process of setting up a similar enterprise. 'Thank you for coming,' she said as she opened the door for Maddie. 'This will all be so helpful for Sally.'

As a result, Maddie was in a foul mood. She had arranged to meet Amy for a drink and looked forward to offloading her bile. When she arrived at the pub Amy had suggested, she had a text from her friend to say she'd be a little late. Maddie bought a large glass of red wine and by the time Amy arrived, she'd finished it.

'I'm sorry I'm late,' Amy said, bursting in on Maddie's gloomy solitude. 'Let me buy you another — I won't be a moment!'

In retrospect, Maddie should have recognised the warning signs. That Amy's obvious exuberance only exacerbated her bad mood was an indication that she should take a deep breath before saying anything. At the time though, Maddie could only recall the irritation Amy had expressed on the one occasion Maddie had been a few minutes late. She should also have realised that a glass of red wine drunk in a state of quiet fury should never be followed by a second.

'Here you are,' Amy said, returning with drinks and crisps. 'I'm truly sorry I'm late. Life's a little insane at the moment. How are *you*?'

'I'm glad you asked,' Maddie said. 'Today I've wasted a good three hours on two appointments on which I'd already done a huge amount of preparation and which without any doubt at all have proved . . . ' She stopped. 'Amy, what are you drinking?'

'Lime and soda,' Amy said. 'It's not bad, actually.'

'Is this a New Year's resolution? Have you given up alcohol for the year?'

'Sort of.' Amy's eyes sparkled.

'Amy,' Maddie said, 'please reassure me that there is no profound reason for your decision to drink lime and soda tonight. I'm sure there can't be. You did, after all, promise not to get pregnant for at least six months and you do have another eight weeks to go.'

'I agreed I'd spend six months trying to find a man,' Amy said. 'Well, I've found one and we're going to have a baby.'

'Well then,' Maddie said, 'congratulations. Who's the lucky man?'

Amy's chin rose as if gearing herself up to withstand a titanic storm. 'You know who it is.'

Maddie took a deep breath. 'When I suggested you find a man, I didn't mean you should copulate with the first man you see. You're pregnant with Coulsdon Man? You've allied yourself with a Belfast sink! You're pregnant with *Warren*?'

Amy's face took on the colour of an overripe strawberry. 'I can't believe you sometimes. You are the most appalling snob. You should hear yourself: *You're pregnant with Coulsdon Man?* What's wrong with Coulsdon? Is it because it's a suburb and even worse, a suburb in Surrey? I suppose Crystal Palace is the most cutting-edge, cooler than cool, hottest place in south London? Come to think of it, what's wrong with Belfast sinks? I like Belfast sinks and I think it's pretty impressive that Warren installed it without any help. It's a far better skill than acting in boring plays that no one sees. I expect you'd find his house terribly dull, which is a pity because I'm moving in there in a few weeks' time.'

'Amy, Amy, Amy, I'm sorry . . . There's nothing wrong with Coulsdon. I'm sure it's a place with any number of interesting qualities . . .'

'No, you're not. You wouldn't say that if you thought it, and the really irritating thing is that I bet you've never actually been to Coulsdon in your life and yet here you are putting on that voice . . .'

'I'm sorry.' Maddie sliced the air with both her hands. 'Possibly, I am guilty of dismissing Coulsdon out of hand. Possibly, I am guilty of underestimating Warren. I can only repeat how sorry I am. I've had a bad afternoon and I've taken it out on you. I'm sorry. It's fantastic about the baby. I wasn't expecting it, that's all. I hope you'll be very happy. I'm sure you will be.'

'And you'll come and visit us?'

Already Amy had become an *us*. Maddie could imagine ringing the doorbell and being greeted by the triangular shape of Amy, Warren and baby. 'Of course I will,' Maddie said. She would go once. She would make a point of admiring the house and cuddling the baby. She was getting quite good at cuddling babies. She would go and she wouldn't come back. She was aware she felt a furious and quite unjustified resentment towards Amy. She was angry with her for being late this evening; she was angry with her for plunging headlong into pregnancy and dragging poor Warren along with her; and even that was unfair since perhaps poor Warren was only too happy to plunge. Most of all she was angry because she knew she and Amy no longer had anything in common.

★ ★ ★

When Friday came, she was travelling across London all over again, this time to have supper with Laura and Ted, an occasion Maddie would normally anticipate with pleasure. A few days ago, Maddie had asked Gregory if he was going and Gregory had taken some time to utter the one word, 'No.'

'Why not?' Maddie persisted. 'They always ask us together.' She watched Gregory's face twist into a strange gurning shape, a sure sign that he was unhappy with the conversation. 'Did you know I'd been invited? You did, didn't you? So why aren't you going?'

Gregory pulled at the neck of his jumper and reluctantly met her eyes. 'They want to have you on their own,' he said.

'Really? Why?'

'I think Ted might want to have a word about Joe and find out how things are with you two. You know what Ted's like. He worries about things.'

'Joe is twenty-seven. He's a big boy now.'

'I know,' Gregory said. 'But you are thirty-six.'

Maddie pushed away the low table on which her laptop sat, stood up and went across to Gregory. 'How old are *you*?'

'I'm thirty-six.'

'And how old is Minty?'

'She's twenty-five.'

'Right. Tell me, Gregory, do you have any comment to make about my relationship with Joe?'

'Absolutely not,' Gregory said.

230

Maddie rang the doorbell, listening to the barrage of sounds from within the house. Eventually she heard Laura's voice call, 'I'm coming!' A minute or so later, the door was flung open and Laura appeared with a red-faced, half-naked baby in her arms. 'Hi, Mads, Ted's dealing with Billy, I won't be a moment. Help yourself to wine, you know where it is . . . '

She disappeared up the stairs with the baby squirming in anger. Maddie could hear Billy shouting, 'No, Daddy! No, Daddy!' and decided that now would not be the time to say hello to her godson. She took off her coat and hung it up before going through to the kitchen. In Ted's usual meticulous way, all the ingredients for the meal were set out: flour, lasagne, cheese, tomatoes and a solitary onion on the chopping board. Maddie picked it up and peeled it. She heard the doorbell ring, set down the onion and went through to the hall, calling out, 'I'll get it!'

It was Freddy. The beard had gone and his hair was shorter than it had been at his wedding. He stood in the rain, hugging a bottle of wine to his chest. 'Hello,' he said. 'You're supposed to be here tomorrow.'

'No, I'm not. What are you doing here?'

'They invited me to supper. You should be here tomorrow.'

'I wish you'd stop saying that. I was invited for tonight. They wouldn't invite us together, would they?'

'Of course not. They want to talk to you about

your treatment of poor young Joe.'

'I don't believe this. Look, Freddy, you've obviously got the wrong night . . . '

'I'm getting very wet,' Freddy said. 'Can I come in please?'

Maddie gave an ungracious grunt and stepped aside. 'Does *everyone* know about me and Joe?'

★   ★   ★

'I'm afraid so,' Freddy said cheerfully, shutting the door behind him. 'Can you take my bottle while I get this wet mac off?'

'Freddy?' Ted appeared at the top of the stairs. 'What are you doing here?'

Maddie directed a triumphant glance at Freddy. 'I told you,' she said.

Freddy was unabashed. 'Hello, Ted. I've come for supper. You invited me.'

'That was for tomorrow.'

'It was definitely tonight. I'm going down to my parents tomorrow.'

'But we've got Maddie here . . . '

'For goodness' sake,' Maddie said, 'it doesn't matter. I don't mind if Freddy's here.' She could hear Billy upstairs calling for his father. 'Go and see to your son. I'll get started on the dinner.'

Ted stared anxiously at them both, uttered a heartfelt expletive and went back into the bedroom.

Maddie brushed past Freddy and went straight through to the kitchen. She picked up the kitchen knife and began to slice the onion. She did not look up when Freddy joined her.

'You want to slice it thinner,' he said. 'And you'll need another onion. I'll get it for you.' He opened the door of the fridge and pulled out a bottle of Sauvignon. 'Do you want a drink?'

'Thank you. And perhaps, since you're such an expert, you'd like to carry on preparing the onions while I make the cheese sauce?'

'I'd be delighted.' He opened the bottle and poured them both glasses. 'Cheers.'

Maddie put down the knife and picked up her wine. 'You're enjoying this, aren't you?'

'If you mean, am I pleased to see you . . . '

'You know very well what I mean. 'Poor young Joe . . . ' Give me a break! He's at least a year older than your very young wife.'

'That's true,' Freddy said, 'but as you've often told me, women mature quicker than men do.' He watched her take the slab of Cheddar out of its wrapping. 'You will grate lots of cheese, won't you? You never make it cheesy enough.' He began to cut the onion. 'I haven't seen you since the wedding. I thought you looked fantastic, by the way. I loved the dress.'

'I didn't think you'd noticed.'

'I always notice what you wear.'

She raised her eyebrows and it was perhaps fortunate that Ted and Laura walked in at that moment, full of apologies for the delays. 'Maddie, it's lovely to see you,' Laura said. 'Freddy, we thought you were coming tomorrow.'

Freddy beamed at her. 'Did you?'

'I mean it's lovely to see you but perhaps it's better if . . . '

'It's fine,' Maddie said. 'I mean for heaven's

sake . . . He's married, and I've moved on . . . '

'We all know that,' Freddy murmured.

'Shut up, Freddy. I only suggested you stay because hopefully your presence will stop Ted giving me a lecture about Joe.'

'I wouldn't,' Ted protested. Rather spoiling the effect by adding, 'It was only that Joe is pretty upset and . . . '

'Listen,' Maddie said, 'when we got together I told him it was nothing serious and to be honest I don't see that it's any of your business anyway . . . '

'I think,' Freddy said helpfully, 'Ted's just looking out for his little brother.'

'Freddy, if you say another word, I swear I'll throw this grater at you.'

'Look, Maddie,' Ted said, 'I didn't mean to upset you and of course . . . ' he threw a furious glance at Freddy, 'we didn't invite you here just to talk about Joe. Let's all have some wine and start again. I need some alcohol.' He took down a couple of glasses. 'Freddy, since you're apparently staying, how are you?'

'I'm extremely well. I'm off to America in three weeks.'

'Oh my God,' Laura said. 'It's definite then? You're in the zombie thing? That's incredible. So what does it mean? Are you going out to live there or what?'

'I'm not taking anything for granted after the last time. But I'll definitely be there for the next eight months and then we'll see what happens. Victoria's got a couple of jobs here for the next three months but then she'll join me.'

'That's amazing news,' Ted said, putting an arm round Freddy. 'My friend, the TV star. It's actually going to happen!'

'I hope so,' Freddy said. 'You must all come out and visit me. It's pretty scary. I won't know anyone out there.'

'Give us a year or so,' Laura promised. 'I need to get used to having two children before we make any big holiday plans.'

'What about *you*?' Freddy asked Maddie. 'Do you fancy coming to California for a holiday?'

'I couldn't afford it,' Maddie said.

'I'll pay for you,' said Freddy. 'You wouldn't believe what they're paying me.'

The room fell suddenly silent. Maddie could see that neither Ted nor Laura was fully convinced that Freddy was joking.

'Funnily enough,' Maddie said, 'I think I'll say no to your very attractive offer. I can't imagine Victoria would be happy to have you fly out an ex-girlfriend.'

'She knows I miss your friendship,' Freddy said. 'We are still friends, aren't we?'

Maddie smiled. 'That's very sweet, Freddy. Given that we've not seen each other for at least a year, apart from a short and not terribly interesting conversation I had with you and your wife at your wedding, I would say, on balance, that, no, we aren't.'

★ ★ ★

When Maddie woke the next morning she reached for her phone. Walter had sent her two

235

more texts since his 'Can we start again please?' The last one, four days before, had suggested dinner. She'd been put off by his choice of location.

She found herself returning again to the conversation last night. Freddy had been in one of his wilfully provocative moods, throwing out comments like a fisherman casting his line in random directions in the hope of catching something. She wasn't convinced he *had* got the dates mixed up and it was impossible to tell whether he genuinely thought they could have some sort of friendship. Either way, it didn't matter.

She looked at Walter's latest text: 'Dinner at my place? Please?' She took a deep breath and sent him a one-word answer. 'When?'

20

Henry had had second thoughts about the book group and Pilates. To be strictly accurate, it was his mother who had the thoughts which she expressed with great force in a long conversation down the phone. She was suffering from another bout of flu and had forbidden Henry to visit her. 'Violet's looking after me,' she said. 'You know what I'm like when I'm ill. I like to hide away and be very quiet. I'm too feeble for conversation.'

'You wouldn't know it at the moment,' Henry said.

'That's because I'm in bed and I've been thinking. You never used to be a quitter, Henry. Violet does Pilates. She says her back was transformed after just one lesson.'

'So was mine. I could hardly walk for a week.'

'That was because you didn't pay attention to your instructor. Try again. And I don't understand about the book group either. You were so enthusiastic at first.'

'I told you, Granty, I feel awkward. I'm the only man there . . .'

'Good. That's the idea. You are there to meet women.'

'Well, I've met them and, trust me, romance with any of them is out of the question.'

'You get to know them and they introduce you to more women. And meanwhile, you're flexing your social muscles and, heaven knows, they do need flexing.'

In fact, Henry felt guilty about the book group. Tessa had rung after he'd missed the last one the week before and asked why he'd not been there. When he tried to explain that he thought he'd be unable to come again due to unforeseen commitments, she'd been quite upset. Everyone appreciated his contributions, she said, and if he wasn't excited by the February choice, he might like to know that in March it would be *The God Delusion* by Richard Dawkins.

'It's a very masculine book, don't you think?' she asked hopefully.

Henry had no idea but he made a vague promise to look into it.

The following evening he had a call from Becky.

'Tessa gave me your number,' she said. 'I hope you don't mind.'

'Not at all,' Henry said, before remembering the circumstances of their last meeting, and adding with forced geniality, 'A belated happy new year to you!'

'Thank you. I want to say — I hope you don't take this the wrong way — but I'm worried that you've decided to leave the club because my husband was rude to you.'

'Oh well . . . ' Henry started walking round the kitchen table, one hand clutching the phone, the other skimming the tops of the chairs.

'Because if you have, I shall be even angrier with my husband than I am already. He was very offensive to you and you did nothing to deserve it. He was only like that because he was jealous. He thought you and I were having an affair.'

'But that's ridiculous,' Henry exclaimed. 'I'm old enough to be your father!'

'That's sweet of you to say so but I don't think it's true. The fact is, he's in no position to accuse me of anything since he's been seeing a student who certainly *is* young enough to be his daughter. We're going through a rather difficult time at the moment, and to be perfectly honest, if you give up the book group because of him I shan't answer for the consequences. I've told him I want him to call on you and give you a direct apology.'

★ ★ ★

Henry was revolted by the idea. 'No, that won't be necessary. Please don't even think of it. I would find it excruciating.'

'But if you won't come back . . . '

'I will,' Henry said quickly. 'I promise I will.' Anything, he thought, would be preferable to a visit from the wild husband.

After Becky had rung off, Henry went upstairs and stood in front of the mirror. He tried to see himself through the eyes of Becky's husband. He pulled his shoulders back and raised his chin. He suspected Becky's husband was a little mad but he couldn't help smiling at his reflection.

★ ★ ★

He got back from work a few days later to find a message from William on the answerphone. Perhaps he imagined it, but he felt he detected an uncomfortable note in William's voice. 'Hi, Henry, just a call to say hello and exchange news. I'm up to my ears in work at the moment but it's time we got together, so give me a ring when you can and we'll fix something up. I warn you, I intend to keep trying! Bye for now!'

Henry had no intention of ringing William, much less exchanging news with him. He could imagine only too easily how *that* conversation would go:

WILLIAM: So, I have a new book out in April, the ratings for my TV show are going through the roof and Ellen and I are madly in love and can't keep our hands off each other. What about you?

HENRY: I'm thinking of rejoining my book group.

Henry had no wish to hear about the delights of William's new lady friend. While heating up the remains of Monday's Irish stew, he stood with his arms folded, recalling the moment William's smile worked its extraordinary magic on Ellen. While he ate his supper he tried to plan his response in the event of a further call from William: it would be measured but a little cool, he thought, though actually such subtle nuances would be lost on William.

The phone rang while he was washing up. He dried his hands on the towel and murmured, 'Measured but cool,' before picking up the handset.

'Hello, Dad. I'm glad I caught you before you left.'

Henry frowned. 'Nina? Am I supposed to be going somewhere?'

'Don't worry, that's fine. You can put away your car keys. You needn't come over tonight after all. Something's come up and I can't go out.'

'Nina, I'm sorry. I have no idea what you're talking about. When you . . . '

'No, really, I can do it another time. Do me a favour and ring Cindy for me, will you? Tell her I'm all right and I'll ring her soon. Don't forget, Dad. *Ring Cindy! Tell Cindy I'm all right!*'

The phone went dead and Henry regarded it with consternation. Had he offered to babysit tonight? And who the hell was Cindy? He was about to ring back when everything fell into place and he felt a sharp contraction of his heart. Steady, he thought, steady. Don't panic. Keep calm. Get the car keys and keep calm.

★　★　★

Cindy had been at school with Nina. When Nina was seventeen they had gone to a party together. Marianne had been a little concerned because Cindy's companion, Jake, was driving them there. The two of them had come into the house for a few minutes and, according to Marianne, Jake had resolutely failed to meet her eye when she said hello. Afterwards, Marianne blamed herself for not acting on her instincts but, as Henry said, one couldn't stop a young man

241

driving one's daughter to a party simply because he had no discernible social skills.

A few hours after they'd gone, Nina rang. She was almost hysterical and at first it was impossible to understand her. Eventually, she managed to say she was at Ipswich police station.

It transpired that Nina had sensed something was wrong as soon as they arrived at their destination, a square brick house on the outskirts of Ipswich. Neither Cindy nor Jake seemed to know who was throwing the party and the energy with which the young man tried to press pills on to Nina made her first wary and then frightened. Nina knew no one there apart from Cindy and all of the men seemed to be much older than them. It was, she told her parents later, only after she'd seen Cindy being led up the stairs by a man with a paunch that she wanted to ring them. But there were people all around her, she wasn't sure what to do and anyway, the police arrived a few minutes later.

Apparently the police had been interested in Cindy's friend for some time. It emerged that Jake had a lucrative sideline in bringing young girls to parties and ensuring their compliance with the help of industrial quantities of dope. It was impossible to be angry with Nina and, as Henry said later, there was really no need to rebuke her for the ease with which she'd accepted the invitation of a girl she'd never much liked. In the car on the way back home, Nina lacerated herself with furious denunciations: how could she be so stupid? Why hadn't she asked more about the party? Why had she thought that any party suggested by Cindy would be any good anyway?

Marianne had been struck by the fact that Nina had wanted to ring them but felt constrained by the other people around her. She came up with the suggestion that if ever Nina was in a situation that frightened her, she should ring them, say where she was and simply add, 'Tell Cindy I'm all right.' Then, Marianne assured her, they would know what to do.

For at least a year after that, both Nina and Maddie took to ringing their parents, gasping, 'Tell Cindy I'm all right,' and then hooting with laughter as their mother scolded them for making fun of her brilliant idea. But that was then and this was now. Nina was in trouble and as Henry sped towards Ipswich, he found himself chanting again and again, 'Tell Cindy I'm all right.'

When he arrived at the house, he could hear Nina arguing with someone inside. He took a deep breath and rang the doorbell. There was a brief silence and then there were a few words spoken in a low, masculine voice. He rang again and this time he could hear Nina, loud and clear. 'If the bell keeps ringing, the children will wake up. I have to answer it.'

When she opened the door, she mouthed silently, 'Thank you,' and then said loudly in a queer, strained voice, 'Hello there, Dad! I told you, you didn't have to come over.'

'I'm sorry,' Henry said, 'I didn't understand. Now I'm here, perhaps I could have a cup of coffee before I go home again.' Perhaps she'd

243

surprised a burglar and he was holding her hostage. He directed a carefully benign smile at the intruder. The man was tall, rather good-looking, probably in his early forties, with straight black hair brushed back from his face and one of those half-hearted attempts at a beard. 'Haven't I met you before?' Henry asked.

'You might have seen him at parent-teacher meetings,' Nina said, still in that artificially cheerful tone, as if she were at a particularly difficult drinks party. 'He teaches Geography. He's Deputy Head now.'

'You came round that first night I babysat,' Henry said. He extended a hand to the Deputy Head. 'I'm Henry, Henry Drummond.'

'Stephen.' The man's grip was firm. 'Stephen Castleford.'

'It's nice to meet you, Stephen.' He wished he knew what Nina wanted him to do. He couldn't believe a deputy headmaster could be a hostage taker. He sat down on the sofa.

Nina's hands twisted together. 'Now that Dad's here, Stephen,' she said, 'perhaps you should go.'

'I told you,' Stephen said gently. 'I am staying till Robbie gets back.'

Henry could imagine this man in class, patiently repeating instructions to wayward pupils. He reminded Henry of a Science teacher he'd once had, a soft-spoken man who had an iron-clad conviction that he was always in the right. He glanced up at Nina. 'Why don't you make that coffee while Stephen and I have a chat?'

Nina nodded and went out. Once she'd gone, Stephen settled in the armchair opposite Henry. 'Nina and I are old friends,' he said.

'That's nice.'

'There was always a spark between us. I knew she liked me. Of course, I did nothing. I was married. And I was her teacher, after all.'

'Quite right,' Henry said. He was beginning to find Stephen's fixed attention on his face a little unnerving.

'My wife and I live round the corner. We moved here a year ago. Six months ago, I spotted Nina in the street. She saw me and gave me the most wonderful smile. It made me catch my breath.'

'Both of my daughters have always had lovely smiles.' Henry looked down at his hands and then cleared his throat. 'Do you have children of your own, Stephen?'

'Three sons: thirteen, fourteen and sixteen.' He gave a sudden chuckle. 'They're all pretty sullen and spotty at the moment. It's not easy sharing a house with three adolescent boys. My wife adores them, of course.'

'I'm sure she does.'

Stephen leant forward suddenly. 'I want to assure you, Henry, I have only honourable intentions towards your daughter. I intend to leave my wife. We've not been getting on well for a long time. Nina and I want to be together.'

Glancing straight ahead of him, Henry could see Nina standing, listening in the dining-room. She fixed him with intense eyes and shook her head furiously.

Henry said carefully, 'But Stephen, Nina has a partner already and she and Robbie *do* get on well. She loves him.'

Stephen gave a brief chuckle. 'I don't want to embarrass you,' he said. 'So let me just assure you I have reasons, very sound reasons, to believe differently. I've come here tonight to explain them to Robbie.'

Henry's fingers curled into the palms of his hands. 'I bow to your superior knowledge, of course, but it strikes me that Nina would rather you left now. When Robbie comes home he'll be tired. Your news will upset him and he may well lose his temper. Voices will be raised, the children will wake and Nina won't thank you. I have to say I think it's possible that you've misread the situation. She and Robbie have always been very close to each other.'

Stephen smiled. He sat back in his chair and crossed his legs. 'May I speak frankly? I have often observed in my career that parents can be amazingly blinkered where their children are concerned. Most people who look at Nina would assume she is a happy, self-confident woman. I know a different Nina: insecure, unsure of herself, scared of Robbie and scared of voicing her own feelings.'

'I have to say,' Henry said, 'that I've never known Nina to be backward in voicing her feelings.'

'That's because you don't know her as well as I do.'

'You might be right,' Henry said, 'but one thing I do know is that she hates to be forced into a corner. If she feels you're forcing her hand she won't forgive you.' For the first time he thought he detected a flash of uncertainty in Stephen's eyes. He pressed home the point. 'You must let *her* decide when and where she reveals the truth to Robbie. She's never liked being bullied.'

Nina came back in with a tray containing three small mugs. 'So,' she said, 'here's the coffee!'

Stephen stood up. 'I've told your father about us,' he said. 'He thinks it would be best if *you* told Robbie.'

Nina stood in front of Henry with the tray and rolled her eyes before saying cheerfully, 'I think that's best.'

Henry took his coffee and had a sip. As Nina sat down beside him, he reached across to grasp her hand. They both watched Stephen take a gulp of his drink. If this were a Hitchcock film, Nina would have slipped a sleeping potion into his mug and they would both watch silently while his eyelids started to close. Henry wished they *were* in a Hitchcock film.

Stephen gave a satisfied nod. 'This is excellent coffee,' he said and now Henry *knew* he was mad because the coffee was appalling and at some future date he would have to sit his daughter down and teach her how to make it properly.

There was the sound of a key in the door and all three of them froze. A moment later, Robbie stood in the room, directing a slightly bewildered smile at the unexpected guests.

Henry put his mug down and stood up. 'Stephen and I were just leaving, Robbie.'

Stephen mirrored his actions. 'Good evening, Robbie,' he said. 'My name's Stephen. Stephen Castleford.'

'So there we are.' Henry clapped his hands together. 'Stephen, shall we go?'

'Right,' Stephen said and then as Henry pulled out his car keys, he put up a hand. 'I'm sorry, Henry. I have to say something to Robbie. It's not fair to keep him in the dark.'

'I think we should go, old chap,' Henry said. 'Robbie looks exhausted.'

'The fact is,' Stephen said, 'Nina and I have something to tell you.'

'No,' Nina said, 'we don't.'

'He deserves to hear the truth,' Stephen said. 'I'm sorry, Robbie, but Nina and I are in love.'

'We're *not*!' Nina said.

Robbie gazed at her. 'What is all this?'

'It's nothing!' Nina put one hand up to either side of her face. 'He's drunk! He's delusional! Dad was about to take him home.'

Robbie nodded at Stephen. 'That's probably a good idea,' he said.

His tone was gentle, almost kind. Later, Henry thought that it was that very sympathy that probably hardened Stephen's resolve.

'I don't wish to burden you with the details,' he said, 'but a few months ago I discovered that Nina loved me as much as I do her.'

Robbie set his bag down. 'Feel free to burden me,' he said.

'I came round to see her. We had a bottle of wine. We sat together on the sofa. She wore a blue denim dress with poppers.'

'Listen,' Henry said, 'we don't want to hear this . . . '

'Please, Henry, let the man speak.' Robbie nodded at Stephen. 'Carry on.'

'Robbie,' Nina pleaded. 'Can we stop this? Stephen came round and we did have some wine but . . . '

'She wasn't drunk,' Stephen said. 'Neither was I.' His voice was low, steady, relentless. 'I kissed her. I pulled at her dress and it opened like a book. I kissed her breasts . . . '

'For God's sake!' Henry exclaimed, 'That's enough!'

'I kissed her breasts,' Stephen continued, 'and then we fell onto the floor. I have often had sex but this was the first time I made love, real love. When I entered her, we moved in perfect unison together. We came at the same time and when I looked in her eyes I knew she loved me as I did her. That is the truth, the whole truth and nothing but the truth.'

Henry saw Robbie's face and instantly leapt between the two men. 'Robbie, if you hit him, there'll be noise and the children will wake. Think of Chloe and Megan.'

Nina was crying now and calling to Robbie but he seemed not to hear her. He spoke softly to Stephen. 'Let Henry take you home. Now. If you don't go, this moment, at once, I will drag you outside and I promise I will throw you in the gutter.' He turned to Henry. 'Don't come back, Henry. Nina and I need to talk.'

Henry glanced at his daughter. She nodded.

Henry tugged at Stephen's sleeve. 'Come on,'

he said. 'You've done what you set out to do.'

Stephen's terrifying self-righteousness had left him. He allowed himself to be led out of the house and into Henry's car and, when Henry drove away, told him quietly that he was grateful for the lift and that all Henry had to do was to turn left and then left again and then drop him at the post box.

Henry's hands were shaking with the effort to contain his rage. He couldn't bear to have the man in his car. Tomorrow, after work, he would go to the garage and vacuum the entire interior. He drove in silence and as soon as he'd dropped off his passenger, he turned and drove back to Nina's street, parking a few yards from the house.

He hovered by the front door. The light in the sitting-room had been switched off and he could hear no voices. Robbie had told him not to come back. Nina had nodded her agreement. He had never felt more useless or indecisive in his life. He waited another couple of minutes and then walked back to the car and drove home.

21

Maddie had forgotten how complex romance could be: one needed the sensitivity of a diplomat and the tactical skill of Napoleon. Walter had apologised for his initial presumption but had overreached himself again by inviting her to supper at his flat. In a moment of madness which she could only blame on Freddy, she had accepted his invitation, and now here was the result: a brisk, confident reply giving a date, a time and an address.

'The trouble is,' Maddie said to Gregory during one of their coffee breaks, 'I know he should have chosen a neutral location but if I point that out *now*, it makes me sound nervous and indecisive and paranoid. Plus there is also the possibility that he wants to make amends by cooking me a meal . . . '

'Let me see the text,' Gregory said, taking the phone and reading the message. He passed the phone back and stared solemnly at Maddie. 'This might just be fate,' he declared, a pronouncement the old Gregory would have deplored but one that he'd used more than once since the arrival of Minty in his life. 'Minty's brother lives on the same street. If that isn't a sign I don't know what is. We'll go and have supper with him and drop in on you at ten to make sure you're all right.'

'Why would you do that? How would I explain

it? 'Oh, by the way, Walter, some friends of mine are calling here later just to say. hello.' That sounds very weird. He'll see through it at once.'

'Tell him I need to give you an important document.'

'Why wouldn't you email it to me?'

'Details, details. It's an excellent idea. You can go safely to supper and we get to see Walter. I've never met anyone called Walter before.'

'Neither have I.' Maddie stared out of Gregory's window. Since his was a lower ground-floor flat, pedestrians could only be seen from the knees down, which could be surprisingly interesting. The woman currently walking along the pavement wore bright pink boots that could barely contain the legs inside them. Maddie glanced across at Gregory. 'Did you know that Freddy's off to California in a couple of weeks?'

Gregory nodded. 'Minty speaks to Victoria most days.'

'How does Victoria feel about it?'

'She's thrilled. Her own career is going pretty well at the moment. She's doing a film in Berwick-on-Tweed and then she starts a TV crime serial. She's flying out to join Freddy in May.'

'How exciting,' Maddie said.

'You sound like my mother. Every now and then she asks me to tell her how the business is going and I tell her all about it and then she says, 'How exciting' and changes the subject.'

'Tell me,' Maddie said, 'has Minty begun to find you annoying yet?'

252

'Of course she hasn't.'
'She will,' Maddie said.

★ ★ ★

For once, Maddie was early and decided to explore Walter's home environment before calling on him. She stared up at The Shard — all two hundred and forty-four metres of it — and wondered whether she loved or loathed it. On balance, she decided, she loathed it. She stood outside the Design Museum, currently celebrating the anglepoise lamp amongst other iconic creations. If she'd had the time she could have visited Tate Modern or even Shakespeare's Globe Theatre. One could never be bored round here, though without a good income it might be frustrating. Would she have felt differently about Coulsdon Warren if he'd been living here? She had an unpleasant feeling she might have done.

Walter's flat was in a new development that used a combination of red bricks, wooden slats and vast windows to produce an extremely stylish building. The residue of guilt she felt about Warren prompted a sudden revulsion against it. Everything here was rich and privileged; she found herself yearning for Crystal Palace with its eccentric park with its dinosaur sculptures, its shabby shops and its friendly cafes.

She pressed the button of the intercom entry system and Walter's voice said, 'Hi, Maddie, come on up.'

In her own house, human voices made the

intercom crackle and she always had to go down the creaky stairs to let visitors in. Here the door opened automatically and she stepped into a mirrored lift that did nothing to lift her spirits since it reflected a stain on her dress that she had somehow failed to notice earlier. Already she had decided this date would be a disaster.

Unwittingly, Walter saved the day, or rather the evening. When he flung open the door of the flat, he voiced her thoughts, 'This is going to be a disaster. I should never have asked you here.'

She wondered if he had telepathic powers.

'I thought I'd do something easy,' he said, 'pork escalopes in a nice creamy sauce and now I've made it — I swear I left it for only a few seconds — it's burnt to nothing in the pan and I've used up all the cream and it's all doom and destruction and we should have gone out somewhere . . . '

'Walter,' Maddie said, 'take me to your kitchen.'

By the time Maddie had saved the meal — she made a new sauce with wine, lemon juice and tarragon — she was ready to forgive him for the splendour of his apartment with its shiny white units, submerged lighting and outside terrace. Walter told her he'd be paying off the mortgage on his death-bed but he had enough spare cash to hang expensive-looking prints on the walls. Of much greater interest to Maddie were the three framed photos of Walter with a stunning-looking woman who closely resembled Charlotte Gainsbourg.

'She's beautiful,' Maddie said.

'Yes,' Walter said, 'she was.'

'She *was?*'

'We were married for three years. And then one day she flew back from Germany. There was a freak accident and suddenly I wasn't married any more.'

Maddie stared at him with new eyes. In a few seconds he had gone from being an excessively wealthy accountant to a man of infinite tragedy. 'Oh Walter, I'm sorry. You look so happy together.'

'We were. But life goes on and one can't mourn forever. Shall we eat?'

Over supper he asked about her job and she reminded him she'd talked about it on their first date.

'I know,' Water said, 'but I wasn't paying attention. Tell me again.'

'How do I know you'll listen this time?'

'The prospect of sex is very distracting. I don't expect it this evening so will give you all my attention. Tell me about your job.'

'I have a business with my friend, Gregory. We run Plug Clubs.'

'Are you plumbers?'

'We call them Plug Clubs because they plug the gaps in our education system. We run clubs after school and encourage the children to talk and discuss and debate, we offer philosophy and team games and . . . I can't believe you didn't take all this in last time.'

'I'm taking it in now. Have you known Gregory for long?'

'We were at university together. In fact,'

Maddie paused to finish her wine, 'I hope you don't mind but Gregory and his girlfriend, Minty, are popping in here at about ten because Gregory has some papers for me to sign.' She cleared her throat. 'They happen to be in the area tonight . . .'

'That's convenient,' Walter said politely.

'They're having supper with Minty's brother. He lives down the road from you.'

'That's a coincidence,' he said in the same measured tone.

'I suppose it is.' Maddie heard her phone ring and instantly sprang up. 'I'd better take this — in case it's them.' She checked her mobile and then put it back in her bag. 'That was my father. I'll ring him back tomorrow.'

'Perhaps he'd like to call in on us too,' Walter said. His voice was polite and affable and didn't fool her for a moment.

As always when Maddie felt she was somehow in the wrong, she became defensive. 'You can't blame me for taking precautions. I've only met you once before and besides, Minty's brother *does* live round here.'

'I'm a little appalled that you think I might be the sort of man who would force myself on an unwilling dinner companion.'

'I don't. But the trouble with these sorts of things is that we know so little about each other and there are some very odd people around.'

'That's true. Is there anything you wish to tell me about your own special habits?'

'Look, I'm sorry. I'll ring Gregory now and . . .'

'I shall be delighted to meet them, if only to clear my character.'

'I think you'll like Gregory. I've actually only met his girlfriend once, at a wedding but she's very young and pretty.'

'You don't have to sell them to me. I really don't mind.'

Maddie stared at him and frowned. 'Oh, for goodness' sake,' she said. She pushed her chair back, stood up and then bent down to kiss his mouth. It lasted far longer than she'd intended and when they finished, they both stared at each other a little breathlessly.

'Wow,' Walter said, 'that was nice.'

'I think,' Maddie said, 'I might ring Gregory after all.'

In the sitting room the front door slammed, a voice called out, 'Walter?' and a few moments later a woman looking remarkably like Charlotte Gainsbourg appeared in the doorway.

'Josie!' Walter gasped.

'Is that your wife?' Maddie asked and, seeing him nod speechlessly, added, 'I thought she was dead?'

'So you killed me off, did you?' Josie swept over to one of the units and took out a glass. 'How did I die?'

'You were on a plane flying over Germany,' said Maddie.

'That's inventive.' Josie took a seat at the table and reached for the bottle. 'I am so thirsty,' and staring at their plates, said, 'I am so hungry.'

'You can finish this if you like.' Maddie passed

over her plate. 'I seem to have lost my appetite.'

'Thanks.' Josie pulled the plate towards her and loaded the fork with the last big piece of escalope. She looked at Walter. 'Are the two of you together?' she asked.

'No,' he said, 'she's just a friend. What are you doing here? You said you'd never come back.'

Josie spoke through a mouthful of pork. She might look like Charlotte Gainsbourg but she had appalling table manners. 'I know, I know! I tried to love Berkshire and I tried to love Philip but he and Berkshire are made for each other. I've got my old job back and now I'm staying with Bridget . . . '

She stopped at the sound of Gregory's loud voice speaking through the intercom. 'Hello. This is Gregory with a document for Maddie.'

'I'll let him in,' Maddie said. She ran through, hissed into the intercom, 'Come on up, Gregory, as fast as you can,' and pressed the buzzer.

She could hear Walter saying, 'I can't believe you didn't ring — I can't believe you just walked in . . . '

Maddie opened the door as soon as Gregory thumped on it. He stood poised for action, while behind him Minty gazed at Maddie with nervous sympathy.

'What's happened?' Gregory asked breathlessly. 'Are you all right?'

'I am so glad you're here. Come and say hello and then let's go.' She led them through to the kitchen. Walter and Josie were now sitting next to each other. Maddie's plate was empty as was Josie's glass. Maddie said, 'Josie and Walter, meet

Gregory and Minty. Gregory and Minty, meet Walter and Josie.'

Josie swept back her mane of shiny chestnut hair. 'Hi,' she said, without curiosity.

'I have to go,' Maddie said, sweeping up her bag and coat as she left. She was careful not to look at Walter. She was almost certain he would be far too busy staring at his un-dead wife to offer her the slightest apologetic glance but she had no wish to confirm the suspicion. In the lift going down she explained what had happened. 'Walter and I had supper together. He showed me photos of his wife. He said she was dead. Then she burst in and was obviously alive and sat down at the table and they both ignored me.'

'Oh my God,' Minty said.

★   ★   ★

As the lift stopped, Maddie noticed that Gregory was sucking in his cheeks and his body was moving strangely backwards and forwards.

'Gregory,' she told him, 'this is *not* funny and if you mention this to anyone, you are *dead*.'

★   ★   ★

Maddie was woken by her phone the next morning, reaching for it in a half sleep and mumbling a hello.

Her father's voice was apologetic. 'I'm sorry, Maddie. Have I woken you?'

'It's all right.' Maddie glanced at her alarm clock. 'It's way too late anyway. How are things?'

There was a brief silence as if her father was trying to work out what to say. 'Are you free next weekend? Can you come up?'

'I think so.' Maddie sat up, fully alert. 'Dad, are you all right? What's happened? Is anything wrong?'

'Yes,' her father said. 'Everything is wrong.'

22

Henry rang Nina three times on the Thursday morning before she picked up. 'Hi, Dad. I've been meaning to ring you . . . '

'I was worried,' Henry said. 'Are you and Robbie all right? After what that man said . . . '

'You didn't believe any of that stuff, did you? He's flipped. He should be sectioned or something. I was really pleased to see him at first and then he kept coming round and it became embarrassing. I suppose I should have told someone but I felt partly responsible. I mean, I did invite him over in the first place. Anyway, I hope it's all over now. Robbie and I are fine. I'm just sorry I got you involved . . . Chloe's with me. She'd love to speak to you. Would you like to have a word?'

Henry could hear Chloe breathing into the phone. 'Hello, Granda!'

'Hello, Chloe!' In the background, he could hear Nina urging her to sing to him.

Chloe took a deep breath. 'I'm a troll, fol-de-rol and I'm . . . EAT you up!'

'Well, Chloe, that's just lovely,' Henry said. 'Well done!'

'Thanks!' Chloe said carelessly. 'Bye, Granda!'

Now Nina was back. 'Dad, thanks so much for ringing. And I'm sorry about yesterday. I'll talk to you again soon. Bye now!'

Henry put the phone down. Nina had

261

sounded more or less normal. Perhaps every-thing *was* normal. It was clear that Stephen Castleford was disturbed. Everything about him had been odd. The more Henry thought about it, the more obvious it was that his graphic fantasy of lovemaking with Nina was the sign of a deeply deranged individual. Thank goodness Nina had made Robbie see that. What worried Henry now was that the man might try to bother Nina again. He would ring her at the weekend and suggest that perhaps she should contact Castleford's wife or even the police.

For the rest of the day he found it difficult to concentrate on work. In the night he had a horrible dream in which Stephen Castleford, looking like Jack Nicholson in *The Shining*, tried to break Nina's door down with an axe. He woke in the morning feeling exhausted and was glad he had the day at home. He spent the morning unleashing his feelings on a tree that had fallen in a storm the week before, chopping it into neat piles of logs. The garden was sodden and subdued, its flowerbeds covered with leaves, while random branches were strewn across the lawn.

He went in around midday and had just taken off his boots when the phone rang. He hit his hip against the table in his haste to get to it and made a silent howl of protest as he picked it up.

'Dad, I rung you earlier but you weren't there . . . '

'I'm sorry, Nina, I've been in the garden. How are you today?'

'I'm fine. I wondered if I could come and stay with you tonight.'

'Of course you can. It would be lovely to see you and the girls . . . '

'It would be just me, I'm afraid. Robbie will have the girls at home with him.'

Henry pulled out a chair and sat down. 'I don't understand. I thought . . . '

'I'm sure it's a temporary thing. He's a little upset by what happened and Clive has a spare room so he's moving there on Sunday. He wants to have the girls to himself at weekends so I said I'd come to you . . . '

'But that's appalling! Surely he sees that . . . '

'He will do. He just needs a bit of time, that's all. We'll be fine. Soon, we'll be fine. If I can't stay with you, I can easily go somewhere else . . . '

'Don't be silly, you know I'd love to have you here whenever you want. I'll make a nice supper.'

'Great! And Dad, there's no need to tell anyone about this. It'll all blow over.'

Henry put the phone down. Everything was happening so quickly. How could Robbie take that man seriously? He stood up and made coffee and then remembered he was supposed to be visiting his mother tomorrow. He had no idea what he was going to say to her.

★   ★   ★

Granty was fully recovered from her flu. 'Henry,' she said, 'what do you think of fracking?'

'I have no idea,' he said. 'I know very little about it.'

'Well, you should find out. I read a fascinating article this morning which described it as 'fracturing the earth'. Isn't that poetic? I've written a letter to my MP and you should write one too. It's untried and untested and . . . '

All Henry had to do was put in the odd grunt here and there. Perhaps he should just say that his car was out of action or that another tree had fallen or he had a hugely important case to work on. The trouble was that she would want to know the details and Henry was never very good at making up details.

'Henry,' his mother said, 'you're not listening to a word I'm saying.'

'It's a complex subject . . . '

'I shall give you this article tomorrow. It's very clear.'

'Ah!' Henry cleared his throat. 'That's why I rang you. I'm afraid I can't come tomorrow. Nina's driving over tonight. She and Robbie decided it would be nice for him to spend some time with the girls on his own and so . . . so, there it is.'

'But that will be lovely! Bring Nina with you. The three of us can go out to lunch.'

'That would be nice but . . . Nina's a little under the weather. That's why she's coming here. She needs to have a . . . a rest from the children.'

There was a long, pregnant pause. 'Henry, you are so bad at lying. You always were. What's happened?'

'I can't tell you,' Henry said, and even as he said it he knew that this small solid declaration would have no chance of survival in the face of Granty's tank-like determination. 'I promised I wouldn't say anything to anyone . . . '

'I'm not anyone. I'm a grandmother. Tell me.'

Henry sighed. 'Nina rang me on Wednesday evening. She made it very clear she wanted me to come over right away. There was a man there. He was . . . an acquaintance of Nina's and he was obviously unhinged. Then Robbie came back and the man claimed that he and Nina were in love. Nina kept saying it was ridiculous and I'm sure it *is*, but . . . '

'Have you talked to Robbie?'

'Not yet. Nina says he's moving in with his friend Clive on Sunday evening. She says it's only temporary. I think Robbie just needs to take a step back, look at the situation objectively and then he'll realize he's made a mistake. Obviously, if things don't change I'll have a word.'

'You know what happens when you mix cement? It soon sets hard and then it's impossible to do anything with it. That's what the brain is like. Once people think the unthinkable it soon stops *being* unthinkable. Time is of the essence, Henry. Use this weekend to talk to Nina and make sure you *do* talk to her. And then you need to talk to Robbie.'

★   ★   ★

It was all very well for Granty to blithely issue impossible instructions. Nina had always been

265

someone who only revealed information when she wanted to reveal it. She arrived on Friday evening in a mood of such rigid good humour that it was impossible to dent it. Over supper she switched relentlessly from one uncontroversial topic to another: Megan's third appearance this term on something at school called The Wall of Excellence; Chloe's ever-expanding vocabulary; a sponsorship run she was organizing for new games equipment. It was only when Henry said for the second time that he would like to know what was going on with Robbie that she fell silent.

'Nina?' Henry prompted.

'Dad, I know you're worried but I can't talk about it at the moment. I have no idea what's going to happen. Stephen Castleford might be mad but he was very convincing. While Robbie continues to believe him, there's no future for us. All I can do is hope that he sees sense and . . . '

'Would it help,' Henry asked, 'if I were to go and see Stephen? If I could persuade him to admit the whole story was a fabrication . . . '

'You don't understand, Dad. Stephen's convinced himself it *is* true. I know you want to help and if there's anything you can do, believe me, I'll ask you. Now, let's wash up the supper and then we can watch something silly on the telly.'

They watched *Saving Private Ryan*, which wasn't silly at all. Within the first ten minutes, Nina was curled up on the sofa beside her father, one arm wrapped in his, her attention totally captivated by the celluloid depiction of the World War II Normandy landings. Afterwards, Henry offered up silent thanks to the genius of Stephen Spielberg that enabled Nina to forget for three and a half hours that the father of her children had decided to leave the family home.

★   ★   ★

On Saturday, Henry went into town to do a food shop while Nina said she would catch up on some work. When he came home her eyes were swollen. She told him she'd been invited to go out for a drink in the evening with Alison and Crystal. Henry said a little too enthusiastically that he thought that was a splendid idea. He couldn't understand why Nina, such a natural fighter, appeared to be so supine about Robbie's defection and Stephen Castleford's lies. Perhaps her friends would convince her to let him go round and confront the man. In the afternoon he went out into the garden to vent his frustrations on the leaves. When he came in he found Nina asleep in front of the television.

They had an early supper and Nina went off about eight. At least she'd made an effort with her appearance, which was a good sign, Henry thought. Throughout the evening he kept the phone by his side but no one rang.

He heard Nina stumble up the stairs at one. Half an hour later he heard her being sick in the bathroom. I have to do something, he thought. Tomorrow, I must do something.

And so, at ten the next morning, with Nina still safely in bed, he rang Maddie.

She sounded half asleep. 'Maddie here.'

'I'm sorry, Maddie,' he said. 'Have I woken you?'

'It's all right. It's way too late anyway. How are things?'

He thought for a moment. Nina had told him to tell no one and already he had told his mother. He asked, 'Are you free next weekend? Can you come up?'

'I think so. Dad, are you all right? What's happened? Is anything wrong?'

'Yes,' Henry said, unable to help himself. 'Everything is wrong. Do you remember a teacher called Stephen Castleford?' 'Mr Castleford? Of course I do. We were all in love with him. Nina was *obsessed* with him.'

'Was she?' He wished he hadn't heard that. 'Did he ever take advantage of that?'

'Despite her very best efforts, I gather he behaved impeccably.'

'I see.'

'Dad? Why are we talking about him?'

Henry lowered his voice. 'Nina doesn't want anyone to know,' he said, 'but I have no idea what to do. I'm out of my depth here. Perhaps you can talk to her.'

'About Mr Castleford? Has she been seeing *Mr Castleford?*'

'She says she hasn't. He says she has. Of course I believe her but he seems to have convinced Robbie . . . And now she's agreed to stay with me every weekend so Robbie can see the children and tomorrow Robbie is moving in with Clive and Nina seems to be . . . just accepting it all.'

'I'll come up next weekend. You'd better not tell Nina. We haven't spoken since Christmas.'

'Why not?'

'We had a stupid argument. We're both waiting for the other to ring. Look, I can't talk now, I'm going out in half an hour. It's just as well you woke me. I'll see you on Friday. I'll get a taxi from the station'

'That might be better,' Henry agreed. 'Do you think I should tell Nina you're coming?'

'Don't say a word. I'll handle the explanations when I arrive.'

'All right. I'd better let you get on. Are you going anywhere nice today?'

'I don't know. Possibly. I'll see you Friday.'

★   ★   ★

Nina came down in her dressing-gown at midday and asked weakly for coffee.

Henry reached for the kettle. 'I heard you last night,' he said. 'Have you been sick again this morning?'

'Oh God, I'm sorry.' Nina put her head on the table. 'I shouldn't drink shots any more. I can't take them.'

The sound of the door knocker echoing loudly throughout the house surprised them both. Nina raised her head and stared at Henry. He said gently, 'Don't get your hopes up. I'll go.'

It wasn't Robbie. He could hear William outside, remonstrating with someone as he reached the door. When he opened it, Ellen stepped forward. 'Henry, I'm sorry to gate crash you like this. William's in a foul mood and I suggested I could walk to my house from here so that William can stay and talk to you. Do you have guests with you today?'

'I've got my daughter, Nina, here . . . '

Nina!' William called, 'Beautiful Nina! Ellen, you have to meet her before you go. Where is she, Henry? In the kitchen?'

'Yes but . . . '

It was too late. William had already charged ahead and Henry could only follow along with Ellen. He found Nina submitting herself to one of William's bear hugs while protesting that she didn't look beautiful at all. 'I actually have a pretty amazing hangover.'

'You and your mother,' William told her, 'are the only women I have ever known who can still look beautiful when ill. This is Ellen, and I'm sure she's the same but I have yet to see her with a hangover so the jury's still out.'

Ellen smiled at Nina. 'You're Henry's younger daughter, aren't you? It's nice to meet you.' She glanced at her watch. 'I'd love to stay but my family are coming over at one. We're all going out to lunch. My granddaughter is about to go to Paris for three months to be an au pair.'

'I'm sorry,' Nina said. 'I don't believe you're old enough to have an au pair for a granddaughter.'

'Thank you for saying so but it's definitely true. William's in a sulk because he wants to come out with us and I won't let him. I don't see enough of my son and my granddaughter and it's an important family occasion. And now I

270

really must go . . . '

'I'm happy to drive you home,' William said.

'Certainly not,' Ellen said. 'After the meal we ate last night I need the exercise. Goodbye, everyone!'

William stared after her and sighed. 'She's already forgotten about me,' he complained. 'She can't wait to see her family.' He glanced across at Henry's joint of beef on top of the stove and said hopefully, 'That looks a nice bit of meat, Henry.'

'Well, you can't have any,' Henry said. 'That's for Nina and me.'

'Poor Uncle William!' Nina said. 'Let him stay. I'm not sure I can eat anything today anyway.' She took a glass tumbler from the draining board and filled it with water.

'The last time I saw you,' William told her, 'you were sitting at this table like some serene Madonna, feeding a baby.'

Nina sat down again. 'She walks and talks and goes to nursery now.'

'I hate how time flies,' William said. 'She was a lovely little baby. Where is she?'

Nina stared at her glass. 'She and her sister are with their father.'

Henry poured boiling water into the cafetière and watched William take a seat next to Nina. If there was one thing William liked more than talking about his personal problems it was listening to someone else's personal problems. Henry remembered a supper party they'd had once with William and a couple who weren't getting on well. William had started asking

271

questions and the meal had degenerated into an analyst's couch session. It had been very uncomfortable and neither he nor Marianne had been surprised when the pair announced their separation soon after. Later, William said he'd attempted to lance the marital boil and Marianne had told William that he couldn't lance a boil with a pickaxe.

Perhaps William remembered that too. He waited for at least three seconds before asking, 'Has there been a falling-out?'

Nina shrugged. 'You could say that.'

William gave a sympathetic nod. 'I take it you have a lover in the wings?'

'For God's sake,' Henry exclaimed, 'that is completely out of order.'

'I'm sorry,' William said. 'But I've known Nina all her life and I can't believe any man would leave her unless he thought she had someone else.'

'Thank you for the compliment,' Nina said, 'if it *is* a compliment. He's not a lover. He's a stalker.'

'Really? How very interesting.' William leant forward. 'Tell me more.'

'Don't tell him,' Henry said. 'He'll bring it out as an anecdote for one of his lectures.'

William beamed at Henry. 'That coffee smells wonderful.'

Henry, with great ill-grace, put two mugs down on the table.

'So tell me, Nina,' William prompted, 'how did you meet the stalker?'

Nina tightened the belt of her dressing-gown

and pushed back her hair. 'He used to teach me Geography at school. For most of my last year I had a monumental crush on him. Nothing happened of course, but he was very beautiful.'

A few moments ago, Henry had been ready to throttle William. Now he almost loved him. Nina was talking at last and the fact that she could mention her past infatuation so easily was proof beyond doubt that it hadn't lingered into the present. He put the cafetiére on the table. He dared not look at his daughter. He took out the bag of sprouts and put them on his chopping board.

William was fully engaged. 'And I take it you met him again? What's he like now? Bald, fat and sweaty?'

'No. He's still very good looking. I bumped into him in the autumn. He and his family live round the corner from us. He was very pleased to see me.'

William raised an eyebrow. 'I bet he was.'

'To be fair, I was pleased to see *him*. I was on my way to pick up Chloe from nursery. I told him he should come round sometime and meet my girls. He came over the next evening and he was sweet with them and nice to me . . . '

'I bet he was,' William said again. 'I can imagine the chemistry zinging its way round your kitchen.'

Henry cast a furtive glance at Nina and was relieved to see she had not taken umbrage.

'In my defence,' she said, 'Robbie is hardly ever at home. He's a complete workaholic. It was flattering to get some masculine attention for

273

once, that's all. I didn't want anything more. And besides, I knew he was married with children.'

'Fair enough,' William said. 'It's all very understandable. So I imagine he starts increasing his visits and . . . What's his name?'

'Stephen — Stephen Castleford.'

'So I imagine poor Stephen was soon hopelessly smitten.'

Nina poured out the coffee. 'By the time I realized what was happening, he'd convinced himself we were madly in love. He came over on Thursday evening. I managed to ring poor Dad who came over straightaway. Basically, Stephen refused to go until he talked to Robbie and when Robbie arrived, he told him a stream of lies and . . . '

'Robbie believed him?' William nodded. 'I do have this problem with infidelity.'

Nina looked at him sharply. 'I didn't say I *was* unfaithful!'

'I know. I'm talking about Robbie. I'm always amazed when someone will throw away a happy domestic life because of a momentary error.'

'William,' Henry said, 'the man was telling *lies*.'

'In a way, that's irrelevant. As far as Robbie's concerned, they are true. All I'm saying is that there are far worse things than infidelity.' He smiled at Nina. 'I remember observing you and your family last time I saw you. It was obvious that Robbie was very proud of you and the children; and yet here he is, prepared to destroy his family simply because he thinks you succumbed to the crazed advances of your old

274

Geography teacher. Shall I tell you what to do?'
He stopped to take a sip of his coffee.

Nina nodded. 'Be my guest.'

'Leave Robbie alone. Don't ring him, don't
text him. Don't apologize. Leave him alone and
he'll soon want to talk. When you see him, be
cool, be calm. I guarantee he'll come back to
you.'

'Are you serious?'

'You're talking to an expert.'

Nina considered him thoughtfully. 'Your
girlfriend seemed nice.'

'She is. Her only fault is that she has a
problem with her priorities.'

Nina laughed and stood up. 'I'm going to have
a shower. Thank you for the pep-talk.'

The two men watched Nina pick up her coffee
and leave the kitchen. William glanced at Henry.
'You're taking forever with those sprouts. Let me
do them. Are we having Yorkshire pudding?'

'Of course,' William said.

'Perfect. Is there a pudding?'

★   ★   ★

'Apple crumble.' Henry walked over to the door,
glanced up at the stairs and came back. 'Do you
really think it will be all right?'

'You've always said he loves her. She's a
brilliant mother, he's a great father. He'd be mad
not to.'

'That's not a definite yes.'

'Nothing's definite where affairs of the heart
are concerned. He needs to take the long view.

275

She had a brief fling with a neurotic teacher. So what?'

'But she didn't,' Henry said. 'The man's a fantasist. You heard her.'

'I did,' Walter said. 'Robbie was never at home. She met up with a man she'd always fancied. He fancied *her*. Think about it, Henry. Of course she slept with him. You know that.'

And the terrible thing was, Henry thought, he did.

23

Of all the things Maddie didn't want to do that day, top of the list had to be going to a family party in Epsom. She still felt shaken by her meeting with Freddy and her disastrous date with Walter. And then, last night, Gregory had come over for supper and arrived at eight with two bottles of red wine and some disquieting news..

'I've told Minty I didn't want to see her again,' he said. He stood outside Maddie's kitchen, legs akimbo, hands clutching the necks of the bottles. He looked like he wanted to hurl them across the flat.

Maddie took them from him. 'Let's have a drink,' she said.

Knowing Gregory's appetite, she had bought crisps and hummus as a prelude to her pasta dish. In the sitting room she sat watching him dig in while she poured the wine.

'We were having supper together . . . ' he began.

'Where were you having supper?'

'Does it matter?'

'I'm trying to picture the scene.'

'You've never been to Minty's flat so how can you picture it?'

'Never mind,' Maddie said. 'You were at Minty's flat. Carry on.'

'We were talking about children. I said I'd like

three boys and possibly one daughter. Minty said two of either would be enough for her and then she said she couldn't even think of babies for at least ten years, given her career and . . . '

'What *is* her career?'

'I've told you already, she's a currency trader.'

'I have no idea what that means.'

'She's a technical analyst of emerging markets.' Gregory took a gulp of his wine and threw an impatient glance at her. 'Do you want me to explain that too?'

'No, thank you, it's clear as day. So, were you talking about having children together or was it just about more abstract preferences?'

'I can't remember how it started . . . I think it was because Minty's brother had just told the family he and his wife were pregnant again. We just got talking about it.'

'So it was a hypothetical discussion and you got upset when Minty said she couldn't think of babies yet.'

'Well,' Gregory said, 'that's what started it.'

'So, basically, you fell out because Minty doesn't want to have babies yet? Why *should* she have babies now? She's only twenty-five. You're lucky. You're a man. You can wait forever if you like.'

'I know all that. I don't mind waiting ten years. It's just that when she said that, I realized I didn't want to wait ten years *with her*. I'd imagined us starting a family quite soon. But if we don't, what will we talk about for the next ten years?'

'Gregory, when have you ever worried about

what to talk about?'

'I don't with *you*. But if Minty and I stay together — without children — for another decade, I think it could get quite difficult . . . '

'What do any of us talk about? You'll grumble about your work, you'll complain about your family, you'll gossip about friends, you'll wonder whether to move in together. You don't worry about *conversations*. If you like being with her . . . '

'I do,' Gregory said, 'but I don't like it *enough*.'

'Did you tell Minty that?'

'Of course I did.'

'Poor Minty,' Maddie said.

On the one hand she rather admired Gregory's certainty and resolution. Hadn't she been appalled by Amy's readiness to accept a man she almost certainly didn't love? On the other hand, Gregory's cold-blooded decision to end the relationship after a hypothetical discussion about the future seemed overly impulsive. What kept Maddie awake that night until the early hours of the morning was that a part of her — an extremely unpleasant part — was heartened by the demise of Gregory's romance. Once again she and Gregory were single together. Normal service had been resumed.

★ ★ ★

On Sunday morning she had forty short minutes to prepare for Epsom. She turned up at Guy's

279

door with moments to spare in a black jersey dress and her ankle-length boots. 'Will I do?' she asked.

'You look perfect,' Guy said, reaching for his car keys, 'if a little funereal.' He looked pretty good himself in a charcoal-coloured suit and matching polo shirt. 'Mind you, so do I. At least we'll go with Aunt Emily's colour scheme.'

Guy's mother and aunt had married within three months of each other. Both couples lived in Epsom and today there was to be a party to celebrate their fortieth wedding anniversaries. Guy had said it would be dire and had asked Maddie to go with him. For some reason, which she could no longer remember, Maddie had thought it would be fun. There was also the fact that she owed Guy quite a lot of favours. Guy didn't much like being on his own and if ever he was in and Leo was out, he'd invariably invite Maddie to keep him company, so he had made her supper far more times than she had made supper for him.

Now, as Guy drove them through south London and out into Surrey, Maddie began to have serious second thoughts. 'Do your parents think we're a couple?' she asked. 'You didn't tell them we were a couple?'

'I simply asked if I could bring you with me. They'll be planning a spring wedding, I expect.'

'Guy, I'm not going to pretend to be your girlfriend . . . '

'You don't have to do anything. Your presence will stop my relatives inviting me to dinner with all their single friends for at least six months.

We'll eat the buffet lunch, we'll toast the happy couples and we'll be home by five.'

'Will there be loads of people there?'

'You'll meet my sister Jenny, who's married to Robert, and my Aunt Emily and Uncle Francis. They have three children, Mary and John, with whom I have nothing in common, and their youngest, Martin, who's home from university. I haven't seen him since he was fifteen but he was a nice boy.'

'I'll never remember all this,' Maddie said. She folded her arms tightly in front of her. '*And* it's raining, it's always raining now. I hate this country sometimes.' She caught Guy smiling at her and said, 'What is it? What have I said?'

'You seem a little out of sorts, that's all.'

'I had a call from my father this morning. There've been huge dramas at home. Nina's had an affair and now Robbie's moving out. I can't believe she could be so stupid.'

'Perhaps she was unhappy with Robbie.'

'She's had no reason to be. He's a wonderful man who's always loved her. They have two beautiful children and a lovely house in Ipswich. She has everything going for her and she's just thrown it all away. She's been so pathetic and self-indulgent. I suspected something was going on at Christmas but she wouldn't tell me anything.'

'I'm not surprised.'

'What does *that* mean?'

Guy shrugged. 'I was brought up in a religious household. I've always found self-righteous anger a little difficult to deal with.'

281

It took Maddie a few moments to unearth the criticism embedded in this comment. 'Are you saying I'm self-righteous?'

'I recognise the vocabulary.'

'I think you're being grossly unfair.'

'Perhaps you're right. I'm sorry.'

Maddie scowled and looked out of the window. They were passing Epsom's racecourse and she could hear Guy's fingers tapping against the steering wheel. They'd been tapping ever since they arrived in Epsom. He was nervous. She'd never seen him nervous before.

'I know I'm in a foul mood,' she said. 'I promise I'll behave at the party.'

He glanced across at her. 'I never doubted it,' he said.

★   ★   ★

As a party venue, Aunt Emily's house had certain glaring deficiencies. The hall was dark and gloomy with a cavernous wardrobe into which Maddie's thin coat disappeared. In the sitting-room, the furniture had been pushed back against the coffee-coloured walls and the room was lit by one excessively bright central bulb in a white plastic lampshade. The walls were bereft of paintings apart from two lurid images of the crucifixion.

The house was crowded with Guy's family and Maddie was passed from one person to another like a prize trophy. Aunt Emily was thin and earnest with prominent teeth. She introduced Maddie to Guy's sister Jenny, whose brown hair was held back by an orange Alice band. Jenny's husband, Robert, had a huge greyish mole on his chin which Maddie tried not to look at. He told Maddie twice that it was a relief to see Guy with a pretty woman friend at last. The first time he did so, Maddie replied that Guy had many pretty woman friends; the second time she just smiled. She did a lot of smiling. Eventually she murmured to Uncle Francis that she needed the Ladies and he told her to go upstairs where she could get a nice view of the garden.

He had told her the bathroom was at the end of the corridor but she stopped outside the second door, frozen by a tune from her childhood which brought back a crystal-clear memory of her mother dancing round the kitchen. Maddie found herself lip-synching the words to 'If I Were a Carpenter' like a karaoke veteran. She couldn't help herself. The music urged her on. She knocked on the door.

Someone called out, 'Come in,' and inside, she saw a young man sitting on a narrow bed, his duvet covered in sheets of paper. He was slight, with a fringe that almost covered his eyes.

'I'm sorry to intrude,' she said, 'but Tim Hardin was my mother's favourite singer. Other children learnt nursery rhymes but my sister and I could chant every line of this. It's so nice to hear him again.'

'Your mother has great taste,' he said.

'She's dead, but you're right. She did.' She saw him glance down at the paper on his lap. 'I'm sorry. I shouldn't interrupt you — I'll leave

283

you in peace. I take it you don't like family parties?'

He stared at her. 'I've been told to stay up here. I'm allowed to come down for the meal.'

'You're not serious.'

He shrugged. 'Apparently I might contaminate the proceedings. Last night I revealed to my family that I am a homosexual.' He emphasised each syllable of the word with an ironic flourish. 'They want me to see a psychiatrist.' He pushed back his fringe. 'Who are you?'

'I'm a friend of Guy. Are you Martin? You must be his cousin.'

He nodded. 'I like Guy. I don't see him very often. He hardly ever comes home.'

'I'm beginning to see why,' Maddie said. 'I can't say I . . . ' She stopped as another voice began to sing. 'Your playlist is incredible: Harry Chapin!'

The young man laughed. 'Did your mother like him too?'

'I don't know but my ex-boyfriend did. It's 'Cat's Cradle', isn't it? He used to play it on his guitar. He said that if ever he had a son he would play it every week to remind him how to be a good father. I *love* your playlist!'

There was another knock on the door and Guy appeared. 'I might have known I'd find you here,' he said to Maddie. 'I bet it's a lot more fun than the party downstairs.' He walked across to his cousin. 'I hear you've been banished,' he said. 'Give me a hug.'

★ ★ ★

284

In retrospect, Maddie should have known Guy would say something. She'd noticed an air of suppressed energy about him as soon as he entered Martin's bedroom.

The three of them went downstairs together and Guy and Maddie kept up a conversation with Martin with such fierce determination that no one dared to come near them. When Uncle Francis clapped his hands and announced that guests could help themselves to egg sandwiches whenever they liked, Guy stood up and clapped *his* hands.

'Before we all attack the generous feast laid out for us,' he said, 'I feel it's incumbent on me to say a few words about the two happy couples we are celebrating today. My parents and my uncle are examples to us all, which may explain why I'm an atheist who's never married.' He beamed at the audience, some of whom responded with slightly uncomfortable laughter. 'I've been encouraged by someone far braver and younger than me to let you in on a secret.' He directed a hand at Maddie who stood a foot or so away from him. 'You've all been very kind to Maddie today . . . ' The atmosphere was electric with anticipation. Guy's mother could barely contain her excitement. 'I suspect that some of you have wondered about the two of us. My brother-in-law asked me directly if I was going to marry her. Well, Robert, the truth is, I can't marry Maddie because I'm already committed to someone else. Leo and I have been together for well over a year now and — with no disrespect to Maddie — he is the one who should be here with

285

me today. Now I can see you're all dying to fall on those egg sandwiches so, without further ado, please raise your glasses to my father and mother and Uncle Francis and Aunt Emily!'

The silence was deafening until Guy's sister stepped forward, directed a furious glance at Guy, and said loudly, 'To the happy couples!'

During the somewhat ragged response, Guy's mother fought her way through the guests to get to Guy. She no longer looked like a fairytale granny from one of Megan's picture books. The twinkling blue eyes had become small blocks of ice and the smiling mouth was a pursed line of fury. 'Thank you for ruining our party,' she said, 'and thank you for mocking everything we hold dear. I am ashamed to have you as my son. You are disgusting. I can't bear to even look at you. I want you to leave at once.'

Guy was very pale but he nodded. 'It's my pleasure to do so,' he said.

His mother stared at Maddie. 'I don't understand what you're doing here,' she said. 'But I do hope you'll be going back with Guy.'

'Goodbye,' Maddie said to her. 'I'm so very glad you're not my mother.'

★ ★ ★

In the car going back, they were silent. Finally, Maddie reached across and put her hand on Guy's knee. 'You were right about me earlier,' she said. 'I *was* self-righteous. If I'm ever like that again, will you remind me of today?'

24

On Tuesday evening, Henry had a glass of whisky after work in preparation for a conversation with his mother. This time, he knew, he had to maintain his resolution however much she might try to persuade him not to. He placed his diary, his pen and his phone on the table in a neat row. Then he sat down, took a deep breath and picked up the phone.

'Granty . . . ' he began.

'Oh, Henry, I've been expecting you to call. What happened? Did you talk to Nina?'

'Yes and she's all right. We've had a very . . . productive weekend. William came over and gave her some excellent advice . . . '

'William gave her advice? You might as well ask Henry VIII for marital guidance! What was he doing there? I thought Nina didn't want anyone to know?'

'She doesn't but William dropped in and could sense something was wrong and, actually, he was very kind and sympathetic. He told her to let Robbie have time to calm down and I think he's right.'

'So do I,' said Granty. 'But she shouldn't wait too long. Remember what I told you about cement?'

'Yes, I remember every word you said and I shall keep your advice in mind. Now, I need to talk to you about something else and I very much hope you'll understand.' He glanced wistfully at his empty whisky glass. 'I don't think — given everything that's happening in the family at the moment — that I can go off on a jaunt to Edinburgh with you in three weeks. I know you're looking forward to it and I would like to see Louise again but . . .'

'I've told you already I can't go,' Granty said.

'What?' Henry was dumbfounded. 'No, you haven't!'

There was a long pause. William could almost hear his mother's brain cells whirring.

'I remember now, I told your brother!'

Henry took off his glasses and rubbed his eyes. 'Which brother?'

'Edward, of course! I told Edward. So now I shall have to tell you. Darling, we have to cancel the trip.'

Henry sighed. 'That's fine,' he said.

'I've been talking to Elizabeth and she's very depressed at the moment which is so unlike her. I've promised to go down for a week and it has to be then. Don't ask me why, Elizabeth did tell me but I can't remember.'

'Why is she depressed? It doesn't sound like her at all.'

'There are many reasons. Her daughter-in-law's driving her mad and has actually suggested that after her last fall, it might be better if she and Luke came to live with her.'

'I'm sure the offer was kindly meant.'

'Of course it was, that's the trouble. If only she was grasping and mean it would be so easy to deal with her. Kindness is something else. I knew

I'd get there eventually! That's why I have to go down then! Luke and Karen are away for that week so we won't have to go over there for supper.'

'I'm sure you'll be a tonic for Elizabeth. Do you want me to drive you down there?'

'I'm still able to catch a train, Henry, but it's sweet of you to offer. What I *do* want is a temporary home for poor Ivan and if you could come over and collect him nearer the time I'd be very grateful. In fact, Henry — let me just check my calendar — If you come on the fifteenth you'd be able to see Edward. He's invited himself to stay for a few days.'

'Has he? Why?' Edward had retired to Avignon with his second wife and since then he and Françoise had only returned to England once — for Marianne's funeral — a decision, Edward had assured Henry gravely, that indicated the depth of their affection for her. Edward was convinced that England was bad for his digestion and every year he put on his Christmas card the same message: 'My digestion continues to do well.'

'I told him I couldn't do France this year,' Granty said. 'Of course I *could* do it but I can never understand a word Françoise says and it's such a long way. You will come and see him, won't you? And you'll look after Ivan?'

'I'd be happy to. Well, if that's all . . . '

'I'd love to chat,' Granty told him, 'but I have a great deal to organize. Are you sure I shouldn't ring Nina?'

'I'm very sure.'

'All right, I'll keep quiet. Keep me informed of developments!'

Henry put the phone down and stared for a long time at his empty glass. 'Sod it,' he murmured and went over to the drinks cabinet.

★ ★ ★

Nina had told Henry that she didn't want him to ring her. 'I promise I'll call you sometime during the week,' she'd said, 'but I want to do it when I'm fit and ready to talk.'

He had to wait till Thursday evening. When she rang he was relieved that she sounded quite animated.

'I had a call from Maddie tonight,' she said.

'Did you?' Henry took a seat at the table. 'That was nice. Did you say anything about . . . ?'

'I wasn't going to but . . . We'd had a row at Christmas and she rang to apologize. She was great, actually. We had a long talk and I suggested she come and join us this weekend. She'll ring when she's on the train. I said we'd pick her up from the station. That's all right, isn't it?'

'Of course it is. I'm glad she'll be here.'

'Funnily enough, she said more or less what William did, and . . . Dad, you'll never guess!'

'Is it Robbie? Has he been in touch?'

'Uncle William was right. Robbie rang me last night and I was very calm. He wants to see me on Saturday afternoon. He says Clive will look after the girls. He suggested we meet at home. That's a good sign, don't you think?'

'It sounds as if it might be,' Henry said. 'How are the girls? Are they all right?'

'They're fine. I've just told them Daddy's working away from home. To be honest, he works so hard every week, they hardly notice he's gone. They're looking forward to seeing him tomorrow.'

'And what about Castleford? He hasn't bothered you again?'

'If he does, I'll call the police. By the way, I've told Colette.'

Henry blinked. 'Have you? Why?'

'She rings every week to talk to the girls. Megan told her I'd been crying and . . . I told her. She offered to come up and visit Stephen. She said she'd be very happy to tell him what she thought of him. She was quite serious. I was very touched but it did make me want to laugh. Can you imagine Colette knocking on his door and laying into him?'

'No,' Henry said, 'I'm afraid I can't.'

★   ★   ★

Henry had prided himself in the last few months on his steadiness in the face of disappointment: his hopes of romance with Ellen had been dashed and he'd been humiliated by Becky's husband. Yet now he was aware that even the slightest thing could throw him off balance. Every time the phone rang, he jumped. On Friday evening at Manningtree Station, he watched Nina leap from the car when Maddie came out of the station. He saw his girls embrace

291

and he felt his eyes smart with tears. They'd always been so different: Nina, so confident with boys, so careless about schoolwork; Maddie, ambitious and much more studious. The one positive result of this whole appalling episode was that Nina could see that when something bad happened, her family would be beside her. He drove home with Maddie and Nina in the back. Maddie described some awful party she'd attended with her neighbour's family and Henry said nothing. He just enjoyed listening to the two of them talking non-stop. He wished Marianne was sitting in the front with him, listening to their daughters.

On Saturday they had an early lunch — Nina ate nothing — and then Nina went off, giving a thumbs up as she drove out into the road. She'd washed her hair, spent ages on her make-up and sprayed herself liberally with Maddie's perfume.

'Let's go for a walk,' Maddie said. 'I don't know about you but I can't face staying in and looking at the clock every five minutes.'

It was one of those February days that encourage fantasies of emigration. It had been raining all morning. At least now it was only cold and damp. Henry and Maddie wrapped scarves round their necks and set off up to the high street, arm in arm and maintaining a brisk pace.

'I can't believe,' Henry said, 'that Robbie could think it right to walk out on Nina and his girls. Even if Nina did have a fling with the Castleford man, it would be inexcusable to break up the family. How could he bear to do it? He's always adored her.'

292

'I know,' Maddie said, 'but from his perspective, he's worked day in and day out to make a good life for Nina and the children and . . . '

'You see, I don't buy that,' Henry said. 'I've known many workaholics in my life and they all say the same thing: 'I'm doing this for the family.' I don't believe it. I never do. If you love your family, you spend time with them. You don't miss the best years of your life together trying to increase your bank balance. I'm not saying Robbie isn't a good father — he's brilliant when he's *there* — but he loves his work and he loves making money. You never hear Nina yearning for a bigger house or a fancy holiday. It's Robbie, it's always Robbie. And meanwhile she spends evening after evening sitting on her own and . . . '

'Dad,' Maddie said, 'you think Nina had an affair, don't you?'

'I think it's possible,' Henry said. 'Don't you?'

'I did,' Maddie said. 'But now — I can imagine her flirting with him, enjoying his attention, but — when I rang her a few days ago she kept insisting Stephen was a fantasist. She was appalled by what he told Robbie. She loves Robbie. She's always loved Robbie.'

'Let's keep our fingers crossed that they sort it all out,' Henry said. 'Shall we . . . ?' His words died as a familiar face loomed in front of him. As the man walked past, Henry exhaled slightly and then he froze again as the man called out, 'Excuse me!'

Henry stopped reluctantly and turned as

Becky's husband, Alex, came up to them. His eyes flittered between Henry and Maddie. 'I want to say sorry,' he said. 'I'm afraid my jealousy got the better of me. I should have known better than to think you were trying to seduce my wife.'

It sounded more like an accusation than an apology. Henry, staring into Alex's glittering eyes, knew exactly what he was trying to do. He assumed Maddie was a lady friend and he wanted to embarrass him. How had someone as sweet as Becky ever got involved with a man like this?

Beside him, Maddie laughed. 'Wow, Dad, that's impressive! You've created a jealous husband! You have my total respect!'

Alex was visibly taken aback. He managed a reluctant laugh before giving Maddie a dazzling smile. 'He deserves it,' he agreed. 'I've been a fool. I have to say it's almost been worth it to meet *you*. Do you live round here?'

'No,' Maddie said. 'I've come up for the weekend. I live in London.'

'That's a pity,' Alex said. 'I do hope I bump into you again.'

Henry said nothing until he and Maddie had turned off the high street into the narrow lane that led to the river. 'I do not believe that man,' he exclaimed. 'He was trying to flirt with you in front of my eyes!'

'I know,' Maddie said. 'He was rather good-looking in a suppressed fire sort of way.' She grinned at Henry. 'So *did* you try to seduce his wife?'

'That,' Henry said, 'is not even slightly funny.'
'How did you meet her?'
'It's your fault,' Henry told her. 'I was trying to do something to report back to you. I joined a book group. I had to read the whole of *Middlemarch*, which I rather enjoyed, by the way. Have you read it?'

Maddie nodded. 'I read it at university. Don't you hate Casaubon?'

'I felt sorry for him. He was out of his depth with Dorothea. She was cleverer than him and he knew it and he couldn't cope. I know the feeling.'

'No, you don't! Can we get back to the subject of the jealous man's wife, please?'

'Becky is in the group. I walked her home one evening and that horrible man drew up in his car and was deliberately offensive. He accused me of being an old-age pensioner . . . '

'That's an interesting accusation.'

'He also suggested I had designs on her. He's a very unpleasant man and I can't understand why she puts up with him. It was all very upsetting.' He sighed. 'In the light of everything that's happened with Nina, it seems rather unimportant. Everything seems unimportant. I think, if it's all right with you, I'll suspend my dating campaign for the time being.'

'I feel the same,' Maddie said. 'We'll wait until Nina and Robbie are back to normal.' She glanced at her watch. 'How do you think it's going?'

★ ★ ★

Six o'clock came and went, and still there was no sign of Nina. While Maddie and Henry prepared the supper they had an exhaustive and ultimately fruitless discussion as to whether this was good or bad. Finally, they heard her car and Henry said, 'Here we go!' He took a bottle of Sauvignon out of the fridge while Maddie put three glasses on the table.

They heard the front door close and Nina call out, 'I'm back!' And then there she was, glancing first at Henry and then at Maddie. 'I should have rung you,' she said. 'But the kitchen needed cleaning and then Robbie collected the girls and they wanted us both to bath them.'

'Sit down, sit down,' Henry said, pouring out the wine. 'You look exhausted.'

'Thanks, Dad.' She almost fell onto a chair. Maddie sat down beside her. Henry stationed himself against the dresser. There were two alternative scenarios buzzing in his head: Nina and Robbie clearing away cups and cutlery, bathing the children together, and then the other: Nina on her own, washing the floor, scrubbing the sink, trying not to cry.

'I should have told him the truth straightaway,' Nina said. 'If I'd told him the truth, it might have been all right. It was that blue popper dress that did it. I should have told him the truth.'

Maddie frowned. 'I don't understand . . . '

Nina sighed. 'Stephen told Robbie I wore my blue popper dress on the evening he came over and . . . Robbie went through my wardrobe last weekend. He couldn't find it. It was the first thing he asked me today. So I told him. I should

296

have told him straight away.' She stared straight ahead, her eyes wide and tragic.

'Nina,' Maddie prompted, 'are you saying you *did* have an affair with Stephen?'

'No,' Nina shook her head fiercely. 'I did not have an affair. I never had an affair.'

'Well then . . . ' Maddie murmured, 'I don't see . . . '

'Robbie is always working!' Nina pushed back her chair and stood up, throwing out her arms. 'I didn't mind when his mother lived round the corner. She'd come over a lot and I'd go out and see friends. It's different now. Every evening, I put the children to bed, I clear up the kitchen and there's no one to talk to.

'And then I meet Stephen and he starts calling round and he tells me I'm beautiful and he listens to my problems and he's an adult and he's company. I like company. He gives me compliments and he looks at me and he listens and that's nice. And then one evening he comes round with some wine and Robbie has rung me to say that he's sorry but he's staying in London because the meeting's run on and Stephen and I drink the wine and he kisses me and tells me he's mad about me and we end up having sex on the floor and as soon as it happens I know it's a mistake and I ask him to go and next morning I throw the dress in the dustbin because I can't bear to even have it in the house. It wasn't an affair. It was one short, stupid fuck, excuse my language, Dad, but that was all it was. And then he keeps coming round and he gets more intense and it begins to get scary and I should have told

297

Robbie because I knew even then that Stephen would do something and he did and now he's ruined us forever.'

'But Nina,' Maddie said, 'if you told Robbie all this, surely he can see that . . . '

'Do you know something?' Nina said. 'I told him I loved him. He said he loves me. He cried in front of me. He cried.'

'So in that case,' Maddie persisted, 'surely he . . . '

'He can't do it! He says it's in his head. He's tried to get it out but he can't.'

'This is ridiculous.' Henry took his car keys from their place on the dresser. 'I'll go and see him. How can he break up his family over one mistake? It's not rational. I'll go and see him. I'll go and see him now.'

'There's no point, Dad.' Nina pushed back her hair and then pulled a sodden tissue from her sleeve and blew her nose. 'Robbie knows it's not rational. He knows I still love him. But you were there that night. Stephen did such a great job. He painted a perfect picture and now it's stuck in Robbie's head. There's nothing you can do. There's nothing any of us can do. It's over.' She began to cry. 'I've lost Robbie.'

Henry took her in his arms and she cried into his shoulder. He glanced across at Maddie, looking for help, for some sign of a solution and all he could see was the same helplessness staring straight back.

25

The rain was relentless. That was how newscasters and weather people kept describing the biblical rain that was flooding sundry parts of the country. When Maddie stomped down the road that morning, with the hood of her parka pushed forward onto her nose, she saw two broken umbrellas lying on the pavement like corpses.

This was the week in which Gregory and Maddie were beginning the year's marketing campaign and a recruitment drive. As the morning wore on, the carpet of Gregory's sitting room became covered with advertising materials, flyers ready for distribution in the relevant areas and new announcements for their website. In the afternoon they would plough through the many CVs sent to them by hopeful applicants. At the back of Maddie's mind, sitting in her subconscious like a present waiting to be unwrapped, was the seed of an idea that she couldn't quite focus on. This had happened to her before and she knew she could only wait for it to reveal itself to her.

Gregory's mother had told him about a brilliant new diet she'd been following: five days of normal eating interspersed with two days of fasting. On fasting days, she said, you should eat only five hundred calories and the weight drops off and the brain becomes infinitely sharper.

Gregory thought that both he and Maddie could do with sharper brains so she'd agreed to an experimental fortnight. Today, she showed him with some smugness the contents of her lunch box: a hard-boiled egg and a tomato. Gregory had a large carton of cottage cheese. He was going to eat a quarter of it now, a quarter tonight and the rest on Thursday.

'That's very boring,' Maddie said. 'For *my* supper tonight I shall eat half a tin of sardines and a small low-fat yoghourt.'

'That's even more boring,' Gregory said.

Maddie bit into her egg and was compelled to admit that without mayonnaise her lunch was pretty dull. She had another bite and stared thoughtfully at Gregory. 'If you were living with someone,' she said, 'and she told you she'd slept with someone else and she wished she hadn't, what would be your reaction?'

Gregory gazed out of the window with narrowed eyes and thought for a few moments. 'I would say,' he said, ' "What have I done to make you need to sleep with someone else?" '

'Really?' Maddie gazed at him with incredulity. 'That's amazing. It's so sensitive and thoughtful and considerate and . . . unbelievable. There's no way you would ever say anything like that.'

'You may be right. It's what Minty told me I should say.'

'I'm sorry,' Maddie said, 'I don't understand.' She thought for a moment. 'Are you telling me Minty was unfaithful to you?'

'It was in the first week of December. She said

it was because I neglected her.'

'So *that's* why you broke up with her?'

'Of course not.' Gregory looked affronted. 'I told you why we split up. It was a rational decision.'

Maddie put her lunch box down on the table. It never failed to amaze her that Gregory, who was so clever and knowledgeable about so many things, could have so little insight into the workings of his own mind. 'Gregory,' she said, 'it is perfectly obvious that there was nothing remotely rational about your decision to leave Minty. You've been in a permanent good mood ever since you've met her. She made you happy. I couldn't understand why you'd leave her. And now it's crystal clear. You were jealous and hurt and that is why you left.'

'That's rubbish,' Gregory said, 'and I don't want to talk about it.'

'Fair enough,' Maddie said, 'but let me say one last thing. Years ago when Nina and Robbie started seeing each other, Robbie had a very close girlfriend — totally platonic — and Nina took against her. No reason, she said, she just didn't like her. And one evening I went to the pub with them all and the reason was obvious: the friend was in love with Robbie. Nina's subconscious had picked it up and . . . Oh my God, I know what my idea is!'

'What idea?' Gregory demanded irritably. 'You're making no sense.'

'It's been in the back of my mind for ages and now it's come bursting to the front. Listen. I know I was against opening clubs outside

London this year, but what would you say if I told you I know someone in Suffolk who is tailor made to set up and run a new Plug Club there for us?'

Gregory didn't hesitate. 'I'd say: Do it.'

'I'm talking about Nina.'

'I know you are. She'd be excellent. Ring her.'

This was why Maddie liked working with Gregory. He could be difficult and infuriating but he was never afraid to embrace new ideas or make big decisions quickly. She picked up her phone and took it out into the corridor.

'Nina?' she said. 'I want you to listen very carefully. Gregory and I've been talking. We want to extend our Plug Clubs beyond the capital and we thought that Ipswich might be a good place to start. The thing is, we need someone to develop it, run it and nurture it and we wondered . . . '

'Yes,' Nina said.

'Yes what?'

'Yes, I'll do it.'

It struck Maddie that Nina and Gregory would work very well together. 'You know it will be a huge amount of work?'

'That's good. I want a huge amount of work.'

'Great. You can start by having a look at our website. When I come up on Friday, I'll bring an action plan with me. You'll have to look at some stuff on Saturday . . . '

'That might be difficult. Robbie's going away so I'll have the children and Dad won't be around that day. He's got to go and collect Ivan from Granty.'

'That's all right. You can sit down in front of my laptop and I'll take the girls off to the playground for an hour or so.'

'All right,' Nina hesitated. 'Mads, I know why you're doing this and . . . '

'Believe me, there's no altruistic motive here. We both think you'd be perfect. Now let me give you a few dates for your calendar and then this afternoon I'll email you some possible venues — Megan's school might be a good place to begin with . . . '

When Maddie returned to the sitting-room she found Gregory where she had left him, staring into space, one hand holding his massive carton, the other with his spoon in the air.

'Gregory?' she said. 'Are you all right?'

Gregory stirred himself. 'I think so,' he said. Then he stood up and reached for his phone. 'I need to ring Minty,' he said.

He strode off to his bedroom and shut the door behind him. Maddie glanced down at his cottage cheese. He had eaten it all.

★   ★   ★

Like all great ideas, it was obvious once Maddie had thought of it. Nina had a wealth of contacts in Ipswich and Higgleigh, she had a daughter at primary school and she was formidably well organised. When Maddie came up to Higgleigh on Friday she found that her sister had already produced a list of possible caterers, retired teachers, a former professor of Philosophy and Economics and a small band of child-friendly teenagers. She told Maddie that it was just as well it was half-term the following week. Quite a few of her friends were on the list and would have their children at home; they'd be more than happy to arrange to bring them over to see Nina and her daughters.

On Saturday morning, Maddie came downstairs after a modest lie-in to find her nieces busy with crayons and paper at the table, Nina talking into her phone and her father making coffee.

'Hello, girls,' Maddie said. 'What are you doing?'

Megan didn't even look up. 'We're too busy to tell you,' she said.

'Too busy,' Chloe echoed.

'They're doing pictures for Granty,' Henry said. 'I'm off to Southwold in half an hour. Edward's booked a table for half past twelve. Apparently his digestion suffers if he eats later than one.'

'Be sure to give him and Granty my love.' Maddie poured cereal into a bowl. 'Who's Nina talking to?'

'Do you remember Megan's best friend, Sadie? Her family moved from Ipswich to Higgleigh last year so they don't get to see each other as often. Nina's inviting them over here next week. Sadie's mother's a yoga teacher — I think Nina's hoping to enrol her into your Plug Club.'

'Is Nina staying here all through half-term?'

'Not all of it. She's coming over towards the end of the week. She has a whole troupe of friends dropping by over next weekend.'

'I shall definitely stay away then. Are you all right, Dad? You don't mind having the house overrun by children?'

'I don't mind anything so long as Nina's all right. The Plug Club idea has galvanized her. She needs to keep as busy as possible at the moment.'

'I know,' Maddie said. 'I intend to keep her *very* busy.'

★ ★ ★

On Saturday, in Higgleigh at least, the sun came out. It was a very half-hearted sun obscured by menacing clouds but at least it wasn't raining and so, true to her word, Maddie left Nina with a pile of paperwork to read after lunch. It seemed to take a very long time to get the girls ready for their outing to the playground. The paraphernalia surrounding children never ceased to amaze Maddie. Today, a short journey to and from the swings required military planning. Chloe needed spare pants and tights since she had stopped wearing nappies in the daytime three weeks ago; she had to pack bottles of water, packets of raisins, and hats, scarves and gloves in case of a sudden drop in temperature.

Out on the pavement, there was another obstacle. The fiendishly complicated belting mechanism of Chloe's buggy proved too much for Maddie's limited patience and she finally tied a loose knot and hoped for the best.

Megan cast a severe glance at her aunt as they set off on the pavement. 'Mummy *always* fixes it properly,' she told her.

'Mummy's a lot cleverer than I am,' Maddie said, 'and we need to get on because there is so much we have to do. I thought we could go to the playground by way of the river walk and play Hide and Seek.'

'If we go by the river,' Megan said, 'my little sister might fall into the water and then what would you do?'

'I'd jump into the water and beat my chest and say, 'Why, oh why didn't I listen to Megan? Megan knows everything about everything!''

'Hat!' Chloe cried. 'I want my hat!'

Maddie dug into the big bag attached to the buggy and fixed the hat firmly on Chloe's head.

'I don't know *everything*,' Megan conceded graciously. 'That's why I go to school. I learn lots at school. I can say hello in Spanish if you like.'

'You learn Spanish! It's your first year at school and you learn Spanish? Say hello.'

Megan offered a small prim smile and then said, *Hola*.'

'Wow,' Maddie said. 'Can you say anything else?'

'*Uno, dos* . . . '

'*Tres*,' Maddie prompted, '*Uno, dos, tres!*'

Chloe swivelled in her buggy and grinned up at Maddie. '*Tres!*' she said.

'Very good, Chloe,' said Maddie. '*Uno, dos, tres!*'

The three of them chanted the numbers as they turned down the path towards the river walk until a baritone voice called out, '*Cuatro!*'

For a split second, her heart seemed to stop.

She couldn't believe how pathetic she was. It was the man she'd seen on Christmas Day and his eyes were as warm and hypnotic as she'd remembered. He wore the same tartan scarf but he had a different companion this time. She had spiky black hair and very long legs and looked even younger than her predecessor. She and the man were holding hands. Maddie wondered what had gone wrong with the woman in the red coat. They'd seemed so happy together.

'What is *cuatro?*' Megan asked.

'*Cuatro,*' Maddie said, 'is four.'

Megan nodded. '*Uno, dos, tres, cuatro!*'

'*Bueno,*' the man laughed. '*Adios!*'

'*Adios,*' Maddie said and was careful to nod to both the man *and* his companion as they passed. A few seconds later, she couldn't resist turning back. She would have been disappointed if he hadn't also turned back but he didn't disappoint her. Their eyes met and, just as on Christmas Day, he smiled. Once again she found it impossible not to smile back. She felt a small hand tugging at her sleeve and looked down at Megan.

'Was that man Spanish?' Megan asked.

'No,' Maddie said. 'I expect he learnt to speak it at school like you. *Bueno* means good and *Adios* means goodbye.' They had joined the river walk now and the ground was a little bumpy. The river, usually a blueish-grey ribbon, was a swollen, swirling mass of charcoal-coloured water. Maddie twisted and turned the buggy in an effort to avoid the holes and puddles.

'I liked that man,' Megan said.

'Did you?' For no good reason, Maddie was delighted. 'I thought it was just me.'

'Can we stop now?' Megan asked. 'I'll go and hide, and you and Chloe can count to twenty.'

'We'll count to fifteen,' Maddie said. 'Don't go and hide near the water.'

'Of course I won't,' Megan said. 'Shut your eyes.'

Maddie shut her eyes and started counting. She felt quite exhilarated. It wasn't just the man's strong chin or his beautiful eyes, it was that she felt he looked at her as if he was genuinely interested in her, which she knew was stupid. She wondered whether he would have engaged her in conversation if he'd been on his own. The trouble with men like that was that they never *were* on their own. Stop it, Maddie, she thought. Concentrate on the game. 'Fifteen!' she shouted, 'We're coming to find you!' She looked down at the buggy and saw it was empty. 'Megan!' she called, 'Do you have Chloe with you?'

A nearby bush began to vibrate. 'You have to find me first!'

Maddie left the buggy and went straight to the bush. 'Megan,' she said. 'Where's Chloe?'

'She's with *you*,' Megan said.

Maddie swallowed very hard. 'She isn't,' she said, 'I think Chloe has gone and hidden somewhere. We'll find her together.' She took Megan's hand and called out, 'Chloe! Come out, come out, wherever you are!'

They were at the edge of the river now. Maddie tried to quell the rising panic she felt.

308

Why had she ever thought it was a good idea to play a stupid game here of all places? Chloe was wearing a black-and-white panda hat. Maddie scanned the water in search of clues she didn't want to find. She could see nothing and besides, Chloe would have called out if she'd fallen in. Surely she'd have called out? Wouldn't she?

Maddie turned from the river and shouted, 'Chloe! Come out now please!' She could hear her voice, shrill and forced, the hysteria ready to spill out at any moment.

Every second seemed an eternity, as different scenarios ran around her head: Chloe drowning silently, Chloe kidnapped, Chloe crying on her own, Chloe mauled by some huge Alsatian, Chloe in a small, shiny coffin.

Beside her, Megan was getting bored. 'Chloe!' she called. 'We want to go to the playground! Where are you?'

'Chloe!' Maddie called. 'Chloe!' Please God, let her be safe, she prayed, please God, let her be safe. I don't need a man, I don't need babies, I don't need money, I just need Chloe.

'Chloe!' Megan called. '*Uno, dos, tres!*'

'*Tres!*' came a small, wavering echo and then, oh bliss, oh joy, a black-and-white panda hat appeared and there was Chloe easing herself out from a hollow tree trunk. It was — and Maddie knew it always would be — the very best moment of her life.

26

Edward was as tall and thin as Henry. As far as Henry was concerned the resemblance ended there. Edward possessed an air of stern gravitas that engendered a degree of respect and diffidence in all those who talked to him. He had a mane of silver hair, piercing grey eyes and eyebrows that fanned out like bats' wings.

Five years ago he had met his second wife while visiting his first one in hospital. Françoise had flown over from Avignon to visit her ailing brother. Both patients had died within a week of each other and within a month Edward had flown out to Avignon to visit Françoise. On his return he announced he was retiring from the lucrative directorships he'd taken on since leaving the Civil Service; he intended to marry Françoise and move to Avignon.

They bought a large house with a pool, and outbuildings they converted into elegant but comfortable holiday lets. Granty was convinced that their principal reason for doing so was to provide Françoise with a permanent excuse not to visit Edward's family. Henry thought this might well be true but, as he pointed out to Granty, they were always generous with their invitations to France. Edward's son visited with his family every Easter, Granty spent a fortnight there in the summer. He and Marianne had been there a few months before she died; they'd enjoyed themselves hugely which was why Henry had been loath to go back on his own.

Granty might complain about Françoise's refusal to cross the Channel but it was obvious she was glad to have time with Edward on his own. She sat between her sons at their table by the hotel window and said, 'This is so nice, James! I wish you'd come more often!'

'Granty,' Edward said, 'I am your middle son, *Edward*. James is the oldest. He is also bald.' He gave a wintry smile, presumably to indicate he had said something amusing. 'It's good to be here with you both. You're looking well, Henry. I'm sorry to hear about Nina's problems.'

Henry's first reaction was to wonder how Edward knew. His second was to direct an accusing glance at his mother who reacted with a guilty laugh that only incensed him further.

'For goodness' sake, Henry,' Granty blustered, 'who can Edward tell? He only mixes with French people and he's hardly likely to tell any of them, is he?'

'That's not the point,' Henry murmured stiffly. 'Nina was very particular about keeping it to herself.'

'I don't see why,' Edward said. 'Tell her from me that it's nothing to be ashamed of. Roland's wife left him three months ago and he seems quite relaxed about it.' He caught his mother's intake of breath and said, 'Well, it's true.'

'What are you saying?' Granty demanded. 'Are you talking about my grandson? Roland's wife has left him? Why didn't you tell me?'

'I don't know,' Edward said. 'I suppose I

311

forgot. I was a little preoccupied at the time. I thought I had prostate cancer.'

'You told me all about *that*,' Granty said, 'and then it turned out to be *divertissement* something . . . '

'Diverticulitis,' Edward corrected gravely. 'I had a lucky escape.'

'You're always having lucky escapes, Edward. I can't believe you didn't tell me about Roland and Lucy. How could you forget something like that? Why should she leave him? I thought they loved life in Brussels.'

'Roland does,' Edward said. 'Apparently Lucy didn't.'

'So Roland's out there on his own?' Granty put her head to one side. 'That must be so sad for him. Perhaps Nina should visit him. He has a lovely big house out there. They could commiserate together. It might even make Robbie jealous. You should suggest it, Henry.'

'Why would Robbie be jealous of Nina's cousin?' Henry said. 'Besides, it was always Maddie Roland liked. They used to do jigsaws together. Nina couldn't stand doing jigsaws.'

'Perhaps Maddie should go to Brussels then. I'm so sorry about poor Roland.' Granty rose to her feet. 'I must go to the Ladies. If the food arrives, tell them I like lashings of tartare sauce.'

Henry repositioned his chair to let his mother out and then turned back to his brother. 'I'm very sorry to hear . . . ' He stopped as Edward laid a hand on his arm. 'What is it?'

'Did you notice,' Edward murmured, 'that Granty called me James?'

'She always does that,' Henry said. 'Come to think of it, so do I. I call Nina Maddie and Megan Nina. It makes Megan very cross.'

'There's something else,' Edward said. 'Did you know that she rang me weeks ago and asked me quite specifically to come and stay this weekend?'

'She told me you invited yourself.'

'That's not true. She asked me. She said she had something to tell me. When I arrived on Thursday, I asked her what it was she wanted to tell me. Henry, she had no recollection of the phone call.'

'That's nothing to worry about,' Henry said. 'You forgot to tell us about Roland. I see Granty every week. If there was something wrong I'd know.'

'I don't think you would. You've become accustomed to her ways. I haven't seen her for months and I can tell you she's changed. We took Ivan for a walk yesterday and when we came back she'd forgotten her keys. Her neighbour saw us. She had a spare set she keeps for Granty. She told me this wasn't the first time.'

'I lose my car keys at least once a week. Granty's eighty-seven. She's entitled to lock herself out now and then. She's incredibly tough for her age. Do you know she's travelling down to Devon next Friday? I offered to take her but . . . '

'Do it,' Edward said. 'She shouldn't make a long journey on her own.'

'I told you I already offered,' Henry said stiffly. 'She told me she's quite happy to go down on her own . . . '

'Tell her you want to see James. Tell her now. I'll back you up. You could spend the weekend with him and Lorna.'

'Have you ever tried Lorna's cooking?'

'Stay the night then. I don't like to think of our mother roaming round the West Country on her own. If my suspicions are right, we need to make a plan for her future.'

Henry knew what that meant. If Edward was right — and Henry didn't think for a moment that he was — then it would be Henry who would sort things out. Edward had always been very good at issuing instructions while remarkably dilatory at carrying them out.

Their orders arrived and so did Granty. Henry had looked forward to his fish and chips and was irritated with Edward for ruining his enjoyment. With every mouthful he was aware of his brother waiting for him to say something about Devon and the intensity of Edward's gaze irritated Henry so much that he was all the more determined not to bow before it.

'I had a call from James the other day,' Edward said at last. 'He told me he was so looking forward to seeing Granty. He said he hadn't seen *you*, Henry, for nearly a year. He sounded rather upset.'

'Did he?' Henry said. There was no point in resisting Edward; he was implacable. So Henry gave in and put down his knife and fork. 'In fact, next weekend would be a good time for a visit. Nina's coming over with loads of children and girlfriends and it would be nice to get away. I could drive you down, Granty, and then I could drop you off with Elizabeth the next morning.'

'But what about Ivan?' Granty said.

'He can stay at home with Nina and the girls. They adore him. He'll be very well looked after.'

'In that case,' Granty said, 'that would be lovely.' She turned to Edward. 'I feel bad about Henry. Next weekend we were supposed to be going up to Edinburgh to see an old flame of his. Do you remember Louise who lived next door to us, Edward?'

'Yes . . . A pretty young girl with blonde hair.'

'She grew up into a very, very pretty young woman. You'd left home by then. Henry was very smitten by her.'

'You must have been very young when you went out with her,' Edward said. 'You were almost a baby when you met Marianne.'

'I didn't go out with her,' Henry said. 'I had a crush on her at school and it was entirely unreciprocated. Granty arranged this trip and, frankly, I'm glad we can't go. I can't believe Louise has any interest in seeing me now.'

Granty gave a knowing smile. 'I think you'd be surprised, Henry. She was very disappointed when I rang to cancel our trip. I promised I'd arrange another rendezvous in the future.'

'You should come and visit us in France,' Edward said. 'Françoise has some delightful single friends who would be delighted to meet you.'

'Thank you for the invitation,' Henry said. 'If I ever decide to come and live in France with you, I'll be sure to take you up on it.'

So on Friday morning, Henry said goodbye to Nina, the girls and Ivan, and set off for Southwold. He had spent a couple of evenings researching the early signs of dementia. Depression, apparently, was a common symptom, along with a wish to withdraw from the world. Granty showed no desire to withdraw from anything. She had rung him on Monday and persuaded him to give her Robbie's phone number. She said she wanted advice about her boiler but Henry knew it was no such thing. He only gave it to her because the situation was as bad as it could possibly be and Granty couldn't make it any worse.

Granty continued to disprove Edward's thesis throughout the journey. She had rung Roland, she told Henry and had had a long conversation with him and he seemed to be very cheerful. 'I have also,' Granty said, 'rung Louise again. I reported back to her the comment you made about her.'

'What comment was that? I wish you wouldn't do these things.'

'I thought she'd be interested. I simply mentioned that you'd mentioned to me about your unrequited love for her. Do you want to know what she said?'

'No.' Henry glanced at his mirror and moved out into the fast lane of the motorway. After overtaking the white van that had been cruising along the middle lane for the last twenty minutes, he swung gently back into the middle lane. He glanced at his mother. He really must stop telling her things. 'All right,' he said. 'Tell me. What did she say?'

'She said you had no idea. She said she gave you masses of encouragement and you never made a move. She said she adored you.'

'She never said that.'

'Well, she didn't actually say she adored you but she said everything else. You misread the signs, Henry. Aren't you pleased that I found that out for you?'

'I'm not sure,' Henry said.

★ ★ ★

James and Lorna lived in a large bungalow on a steep hill above Totnes. They had bought it when James retired. 'We're thinking of the future,' Lorna had said. 'In ten years' time we won't be able to manage the stairs.' Granty had said to Henry that they wouldn't be able to manage the steep hill either, but since they had already bought the property she'd deemed it tactful to keep her opinion to herself.

Lorna was probably the worst cook Henry knew. He had a theory that Lorna had only accepted James once she knew that he was uninterested in food. Tonight, they ate raddled lamb chops. The onion sauce resembled an old duvet, both in appearance and consistency, while the overcooked onion pieces reminded him of flies trapped in a bowl of cream.

Fortunately, he and Granty had taken the precaution of breaking their journey with a hearty lunch at a country pub. And even if Lorna's cooking was execrable, James' wine was excellent. Granty was certainly enjoying it as she talked about Edward's visit the week before.

'I have some very sad news for you both,' she said. 'Edward just dropped it casually into the conversation as if he were discussing the weather: Roland's wife has left him!'

'I know that,' James said, sawing a chunk of meat from his chop.

'You knew? How did you know? Why did Edward tell *you* and not me?'

'He Skypes me every week,' James said.

'He never Skypes *me*,' Henry said.

'You were never a doctor,' James said. 'For some reason, he's convinced I'm fascinated by any bodily irregularities he thinks he might have. He told me about Roland some time ago. I've been out to visit him.'

'You've visited *Roland?*'

'I do yoga three evenings a week,' Lorna said to no one in particular.

'That's very impressive, Lorna. So tell me, James, about your visit to Brussels. It's unlike you to take off to strange new places.'

'It's a habit I've recently adopted,' James said. 'Lorna and I have discovered we appreciate each other more if we have regular separations. Last weekend she went off to Birmingham to stay with an old schoolfriend.'

'Did you have a nice time?' Granty asked her daughter-in-law.

'We walked along the canal,' Lorna said. 'I never knew Birmingham had a canal.'

'Well, there you go,' Granty said. 'And how did you find Roland, James?'

'He says he misses his children but they're both at boarding school most of the year anyway. It's a big house for just one man, though. I told him to find a new wife.'

Granty shook her head. 'I find it very distressing that none of my grandchildren seem to be lucky in love.'

James nodded. 'Edward told me about Nina.'

Henry turned on his mother. 'You see? You told me Edward would only tell French people.'

'I must say that's not very likely,' James said. 'I can speak far better French than Edward can and that's not saying a great deal.'

★ ★ ★

Late the next morning, Henry drove his mother to Elizabeth's in Exeter. Elizabeth lived in a large white house with a generous porch, a gravelled drive at the front and a big lawn at the back. Although set back from the centre of the city in a quiet residential avenue, it was possible to see the top of the cathedral from the upstairs floor. It was a place that had been designed for comfort rather than elegance and as Henry turned into the drive, it looked much as he remembered it. He helped Granty out of the car and took her bags out of the boot.

The front door opened and there was Elizabeth, holding out her arms and calling, 'Hello there!'

Granty made straight for her and hugged her tightly.

Henry had not seen Elizabeth for ten years. She was smaller and thinner than he remembered but she looked neat and smart in blue trousers and a red jersey and her smile was as warm as ever. 'I know you want to get off quickly,' she told Henry, 'so we'll eat lunch at once.'

In the kitchen, she served out quiche and a variety of salads. 'I made none of them,' she said. 'I've found a wonderful woman who'll make anything I want and deliver it to my door. I still cook for myself but I'd never inflict my offerings on others.'

This was another change, Henry thought. Elizabeth had always been an enthusiastic cook. 'It's so nice to be here,' he told her. 'I always loved this house.'

'I've loved it too. I should have left years ago. It's far too big for me.'

'You forget all your lodgers,' Granty said. 'It's only a year or so since you stopped having them. I remember that young man, Peter. He was very peculiar. I rather liked him because he was obsessed with Doctor Who and if one has to be obsessed with something it might as well be with him. But he was very odd and if it hadn't been for you he'd have probably become one of those sad young men with big dogs and wet sleeping bags.'

'He sent me a Christmas card,' Elizabeth said. 'He works for the National Trust now.' She beamed at Henry. 'Your mother's so good for me. I love her very much, you know.'

And that, Henry thought, was yet another change. Neither Granty nor Elizabeth was given to extravagant declarations of affection. And yet now as he glanced at Granty, he watched her squeeze Elizabeth's hand and say, 'I love you too.'

★   ★   ★

On the long journey back to Suffolk, it occurred to Henry that he had always seen Granty as an adjunct of himself. Throughout his life, she had cared for him, bossed him, and given him — often unsolicited — advice. There had been only one occasion that he could remember when she had shrugged off the maternal role and that had been when his father had died and she had retreated into a rather frightening silence, disappearing off the radar for a few weeks with only Elizabeth for company. But the next time he saw her she was, once again, her concerned and curious self.

He knew she relished her role as the matriarch of the Drummond family but he could also see now that it was one that was definitely circumscribed. There was another side of Granty — he had glimpsed it today — and it made him see that however strong one's love for one's family, one could only be fully oneself with one's friends.

Henry sighed. He had come home to another message on the answerphone from William three days ago and now he felt ashamed he'd ignored it. Life was far too short to indulge in unproductive sulks, particularly where best friends were concerned and even more particularly when William had been kind to Nina. He would ring him this evening. Once again, as she had done so often, his mother had shown him the way.

27

Maddie had been invited to dinner by Gregory on Thursday evening. It was the first formal invitation she had ever received from him; she was not at all surprised when he admitted it had been prompted by Minty. And if Gregory was looking forward to playing host, he was very good at hiding his enthusiasm. In the afternoon he told her rather grumpily to leave work early so that he could do some housework and she stood up at once, assuring him that she couldn't wait to eat his food and drink his wine.

Two hours later, she was back and was very impressed by the changes that had been made in the interval. In Gregory's bedroom a candle had been lit — 'Moroccan Rose,' Minty told her, and it filled the flat with a soft, sweet fragrance. The table in the living room had been cleared of Plug Club papers and had been set for three with glasses and paper napkins.

While Minty put the finishing touches to the dinner, Gregory, as instructed, took Maddie through to the living room and poured out the wine. Maddie sat down on the sofa and picked up her glass. 'I've never been a guest here before,' she said. 'It feels rather odd.'

Gregory took the chair by his computer. 'That's not true,' he said. 'You've eaten here hundreds of times.'

'Yes, but I've always ended up doing the

cooking. It's very nice to have you wait on me. I hope it happens more often.'

'It's Minty's idea. She thinks you're responsible for us getting back together.'

★ ★ ★

'That's very sweet of her. I'm not sure I deserve all this attention.'

'I agree,' Gregory said. 'I had to vacuum the carpet before you arrived.'

'If you're trying to make me feel guilty,' Maddie said, 'it's a waste of time.' But she *did* feel guilty when Minty arrived a little breathlessly with the news that dinner was ready. She was nervous, Maddie realised, which was hardly surprising given that Maddie had never made much effort to get to know her. It was not Minty's fault that she was so much younger than her.

By the time they had finished the curry, Maddie knew that she liked Gregory's girlfriend. She was aware that this change of heart had far more to do with her own state of mind than it did with Minty. The euphoria she'd felt after finding Chloe had continued to linger. For the time being, at least, she couldn't feel jealous of either Minty or Victoria. She was even able to ask quite naturally after Victoria and Freddy.

'Victoria's finished the film in Berwick,' Minty said. 'She's working on a TV serial now. She says the plot's quite ridiculous. The murderer turns out to be the detective's first wife. She likes the director but the leading man's a bit of a problem. They have to do some bedroom scenes together and he's a little too enthusiastic. I suggested she start eating garlic.'

'And what about Freddy? Is he enjoying the States?'

'I think so. There's a photo of him on Facebook. He was coming out of a restaurant with some actress he's working with. The next day Victoria received an enormous bouquet of red roses from him so he obviously feels guilty.'

'*Freddy* sent roses?' Maddie laughed. 'He's only been there a fortnight and already he's behaving like a film star.' She heard her phone ringing and picked it up. 'It's Dad,' she said. 'He never rings after nine. I'd better take it.'

She went out into the corridor and said, 'Hi, Dad. How are you?'

'I'm back in Devon with James,' he said. 'I have to stay on here till Sunday morning. The thing is, Robbie wants to be with the girls this weekend so Nina's coming over to Higgleigh on Friday evening. Is there any way you can come up and be with her?'

Maddie thought quickly and said, 'Yes, I can do that. Why are you back in Devon? I thought Uncle James was bringing Granty back tomorrow?'

'He was,' her father said. 'But that's no longer necessary. There's been a change of plan.' There was a sudden silence and for a few moments Maddie thought they'd been cut off. 'It's Granty,' her father said. 'She's dead.'

* * *

Minty insisted on making sweet tea for Maddie — 'It's good for shock,' she said — and Maddie sat on the sofa with her host and hostess on either side.

'You don't have to tell us anything,' Minty said. 'Just drink your tea.'

The tea was like drinking neat sugar. Maddie put it on the table. 'There's not a lot to tell,' she said. 'I don't understand any of it. Granty's been staying with her friend, Elizabeth. This morning, Elizabeth's cleaner let herself into the house and found a letter addressed to her on the hall table. Inside were instructions to call Uncle James and the emergency services and to do nothing until they arrived.' Maddie picked up her mug with both hands and forced herself to have another sip. 'They found Granty and Elizabeth in Elizabeth's bedroom. They were both in bed and they were dead. There were two empty bottles of champagne and some empty packets of Elizabeth's anti-depressants. James had a long talk with Elizabeth's doctor. He confirmed she'd been depressed and had asked specifically for the pills in question. He said he doesn't often prescribe them but since Elizabeth had been a GP, he presumed she knew what would work for her.'

'Did they leave any letters?' Gregory asked, 'I mean, apart from the one for the cleaner . . . '

'Dad says there's nothing. They'd eaten a chicken casserole for supper and had washed up and clingfilmed the remains of the meal. The kitchen was spotless. No one has any idea why they would do such a thing.'

326

'How's your father?' Minty asked.

'He's shocked, of course, but he says he's all right. Uncle James rang him at work. Dad went home, packed a bag and arrived in Devon a few hours ago. He was only there last weekend. He's been looking after Ivan — Granty's dog — and he's taken him down with him. To be honest, he seems more concerned about Ivan than anything else. He said Ivan wouldn't eat his meal tonight.'

'People do say,' Minty mused, 'that dogs have special senses. When my grandfather died, his Labrador wouldn't eat for days.'

'I don't know,' Maddie said. 'I never thought Ivan had any sense at all.' She took a last sip of her tea. 'I'd better go home and ring Nina. Dad was going to ring her after he rang me. I'm so sorry to break up the evening. It's been lovely. I mean, it was lovely.'

'I'll walk you home,' Gregory said.

'Thanks but I'd like to walk on my own. I'll see you in the morning.'

'Maddie, don't be stupid, you don't have to come in . . .'

'I'd like to. I don't want to sit around all day thinking of Granty.'

'Well,' Gregory said, 'if you're sure . . . Feel free to change your mind.'

'I won't,' Maddie said. 'But thanks.'

It was bitterly cold outside and Maddie wound her long scarf round and round her neck until it covered the lower half of her face. There was a light smattering of rain and a cold wind. As she turned the comer onto the main road, a car drove by, spraying her with water. She kept thinking of Granty at Christmas. She'd been so happy. 'We've got your father back,' she'd whispered to Maddie more than once. 'Isn't it grand to see him like this?' So how could Granty, of all people, take her own life for whatever reason when she must have known what it would do to her son?

★   ★   ★

She had an answer of sorts on Saturday morning. She and Nina were eating cereal in their dressing-gowns when the phone rang. Nina reached across for it. Almost immediately, she stood to attention, face alert and focused. 'Dad? Yes, we're both here and . . . I don't know . . . Hang on.' She put her phone against her shoulder and stared across at Maddie. 'Dad wants to know if the post's arrived.'

'I'll go and see.' Maddie went straight through to the hall and gathered up the assortment of letters in front of the door. She sifted through them quickly and then, her pulse racing, returned to the kitchen. 'Tell Dad there's a letter. Tell him it's from Granty.'

Nina nodded and spoke into the phone. 'Dad, we have it . . . Are you sure? No, that's fine. We'll see you tomorrow. We love you.' She put down the handset. 'Uncle James had one too. Dad wants us to open it and read it.'

They sat down at the table with the envelope between them. Granty's writing, like Granty, was unique, with florid loops and randomly enlarged letters.

Maddie picked it up. 'Here goes,' she said. She pulled out a sheet of paper. Elizabeth's address and telephone number were neatly printed in blue. Maddie put the paper on the table in front of them and they both read it silently.

Dear Edward, James and Henry,

This is NOT a tragedy.

I have a tumour. It's malignant and, because of its position, it can't be taken out. There is a small chance that if I have six months of chemotherapy, it might possibly shrink and could then be removed. But it's ONLY a very small chance and if it didn't work I would have spent the last months of my life being sick and bad-tempered and feeling sorry for myself.

You all know I'm a bad patient. I've marvelled at the bravery of two very dear friends who coped heroically with the indignities and pain of terminal illness. I nursed your father through his final last months. They were tough men, ready to endure horrific experiences in order to live a little longer.

I'm not like that. I'm eighty-seven and I've had a very privileged life. I loved my husband and I love my family, I've never faced poverty or deprivation of any kind. I've enjoyed good health. I'm spoilt. I don't want to fall apart at the first onslaught of uncomfortable physical symp-toms. I don't want YOU to see me fall apart. Perhaps, without Elizabeth, I might have felt I had to soldier on.

Elizabeth says she has Alzheimer's disease. She can no longer drive or concentrate on a book or cook a complicated meal. She is beginning *to find it difficult to remember words when she speaks. She is very good at hiding her condition as Henry will testify. Like me, she has decided she'd rather bow out now while she's still able to do so. And we are so lucky! What can be better than to die with one's best friend by one's side?*

I suspect you will all be very angry with me. What can I say? I'm a physical coward. I always have been. We're none of us perfect after all, so try to understand. I'm sending a letter to Henry at his office regarding funeral arrangements and disposal of my ashes. Goodbye. I love you all. Granty xxxx

★   ★   ★

The funeral was to be held on a Friday at the cemetery outside Higgleigh. Maddie arrived at Manningtree Station on the Thursday night and was surprised to see her cousin Roland standing waiting for her by her father's car. The last time she had seen him had been at her mother's funeral. He and his wife had been the best-dressed couple there and tonight he looked as suave as ever in a black coat, red scarf and grey trousers. He was like one of those old matinee idols with his slicked black hair and strong, smooth jaw.

'Roland,' she said, kissing his cheek and breathing in a gorgeous scent of musk, 'it is very kind of you to collect me.'

He took her bag and threw it into the back seat before opening the passenger door for her.

He certainly had the manners of a matinee idol. 'To be honest,' he said, 'I was glad to get out of the house. Dad and Uncle Henry have already got into the red wine and are striding round the kitchen like a pair of growling bears. They were grumbling about Granty's ashes when I left.'

'What about Granty's ashes?'

'Uncle Henry must have told you.' He climbed into the driver's seat and turned on the ignition.

'He hasn't told me anything. It's taken him years to get over Mum's death and the last few months he's been so good and now he's gone right back into his shell.'

'Well,' Roland paused as he drove down the sliproad and progressed to the roundabout, 'Granty wants them to throw her ashes in the same place as Grandpa's . . .'

'That was the Scilly Isles, wasn't it? She and Grandpa had their honeymoon there.'

Roland nodded. 'She wants them to do it on her wedding anniversary. That's next week. Dad's been in charge of the arrangements. I said I thought it would be an excuse for a nice jaunt and the two of them stared at me as if I were mad. Quite frankly, Granty could have suggested the local tip and they'd still complain. I don't think they'll ever forgive her for all of this.'

'Is Uncle James there?'

'He and Aunt Lorna arrive tomorrow. So tonight it's just you and me and the two bears. Perhaps over supper we should discuss my failed marriage. That might distract them.'

'Oh, Roland,' Maddie said, 'I'm so sorry about

331

Lucy. Is there any chance she might come back?'
'Good God,' Roland said, 'I hope not.'

★ ★ ★

Nina had briefly toyed with the idea of bringing her daughters to the funeral. Then Robbie's parents had offered to come up on the Thursday evening and Nina had accepted the offer gratefully. As she whispered to Maddie while they waited for the coffin to arrive at the crematorium, she was glad the children weren't there. 'This place is so grim,' she whispered. 'It's times like these that I wish we'd been a religious family.'

Maddie nodded. The plastic lilies on the left of the dais had dust on them and the rows of chairs on either side of the aisle were small and uncomfortable. Maddie and Nina sat on the front row to the right. Behind them they could hear Colette talking earnestly to Granty's cleaning lady and her husband about Granty's cat. 'It's so good of you to have her,' she said. 'I was always a little nervous round Lupin. She's a very *superior* cat, if you know what I mean.'

The mealy-mouthed tinned music was abruptly replaced by the sinister notes of the second movement of Beethoven's Seventh Symphony. Colette leant forward and hissed, '*Zardoz*.' Maddie nodded. This had been the soundtrack to *Zardoz*, a futuristic sci-fi film about people condemned to immortality who longed to die. Was this why Granty had chosen it? Maddie very much hoped it wasn't.

The coffin arrived, borne aloft by Granty's

sons, her grandson and a couple of pall-bearers. A small mound of lilies — real ones — lay on top of the coffin and wobbled slightly as it was set on its stand. Maddie watched the three brothers take their places next to Aunt Lorna on the front row on the other side of the aisle. Nina stood up to let Roland through to his place between her and Maddie.

Just as they had reassembled themselves, another man arrived: Robbie, in his best black suit, looked down at Nina with a slight embarrassed smile, and as they all moved chairs yet again, Maddie saw him take Nina's hand.

Granty had suggested in her funeral instructions that her youngest son might like to give the address since he had seen most of her in the last forty years. Henry had resolutely refused to do so and neither of his brothers had showed any desire to assume the responsibility. So it was left to Aunt Lorna, who walked up onto the dais and proceeded to give one of the most boring speeches Maddie had ever heard: a stream of chronological details shorn of any hint of Granty's personality. The readings chosen by Granty went some way to make up for Aunt Lorna's shortcomings.

Roland had been given a joyous poem, 'Pied Beauty' by Gerard Manley Hopkins. Nina had 'Remember' by Christina Rossetti while Maddie read out a Sanskrit proverb and as she finished with the last rousing sentences she could almost feeling Granty cheering her on.

' . . . But today, well lived,
Makes every yesterday a dream of happiness,

And every tomorrow a vision of hope.

Look well, therefore, to this day.'

She had barely sat down when the small curtain opened and the coffin began to slide forward with ghastly, inexorable slowness. She bit her lip. Behind her, Colette blew her nose fiercely. It was only now that the full enormity of Granty's absence took hold for Maddie. As the coffin disappeared from view, the familiar sounds of the *Doctor Who* theme music resounded through the room.

It was a pity, Maddie thought, that Granty couldn't know that her death had prompted the return of Robbie to Nina. Certainly, it lifted the spirits of everyone. Even those who didn't know about the schism could see Nina's radiance. It was impossible not to be affected by it. Back at home, as Maddie passed round sandwiches, she watched her father circle the sitting room, chatting to Granty's book-group quartet, her cleaning lady and the frail old couple who used to live next door to Granty in Higgleigh. Every few minutes his eyes would fall on Nina and Robbie chatting to guests, side by side.

★ ★ ★

After the polite restraint of the funeral tea, the extended family appreciated the arrival of alcohol in the evening. For Maddie, there were three images she knew she would always remember. The first was the sight of Robbie sitting in a corner of the kitchen with her father, talking nonstop in low, earnest tones, one hand waving his can of beer, the other repeatedly pressing Henry's knee. The second was at midnight when everyone else had gone to bed and she and Roland sat in the sitting room by the fire with one last glass of wine and Roland put his arm round her and told her he'd been in love with his squash partner for over a year.

The final snapshot occurred in the early hours of the morning. Maddie woke and thought she heard Ivan barking. She went downstairs and stopped on the threshold of the kitchen. There sat her father, Ivan stretched across his lap, his hand gently stroking Ivan's fur and tears falling down his face.

28

The two remaining members of the party were late. Henry stood by the ticket desk, a small distance apart from his companions, his gaze fixed on the entrance to the airport. Edward and James both wore flat caps and green Wellington boots. Edward had bought his pair yesterday. They made an incongruous pair: Edward, tall and hawk-faced, constantly checking his watch, his dark jacket opened to reveal a brown waistcoat, orange shirt and tweed tie. James, short and rotund, his glasses on his nose, lost in his newspaper crossword. Sitting on a bench nearby was Lorna, in the knitted hat she had worn since their early breakfast, reading a biography of Charles Dickens.

Edward came up to join Henry. 'This is isn't good enough,' he said. 'I gave strict instructions that we should *all* be punctual. The wind's getting up now. If we don't go soon, they'll cancel the flight. I know these people. Give them the slightest excuse and they'll cancel the flight.'

'There's still time,' Henry said. 'They'll be here soon.' His face relaxed and he added, 'Here's one of them now.'

Colette, in denim jeans, a green jumper and a blue anorak, scurried through the doors with a suitcase in one hand, a bag in the other. 'I'm sorry,' she said, 'I'm so very sorry. I've been staying with a friend. She said we had plenty of time and I knew we didn't but I couldn't say a word when she's put me up and driven me halfway across Cornwall. I'll check in right away. You haven't been waiting long, have you?'

Henry got in quickly before Edward could speak. 'That's fine. We're still waiting for the last . . . ' He stopped as a tall, slender woman with short blonde hair, green trousers and a calf-length camel coat came towards them. She stopped opposite Henry, her sky-blue eyes considering him with a quizzical, almost challenging air. 'Hello, old friend! I'd recognise you anywhere! Please tell me I haven't changed!'

'Louise,' Henry breathed, 'you haven't. It's wonderful to see you.' He swallowed hard. 'You probably don't remember my brother Edward? And this is my sister-in-law, Colette. You should both check in right away.'

Louise smiled down at Colette. 'So you're late too? Thank heavens I'm not the only one.' She beamed at Edward. 'I do remember you, you know. We won't be a moment, I promise you.'

'Well,' Edward murmured, looking after her with approval, 'I can see why you liked her, Henry! She's delightful.'

Unfortunately, his newly restored equilibrium didn't last long. As they arrived at the customs desk, the official told Edward that his group were the last of the passengers to go through. He seemed quite relaxed as he said this but Edward had an innate dislike of people in uniform and instantly stiffened.

The man looked through his passport and said, 'Could you please take your boots off, Sir?'

337

'I beg your pardon?' Edward asked with heavy irony. 'Do you suspect me of trafficking drugs? Do you think I might be hiding a gun or a knife between my toes?'

The official attempted an uncertain smile. 'I'm sorry, Sir, but we ask everyone to do this . . . '

'Please forgive me if I'm wrong,' Edward said, 'but the last time I checked, the Scilly Isles were still part of the United Kingdom and . . . '

'Edward,' Henry murmured, 'if you carry on like this, we'll all miss our flight. Why don't you just sit down and remove your boots?'

Edward grunted but agreed to sit down and do as Henry suggested. The others proceeded through without any problems while Edward continued to pull at his footwear. 'I can't get them off!' he shouted, 'I shouldn't have to get them off. Are we in a police state?'

Henry and Colette, united in horror in the presence of such intemperate behaviour, raced through to the seating area and sat down quickly. James sauntered towards them with Lorna and said, 'Louise is staying with Edward to see if she can help.'

Louise's efforts were obviously unsuccessful. After ten minutes a voice came through the tannoy system apologizing for the delay. Colette put her head in her hands and Henry stared up at the ceiling.

Another ten minutes went by and then Louise appeared. Behind her, the official pushed Edward in a wheelchair. Edward leapt out of it, gave a regal nod and said, 'I believe we are ready to go.'

'For goodness' sake, Edward,' Henry muttered, 'you've been quite impossible.'

'Nonsense,' Edward said, 'I was perfectly reasonable.'

Louise's mouth twitched. 'You called that poor man a Nazi.'

'Well so he was,' Edward said. 'I was compelled to point out that I've served Queen and Country throughout my adult life and . . . '

'You've done very well out of Queen and Country,' Henry said. 'And why did you need a wheelchair?'

'In my efforts to pull off my boots,' Edward said, 'I hurt my knee.'

'You never did pull off your boots,' Louise reminded him.

A voice on the tannoy system announced that the Skybus was ready for boarding. As they boarded the tiny plane, it was impossible not to notice the aggrieved looks directed at them by the other passengers. James and Lorna sat together as did Louise and Colette which meant that Henry was forced to sit next to Edward, immediately behind the pilots.

One of them spoke into his microphone. 'I apologise for the delay,' he said. 'This was due to a disagreement with a passenger which, I am glad to say, has now been resolved.'

Henry shut his eyes but opened them again when the plane took off. The journey was a short one but the sight of the five islands scattered across the smoky blue sea was impressive. The plane did seem very fragile though and Henry was glad when they landed.

Colette, he noticed, looked pale.

Edward, good humour fully restored, hailed taxis and barked instructions. On arriving at their location, a mere ten minutes away in Hugh Town, he was the first to stride into the hotel and greet the proprietor, a mild-mannered man called Mr Harris.

'We were here nine years ago,' Edward told him, 'but that was in the summer.'

'You'll find it much quieter now,' Mr Harris said. 'We only opened for the season last week and at present you're our only guests. We serve breakfast, of course, and you're welcome to use the lounge in the evening.'

'You don't do lunch or dinner?' Edward asked.

'At this time of year, I'm afraid we don't,' Mr Harris said, 'but there are plenty of pubs down the road.'

Henry held his breath but it was Colette who spoke. 'That sounds perfect,' she said. 'It will be such fun to have the hotel to ourselves.'

Edward raised his eyebrows but merely said that they'd better go to their rooms right away before grabbing a quick bite to eat.

Safely in his bedroom, Henry relaxed at last. He had been excruciatingly embarrassed by Edward's behaviour at the airport and wished he could ignore it like James and Lorna or find it amusing like Louise. He sat down on his bed and thought of Louise. When he had first read Granty's request for her inclusion in the party, he had felt exasperated by her heavy-handed attempt to play matchmaker beyond the grave. Since then he had felt, by turns, anxiety, curiosity, excitement and finally trepidation. He wondered if one could use trepidation as a verb. If so, he was now deeply trepidated. He had almost hoped she would not live up to expectations. She might have lost her looks, acquired irritating habits, even proved to be unpleasant.

But here she was, still beautiful and charming. In the plane he had glanced back at her briefly and seen her chatting to Colette who had looked both relaxed and entertained. He wasn't sure why Colette's response proved that Louise was a nice woman but somehow he felt that it did. So now, Henry thought, Louise had lived up to expectations and he didn't know what he felt. Or rather he did: he felt trepidated.

★   ★   ★

Granty used to say that Edward and James were like weather-clock figurines: when the sunny one came out, the rainy one withdrew. When Edward was good, James was bad. So it was today in the pub. Edward was as good as gold and James was not. James, who would eat without comment anything Lorna served, however grisly, felt it incumbent to criticize his food when dining out. This afternoon, he told the barman that the chips were too fat. When the barman replied that the chef always made fat chips, James said loftily that it was a pity the chef could not show more flexibility. He then proceeded to eat every one of his chips and most of Colette's. It was just as well, Henry thought that they were only spending two nights here. If they stayed any

341

longer, every hostelry in town would refuse to serve them.

After lunch they set out to discharge Granty's ashes. Though the wind was fierce, at least it didn't rain. The party trudged along the road and up along the cliff towards the golf course, their heads down against the cold rush of air. Finally Edward said, 'This seems as good a place as any. Henry, do you want to do the honours?'

'Shouldn't we say something first?' Henry asked. 'It seems a bit feeble to come all this way and not say something.'

'I suppose we should,' James said. 'We all said something for Dad after all. I think a few words from the three of us would be appropriate.'

'Very well.' Edward took off his cap and stood with his hands together in front of him. He looked round about him, as if searching for someone. 'So, Granty, we're here to say our final goodbye to you and I won't pretend that your manner of passing has not been extremely distressing. I, for one, find your behaviour difficult to understand. You have a son who is a very able doctor . . . '

'Retired,' James murmured.

'You have a son who is a very able retired doctor who would have been happy to discuss your medical condition and yet you failed to consult him . . . '

'This is stupid, Edward,' Henry protested. 'She can't hear any of this . . . '

'She *might*,' Edward said, 'and it needs to be said.' He raised his eyes up to the sky, his white hair flying away from him. 'I can't pretend I'm not disappointed, very deeply disappointed. You've let down your grandchildren. There's Roland who needed your support and Nina . . . '

'This is hardly appropriate,' Henry said, 'Besides, Nina's fine now, and we're all cold up here. Can't you just say something short and to the point?'

'And so, Granty,' Edward intoned, as if he had never heard Henry's interruption, 'I will say goodbye and I will try to forgive you.' He jammed his cap on his head and murmured, 'There. I've done it.'

James stepped forward. 'Well,' he began, 'Of course we'll all miss you . . . ' His face abruptly crumpled and Lorna grabbed his hand saying, 'That's very good, James.' She nodded fiercely at Henry. 'Say something quickly.'

Here they were, Henry thought, three old men in their sixties, all totally bereft because Granty had always been there for them and now she wasn't. 'Goodbye, Granty,' he said. 'We will miss you very much. You loved us all and we loved you.' He could see Edward clapping his hands together. 'And now, unless anyone else wants to say something . . . ' Henry glanced at the three women, all of whom shook their heads, their faces blue with cold. He stepped as near to the edge of the cliff as he dared and hurled what was left of Granty out onto the sea.

★ ★ ★

In the evening, they visited a different pub; it had a nearly identical menu to the place they had visited at lunch. The events of the afternoon had had a sobering effect on the party and even James accepted his fat chips without comment.

'It's been a funny sort of day,' Louise said. 'I'm very touched that Aunt Teresa wanted me to come. We always had such fun when we saw each other but the last time was eight years ago. To be honest, I'm a little baffled. I can't imagine why she was so keen for me to be here.'

'I can tell you the answer to that,' Edward said.

Henry's eyes bore into his brother's. To his surprise, Edward's face suddenly twisted, his complexion reddened and he murmured, 'Actually, I can't.'

Colette was quick to fill the curious silence that followed. 'Granty often talked about you,' she told Louise. 'She was very proud to be your godmother. She often said she was so happy in Higgleigh when you and your parents lived next door.'

'She never forgot my birthday,' Louise said. 'And when my husband died, she sent me a beautiful letter. I have it still. Things like that mean a lot.' She caught Henry's eye for a moment and then smiled at Colette. 'So tell me, why are you here?'

'I'm not sure.' Colette looked a little taken aback. 'Granty was always very kind to me and . . . '

'Colette and Granty were great friends,' Henry said. 'Granty was an enthusiastic film buff and so is Colette. She can tell you anything about Hitchcock's films. She has an amazing memory.'

344

He gave an encouraging nod. 'Go on, Colette. Tell them something.'

'Well . . .' Colette thought for a few moments. 'Have you all seen *Rebecca*?' She glanced around the table. 'So you know that Joan Fontaine played the part of the second Mrs de Winter. But there was another very unlikely candidate for the role. Who was it?'

'I have no idea,' Edward said.

'Granty would have known,' Henry said.

'Granty did,' Colette said. 'Laurence Olivier played Maxim and wanted Vivien Leigh to act opposite him. And did you know that David O. Selznick wanted Vivien Leigh to play the part of Alicia in *Notorious*?'

'Never heard of it,' James said.

'Oh James, you must have done!' Colette was shocked. 'It's one of the best films ever made.'

'Did Vivien Leigh play the part?' he asked.

Of course she didn't! It was Ingrid Bergman. You have to see it. Claude Rains is wonderful and the actress who plays his mother is terrifying. Of course in real life she was only four years older than him but you'd never know . . .'

Granty, Henry thought later, would have loved the evening. She'd have swooned over Cary Grant and complained about James Stewart — he must ask Colette why she'd never liked him — and she'd have noted every occasional glance Louise threw at him. He could imagine her urging him on: 'Speak to her, Henry, tell her what you think,' which did rather presuppose that he knew what he thought.

345

James had organized a trip to the nearby island of Tresco for their final full day. It was, he told them, a family-owned island with outstanding tropical gardens. At breakfast — during which he sent his bacon back twice — he announced that they should all meet at St Mary's Quay at eleven. Until then, he said magnanimously, everyone was free.

At three minutes past eleven all but one of the party had assembled at the quayside. 'As usual,' Edward said, a little unfairly, 'someone is late.' Henry was about to offer to go on a search when Louise raced into view. 'I'm sorry,' she called, 'I'm so very sorry!' She stopped beside Henry and strove to catch her breath. 'I've been buying T-shirts for my grandchildren and I'm afraid I got carried away . . . '

'Never mind that,' Edward said, 'Let's just go! We don't want to keep the skipper waiting any longer.'

The skipper seemed quite unconcerned. He helped each of them into the small wooden boat, warned them it might be a little choppy and started the engine. In fact, the journey was fairly smooth and it was impossible not to be excited by the sight of empty golden beaches as they came close to shore.

'We'll do the gardens first,' James said. 'If we walk briskly we can cover most of them before lunch.'

It turned out to be more like a march than a walk, with James barking out information about

346

the subtropical climate and the two thousand species of plant life. They passed a number of walled enclosures and, had he been on his own, Henry would have liked to explore all of them.

It appeared that Louise had similar ideas. 'I want to explore those steps,' she told James, 'the view at the top must be great.'

'There's nothing you can't see down here,' James assured her, 'and we need to get on if we're to see the shipwrecked figureheads. Now they really are worth seeing.'

'I'll catch you up,' Louise said and set off at a quick pace before turning back to Henry. 'What about it, Henry?' she asked. 'Are you coming with me?'

Henry, aware of four pairs of eyes silently watching him, awarded them with a casual wave before scurrying after her.

'There is something about your brothers,' she murmured as they climbed the steps, 'that makes me want to misbehave. And oh,' she breathed as they stopped halfway up, 'look at this view. It's like the Garden of Eden!'

She was right. Apart from the odd stone wall and rustic bench, all one could see was lush vegetation, towering palm trees and vivid splashes of colour. She beamed at him. 'I'm so glad I'm here.'

'Me too,' Henry said. 'It's beautiful.'

'It is,' Louise said, 'but what I mean is that I'm glad I'm here with *you*.'

'Well,' Henry said, 'so am I.'

She laughed. 'Oh Henry, you haven't changed! I remember walking back from school with you years and years ago and I said that you were the best-looking boy in our year. I've never seen anyone look so uncomfortable! You won't remember that of course.'

'I remember it very well. You were making fun of me.'

'I meant it though. When my Douglas died, your mother wrote and told me how much you missed your wife. I often thought about ringing you.'

'I wish you had done.'

'I'm glad I didn't. I was very over-emotional at the time. You'd have been embarrassed.' She loosened the scarf round her neck. 'We'd better catch up with the others. If we don't go now we might never find them and then you'd have only me for company.'

'I wouldn't mind that,' Henry said.

'Neither would I,' she said.

29

Maddie's coleslaw salad was one of the most charisma-free meals she had ever made for herself. Coleslaw with too little mayonnaise was like apple crumble without brown sugar. I can't work and diet, Maddie thought, particularly when I have to watch Gregory eating his way through a plate of ham-and-pickle sandwiches.

He felt her eyes on him and looked across at her. 'Do you want to hear some gossip?'

The humanization of Gregory was gathering apace. Pre-Minty, he would have never asked a question like that.

'Of course I do,' Maddie said.

'Minty was looking at Freddy's Facebook page last night and there was another picture of him with the zombie actress. He was walking down a street with her. He had her little girl on his shoulders.'

'Why the hell does he post these photos?' Maddie asked. 'What exactly is he trying to prove?'

'He is raising his profile,' Gregory said. 'The zombie actress is, according to Minty, a rising star.'

'Well, if I were Victoria,' Maddie said, 'I'd take the first plane out to California and throw my wedding ring at him.'

'She can't,' Gregory said. 'She's working. And she knows how the industry works. And besides, she has an admirer of her own.'

'Really?' Maddie put down her coleslaw. 'Who?'

'Apparently,' Gregory bit into his sandwich, 'she's been seeing Joe.' He gave Maddie a significant nod. '*Your* Joe.'

'He never was *my* Joe, and I don't believe it. She can't be. I spoke to Laura on the phone only last night. She didn't say anything.'

'I'm not surprised,' Gregory said. 'Think about it. They were cross with you for taking advantage of poor innocent Joe and now Joe's taking advantage of poor absent Freddy. Apparently.'

'I don't believe it. I mean I can believe he'd like *her* but I can't believe she'd like *him*. She loves Freddy. And Joe's a ridiculous boy who takes himself far too seriously.'

'I totally agree,' Gregory said, 'I never understood what you saw in him.'

'My relationship with Joe, if you can call it a relationship, was based on very specific expectations. Victoria has Freddy. And she's sweet and kind and beautiful. If they *are* seeing each other I bet it's only because she's upset with Freddy. Don't you find all this depressing? Six months ago we watched Freddy and Victoria tell the world they were soulmates and now there's all this gossip swirling about them. It's enough to make you give up on love forever.'

'I thought you *had* given up on love.'

'I had. And now I shall give it up all over again.'

Gregory took another bite of his sandwich. 'I shan't,' he said.

Guy had invited Maddie over to supper again and, since he was an excellent cook, she felt it was a good time to put an end to the diet she'd long wearied of. Once Gregory crumbled, she'd known it was only a matter of time. She sat at Guy's kitchen bar, sipping Prosecco, eating olives and watching him cut up skinless chicken fillets.

'There's something very satisfying about slicing these things,' he said. 'It's something to do with the texture. They squelch and they're easy to cut.'

'I like watching you cook,' Maddie said. 'You're very precise.'

'I know. It drives Leo mad. He likes to throw everything in and see what happens.'

'How *is* Leo?'

Guy put the last strip of chicken onto a plate and took the chopping board over to the sink. 'He has an important obligation tonight. He's meeting Jess's boyfriend.'

'She has a boyfriend? Jess has a boyfriend? When did that happen? She only had a baby last week.'

'She had Phoenix three months ago. A lot's happened since then. Did you know she enrolled with a dating agency?'

'I had no idea. And she's met someone already? I'd love to know her secret.'

'You should talk to Leo. He was the one who wrote her profile and chose her photo. She went out for a drink with a man called Simon and then a few days later they went out to dinner and then he invited her over to supper and tonight she's cooking *him* supper and introducing him to Leo.'

'It's like fast-forwarding a film. No one gets that serious that quickly.'

'Jess would beg to differ.'

'Wow.' Maddie stared across at the small mound of chicken strips. 'How does Leo feel about it all?'

'He's very nervous about tonight. He really wants to like Simon. If he doesn't he has no idea what to say to Jess.'

'There must be something wrong with him,' Maddie said.

'Who? Leo?'

'No, Simon. I bet he's been married five times or he lives with his mother.'

'He's a widower with two teenage sons. He's a general surgeon at St Thomas's Hospital. He used to work for *Médecins sans Frontières*.'

'He sounds too good to be true,' Maddie said. 'Perhaps he just wants a nanny to care for his horrible sons.'

'Jess has met his sons. She says they're lovely. And Simon, apparently, looks like George Clooney.'

'He's obviously perfect.' Maddie bit into her third olive. 'Of course I'm thrilled she's found a nice man and I'd like it put on record that I'm neither bitter nor jealous but I would like to know how it is we both join dating agencies and I meet perverts and liars and she meets a heroic doctor who loves children and looks like George Clooney.'

'You've just had bad luck,' Guy said. 'You should be inspired by this. Somewhere there's a brave kind doctor just waiting for you.'

'Thank you for your confidence. You must admit it's a little depressing to be beaten in the dating game by a woman who's over forty and has just had a baby.' Maddie sighed. 'To be honest, I can't summon much enthusiasm at the moment. Apart from anything else, there's too much else going on. Did I tell you Nina and Robbie are getting married in May? Nina's coming to London on Saturday and we're going to look for a dress for her.'

'Weddings,' Guy said, 'are perfect for meeting new people.'

Maddie shrugged. 'I know all the guests. I managed to upset most of them over Christmas. Do you want me to slice those mushrooms?'

'Quarter them, will you? I'll prepare the broccoli and then everything's ready.' He refilled their glasses. 'I have something to suggest to you.'

'It sounds serious.'

★   ★   ★

'I don't know if it is or not. It's not really a suggestion. It's just a thought. It's an embryonic thought. That's a pun by the way.'

'Is it? Are you talking about babies?'

'Leo and Jess have talked about having another one in a couple of years. If Simon stays around that might all change. Even if it doesn't,

353

it's set me thinking. I have a very, very hypothetical proposition to put before you. Supposing you're still single in a couple of years, how would you feel about having a baby with me? I mean, I know Phoenix is only three months old but Leo and Jess seem to make it work and . . . It's only an idea, of course. Feel free to laugh at it. Feel free not to respond at all. It's quite unnerving having you look at me like that. I feel I've just dropped my trousers or something . . . '

'I'm sorry,' Maddie said. 'I was thinking. I reckon you'd be a fabulous father.'

'It's just a suggestion. I mean anything can happen in a couple of years.'

'I know. It's a hypothetical proposition. But it's a very interesting one.' She glanced across at Guy's film poster. 'You'd have to promise me one thing though. If we were to have a boy, there's no way I'd agree to call him Montgomery. Now Blane on the other hand . . . '

'We would never call him Blane.' He picked up the broccoli and then put it down again. 'By the way, I misled you about Simon.'

'You mean he's not a doctor or a great father or a member of *Médecins* . . . '

'No. He's all those things. But he doesn't look like George Clooney.'

Maddie smiled. 'I knew it!'

'What Jess actually said was that he's a dead ringer for Liam Neeson.'

★　★　★

That night Maddie sat in bed with her laptop on her knees and studied Freddy's Facebook page. The girl beside him was very pretty and her little daughter looked quite at home on Freddy's shoulders. But then, he'd always been good with children. It was weird to look at the photo and find she no longer loved him. There was a time not so long ago when she believed he was her soulmate. Perhaps he had been. Perhaps he would be still if he hadn't been offered the part in California, if she hadn't lost her temper, if he hadn't lost his, if he hadn't slept with Esther, if she'd taken him back. There were so many ifs and none of them mattered anymore.

Freddy had married Victoria and now he'd gone to California and was consorting with sexy starlets. She was still working with Gregory and they were at last beginning to make proper money. She'd met a couple of odd men but she'd also made a good friend in Guy; she'd discovered the beauty of babies and learnt that nothing could beat the safety of her niece. What else was there? She'd lost her beloved Granty but she was closer than ever to her father and her sister. She'd moved on from Freddy and she'd survived. Life had changed, the future was uncertain, but it no longer hurt that Freddy wouldn't be part of it.

In the six months since Freddy's wedding, Maddie had felt like a customer in a clothes shop trying on different outfits. There had been the single-minded career-girl suit, the low-cut party-time frock, the universal-godmother suit and, finally, the big maternal cardigan. She had more or less given up on *that* dream when Chloe emerged from the hollow tree trunk. God had given her niece back and in return she had forfeited any idea of having a daughter as well. It was, Maddie saw now, an irrational response to a brief scary episode. Maddie didn't believe in a God who would threaten to extinguish one small life in order to stop her creating another.

★ ★ ★

Now Guy had offered her the vision of a unique designer costume. She was a thirty-six year-old woman with a business she cared about. She had no wish to spend the next few years seeking out the odd and very rare man who wasn't psychologically flawed or attracted to much younger women. She allowed herself to dwell for a few moments on the undeniable attraction of the tartan-scarf man in Higgleigh. Colette was right. Romantic love was an unreliable emotion. Friendship on the other hand, was not.

Maddie woke the next morning with the feeling that her life was on track once more. She was in control. And then, just as she was leaving for work, she had a phone call from Bryony Adams, the nice woman who ran the Forest Hill Plug Club. Her son, Eddie, had been knocked off his motorbike the night before. She was very sorry but she wasn't sure she could . . .

'Don't even think about it,' Maddie said. 'I'll take your place this afternoon. Don't worry about a thing,' which was, she thought after she eventually came off the phone, a singularly stupid thing to say to a woman whose son had broken his leg in at least three places.

When she finally arrived at Gregory's flat, she could hear him talking on the phone. By the time she'd shaken her umbrella and taken off her wet mac, she found him staring at his screen, apparently unaware that she was at least forty minutes late. She told him about Bryony's phone call and poor Eddie's accident and he grunted. The humanization programme appeared to have stalled.

'Gregory,' she said, 'have you heard a word I said?'

He looked at her then. 'I've had your sister on the phone. We should have brought her in a long time ago. Her programme for the Ipswich club is the best we have.'

'I know that . . . '

'And now she's come up with something else. She says we should expand our horizons. She said she was out last night and saw a group of teenagers sitting in some bus shelter. She said they're always there. She said we should have Plug Clubs for teenagers.'

'That's a totally different concept.'

'I know but it's a good one. We should think about it. Oh, and she told me to tell you your father's marooned in the Scilly Isles. Nina's very worried.'

'About Dad?'

'About your grandmother's dog,' Gregory said. 'Nina's looking after him and he's pining.'

30

Henry had always seen himself as someone who was slow to judge and he was rather shocked to find that he wasn't. But in this case, he knew he was right and it was all the more shocking since the day had seemed to hold such promise.

When they came back from Tresco, Lorna had suggested that before setting out for their final pub meal, they should meet for a drink in the hotel lounge. James volunteered to buy the wine and they all agreed to meet at seven.

Henry came downstairs to find James and Colette taking glasses from the cupboard on the wall. 'I can't find any staff here,' he said. 'I wanted to see Mr Harris about the taxi tomorrow but there's no one at the desk.'

'He goes home at night,' Colette said. 'We're the only ones here. I love it. It's so surreal. I feel like we're in *The Shining.*'

'Except,' James said, 'the place isn't haunted, we're not cut off by snow and none of us is mad.'

'As far as you know,' Colette said.

Edward appeared in the doorway looking triumphant. 'The wine is now presentable,' he said. 'I've had it in the hotel fridge for the last hour. Where's the bottle opener?'

'I assumed,' James said, 'that you'd bring one back from the kitchen.'

'I couldn't find one. I assumed you'd found one yourself.'

'I'll go and look,' Henry said. 'There has to be one somewhere.'

'I'll come with you,' Colette said. 'I've never been in a hotel kitchen before.'

She and Henry walked through the corridor, down a couple of steps and into the dining-room. It took a few moments to locate the dining-room light switch and when Colette did so she walked between the tables, holding her arms out. 'Oh Henry, I love this! We have the entire place to ourselves. I love Mr Harris for trusting us to be here on our own.' She marched through to the kitchen and threw open the door. 'Look at this! It gleams. You must remind me to congratulate him tomorrow after breakfast.'

'I will,' Henry said, 'but only if I can find the corkscrew. It's a funny thing but as soon as I know I can't open a bottle I find I'm desperate to have a drink'

They went through all the drawers and Henry was beginning to despair when Colette found one hanging on a hook next to the fridge.

'Colette,' Henry said, 'I am very glad you're here. Let's go. I'm dying of thirst.'

Lorna was coming down the stairs and the three of them converged on the lounge together. 'Have you done your packing?' she asked them. 'We have to be at the airport by half past eight, you know.'

'I'm sure we don't,' Henry said. 'The airbus doesn't go till twelve.'

'It goes at nine,' Lorna said. 'I'll check with James.'

In the lounge, a strange sight greeted them.

Louise's body, dressed in black trousers and matching polo neck, made a perfect n-shaped curve while on either side of her James and Edward, their complexions red with effort, were trying without success to touch their toes.

'What's going on?' Henry asked.

Lorna, a single-minded woman, said, 'James, Henry says the sky bus goes at twelve.'

'My ticket says that too,' Colette said.

★ ★ ★

'I did tell you all,' James said, straightening himself with difficulty, 'to book the morning flight. We're going at nine.' He glanced at Louise and Edward for confirmation and they both nodded.

'I did book the morning flight,' Henry said, picking up the bottle of wine and applying the corkscrew to it. 'I presumed you meant the midday one.'

'Midday, Henry is *after* noon. I can't believe you made such a mistake.'

'Well, I did too,' Colette said. 'It doesn't matter. Henry and I can share a taxi to the station at Newquay.' She sat on one of the chairs round the small table. 'What were you doing when we came in? It looked very strenuous.'

'We were trying,' James said, 'to touch our toes.'

'It's my fault,' Louise said. 'I was telling them my beauty routine. First, I do press-ups — they refused to try those — and then I touch my toes. I bet them both a glass of wine at the pub that they wouldn't be able to do it. They couldn't.'

'I can,' Lorna said. 'I do it in Pilates.'

'I intend to do Pilates,' Colette said. 'I shall take it up when I retire.'

'The sooner the better,' Louise said. 'We need to take care of ourselves *now*. That applies to our faces as well as our bodies.' She took a seat next to Colette and gazed at her earnestly. 'Gravity drags everything down as we get older. The skin's ability to produce collagen diminishes with age, it loses its firmness. I noticed it with you last night in the pub. When you don't talk, your mouth drops downwards. It makes you look grumpy.'

Colette went rather pink. She murmured, 'Oh dear. How very alarming.'

'It's easily done,' Louise said graciously. 'There are facial exercises I could show you but the best thing to do is to smile all the time. It's a lot cheaper than double-jaw surgery!'

She smiled at Henry but he didn't smile back. He was astounded by her behaviour. How could she pick on Colette of all people? Colette, who had been so happy and cheerful, now sat in frozen silence. It was wrong, Henry thought. It was wrong, it was mean, it was cruel.

★   ★   ★

He and Colette came down to see the others off the next morning. Louise hugged him and whispered, 'Come and see me,' and Henry was grateful for Edward's excessive regard for timekeeping; his frenzied determination to

361

shepherd his companions into the taxi put a stop to any further conversation.

Breakfast without his brothers was a pleasant experience. The waitress, who only yesterday had deposited their orders with silent, scared speed, was happy today to suggest local places to visit before their departure. She picked up one of the brochures Colette had brought down from her room and gave an authoritative nod.

'There's a lovely bay at Old Town, full of golden sand. And you can walk past Harold Wilson's house. He was a British Prime Minister a long time ago and he had a holiday house here. You'll enjoy that.'

Henry stared after her retreating figure. 'Did you hear that? 'A long time ago . . . ?' I remember Harold Wilson being elected. I thought he was the most exciting leader we'd ever had.'

'He was never exciting,' Colette said. 'He smoked a pipe and had bad teeth.'

'Everyone had bad teeth in those days.'

'And he let himself be bullied by Marcia Falkbender.'

'I'm quite sure that wasn't her name.'

'I'd like to see his house,' Colette said, 'and it doesn't look too far to walk.'

'A gentle stroll would be very nice,' Henry said. 'One can't have a gentle stroll with James at the helm.'

When they came down to the desk with their suitcases, Mr Harris had some startling news. Although the Skybus had left without incident at nine, their own flight at twelve had been cancelled due to bad weather. 'I'm afraid,' he said, 'you'll be spending another night here.'

It could have been worse, Henry thought. He might have been marooned with Edward and James.

When they set out on their walk, they agreed they were glad not to be flying. The sky was thunderously grey and the wind stung their eyes. 'However,' Henry said, 'you can smell the sea and that's such a good smell.'

'I'll take your word for it,' Colette said. The hood of her anorak was pulled tight round her face and her thick scarf obscured all but her eyes and nose.

In this weather, a gentle stroll was out of the question. They walked hard and fast, stopping only to watch a group of men, armed with ropes, trying to salvage a small boat that had cut loose from its moorings and was straddled precariously on the side of a rock.

'Do you think we should help them?' Colette asked.

'The point is we *wouldn't*,' Henry said. 'I only have to look at a rope to feel helpless.'

'When I was at school,' Colette said, 'we had to climb ropes in the gym. I could never do it.'

'Neither could I,' Henry said, 'and I don't intend to start now.'

Harold Wilson's house was a disappointment. Small, grey, dour and curiously exposed for a Prime Minister's residence, it was set back from the beach on an expanse of grass.

'I suppose it made a change from Downing Street,' Colette said. 'Henry, I hate to be a killjoy, but it's raining. I'd be happy to change the smells of sea air for those of a nice warm pub.' Henry agreed and took Colette's arm as they turned into the wind. She looked as if she might be carried away at any moment.

When they finally sat down in front of a fire with two large glasses of wine, steam rose from their wet trousers.

'I have to tell you,' Colette said, 'if you want to go walking again today you're on your own. I'm staying here. It's bliss.'

'I agree,' said Henry. 'But look at it this way. If we hadn't been out, we wouldn't appreciate being in.'

Colette gave one of her pistol-cracking laughs. 'I don't need a walk to make me appreciate a coal fire and a glass of Merlot.' She raised her glass in front of her. 'I think we should drink to Granty. She always liked a good fire.'

'To Granty,' Henry said and took a deliberate gulp before setting his glass down. He was glad he had Colette to himself. He had a sudden overwhelming urge to confide in her. Now he thought about it, she was, he realised, the only person in whom he possibly *could* confide. 'Colette,' he said, 'that night of the funeral, I had a long talk with Robbie.'

'I noticed,' Colette said. 'You both looked very serious.'

'It was rather upsetting. He'd had quite a bit to drink but he wasn't drunk. Well, he wasn't very drunk. He told me that Granty had rung him just a few days before she died. She had something rather shocking to tell him. Many years ago, Dad was in Paris at some convention and we were all at boarding school. She heard a phone-in programme on the radio. A man was talking about the loss of his wife and the fact that his small son was sad because he was beginning to forget what his mother looked like. Granty told Robbie that she recognised the caller. He was an old boyfriend. After the programme she rang him on an impulse and he suggested they meet for lunch at his house in Cambridge.' He noticed Colette frowning. 'Did she ever tell you about this?'

'No, not at all. Carry on please.'

'Apparently they had a very intense lunch and then . . . ' He paused but now that he'd started — why had he started? — he had to go on. 'Granty told Robbie they had sex on the kitchen table. She said it was a moment of madness and that she confessed it all to Dad who apparently was very good about it. The thing is . . . '

'What?'

'It seems so incredible. She adored Dad. And she'd never have let him go off to Paris without her. The whole story is incredible.'

Colette sat back in her chair and folded her aims. 'Oh Henry, you've seen *Sleepless in Seattle*, haven't you?'

He stared at her blankly. 'Yes, but . . . I don't see that . . . Are you saying that . . . ?'

'You don't believe Granty's story for a moment, do you? It's straight out of *Sleepless in Seattle*. As far as the sex on the table is concerned, I *think* it might come from *The Postman Always Rings Twice* with Jessica Lange

365

and Jack Nicholson. Such a clever thing to say, it's such a very graphic image which, presumably, was Granty's intention.'

'She made the whole thing up? But that's . . . ' Henry struggled to find the right word. 'That's preposterous.'

'I'm not sure I agree. If Granty had simply preached the virtues of forgiveness, Robbie would have remained unmoved. But she tells him a story in which a man he respected endured the same indignity as he did but responded with grace and compassion.'

'But if it wasn't true,' Henry protested, 'she told Robbie a lie!'

'And now he's back with Nina,' Colette said. 'So it worked.'

'But it's based on a fantasy! You don't think that's wrong?'

'Well, you know what I'm like. I've been living with a fantasy for years.'

'But that's . . . ' Henry stopped and stared at Colette.

She looked at him with eyes that were an odd combination of defiance and sympathy. 'I'm sorry, Henry, I didn't mean to embarrass you. You've always been so kind and tactful. I shouldn't have said that.'

'No,' Henry murmured. 'I can't pretend I ever understood but . . . '

'Granty did. The day I heard she'd died, I went to my bedroom and took down all the photos and posters. I thought: if Granty could do what she did, then it was time that I got rid of Hugh.'

'You sound like you admire her for what she did. She left us all, Colette, she never said a word, she never gave us a chance to say goodbye . . .'

'I know. I know you and James and Edward are very upset by that . . .'

'Upset is putting it mildly. She *left* us.'

'I know. It's very hard. But she hated being ill and she hated people seeing her ill. It takes bravery to do what she did. And she did it in style: champagne and her best friend by her side. That's what she wanted to do. And before she went she rang up Robbie and quite obviously gave the performance of a lifetime. What's not to respect?'

Henry didn't answer. He sat and sipped his wine. 'I wish,' he said eventually, 'that I spoke at her funeral. It's what she wanted. I shall always feel guilty about that.'

'She'd have understood.'

'That's not the point.'

Colette stared down at her glass. 'I'm an expert on guilt,' she said. 'And you don't need to feel it.'

'What have *you* done to feel guilty about?'

★   ★   ★

'I've done plenty.' Colette sat up very straight and looked directly at Henry. 'In September, my first husband wanted to see me. You probably don't remember Alan.'

'Not really.' Henry and Marianne had only met him once, at the small civil wedding

367

ceremony in London. He was a sullen and taciturn bridegroom. Immediately after the ceremony he had taken Colette off to Newcastle and in the next few years she had rebuffed all attempts by Marianne to get them down for a visit. 'What did he want after all this time?' he asked.

'He was dying. His wife said he was desperate to talk to me and tell me he was sorry. I wouldn't go.'

'You must have had your reasons.'

'Oh yes. He used to hit me when he was drunk. But I should have gone to see him.'

'Good God, of course you shouldn't. Why didn't you tell Marianne? Why didn't you tell both of us? You should have come to us.'

'I wanted to sort it out myself. And I did. I left him. I got another job and then I married Robert.'

'I remember Robert. He was a nice man. I liked him. He was very sweet with the children.'

'He is a nice man. And now I've hurt him too.'

Henry was finding it difficult to follow all these revelations. 'I don't understand. Are you still in touch with him?'

'I see him once a year. I saw him in January. So did you.'

'I'm sorry, Colette, you've lost me . . . '

'You were in a restaurant in London with Marianne's old friend and I was having a meal with Robert.'

Henry downed his wine and put his glass to one side. 'You were in a restaurant with *Robert*? That was *Robert*?'

'Yes. I can see why you didn't recognise him. I wish he wouldn't wear that wig. The colour's not right at all. He's a very nice man and he was a very kind husband. It was my fault we broke up. I just couldn't find him attractive in a dress.'

'I should think you didn't! He wasn't attractive at all. I remember thinking he . . . she . . . he was very odd indeed. You can't feel guilty about that.'

'It's not *that* I feel guilty about. He was always very fond of you. He expected me to tell you who he was and I couldn't. I was embarrassed and he saw that and it hurt him. I feel bad about that. He lives in Canada now and he comes over once a year to see his mother and he always takes me out and . . . that hurt him.' She moved her chair back and stood up. 'I need to go the Ladies now.'

Henry went to the bar and bought two more glasses of Merlot. He took them back to their table and sat down. He was stunned by Colette's candour. But then he had surprised himself by telling her about Robbie's last conversation with Granty. Perhaps their enforced sojourn on the island was responsible. It was as if they were outside time, outside their normal lives.

He was humbled by her revelations. While he and Marianne had brought up their girls, dropped in on his parents and seen their friends, Colette had coped with first a wife-beater and then a transvestite. After Marianne's death, while he had been absorbed in his loneliness, Colette, who had been on her own for decades, had regularly driven up to Ipswich to see Nina and

369

her girls — which was how she'd known about the troll song, of course — been a rock to Maddie, and a good friend to Granty. While he'd been looking for love he'd never once thought why it was that Colette needed a fantasy boyfriend.

He would be different now, he thought, he would try to be more of a support to her. He could start by helping her to feel better about Robert. Perhaps he could offer to join them for lunch next time he came to England.

Colette came back to her seat with rather red eyes and a very determined smile. 'Oh Henry,' she said, 'that's a very big glass. I shall be quite hopeless for the rest of the day.'

'We've nothing to do for the rest of the day so it hardly matters.' He leant forward. 'About Robert, Colette . . . '

'Henry,' she said, 'I don't like talking about myself and now I know why. It's very depressing.' She stared at the pocket of his jacket. 'I think that's your phone beeping. You ought to look at it.'

Henry pulled it out and read the message. 'That's odd,' he said. 'It's from Edward.'

'What does he say?'

' "Tell Colette my ankle still hurts" ' He looked up in time to see the ghost of a smile around Colette's mouth. 'What does that mean?'

'I have no idea,' Colette said, taking a sip of her wine.

Henry stared at her. 'I remember!' he cried. 'On our first night here we were at the pub and Edward was about to tell Louise why Granty had

370

wanted her here and he suddenly looked as if he'd been hit very hard. Colette, that was you! You *did* hit him very hard!'

'I simply tapped his ankle. He was going to spoil everything.'

'Well,' Henry said, 'there was nothing to spoil.'

'But you got on so well . . . '

'Well, I . . . What did *you* think of her? Did you like her?'

'I thought she was very beautiful.'

'That doesn't answer my question.'

'I could see she liked *you*, Henry, and that's what counts.'

'You didn't like her.'

'I didn't say that.'

'You don't have to. To be honest, I knew as soon as she went on about uplifting facial exercises that we had nothing in common. And if ever I catch you doing a uplifting facial exercise, I shall be very angry.'

'She meant well . . . '

'I don't care. I found it very annoying. I've found these last two days very enlightening. When Louise walked into Newquay airport, I was horribly nervous. I was nervous every time we talked. And now I realise I don't need a new wife. I have my friends and my family. Did I tell you that Nina and Robbie are putting their house on the market? They want to come back to Higgleigh. If they do, I shall be on hand to babysit. I want that. I'm relaxed with that. I like being relaxed. If I had the choice of sitting here with you or sitting here with Louise I'd pick you every time.'

371

Colette had gone a little pink. 'Thank you, Henry. That means a lot. We *are* friends, aren't we?'

'We certainly are. We must see each other more often. I can't believe you kicked Edward's ankle! Are you free next Saturday?'

'Well, yes. I suppose you could come down for lunch.'

'No,' Henry said. 'I can say this because we are friends. On the very few occasions you cooked for Marianne and me, we could see that you found the process of cooking a meal a laborious one. I will come down next Saturday and take you out to lunch and we shall put the world to rights. If Maddie's free, she can come too.'

'Well,' said Colette, 'I would like that very much.'

'I'll tell you something else,' Henry said. 'Do you remember that lady I saved back in September? Her daughter's getting married in May and has invited me and a friend to the wedding. Would you come with me?'

'I like weddings,' Colette said. 'I'd be happy to come. It sounds like fun.'

'It will be now I know I won't be on my own.' Henry said. He raised his glass. He felt as if he had made an extraordinary discovery. 'Here's to friendship,' he said, 'to plain and simple friendship!'

31

Apart from a nagging, minor anxiety, Maddie had been keenly anticipating Nina's wedding party.

The civil ceremony had taken place the day before with only parents and best friends attending. As far as Nina was concerned it was the party tonight that counted, on this, the longest day of the year. So Maddie had come up from London and today she and her father were looking after the children while Robbie's very capable parents and an army of friends transformed the town hall.

Now as people began to arrive, everything was ready. Caterers manned the bar, music played and plates of sandwiches and pastries were laid out in the other room. Tealights lit up the tables against the walls, bunting straddled the beams and paper hearts dangled from the ceiling. Nina looked stunning in a sparkling silver dress and Robbie resembled a jovial gangster in black shirt, black trousers and scarlet tie. The only slight worry was that Colette, who was driving down from a business appointment in Durham, had so far failed to show up.

Maddie spotted the arrival of Uncle William and his girlfriend and she set off across the floor to meet them. She knew the history of The Smile and looked forward to meeting the beautiful Ellen face to face. Halfway there, she was waylaid by the nagging, minor anxiety. He'd lost weight and looked rather fine in his grey trousers and pink-and-white striped shirt. In other circumstances she'd have wanted to congratulate him.

'Clive!' she said, gearing up for yet another apology.

'Hello, Maddie,' he said. 'I thought I'd have seen you at the registry office.'

'I wasn't invited,' she said. 'I gather it was very exclusive.'

'I suppose it was. Just parents and best friends.' He emphasised the last two words. 'We had a great time. Robbie brought along some champagne. I went with Verity. We've been together for a while now.'

'Really?' Maddie said. 'That's great news. Where did you meet?'

'At the gym,' he said. 'I joined it in January.' Accusation oozed from every pore. 'Someone told me I needed to lose weight.'

Maddie's heart plummeted. 'Clive, when I said those things back at Christmas . . . '

'Here she is now,' Clive said. He held out an arm to a tall, generously built woman in a very short dress. She held a very full glass of wine.

'Hi,' she said, 'I'm Verity. I love your outfit.'

'Thank you. I bought it for my ex-boyfriend's wedding last year. It's nice to have a chance to wear it again.'

'Verity,' Clive said, 'this is Maddie.'

Verity had a singularly sweet smile that closed like a trap as soon as Clive mentioned her name. 'Clive's told me about you,' she said.

'I'm sure he has.' Maddie offered an ingratiating smile that was received with stony expressions by both Verity and Clive. 'I'm afraid I behaved badly last time I saw him. I got very drunk and was upset about something I can't even remember. Poor Clive got caught in the crossfire.'

'He was very upset,' Verity said. 'You told him he was fat.'

'That was very wrong of me and I feel very bad about it.'

'Yes, it was,' Verity said. 'It's not nice to tell people they're fat.'

Clive's arm tightened round Verity's waist. 'I'm very lucky with Verity,' he said. 'Do you have a boyfriend here tonight?'

'No. I'm still a sweet single girl!' Maddie's phone rang and she pulled it from her shoulder bag as if it were a lifeline. 'I'm sorry, I'd better take this.' Colette had earned her undying gratitude by choosing that moment to ring her. She caught sight of her father, standing near the bar with Lorna, shooting a concerned expression at her.

'Maddie?' Colette sounded breathless. 'I've just left Henry's house. I'm so sorry I'm late. There was an accident on the motorway and the queues were horrendous. And then I got to Henry's and the babysitter was about to put Megan to bed and she wanted to say goodnight and then I had to change . . . '

'Don't worry, everything's fine. The party's hardly got going. Do you know where to come?'

'It's just off the high street, down by the

graveyard, isn't it? I'll find it.'

'I'll come out now and look for you. See you in a moment.' Anything, she thought, to get away from Clive and Verity. She gave them another apologetic glance before fleeing towards the door.

Her father caught up with her as she stepped outside. 'Was that Colette? Is she all right?'

'She got stuck in a traffic jam. She's been home and is walking over here. I'm on my way to meet her.'

'I'll come with you,' Henry said. 'I was trapped by Lorna. I swear she's as bad as James these days. She wanted to know what time they should arrive for lunch tomorrow. I said that Nina and Robbie are staying the night in The Woodland Hotel and that I promised I wouldn't serve up till two. Do you know what she said? She said: 'James and I always eat at one.''

★ ★ ★

Maddie laughed. It was good to be outside. It was a perfect summer's evening. There was a gentle breeze and a faint smell of lilac coming from the graveyard.

'So then,' Henry said, 'I explained that her B&B was famous for its breakfasts and so she wouldn't even *want* to eat till two and she proceeded to give me a very long lecture on the importance of regular mealtimes.'

'At least they made the effort to come. It's a long way from Devon.'

'There was an ulterior motive. They're very

keen to pick up Granty's bedroom lamps for their spare room.'

On the other side of the road, Colette called out to them and they both looked up. A man in a tartan scarf and padded sleeveless jacket was staring at Maddie but it was only later she remembered that. In the next few moments, everything seemed to happen in terrifying slow motion. Colette stepped out onto the road as a black mini careered towards her. They had only time to shriek a warning at her. The man in the tartan scarf leapt out and grabbed Colette by the waist, pulling her back onto the pavement where they fell in a tangle of limbs.

Henry, paying no regard to traffic, dashed across the road and nearly got run over himself. Maddie followed behind and saw him fall to his knees and take Colette into his arms.

'Colette!' Henry said. 'Speak to me, Colette!'

It was horrible. Her eyes were closed, her face was white, her body as limp as a rag doll.

'Colette,' Henry cried. 'Come back to me!'

The man in the scarf eased himself slowly and painfully into a sitting position. 'Shall I call an ambulance?' he asked. 'Shouldn't I call an ambulance?'

'Colette!' Henry said. 'Colette!'

Maddie held her breath, not daring even to blink. And then, miracle of miracles, Colette's eyes flickered, she whispered, 'Henry,' and he crushed her to him.

Maddie looked away because she didn't want to cry. It was now that she registered the man who'd rescued Colette. 'Thank God you were here,' she said. She took him by the arm and helped him to his feet. 'Are you all right?'

'Yes, I'm fine.' He pulled out a phone from his jacket. 'What about an ambulance?'

Colette's voice was stronger already. 'No, please, no. I just blacked out for a moment. I have a horror of hospitals and I'm really quite all right. I landed on you, after all. I hope I haven't broken your back.'

'This jacket's very thick and you are very light. Can I help you up?'

Between them, Henry and the man levered Colette to a standing position.

'Look!' she said, 'I'm fine.' She stumbled slightly and Henry's hand instantly shot out to steady her.

'If you take her arm again,' he told the man, 'we'll get her to the bench in the car park. I'll sit with her a while. She needs to rest.'

They set Colette carefully at the end of the bench. Henry took off his jacket and draped it over Colette's shoulders, ignoring her protests. 'Don't try to talk,' he told her. 'Just sit there.' He sat down beside her and took her hand in his. 'If it weren't for our saviour here . . . ' He looked up at him. 'I want to thank you,' he said. 'You were amazing and . . . ' He bit his lip for a moment. 'I'm in your debt. I think Colette and I will stay here for a little while to catch our breath. We're having a party across the road at the town hall. I'd be very grateful if you'd accompany my daughter back there.'

'Dad, that's really not necessary. I'm sure he needs to get on . . . '

★ ★ ★

'I don't,' the man said. Maddie stared a little helplessly at Colette. 'Shouldn't we get you to the hall and give you sweet tea or something?'

Colette shook her head. 'I hate sweet tea,' she murmured.

'We'll stay here for a while,' Henry repeated. 'Go on, Maddie, off you go. And give our friend a drink when you get there.'

Maddie hesitated. It was obvious Henry wanted to be on his own with Colette. She bent down to kiss Colette's cheek. 'Don't be brave. If you feel faint again, let Dad call an ambulance.'

The man took her arm and shepherded her back towards the high street. 'Are *you* all right?' he asked. 'You look very pale.'

'It was just rather a shock. I thought she was dead. She looked so white.'

'She'll be all right.' He glanced back towards the car park. 'She's in good hands. It's very touching to see a couple of that age still so much in love.'

'It's not like that,' Maddie said. 'Colette is my aunt. Of course my father's very fond of her.'

'I see.'

'You weren't to know. My grandmother died in February and Colette's been a great support to Dad. They've seen quite a lot of each other lately. They went to a wedding together last month and . . . ' She glanced up at him. 'Did you really think they were in love?'

'He was obviously very upset by what happened. As you were. He did seem . . . '

379

'Yes,' Maddie agreed. 'He did.' She shivered and hugged her arms to her chest. 'You saved her life. I can't bear to think what . . .'

'Then don't. I'm glad I was there.'

They had reached the door of the hall and she stopped at the bottom of the steps. 'I need a drink,' she said. 'Would you like to have one with me?'

'I'd like that very much.'

They entered the hall, took their drinks and found a table near one of the windows. Maddie studiously avoided eye contact from everyone but her present companion. 'I should go and tell my sister what's happened to Dad,' she said, 'but I need to sit here for a minute and get some wine down me. It's ridiculous. My hand's still shaking. Look.'

He took her hand in both of his and she felt the warmth of his palms. 'Is that better?' he asked. 'I'm quite happy to hold your hand for as long as you like.'

She laughed. 'That's kind but I need it to lift my glass.' She took a sip of her wine. 'My name's Maddie, Maddie Drummond.'

'I'm Adam. Adam Anderson.'

'Hello, Adam. I've seen you before. I recognised the scarf.' And the brown eyes. And the chin. And the shoulders

He nodded. 'Every time I come to Higgleigh, I look out for you. The first time I saw you was at Christmas. You wore a leather jacket and brown trousers.'

'And you wore that scarf. Your companion wore a beautiful red coat.'

380

'That was my sister,' Adam said. 'She's fond of that coat.'

'It's a very nice coat,' Maddie agreed. She was his sister!

'And the next time I saw you was in February. You were walking towards the river and you were teaching your children Spanish.'

'That's not quite accurate. Megan was telling me the Spanish words she knew and . . . ' The full inference of his words suddenly hit her. 'They're not my children. They're my nieces. I mean I would like children sometime but . . . '

'Maddie,' he began.

'And *you*,' Maddie continued inexorably, 'were with a very pretty young girl . . . '

'That's right. I was with my daughter.' He stared at her. 'You thought she was my girlfriend? Please, please tell me you didn't think she was my girlfriend! Oh my God, you did. My daughter will be horrified when I tell her.'

'I did think she was rather young for you.' She was his daughter!

'Actually, she's amazingly grown up for her age but I know what you mean.' He put his hands on the table. 'Can I ask you a very personal question? Are you seeing . . . Do you . . . ?'

'No,' Maddie said, 'I'm completely single.'

'So am I.'

They smiled at each other. Maddie felt a little breathless, as if she'd just climbed the Matterhorn and could see the sun on the other side. She was aware of her name being called and, turning, saw Nina at the back of the platform, holding a microphone and tapping her watch.

'Maddie!' she called. 'I need you up here to . . . ' She stopped as she took in Adam's presence and the surprise on her face was almost comical.

'I'm coming!' Maddie promised and turned back towards Adam. 'I'm sorry but . . . '

He was looking in the opposite direction. 'That's my mother over there with her boyfriend,' he said. 'She told she was going to a wedding party tonight.'

Maddie followed his gaze. 'Your mother is Uncle William's girlfriend?'

'Is he really your uncle?'

'No, he's my father's best friend. They're smiling at us.' Maddie gave them a wave. William gave an energetic wave back. Adam's mother gave a slightly awkward one.

Adam unbuttoned his jacket. 'This is very funny. I can read her like a book: I'm here, chatting up an extremely attractive woman and she's desperate to know what's going on. She's equally desperate to show that's she's *not* desperate to know.' He took a gulp of his drink. 'I'd better go and say hello in a minute.'

'And I ought to go and see Nina.'

'I'm beginning to feel uncomfortable,' he said. 'That couple over there are looking at us now. I suppose I'm not dressed for a party.'

Maddie caught sight of Clive and Verity. 'It's not that,' she said. 'They're wondering who you are, that's all. Clive's an old friend. I was horribly rude to him at Christmas. You should know I have a temper.'

He took a gulp of his wine. 'This is all so very odd. Just before that car came along, I saw you on the other side of the road. I thought: how can I go and introduce myself to her without sounding like an idiot? And now here I am and here you are . . . ' He grinned and put his hands through his hair. 'I should probably stop talking now.'

'I like you talking.' He had such beautiful eyes and a small scar above his left eyebrow. She could look at him forever. 'But I really ought to go . . . ' She glanced a little guiltily across at her sister.

But Nina was no longer looking at them and neither were William and Ellen, nor even Clive and Verity. All of them were staring at the door of the hall. Henry and Colette stood in the entrance, hand in hand, looking as radiant as any bride and groom.

Adam smiled. 'I think,' he murmured, 'we've just been upstaged.'

We do hope that you have enjoyed reading this large print book.

Did you know that all of our titles are available for purchase?

We publish a wide range of high quality large print books including:
Romances, Mysteries, Classics
General Fiction
Non Fiction and Westerns

Special interest titles available in large print are:
The Little Oxford Dictionary
Music Book
Song Book
Hymn Book
Service Book

Also available from us courtesy of Oxford University Press:
Young Readers' Dictionary
(large print edition)
Young Readers' Thesaurus
(large print edition)

For further information or a free brochure, please contact us at:
Ulverscroft Large Print Books Ltd.,
The Green, Bradgate Road, Anstey,
Leicester, LE7 7FU, England.
Tel: (00 44) 0116 236 4325
Fax: (00 44) 0116 234 0205